"As incisive as any news report on the trials bedeviling today's politically correct military. . . . A must-finish thriller and revelatory look behind the khaki curtain."

—*King Features*

"A tense, brilliant novel. Kara Guidry is a character who will stay with you long after you've finished *Heart of War*. It's hard to imagine how Truscott's novel could be more topical."

—*Castro Valley Forum*

"Couldn't be more timely. Truscott offers a riveting insider's perspective of today's Army while humanizing the soldiers and officers. Kara Guidry [is a] fascinating protagonist. One of the most clever, most committed and humane characters to be found in the murder mystery genre. An important and relevant thriller."

—*Hartford Courant*

"Truscott's characters are focused and driven and thoroughly believable. His exploration of military-social issues is thoughtful, without slowing down the plot. An absorbing, thought-provoking thriller."

—*Herald Sunday* (Portsmouth)

"A stunning interweaving of contemporary issues built into a love story, a murder mystery, and courtroom thriller. A good, enjoyable read. Satisfying."

—*Times-Picayune* (New Orleans)

"Truscott twists his plots and subplots into a final military courtroom scene where justice actually is done. *Heart of War* gobbles today's headlines about sex between the ranks."

—*Kansas City Star*

HEART
OF WAR

Lucian K. Truscott IV

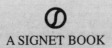

A SIGNET BOOK

SIGNET
Published by the Penguin Group
Penguin Putnam Inc., 375 Hudson Street,
New York, New York 10014, U.S.A.
Penguin Books Ltd, 27 Wrights Lane,
London W8 5TZ, England
Penguin Books Australia Ltd, Ringwood,
Victoria, Australia
Penguin Books Canada Ltd, 10 Alcorn Avenue,
Toronto, Ontario, Canada M4V 3B2
Penguin Books (N.Z.) Ltd, 182–190 Wairau Road,
Auckland 10, New Zealand

Penguin Books Ltd, Registered Offices:
Harmondsworth, Middlesex, England

Published by Signet, an imprint of Dutton Signet,
a member of Penguin Putnam Inc.
Previously published in a Dutton edition.

First Signet Printing, May, 1998
10 9 8 7 6 5 4 3 2 1

 REGISTERED TRADEMARK—MARCA REGISTRADA

Printed in the United States of America

PUBLISHER'S NOTE
This is a work of fiction. Names, characters, places, and incidents either are the
product of the author's imagination or are used fictitiously, and any resemblance to
actual persons, living or dead, events, or locales is entirely coincidental.

To my mother
Anne Harloe Truscott

Then again, I'll tell you what we could do
You be me for a while, and I'll be you.
—Paul Westerberg
The Replacements
"I'll Be You"

Chapter One

Kara Guidry was stunned by her indecision.

They had been together only a few months, but already she loved to lie next to him in bed and lean on her elbow and watch him sleep. With his eyes closed, he looked like a boy, except for the curly brown hair on his chest that became a light fuzz at his belly button and got darker and more wiry going down, swirling and twisting at the sinuous juncture of his thighs in a passionate calculus of the flesh.

She wanted to reach out and stroke his belly and rub her fingers in the thickening sworls of his masculinity, but if she touched him, he would wake up, and she wanted him to sleep so she could lie there and gaze at him. Her dilemma was delicious, made her feel like a girl instead of the woman she was.

The first time they spent the night together she had been watching him sleep and had absentmindedly run her fingernail down his belly, and he jerked awake full of fire. In the dim light she thought she saw yellow in his eyes, and from somewhere deep in his chest came a low, guttural growl. Then he rolled gracefully over on top of her, and he looked into her eyes and the yellow was there, she could see it clearly now. He growled again and chewed on her shoulder, sending shivers down her legs. He burrowed his face into her neck, and he held her breast in his hand like a hunter in possession of prey. As he nibbled her lips, she looked up into his eyes and they flashed hungrily and he started licking her, grooming her like a cat. His tongue searched for pockets of sweat, and when he found them, he drank deeply. She hoped he would never stop, and he didn't, not for a long, long time.

She looked over at the bedside clock radio. 10:30. She whispered his name.

"Mace. Mace Nukanen. Wake up."

He stirred, threw an arm over his forehead, and settled back into a deep sleep. She got up and tiptoed across the room, and stood at the big motel mirror filling one wall of the bathroom and ran her fingers through her blond hair.

Must be those reveille runs, she mused.

She looked pretty damn good for a thirty-five-year-old woman who had spent a third of her time on the earth in the United States Army. She weighed exactly the same as she had on the day she graduated from West Point thirteen years ago. Maybe her elbows were a little sharper, her smile lines a little deeper, but her body had survived pretty much intact. Her hips curved gracefully into tight, sinewy thighs, and her waistline was nothing to be ashamed of. She remembered with some distaste that a few years ago when she had been in law school, studying maybe eighteen hours a day, she had given up running and gained ten pounds that had settled around her midsection like a thick winter coat. Immediately she had carved two hours from her studies and went back to running every morning. She had never stopped.

She splashed water on her face. She had her father's strong jaw and serious brows and her mother's pointed chin and slender, elegant nose. Her deep-set, large brown eyes looked perpetually skeptical, darkly witty, and when they flashed, they could make dogs bark and small children hide their faces. Her smile was like her voice, warm and just a little husky and worn.

She heard a step, saw him in the mirror, turned in time to catch him around the waist. "We've got to go. It's almost checkout time."

He pulled her toward him. "No, we don't. We can stay another day."

"I've got that court-martial on Tuesday, and I've got to spend tomorrow prepping for it."

"Right. Corporal Richards. That thing in New Orleans. You going to get him off?"

"I won't stand a chance if we don't get ourselves back to Benning today."

He was taller than she was, stronger. He turned on the shower, picked her up, and stepped in. Water cascaded into their faces as he kissed her, sliding his hands down, grabbing her ass. She lifted her knees, wrapped her legs around his waist, leaned back against the shower wall. All she could hear was the rhythmic pounding of the shower and his hot, wet breath on her breasts. She knew why she surrendered herself to him. He did care about her; he cared about her in a way she had never experienced before, and he had insisted that she understand this even though she knew it was dangerous for both of them.

He was younger than her by several years; she had never bothered to ask how many. The absence of gray hairs in his crew cut told her what she needed to know. So did his skin, which was smooth and unlined, and his eyes, which sparkled with eager intelligence, and his hands, as big as omelet pans, which he carried at his sides awkwardly like a teenager.

She had met him canoeing down a river in north Georgia. It was the middle of the week, and they were alone on the river, each in their own canoes, and they fell into following each other, taking the same line through the rapids, leaning back sunning themselves through the slow stretches. Ten miles had gone by before he asked her what she did. She told him. She asked him. He told her. Another five miles passed before he asked her what rank she was. It was already too late.

She was out there on the river with him, and she had

watched his broad, tanned back glistening in the hot sun, the easy stroke of his paddle. He knew the river, embraced it like a lover, pointing at a turtle sunning on a log, a muskrat diving from the bank, swimming into its lodge, the swirl of a smallmouth bass rising for a cricket caught in a ripple behind a sunken stone. They rounded a bend, and he pulled his canoe to the side of the river and climbed up the bank and slid down the muddy bed of a feeder stream into the river with a huge splash. He stood up grinning, and she did the same thing, and there they were, diving on their bellies down a muddy stream into the river like a couple of otters. She ran up the bank and slid down again. Her top came off, lost in the rushing water of the river. She laughed. Then they both ran up the bank, and he slid down and then she belly-flopped onto the mud, and when she squirted into the river he caught her in his arms. Later on, they set up camp on a sandbar and sat staring at the fire as darkness fell. He poked it with a stick, sending sparks flying into the night.

"What are we going to do? I'm a sergeant. You're a major. They've got fraternization rules against what we're doing. They'd discharge both of us if they found out we were out here on this river together."

She walked to the riverbank, threw a rock into the water. "Have you ever thought of signing up for Officer Candidate School?"

He laughed. "Me? You see me as a lieutenant?"

"It's just a thought."

"Hey, I've been a sergeant for twelve years now. I've only got eight left for my twenty. I like being a sergeant."

"It'd solve the fraternization problem, is all I was thinking."

"It's not a problem yet, is it?"

"I guess not."

He walked over next to her, picked up a rock, tossed

it in his hand. "Wanna bet I can't hit that flat spot out there behind that rock in the middle of the river?"

She looked at the river. A large boulder had formed a V-shaped ripple that glistened in the moonlight. He was grinning. "How much?" she asked.

"One kiss."

"You're on."

He wound up like a baseball pitcher and threw. The rock landed dead center, exploding the riffle in a spray of bright water. "Close enough for government work?"

She took his face in her hands and kissed him on the mouth. Smiling, she said, "See? It's a problem already."

That night they slept next to each other in sleeping bags near the fire, and in the morning they stripped naked and bathed in the river and cooked scrambled eggs and looked at each other across their tin plates like they'd been doing it every morning of their lives. When they were finished eating breakfast, he took the frying pan and the plates and coffeepot to the edge of the river with a bar of hand soap and did the dishes. Watching him squatting at stream side scrubbing the pots and pans and plates, that was when she decided.

Damn the fraternization rules. The hell with Article 134. He was worth it.

She reached around him and turned off the shower.

"We've really got to check out of this dump."

He grinned. "Dump? The commanding general's quarters is a slum compared to a room with you in it."

She kissed him on the nose, stepped out of the shower, grabbed a towel. A twelve-by-twelve motel room on the Gulf Coast of Florida was the Ritz and she couldn't remember the last time she'd felt this way, couldn't even remember what it meant to feel this way, except for the fact that it meant trouble. Big trouble.

She felt him coming up behind her, whipped around.

"Get your hands off me!" she laughed.

He dove onto the floor, grabbed a foot, started kissing her toes. He was up around her ankle by the time she broke free.

"Coffee? You ever heard of coffee? You want to get some coffee?"

He looked up.

"I get plenty of coffee in the mess hall every day of the week. I only get you on the weekends."

"We can fix that. Move out of the barracks. Get yourself a place downtown. We could spend every night together out at my place."

"Too dangerous. Somebody'd be bound to see us."

He was right, of course. It was one thing to sneak away down to Florida. Quite another to flaunt their illicit relationship, even off-post, around Fort Benning.

She dropped to her knees, grabbed his face in both hands, and kissed him on the mouth. He bit her lip, and she bit his, and they tugged at each other, not wanting to let go. Monday was coming up on them too fast. The real world was about to set in, and they didn't want to let go of what they had, which was unreal; and it was illicit and it was hot and it was undeniable, and because it was all those things it was dangerous and hugely wonderful.

"I'm going to pull rank on you."

"Try it."

She stood up, looking down at him. His face was framed between her breasts. His eyes were so dark and huge she felt she could dive into them and never hit bottom. He reached up for her, she jumped back, and he fell forward on his chest on the floor, make-believe groaning.

"It's another goddamned Sunday. I wish Sundays would go away."

"If there wasn't a Sunday, there wouldn't be a Monday, and we'd never start the week and get to Friday, would we?"

"Miss Practicality. Is that what they voted you in high school?"

"Hey, it works in court, I'll tell you that much."

She patted his head. He felt like a big cat, ready to pounce. He leaked desire, every muscled inch of him was blazing soaking glowing red with it. It felt good, a man in heat at your feet. She wondered why so many years had passed before this man had come along and made her feel this way, and then she looked down at him and he smiled at her, and she stopped wondering and she kissed him and she pulled him to his feet and she shoved him toward his overnight bag.

"We've got a long drive ahead of us."

He stepped into his jeans and pulled a sweater over his head. "I'll take the bags down to the car." He grabbed them and went outside. Down the way a door opened, and a crew-cut man stepped out of his room, heading for his car. Mace turned and went quickly back inside.

She was standing at the mirror, her back to him. She turned around and saw him standing at the window, peeking through the curtains. "What's the matter? I thought you went out to the car."

"I just saw Lieutenant Parks getting into his car."

"Your platoon leader? He's *here*?"

"Yeah. He almost saw me."

"So? He signed your pass. You're allowed a weekend at the beach."

"Not staying in a room with a Jeep Cherokee with an officer's sticker on the bumper, I'm not."

She walked up behind him and peeked over his shoulder. Across the highway, the Gulf was choppy under heavy December skies. A car started, pulled out of the motel parking lot, turned down the highway, and disappeared into the misty distance.

"He's gone."

"That was Parks?"

"Yeah."

"That was close."

"Yeah." He opened the door, and she stepped into the parking lot. An icy wind off the Gulf of Mexico hit so hard it took her breath away. Clouds over the water had turned into a black wall across the horizon, gray curtains of rain below slanting darkly into the Gulf.

"That's some storm out there," she said.

She unlocked the door of the Jeep Cherokee and climbed in the driver's seat. He climbed in the other side. "We can stay ahead of it if we don't stop for breakfast."

"Let's go."

She pulled out of the motel parking lot and turned up Route 41, heading north, toward Georgia.

Tall trees at the edge of the parade field were bent horizontal, whipping the ground with low limbs. General William Beckwith stood at the window of his office in Headquarters. He was wearing a white shirt with a black bow tie and his drawers. His white legs disappeared into black over-the-calf socks. Outside, a lone soldier leaned hard into the wind as he made his way down the sidewalk into Headquarters.

Phone calls were starting to come in about the weather. Control was everything in the Army, and weather was just about the only thing a commanding general couldn't control, and he wasn't happy about it. The phone calls meant problems, and problems meant the General had to find people to solve the problems for him, and the kind of people you could count on to solve problems for you were getting damn hard to find in the Army.

The storm outside was whipping through the post with more than winter's usual discontent. Trucks in the motor pool rocked noisily on their shocks, canvas tops whipping against steel frames like snare drums. M-1 tanks pinged and creaked as frigid air contracted their heavy iron turrets imperceptibly but noisily. Teenagers leaving the early movie were hit hard by the wind, clutched at each other, screamed soundlessly into the teeth of the storm. A girl fell, a boy tried to help her, fell on top of her; they skidded on the icy walk. A light pole snapped, crashed to the ground, its halogen bulb exploding next to them. Someone screamed. Blood stained the sidewalk. MP's arrived, brandishing flash-lights. An ambulance drove up, lights spinning, siren wailing. Over at the post hospital emergency room, two medics went through a dozen needles and two packs of suture thread stitching up cuts.

Flooding had started across the post, near the river. The water was over the curb, up to the front steps of barracks in some areas. The chief of staff, a florid-faced colonel by the name of Roberts, entered at a run.

"Sir, we're getting calls. People are wondering what you're going to do about the flooding."

Beckwith barked his displeasure. "They want me to stop a goddamned flood? The goddamn weather isn't my responsibility! They should take their complaints to the big man upstairs."

There was a long pause as Colonel Roberts thought about what he was going to say. Finally he settled on an old military axiom. When in doubt, flatter.

"Sir, to them you are the big man upstairs," the chief of staff replied without irony.

A thin, self-satisfied smile played across the General's handsome features as he looked out his second-floor window. Roberts' ploy had worked.

The big man upstairs. Yes, indeed.

General Beckwith wasn't physically a big man; he stood five nine, he had narrow shoulders, a thin face with sharp features, but the way he filled up a room, even standing there in his drawers, had been remarked upon since he was a lieutenant. He was quick and direct, and his voice boomed when he addressed the target of his attentions. At West Point, instructors in the Tactical Department had called it "command presence," and Bill Beckwith had it in spades, even as a plebe.

He turned around. His aide, Captain Randy Taylor, was standing in the door, a pair of uniform trousers over his arm. "Sir, your dress blue trousers are ready."

"Put 'em down, Randy," boomed Beckwith. "I need a drink."

Randy neatly folded the General's trousers over the back of a chair and opened a mahogany cabinet, exposing a built-in wet bar. He filled an old-fashioned glass with ice and poured it half full of gin and dropped an olive into the mix. He picked up a cocktail napkin decorated with Infantry crossed rifles and handed the drink to Beckwith.

"Your martini, sir."

"You didn't put too much goddamned vermouth in this thing, did you, Randy?"

"No, sir."

Beckwith took a sip, smacked his lips. "Damn good martini, Randy. You're getting it down."

"Thank you, sir." There was a knock at the door. The General's secretary, Miss Flaherty, walked in. She was nearly six feet tall, and when she spoke, the windows shook.

"Wife for you on line two, sir!"

"Tell her the car will be there at 1900."

"I reminded her of that fact, sir! She wants to speak to you anyway, sir!"

Beckwith walked over to the phone, waved his hand, dismissing his secretary. Randy was about to walk through a connecting door to his office when the General stopped him. "Just a minute, Randy. I'm going to need you." He picked up the phone. "What's going on, hon?" He listened for a moment, nodding his head. "I'll see what I can do. Right. Okay. See you at the club." He hung up and collapsed on a leather sofa, ran his hands through his hair. When he looked up, Randy could see his eyes were red, and his face had lost some of its color.

"Answer me this, Randy, will you? God is fixing to dump about twelve inches of water on this Army post with which he has entrusted me, and he's already knocked down about thirty trees, and we've got an overflowing emergency room over at the hospital, and my wife calls up and tells me Colonel Sumner's wife next door is going to wear the same dress she's wearing to the club and what can I do about it."

Beckwith walked over to the window, which was being pelted with rain.

"The President is about to pick the next Chief of Staff of the United States Army, and I'm on his short list. I've got the Sec Def coming down for a private inspection tour next week, and the biggest problem I've got is Mrs. fucking Colonel Sumner and her goddamned dress."

Randy stood before the General as though he'd been training for this moment all his life, what to do when an irate general appears to be reaching the end of his tether. In the old Army, the Army of his father and his grandfather, they'd tell you to make a quip, get a laugh, help the old man over the hump. Grin and bear it. His father had been a general's aide when he was a young man, and his grandfather had been a general. Randy had been in the room hundreds of times when moments like this were shared by men who considered that the world was a place full of people who had no understanding of those who were part of the warrior caste, those who formed a Brotherhood of the Gun, those who gathered together under the banner of Duty, Honor, Country, to guard against all enemies, foreign and domestic. But this was the new Army, and this was a new kind of general. He didn't want brotherhood; he wanted confirmation and most of all, he wanted help. He wanted his trousers pressed and his martinis mixed. He wanted his tie adjusted and his wife subdued. He wanted his shoes shined, his ego massaged.

He wanted his way smoothed, and his life not just validated by companionship and camaraderie, but managed the way "handlers" groom and buff modern American politicians.

And so Captain Randy Taylor, who was six feet tall and wise beyond his years, and had long since realized he was a handler, once again endeavored to handle the life of General William Beckwith, the commander of the Third Army at Fort Benning. He picked up Beckwith's martini.

"Let me back that up for you, sir."

He dropped in a couple of ice cubes, topped it off with gin, handed it to him. Beckwith drank eagerly.

"I'll pick up Mrs. Beckwith, sir. I'll take Corporal Weyerich with me. He's the clerk who used to work in a hair salon."

Beckwith, wearily: "Right. Weyerich. Of course."

"Corporal Weyerich will comb out her hair. I'll fix her a Manhattan. While Weyerich is doing her hair, I'll give Mrs. Sumner a call and tell her she's not to wear the same dress as Mrs. Beckwith. I'll coordinate with your driver and make sure we arrive at the club the same time you do, so she won't have to stand around waiting."

Randy handed the General's dress blue trousers to him. Beckwith stepped into the trousers, pulled the suspenders over his shoulders.

"I guess the question I ought to be asking myself is, What would I do without you, Randy? Order myself up a concierge, I guess."

A knowing smile: "I don't believe Army commands come equipped with a concierge. Not provided for in the TO&E, sir."

Beckwith laughed, threw an arm around Randy's shoulder. "Listen to me, now. I want to get this thing tonight over with as quickly as possible. I give my speech to the ladies at the club at 2100. I'll conclude at

2120 and circulate. I want you to get word to me by 2130 that there's a power line down, or lightning has hit some fucking building, or the parade field's waist high and rising, something that will require my immediate attention."

Randy nodded. "I'll call Peters, sir. The O-club manager. He'll give you the message."

"Good work."

Beckwith walked over to the wardrobe stand, where his dress blue jacket hung. Lovingly he ran his fingers over the ribbons above the left breast pocket, touched the stars on the jacket epaulets. Randy started to leave. Beckwith stopped him.

"Who's driving me tonight?"

"Sergeant Taylor, sir."

"Tell Taylor to leave the staff car in front of the club for me. I'll drive myself home."

Despite the fact that Army policy required an enlisted man to drive the General's staff car, this was a request that General Beckwith had made before, and Randy didn't hesitate. "Right, sir. I'll tell him."

"You'd better get a move on if you're going to get the missus over to the club at 1900."

"Yes, sir."

Randy scooted through the door to his office and picked up the phone. "Weyrich? I've got a mission for you." He grabbed his overcoat and was out the door.

The storm caught them just outside of Eufaula, Alabama. The road was obliterated by blinding sheets of rain that slowed them to twenty miles per hour. Mace was driving. It took nearly an hour to make the fifteen-minute drive from Eufaula to Phenix City, just across the Chattahoochee from Fort Benning. Mace could barely make out the edge of the road. The defroster was on full, and failed utterly to clear the inside of the windshield. Kara swiped the windshield with a paper towel, but it fogged again quickly, so she tore off another towel and kept wiping, a pile of wadded-up paper towels growing at her feet.

Mace squinted into the gloom. "This stuff is going to play hell with training tomorrow. We're supposed to run the confidence course at 0800. There ain't a chance it's going to let up."

"Don't worry. Your battalion commander will call it off."

"Not a chance. They've got some new policy, came down last month, that no training was to be canceled due to weather. A friend of mine told me they had him practicing river crossings last week. It was forty-five outside. The water was fifty degrees, and they had them in there all day."

Kara peered into the rain. "I think this is the turnoff for the bridge. Can you see the sign?"

He squinted out the side window. "Yeah, this is it."

He made a right, and the Cherokee started up the long ramp leading to the bridge. Below them the Chattahoochee was swollen, surging over its banks, filling the sloughs and low spots along the river.

"Christ, you see that?" Mace pointed out the window. "Half the damn north end of the state is dumping runoff down that channel. I've never seen the river this high."

"Me either."

"Let's turn on the weather." He fiddled with the radio until he came up with an all-news station out of Atlanta. The radio announcer's voice was edgy, tinged with excitement.

". . . power is out to twelve thousand homes in the Atlanta area . . . six inches have fallen in the last two hours, and rain is not expected to let up until Monday afternoon . . . Georgia Electric has crews on the move all over the northwest side . . ."

They listened for a minute, then he turned off the radio. "I've seen storms like this before come boiling out of the Gulf. It's going to get worse before it gets better."

"I wonder how things look out at the post."

"They probably called an alert, got everybody in full field gear, waiting for orders to fill sandbags."

He slowed the car at a light. The intersection was flooded, water flowing over the curbs. He turned left. The Cherokee plowed through, found clear pavement, and accelerated.

"Which way are you going?"

"South gate. It's quicker. Artillery Drive comes up right behind my barracks."

He turned left, drove a half mile, made another left. They were on a two-lane blacktop out near the edge of Columbus. The headlights of the Cherokee found a small sign: FT. BENNING SOUTH GATE. He made the turn onto the military reservation, driving down a narrow road lined on either side with thick pine forests.

"Aaahhh. No place like home," said Mace.

"How'd you manage to get yourself stationed here at Benning for so long?"

Smiling: "They do stuff like that for sergeants."

"The longest duty I ever had was two years. I've done my share of one-year tours."

"That's what you get for not being married. They'll ship you anywhere anytime, they know you haven't got a family to lug around."

"So? You're not married, and I don't see them bouncing you between Army posts like a damn ping-pong ball."

"Like I said. You get good deals when you're an NCO."

She laughed. "I see. God made you a sergeant first and a man second. I call that the luck of the draw."

"I don't know you'd call five years at Benning luck." He took a swipe at the windshield and sat forward, straining to see out. "Jesus. Look at the rifle range."

He slowed the Cherokee to a stop. They could make out the corrugated steel sheds and control tower of the rifle range standing in the middle of a lake covering several acres.

"Incredible."

"I've never seen rain this bad at Benning," said Mace. "I mean, this is really something. And it's starting to come down harder."

The wind shifted, and rain pelted the Cherokee like a shower of BB's. The ditches on either side of them were flooded, water rushing beside them in wide brown streams. They crossed an old concrete bridge that usually stood a good thirty feet above the creek bed. Water flowed less than a yard below the roadway.

As they started up a hill on the other side of the bridge, he reached down to drop the Cherokee into a lower gear, and Kara touched his hand. "Maybe we'd better turn around, head back, and go through the main gate. We're going to get stuck out here."

"Nah, we'll do okay. We've only got another couple of miles to go."

"I mean it, Mace. I want you to turn around."

He pulled to a stop at the crest of a hill, staring straight ahead. His voice was icy. "You pulling rank on me?"

"Don't start, Mace. All I'm saying is—"

"It's your car, huh? You're the major, you're the one gets to decide where we go? You wanna drive? Here." He opened the door. Needles of rain stung her face.

"Mace, don't be ridiculous . . ."

He slammed the door. He was walking around the front of the car when he started running down the hill. She lost sight of him, and then suddenly he opened the door and climbed behind the wheel.

"Look down there! You see it?"

Kara squinted into the darkness. "Where?"

He put the Cherokee in first and eased down the hill. The river had overflowed its banks, flooding the road. The Cherokee was axle deep when he shouted: "There!"

Water rushed by in a violent torrent, nearly covering a car stalled about twenty yards ahead of them. A woman was hanging out of the window of the car, her dark hair blowing wildly in the wind. Mace stepped into the rushing water. Kara knew he was yelling, but she couldn't hear him.

Captain Taylor's fingers found the levers on the control panel in the dark control booth. Below him a woman with truly huge hair was finishing her introduction. The applause was deafening as General Beckwith stood up and approached the podium.

Slowly Randy pressed two of the levers up their slides a notch. Down on the stage of the officers club ballroom, the effect was subtle but real. General Beckwith's face took on a healthy glow in the spots thrown through red and blue gels. Randy turned to the man sitting next to him.

"He'll start moving around in a minute, Weyrich. Follow him with the white spot. Widen it out from waist up. Take him head-to-toe when he moves. You'll wash him out if it's too intense."

"Got you, Captain."

Randy opened the door and walked down a set of narrow stairs, opened another door into a back corridor in the officers club. He passed through the kitchen, stopped and poured himself a cup of coffee, and gnawed on a dinner roll for a few moments. Then he checked his watch and went out the back door to a loading dock. He dropped a quarter in a pay phone and dialed.

"Major, it's Captain Taylor. I need to talk to the General. It's an emergency. This storm is getting worse. There's flooding out near Lawson Army Air Field. They're afraid the Chattahoochee is going to . . ." He waited a moment. "Right, sir. I understand. Tell the General I'll have the staff car outside the front entrance."

He hung up the phone and walked down the steps to a waiting staff car. He drove around to the front of the officers club. The front door burst open. General Beckwith strode purposefully toward the car, surrounded by several officers in their dress blues. One of them opened the back door. Beckwith got in. Randy pulled away.

"What'd you tell them?" asked Beckwith, leaning forward.

"The truth. The whole damn post is underwater."

Beckwith settled back. "Fine job. Damn fine job, Randy."

Randy turned a corner, cut the lights, pulling up behind a car parked behind the movie theater. He got out, holding the door for the General, who walked around and slipped easily behind the wheel. Randy saluted smartly.

"Sir, the radio is tuned to your command frequency."

Beckwith saluted. "See you tomorrow morning, son." Beckwith's staff car disappeared down the alley behind the theater.

Mace was back inside the Cherokee, trembling from the cold. He picked up the cell phone, dialed 911. The phone beeped twice and turned itself off. "Out of range." He threw the Cherokee into reverse and started backing up. "We've got to go for help." He reached the crest of the hill and whipped the wheel, turning the car around. He shifted gears, and the car lurched down the hill. They were at speed, approaching the low concrete bridge, when she screamed:

"Mace! Stop!"

The bridge was flooded. A piece of the side rail broke off and fell into the current.

Mace picked up the phone again, dialing quickly. It beeped, the lighted dial going dark. He cursed. "We've got to try to get her out of there." He pulled a U-turn and headed back up the hill. As they neared the flooded river, they could see that the woman's car had slipped a few feet downstream. She had gotten one of her arms out of the window and was waving.

"You know how to work the winch on this thing?" He rummaged around in the backseat and came up with the shoulder strap off his overnight bag, quickly fastening it around his waist.

"Yeah."

"I'm going to hook into the winch. Play out cable until I get to her. When I get out there and get ahold of her, haul me back in."

"The current's too strong, Mace. Are you sure . . ."

He stepped out of the car. "I'm sure she's going to die if we don't get to her."

Kara slid over to the driver's seat. He waded around to the front of the Cherokee, raised a hand, rolling his wrist. Kara hit the winch release, and the drum started to turn with a loud *whirrrr*. When a few yards had played out, Mace hooked into the strap around his waist. Still facing the Cherokee, he backed slowly away from the car until the winch line was tight. Then he turned and plunged in.

The river knocked him from his feet. He regained his footing, leaned into the current, moved a few yards farther, and suddenly he disappeared. Kara reversed the winch. He bobbed up, went under and bobbed up again, hanging onto the cable with both hands. She jumped out of the car and waded into the river, grabbing the winch line, guiding him in. When he reached his feet, he staggered and collapsed into her arms. He was gasping, spitting water. "You . . . were right. It's . . . it's not going to work."

Kara opened the door of the car, stood on the door sill, looking at the dim figure in the headlights. The woman's head was thrown back. Both arms were out the window now. It looked like she was trying to pull herself free.

Kara shouted at Mace, "See that tree over there?" She pointed at a tall pine about fifteen yards upstream, its trunk awash in the current. "If you get around the tree, you can approach her from upstream. I'll play out the winch. You might be able to swim your way out to her."

"I think you're right."

She got into the car. He leaned in the door. In the dome light his eyes were dark, hooded with fear. "Kara, I'm sorry for what I said . . ."

She kissed him. "Be careful," she shouted. The thrum of rain and wind nearly drowned her out.

He waded through shallow water to the tall pine. Gripping the cable with both hands, he made his way around the trunk of the tree and eased out into the fast current. He let go of the cable and swam a few yards and grabbed onto the branch of a sunken bush. The water was washing over the top of the car now; waves were crashing into the woman's face. He knew she wouldn't last much longer.

The Cherokee's headlights barely illuminated what was happening fifteen yards away from shore. Mace let go of the bush, and the river swept him downstream. He hit the car's front end, bounced on a wave over the hood, and hit the windshield, shattering it. Frantically he scrambled for a handhold, grabbing the A-pillar on the passenger side. The river was about to wash him downstream when slowly he pulled himself up on the roof of the car. Kara hit the winch release button, stopping it. The Cherokee's wipers were struggling against the downpour. She stepped out of the door to get a better view.

Mace had his legs wrapped around the A-pillar of the windshield, the river cascading against him, kicking spray in his face. He reached for the woman, grabbing one of her arms. He couldn't move her. He held onto the A-pillar and slid into the water, still trying to work her free from the passenger window. A huge wave rolled over the car, completely swamping it,

burying Mace in tons of water. Kara waited desper-
ately for him to surface, but he didn't show. She was
just about to hit the winch and start to drag him in
when he burst to the surface. He had an arm around the
woman, waving.

Kara hit the winch, slowly winding in the cable.
Mace clung to the cable with one hand, his other arm
and legs wrapped tightly around the woman's torso. The
winch pulled them a few feet, and a huge wave rolled
through and they were swept under. They were out of
sight for a long moment. Suddenly an arm thrashed out
of the water, and the two of them popped to the surface,
Mace struggling to keep their heads above water, kicking wildly.

Kara jumped from the car and ran through the shallow water. Mace found his footing and stood, carrying
the woman. She was limp in his arms. Kara grabbed the
winch cable, pulling him to her. Together they slogged
through shallow water to solid ground. The woman's
head fell loosely to one side as they laid her down. Her
eyes were closed, her mouth frozen open, her white skin
painted with debris from the water. There was a cut in
her neck, a small one. It wasn't bleeding.

"Oh, my God," gasped Kara.

Mace grabbed the woman's head and jerked it backward, chin up. He shouted to Kara: "You know CPR!
Push on her chest with the heels of your hands between
my breaths!"

Mace knelt next to the woman and, holding her nose
closed, he took a deep breath and blew into her lungs.
Kara pushed hard on the center of her chest, and Mace
blew again. They kept this up for several minutes, when
suddenly above them came the *whap-whap-whap* of a
helicopter. A long shaft of light from a Xenon spotlight
flashed back and forth, searching the water.

Kara stood up, waving her arms. "Over here! Over
here!" she shouted as the wind whipped her face with
stinging rain.

The Xenon moved toward her, bathing her in white light. Kara dropped to her knees and began pressing on the woman's chest again.

The chopper circled, keeping the spot on them, then turned away, hovered, and set down on top of the hill behind the Cherokee. Two medics jumped out and ran down the hill toward them.

"How long have you been doing CPR?"

"A couple of minutes."

They opened a crash kit and went to work. As Mace pulled away from the woman's face to get a breath, the medic placed a mask over the woman's nose and mouth, and began squeezing a rubber air bladder, forcing air into her lungs.

Kara pointed at the wound on her neck.

The medic opened one of the woman's eyelids with her thumb and shined a flashlight. Her eye was rolled back, exposing the bloodshot white.

"May as well put that thing away, Johnson. She's gone." They stood up. A third medic arrived, carrying a stretcher. They lifted the woman's body onto the stretcher and headed back toward the chopper.

"You all had better come with us, ma'am," said the medic.

Kara opened the Cherokee's door. "I'm going to move my car away from the water." She started the Cherokee and backed it up. Behind her the chopper's rotors beat the air. She stopped down the hill from the chopper. The passenger door opened. Mace leaned in.

"Mace, they're gonna want to know what you and me—"

"I'm way ahead of you. Let me do the talking," he said.

One of the medics walked up. "Ma'am, we got to be gettin' outta here . . ."

"I'm with you." Kara turned off the car and followed Mace and the medic up the hill and climbed into the chopper. The woman's body was lying on a stretcher across the middle of the chopper between their feet. The door closed, the rotors picked up speed, and with a shudder the chopper leaned into the wind and banked into a turn, the Xenon spotlight writing on the river like a light pencil.

Kara looked down, trying to find the woman's car in the raging waters below. It was gone.

Chapter Two

"**H**er name was Sheila Worthy." The doctor was a captain, still in his twenties, his eyes rimmed red from lack of sleep. He was leaning against the wall, picking at a thread hanging from the sleeve of his scrubs. He yawned and looked over at Kara sheepishly. "Sorry, ma'am. I mean, it's been a long night."

She smiled. "Was she a soldier?"

The doctor straightened up, pulled a slip of paper from the breast pocket of his scrubs. "Yes, ma'am. Second lieutenant, worked in personnel over in Headquarters."

"Which headquarters?"

"Third Army." He took a deep breath. "I don't know what she was doing out on a night like this. Just one of those things, I guess. Too bad."

He walked through a set of automatic doors. A nurse rushed up, and he broke into a trot as the doors whooshed closed behind him.

The doors opened again, and a spec-4 appeared with a stack of hospital blankets. "Captain Taggert said you all could use these, ma'am."

"Who is Captain Taggert?" asked Kara, wrapping one of the blankets around her shoulders.

"He's the duty doc, ma'am. You was just talkin' to him."

They were sitting on plastic chairs in a waiting area outside the emergency room. Kara wrapped the blanket around her shoulders, shivering.

"Anything else I can get for ya, ma'am? Coffee? Donuts?"

"Do you know what happened to Major Hollaway?"

The spec-4 pointed down the hall at the automatic doors. "He's in there talkin' to Captain Taggert right now, ma'am . . ."

The doors opened on a military police officer thumbing through a manila file folder. He looked up, squinting over a pair of half glasses.

Hollaway was a big, florid-faced man with a salt-and-pepper crew cut and a coal black mustache. As he walked up, he put a friendly hand on her shoulder.

"You look like you've had better days, Kara, you don't mind my saying so."

Kara groaned. "I feel like I'm talking to you from the bottom of a well, Frank."

He pulled up a chair. "It figures you'd be mixed up in this. Which one's your client? The dead girl or the sergeant here?"

Kara shot him a look. He threw up his hands in mock surrender. "Just joking, Kara. Sorry."

"I'm a witness this time, Frank."

He looked at Mace. "Staff Sergeant Nukanen? Did I pronounce that right?"

Mace stood up. "Nukanen. Yes, sir."

Hollaway extended his hand. "You did one hell of a job out there tonight, Sergeant. The incident report says you pulled the young woman out of the water yourself. Mind telling me how you did that?"

Mace shuffled from one foot to another awkwardly. "It wasn't just me, sir. I tied into Major Guidry's winch, and she played me out into the current, and once I got the woman out of the car, Major Guidry winched me back in."

"The medics tell me you and Major Guidry were giving CPR when they arrived."

"We did what we could, sir."

Hollaway peered at Mace over his half glasses, then turned to Kara.

"Just for the record, Kara, what were you and, uh"— he looked down at his file—"Sergeant Nukanen doing out there on the South Gate Road on a night like this?"

Kara started to answer, but Mace interrupted.

"Sir, the major picked me up at a hitch-a-ride shelter. She was on her way to drop me at my barracks. Sir."

Hollaway made a note. "Hellish storm out there to-night. Never saw so much rain. It was raining hard when you picked up the sergeant here?"

"That's right."

Hollaway looked up from his file with a slight smile. "Very commendable. I'll make a note in my report that you are in compliance with the commanding general's policy on ride sharing. Make you look good when the paperwork gets upstairs."

"Thanks, Frank."

"I have one more question. Was the young woman alive when you arrived on the scene?"

Kara glanced at Mace. "Her car was underwater up to the windows. She was hanging out of the window. I thought she was waving at us."

"What did you think, Sergeant?"

"Sir, she looked like she was waving, but by the time I got to her, the car was almost totally underwater. The river was pushing her around pretty bad. One of her legs was caught in the steering wheel."

"Was she alive when you reached her?"

Mace dropped his eyes. "No, sir. Her head was under-water, and she wasn't breathing."

Hollaway shook his head. "These accidental-death investigations really get to you. You've handled them, haven't you, Kara?"

"A few. The way things are today, they'll kick it right back to you if you don't dot every i and cross every t, so we'll be glad to help you any way we can, Frank."

"Okay." Hollaway thumbed through his file for a moment. "It looks pretty straightforward to me. She tried to drive through a flooded spot in the road. Her car probably stalled, the river was rising, and a flash flood overflowed its banks, swamped her car. She got stuck out there with the water coming up. The river was too deep and fast, so she had to stay with the car. And the rest is . . . well. You were there."

Kara sighed. "That's the way it looked to me."

"The only thing that doesn't fit is the wound on her neck. She wasn't bleeding when you all pulled her out, was she?"

"No." Kara wondered where he was going with this.

"Did you see anything that could have caused her wound, Sergeant?"

"I couldn't see that much, sir. The car was full of water, and the river was throwing me around pretty good. I guess she could have gotten hit with something. There was a lot of debris out there, sir. Whole trees were floating past. I saw pieces of a bridge, the roof off a house . . ."

"I asked Dr. Taggert about that. He said the wound entrance was clean. If debris caused the puncture wound, it would have left residue, like a piece of bark, wood splinters, bits of soil. He said the wound was caused by a sharp, pointed object. Metal, or maybe glass."

"The window she was hanging out of was busted out, sir."

"Maybe that was it. The full autopsy will give us microscopic evidence of the wound path. I'm just trying to find something for my report in the morning." He turned to Kara. "You know how it is. They don't want a snapshot. They want the big picture."

Kara was staring off in the distance. Suddenly she came around. "Yeah, I know how it is."

"I called her folks a few minutes ago, talked to her father. A retired colonel." Hollaway checked his file.

"Colonel Worthy, lives up in North Carolina. Asheville, I think . . ."

Kara's head whipped around. "Colonel Worthy? I didn't put it together . . . Sheila Worthy . . . oh, Jesus. I served under him a few years ago. He was one of the good guys, and believe me, good guys were few and far between back then."

"He's on his way down here now. It's going to be a rough day for him." Hollaway stood up. "I'll get an MP car to drop you off, Sarge. Where are your barracks?"

"I'm over in the 2nd of the 29th, sir. Down in South Barracks."

Hollaway turned to Kara. "If you want to wait a few minutes, Kara, I'll drive you home."

"That would be great, Frank."

"Why don't you come with me, Sergeant?" said Hollaway.

"Yes, sir." Mace turned to Kara. "Thanks for the ride, ma'am. I'm sorry things turned out the way they did."

They shook hands. "That's quite all right, Sergeant. Good evening."

"Good evening, ma'am." Mace followed Hollaway down the hall. They disappeared around a corner, leaving her alone in the empty hospital corridor. She was huddled in her blanket, lost in her thoughts, when a voice startled her.

"Major Guidry."

General Beckwith was standing a few feet away in his dress blues. She jumped up from her chair.

"Yes, sir!"

"Sit down. Sit down." Beckwith looked over his shoulder down the hall, pulled up one of the plastic chairs. "It's been awhile."

"Yes, sir. It has."

"I'm sorry we had to run across each other under these circumstances."

"Me too, sir."

Beckwith looked down the hall like he was expecting

someone. He was still looking away from her when he said: "Major Hollaway tells me you were there when they recovered the body."

"Yes, sir."

He shifted around in his chair, adjusting his tie. "A tragedy. Truly. She worked in my headquarters." He paused, seeming to collect his thoughts. "I wish these kinds of things didn't happen. It seems senseless, a fine young officer's life ended, just like that. It makes you feel so helpless, do you know what I mean?"

"Yes, sir. I do."

There was another long pause as he looked down, rocking his left shoe from one side to the other. The shine was marred by a spattering of dried raindrops. He looked up, finding her eyes.

"I had no idea you were stationed here at Benning, Kara. You should have called the office and stopped by."

"I figured they're keeping you pretty busy over there at Third Army Headquarters these days, sir."

Beckwith chuckled. "You've got it exactly right on that score." He paused again, his gaze drifting away. "Why don't we get together for a D-3 company reunion? My aide tells me there are twelve of us here on post. Thirteen, including you. Meet up at happy hour at the O-club some Friday. Swap a few tales about the old days at the academy. How does that sound to you?"

"That would be great, sir."

"Good. I'll tell my aide. His name is Randy Taylor. Good man. He'll make the arrangements."

He stood, straightening his jacket, adjusting the buttons, and Kara got her first good look at him. He was trim, erect, tensed on the balls of his feet, just the way she remembered him. His hair, graying at the temples, was swept back on top, longish for an officer. He paid an inordinate amount of attention to his appearance for an Army man. She remembered her roommate saying that the first male officer to get a face-lift was going to be Beckwith.

"I'll have Randy call you, then. About the reunion."
He flicked an imaginary speck of dust from his sleeve,
and without another word walked away. The small taps
on his heels echoed in the empty hall . . . *tap-tap-tap*.

She shook her head, trying physically to clear from
her mind a conviction that refused to leave on its own:
He knows. He knows about Mace, because he knows
about *me*.

It was the summer of her firstie year at West Point.

She was a platoon leader, training the yearling class
during the two-month summer camp out at Camp Buckner. Beckwith had just arrived at West Point. He was
living in the BOQ that overlooked the Hudson on the
north side of Cullum Hall. They gave him one of the
Camp Buckner training companies to prepare him for
being a company tactical officer when the academic
year began after Labor Day. She saw him early in the
morning that summer, running alongside his company
on their reveille run. He was tanned, athletic, handsome, and he looked younger than his thirty-five years.
She saw him out at the training sites—supervising artillery instruction as the yearlings learned to fire
105mm cannons, or perched on the side of a cliff in a
rope sling, shouting encouragement to young men and
women just beginning their first rappel. Several nights a
week she saw him eating supper with his company in
the screened mess hall on the wooded shore of Lake
Popolopen, the picturesque fingerling lake on which
Camp Buckner was located. More than once she had
heard yearling girls in her platoon talking in the show-
ers about how sexy he was, but that was not a conversation she had ever had with a firstie. She found herself
part of a conspiracy of female silence among her classmates regarding the handsome new major who roamed
among them. The rules against fraternization between
the ranks made him untouchable, of course, but every-

one at West Point knew the first rule of them all, that rules were made to be broken.

During the final week of combat training, she put her platoon through five tough days of Recondo School, run by the 101st Airborne Division at a temporary camp another ten miles out in the boonies. Hand-to-hand combat, night patrolling, helicopter assaults, night attacks through a swamp—Recondo School was a grueling course that stretched the yearlings tight as guitar strings. When it was over, they were force-marched back to Camp Buckner, where the yearlings threw off their combat gear and dove into the lake, and the firsties changed into civvies and jumped in their cars and headed for someplace, *anyplace,* where you could get away from West Point and all things military, drink a beer and listen to some live music, maybe dance a little.

That was the plan anyway. She headed for her favorite bar, out past Central Valley on a two-lane blacktop in dairy farm country, the Ideal Spot, an old farmhouse that had been transformed into a country and western nightclub with a BUD sign flickering over the front door. The place was packed with farm couples and young girls with big hair giggling at goofy, grinning boys who worked under the grease rack down at the local Chevron. She liked the cheap drink smoky feel of the place, and she especially liked the fact that it wasn't full of cadets or officers from West Point, who were much more likely to be found in yuppie watering holes like Bennigans over in Poughkeepsie than in a down-at-the-heels roadhouse on a dusty road out in the country.

So it surprised her when she walked in and saw him at the bar. There was a moment when she actually thought about turning around and getting in her car and driving away. Seeing him sitting alone in an obscure country bar was a risk she shouldn't be taking . . . he might flirt with her, or she with him . . . something might happen. She stood there in the open door, then she shrugged, like so what, and walked in. She had been a cadet for three long years, walked right down the center of the straight and narrow every moment of every day, and it was about time she did something utterly and completely random.

At first she thought he didn't recognize her. Their companies were located across Camp Buckner from each other, and there were maybe a hundred firsties in the cadre, a thousand yearlings in training, and he'd been at the academy only a couple of months, so why should he recognize her? But when she walked up to the bar, he turned and smiled and said hello. She called for a beer and grabbed a pool cue and dropped a couple of quarters in the table, and listened with satisfaction as the balls dropped. She racked them, broke the rack, saw him turn around on his bar stool. She knew exactly what he was going to do. Men were like pieces of heavy equipment. They'd see something off in the distance, and they'd shove aside earth and grass and tall trees, they'd plow a road, bridge a river, do whatever it took to get there. This man, the handsome major, he was no different. He was going to plow straight through the smoky bar and put down a couple of quarters for the next game.

And that's what he did. They played a couple of games of eight ball and drank a few beers, and she knew he'd ask her to dance, and he did, and they danced to the country and western band in the backroom. She knew they wouldn't talk about Buckner or summer training or West Point or the Army, and they didn't. Talking didn't matter. What mattered was the fact that she knew they were going to end up together, but he had no way of knowing this because that intoxicating decision was hers, which must have been why she felt drunk but she wasn't drunk, and neither was he. She could still remember when they danced—she held him tightly and rested her forehead against the stubble of his cheek. She knew he didn't know how to two-step, so she taught him, and the country band put out a deafening wail, and

they drifted through the noise doing the glide she had
learned in Cajun bars outside Lafayette, Louisiana.

She knew all about men, but she didn't know how
she'd feel in his arms. It was like they were the only two
people in the world, a trancelike state where you close
out reason and logic and let the music and the motion
carry you away, and the trance didn't break until the
next morning when she woke up and heard him turn on
the shower in the motel room they had taken down the
road sometime after midnight. He took a long shower,
for which she was deeply grateful, because she still
didn't know how she felt. She stayed in bed wondering
what would happen now. She knew they couldn't go on.
There was too much danger, too much at stake. Then in
a moment of panic it occurred to her that she didn't
know this man at all. There was a rumor he was di-
vorced, or maybe separated, and he didn't wear a wedding ring, but she didn't know his marital status for
sure. As a superior officer, especially in the context of
the academy, he could profoundly affect the rest of her
life as a cadet, make it miserable or delightful or simply
do nothing at all. The panic passed as quickly as it had
come, and with absolute clarity she knew what would
happen: They were going back to West Point in their
separate cars to lead separate lives. For a few hours each
of them had dropped the masks they were wearing—
cadet, officer—and they had behaved as man and woman,
and now they had to pick up the masks and put them on
again, and play the roles that West Point demanded of
them. But she could always hope . . .

Tap-tap-tap . . . he was marching down the barracks
hallway at night, a sharp knock at the door . . . *Room!
A-ten-shun!* He walked through the door like he owned
everything and everyone in sight, and the thing was, he
did. He would stand in the middle of the room looking
at you. Here he was, your tactical officer, and there you
were, ready to receive and obey his orders. If he said
every cadet room in the company would display a black

alarm clock with a white face and black numerals, bingo! You looked high and low until you found one. You got it done. If he issued an order that shoes were to be tied with shoelace loops no longer than one and a half inches the next morning you pulled a ruler from your desk, and you sat down and measured your shoelace loops. His control was absolute. He'd walk over to the dresser and open the top drawer and run the tip of his finger down a perfect pile of your underwear, push his hand slowly under your hose, rolled into tidy little sausages, lift a stack of your meticulously folded bras . . . inspecting . . . inspecting . . . looking for any tiny imperfection. A wry smile cracked the corner of his mouth when he found an item out of place, eleven pairs of hose displayed where there were supposed to be twelve, a bra strap wrapped counterclockwise instead of clockwise. He was sharing a secret with you, a whisper only the two of you could hear. You existed at his discretion. The feeling you got was, by the rules and regulations of West Point, the way they forced you together into a closeness of body and soul unique to a military unit, you belonged to him.

And you did. He knew it and you knew it, and it was a secret between you that each of you would carry to the grave.

Looking back, it surprised her how gently the scales had dropped from her eyes, how calmly she had accepted the knowledge that had come her way. A man could spend a night with a woman and walk away and think nothing of it, and a woman could not, and men knew this. Women might be in control of their own bodies, but their emotions were something else entirely, subject to wistful dreams and frantic intuitions and the tall surf of pure chance. Being a woman at West Point, surrounded by men—there were ten times as many men as women in the corps of cadets—she had learned a grim and disheartening lesson, that sex was doomed to a space between them, not of them, and gentleness was a flower in men that bloomed only at night, if at all.

Tap-tap-tap . . . the sound of his heels on the tiled floor grew faint and stopped. He turned and, smiling, gave her a little wave. "Good to see you!" He walked around the corner and was gone.

"Supertac," she said out loud to herself. That's what they'd called him in Company D-3. That's what she'd called him too. They had never spent another night together, and after she graduated, she had never seen him again, not until this very moment. She had watched the steep and rapid ascent of his career, of course. She had read the stories in the *Army Times;* she had seen him interviewed on *Nightline* after the Gulf War; one of her classmates had faxed her a *New York Times* op-ed piece he wrote opposing gays in the military. She knew from reading a recent article in the *Army Times* that he was on the short list to become the next chief of staff. And now she had seen him, and talked to him, and the feeling she'd had after all these years was a soul-numbing creepiness, like he could see right through her.

"Kara? You ready to go?" It was Hollaway, walking down the corridor toward her.

She slipped the blanket from her shoulders and stood up. "Sure. Anytime you are."

Outside, he popped an umbrella and they ran through the driving rain to an MP car parked across the street. They were headed out Patton Drive, toward the main gate. An MP stepped out of the guardhouse and waved them through. Hollaway drove a couple of blocks and slowed.

"You don't mind if we stop here at the Camelia Apartments for a moment, do you? I've got to inform Worthy's roommate about her death."

"I don't mind."

"You can wait in the car, if you'd like. I won't be long." He pulled into a parking spot and squinted through the windshield. Lights were starting to blink on throughout the World War II vintage brick complex. Reveille was about an hour away. Young officers sharing furnished apartments were breaking starch and blousing trousers and lacing up jump boots. He cut the engine.

"Just a minute. I'll come with you." She opened her door, and driving rain blew into the car.

Hollaway reached into the backseat. "Here. Use my overcoat."

She pulled the overcoat over her head, and they ran up the stairs to a door marked A-5. Hollaway knocked. The outside light came on, and they heard a woman's voice on the other side of the door.

"Who's there?"

"Lieutenant Carrington, it's Major Hollaway and Major Guidry. Open up, please."

The door opened. A young woman with short red hair was standing in the dark hallway, clutching her robe at her throat. "It's about Sheila, isn't it?"

"May we come in, Lieutenant?"

She stepped back. Hollaway and Kara walked inside. Kara pulled the door closed behind her.

"I'll make coffee . . ."

"That won't be necessary, Lieutenant," Hollaway said. "Is there someplace we can sit down?"

She led them into a small, sparsely furnished living room and pointed soundlessly at a sofa that had seen better days.

"Lieutenant, I'm afraid I have some bad news. Your roommate, Lieutenant Worthy, has been killed in a tragic accident."

She sat on a slip-covered armchair. Tears were streaming down her face. "Sheila . . . oh, my God . . . can you tell me how it happened?"

"She was trying to drive through a flooded road, and her car was swamped in a flash flood, and she drowned."

"We're very sorry, Lieutenant," said Kara, kneeling

next to the young woman. "I know how difficult this must be for you. If there's anything I can do . . ."

The young woman wiped her face with the sleeve of her robe. She looked red-eyed at Kara. "I knew. I just knew something would happen to her."

"Do you have any idea what your roommate was doing out on the South Gate Road last night?"

"I told her not to go. She had met him out there before, and I told her it was stupid. If she was going to have this stupid affair with this stupid guy, the least he could do was get them a motel room, but she said I didn't understand, it wasn't like that. She was driving out there to meet him somewhere near the firing range. It wasn't the first time. She's been going out there for over a month now." She turned to Kara. "Would you have done something as stupid as that? I mean, it's a cliché! She's this incredible girl, just starting out on her career, and she falls in love with this married asshole!"

Kara interrupted her. "How do you know he was married?"

"I thought the whole thing was so stupid, and I told her so, because like, he'd never go anywhere in public with her, even like, down to Florida or anything. He had to be married, because he knew if they got caught it would end his career."

Kara was looking out the window at a couple of young lieutenants in battle dress uniform getting into a Camaro. "Not to mention hers. Do you know his name?"

"No, ma'am. She would never tell me. But I kept telling her, I don't care how wonderful he was, I don't care how great the sex was, it wasn't worth it, and she just kept telling me I didn't understand, it wasn't like that."

Hollaway leaned forward. "What time did she leave the apartment?"

"About 2100, sir."

"Are you sure about the time?"

"Yes, sir. I had just gotten home from working late, and she was on her way out."

Kara touched her hand comfortingly. "What do you think Sheila meant when she told you it wasn't like that?"

"She kept telling me I didn't understand, and I guess I didn't. It was like, to me, the whole thing seemed so unbelievably ridiculous, and to her it was like this great adventure, and she just kept telling me how she was like, learning things they never taught you in ROTC, things you couldn't read about in books. She really felt like he was some kind of guide through a part of life she never knew existed. I told her I knew a professor in college just like him, he was like, my mentor, and he was so generous, and I learned so much from him, there's just like, no way I could ever thank him enough. And she said, he's my lover, not my mentor, like there was this big difference that I was too stupid to see."

She took a deep breath, looked at Kara expectantly. "I don't know. Maybe she was right. Maybe I was stupid. Maybe I was jealous. She was so happy when she came back from seeing him. It was like, she was high or something. That was when I knew it wasn't just the sex, because sex couldn't be that good. She had this dreamy look in her eyes, and I knew it was way, way more than that."

Hollaway looked over at Kara and stood up. "Her dad's on his way down here from North Carolina. If you want to take the next couple of days off, I'll call your boss and arrange it."

"Thank you, sir. I'd really appreciate that."

Kara stood up. "I'm over at the Staff Judge Advocate. If I can help you in any way, I'll be more than glad to."

Lieutenant Carrington followed them to the door. The rain was still coming down outside. "I don't know what I'm going to do without her. I can't even afford the rent by myself . . ."

Kara turned, her eyes flashing. "I'll talk to the complex manager this afternoon, Lieutenant. That will be taken care of."

"Thank you, ma'am."

In the car, Hollaway had a quizzical expression as he switched on the wipers and backed out of the parking space. They drove out of the parking lot and were stopped at a light, ready to turn onto Victory Boulevard, when Kara pointed out the window. "I stayed there for six months on TDY one time. We must have gone through a case of roach spray the first week."

"I didn't know you spent time here at Benning," Hollaway said.

"Airborne School. Right after I graduated from West Point. I lived in the apartment on the end, the one with the blinds pulled down. They charged us fifty bucks more because we had a side patio and air conditioning, which worked about half the time."

Hollaway laughed. The light changed, and he pulled into traffic. "You got any thoughts? I mean, this thing is turning out to be more complicated than I thought."

Kara wiped condensation from the inside of her window, turning to get a last look at the Camelia Apartments. "The thing that gets me is, nothing ever changes."

"You mean the Camelia Apartments? They're like a time capsule, a rite of passage—"

"I mean, between men and women," said Kara.

Hollaway drove in silence for a moment. "I'm not sure I understand what you're getting at, Kara."

"We've had years of memos on sexual harassment from Department of the Army, years of raising consciousness in the ranks, years of awareness lectures every six months. Just when you think you're getting somewhere, you come up against this."

"This isn't a case of sexual harassment. We've got an accidental death here, not somebody grabbing ass down in the motor pool."

"What are you? Blind, Frank? You've got a twenty-three-year-old lieutenant having an affair with a superior officer. He could have been the guy who wrote her OER . . . her goddamned job could have depended on whether or not she slept with him. We don't know what kind of pressures he may have been exerting on her."

"Her roommate made it sound like she was the one who was pursuing him."

"See? Nothing ever changes. I see this thing one way, and you see it another, and you're a man and I'm a woman, and I guess that's just the way it's going to be, no matter what we do."

"Well, I'll concede that your experience has been different from mine. But I still don't see how her having an affair had anything to do with her death. The way her roommate told it, she went into the affair willingly, with eyes wide open, even to the point that she refused her roommate's entreaties to give it up and walk away from the guy."

"Women do that to each other. Hell, they do it to themselves."

"Do what?"

"Doubting. Questioning. Wondering. What-ifing."

"Men do it too."

"Yeah, *right*."

Hollaway slowed down, peering out the windshield. "I'm looking for your driveway."

"It's a little farther, around that bend in the road, just past the trees."

Hollaway rounded the bend and turned into her drive and pulled to a stop. "I'm going to need you to come by the office and sign a statement. If you could make it later today, that'd be a big help."

Kara opened the door. "I'll do it. Thanks for the ride, Frank." She stepped out of the car.

"Listen, I'm sorry if . . ."

"Don't worry about it." She closed the door and started to walk away. Then she turned and walked back to the car and tapped on the window. He rolled it down. "Let me tell you, Frank. There's more to this thing than we know. Look at it this way. You've got a negligent homicide on your desk if it could be shown that she was responding to pressure from a superior officer to drive out there and meet him."

"We'll never know that for sure."

Kara grimaced. "Maybe we will. I hope not."

Inside, she took off her coat and put on a pot of coffee. She sat down and pulled off her shoes and rubbed her feet.

She had been born into a different Army, and yet it was still the same. The men who ran the Army did whatever the hell they wanted, and were answerable only to each other. Men around the office still talked about "the little woman" back home. There was at Fort Benning, and on other posts where she had served, the old military ethic that women were supposed to keep their mouths shut and their blouses buttoned and their children at heel.

She leaned back on the sofa and closed her eyes. She remembered the fear in her mother's eyes when she heard the lock turn in the door at night, announcing the return of her father from work. Her mother had spent the last two hours straightening up the house, emptying ashtrays, cleaning out waste baskets, trying to insure that everything was in its place and spotless. It was like their home was an extension of the barracks. She half expected her own father to put on a white glove and run it over the tops of the kitchen cabinets, looking for dust.

It was all about power, but it was more than that. It was about fear. The men in the Army had turned on the television at night and watched the world changing, outside of their control. Women began to act differently. They were on their way in a different world, and soon they would be admitted to West Point and be on their way up the ladder in the Army. Kara remembered how her father had reacted when she told him she was going to apply to West Point. It was like he had just taken a hammer blow to the solar plexis. His eyes bulged, and his cheeks reddened, and he stared at her for what seemed like minutes but was probably a few seconds, and then he got up and left the room. He went to work the next morning and didn't come home until three days later. Her mother had written off his disappearance to "maneuvers" or "Army business" or something like that, but Kara had understood what it was. She was a woman and she was going to enter his world, and in doing so, she was going to change it, and he didn't like it one bit.

Her relationship with her father had always been stiff and formal and distant, but after her appointment to West Point it became downright icy. Her mother had been the one who drove her to the airport the day she left to report to Beast Barracks. After that she saw her father only a few times before he died.

Now she thought of him and the Army he represented. Somewhere out there was a man who shared her father's proprietary instincts about women, that they were things to be possessed and used. Somewhere out there was a man who had been having an affair with the young woman they found in the rushing waters of the swollen river. Somewhere out there was the man who killed her, and his presence was as fresh and real and painful to her as the memories of her own father.

Chapter Three

Captain Randy Taylor was standing at the coffee maker at 0700 when he looked out the window and saw a group leaving the Fifth Army Headquarters across the way. The headquarters buildings of the Third and Fifth armies stood less than a football field away from each other across a grassy parade ground, and they shared a concrete helicopter pad located halfway between them.

Randy knew that it drove Beckwith mad, having the two headquarters located so close to each other. Fifth Army had been headquartered a hundred miles away at Fort Jackson, but downsizing had changed the landscape in more ways than one. Fort Jackson had been closed by the congressional base closure commission, and was now used as some kind of internment camp for youthful offenders. Fifth Army Headquarters had been moved to Fort Benning and now stood just across the way from Third Army Headquarters, so General Beckwith could look out his window at the four-star general who headed up another Army command.

That two such high-ranking generals were headquartered so close to each other was not only a sign of the economic times facing them, it was a recognition that there was a narrowing of room at the top of a shrinking Army. It used to be understood that an Army post was big enough for one commanding general. Now the crowd of flag-bearing staff cars at Fort Benning was large enough to cause a traffic jam in the reserved spaces at the PX parking lot.

Randy watched the group of men as they walked down the sidewalk toward the chopper pad. He chuckled, remembering something his father had told him a long time ago.

You can tell a lot about a general from the solar system of aides who are in perpetual orbit around him wherever he goes. Deputies, usually brigadier generals, are the planetary ring closest to the general's sun. Lesser bodies orbit farther away—a couple of colonels, a moon ring of majors, an asteroid cloud of captains, and in far space perhaps even a frightened lieutenant or two, floating out there like space debris in the command cosmos.

But Randy's father was very specific about the most telling detail of them all. *Pay close attention to the command sergeant major*, he had said. *He's the one who knows where the bodies are buried.*

Randy thought back to a day at the Infantry School, right there at Fort Benning, only weeks after he had received his commission. He was out in the field on a fire-and-maneuver exercise when a helicopter carrying the commander of the Infantry School landed near his training company. Immediately all instruction came to an abrupt halt, and the officers teaching the class in small-unit tactics hurried over to greet the chopper. A brigadier general who commanded the Infantry School got out of the chopper, followed by several aides. He walked quickly toward a shed where the company commander was hurriedly preparing a briefing on the day's training. The general was a good fifty yards from the chopper, which had already shut down its engines, when Randy noticed the command sergeant major climb out. He strolled over to a group of lieutenants who were hunkered down in the shade of a large oak. He plucked a blade of grass and stuck it between his teeth and chewed contentedly.

"Briefing goin' on over there at the shed, huh?" he

asked. One of the lieutenants answered affirmatively. "I don't much like briefings, myself. Guess you all been briefed till your ears hurt, huh?" The lieutenants chuckled nervously, wondering what the sergeant major was getting at. Alone among them Randy laughed so hard it brought tears to his eyes, because he understood immediately that the sergeant major had just told them all they ever needed to know about the general he served under, without saying hardly anything at all.

The blades of a big UH-60 Blackhawk helicopter were beginning to turn as General Bernard King neared the chopper pad. Command Sergeant Major Ted Conklin was walking next to him, an eager spring in his step, an almost devilish grin on his face. They were followed by a clutch of colonels and majors carrying briefcases and clipboards. Conklin leaned in close to the General as they neared the chopper.

"We got this guy's PR people topped off with high-test this mornin', sir. Close as he knows, you've been water-walkin' since your mama said you were old enough to tie your own shoes."

General King laughed. Conklin stopped at the door of the chopper and waited while the General got on. He pulled the door closed, leaving the clutch of aides standing at the edge of the pad, holding onto their hats as the blades of the Blackhawk beat the air.

The big helicopter lumbered aloft at precisely 0702 hours. Four gold stars glinted in the early morning sun as General King pulled on his flight helmet. The intercom crackled, General King adjusted the volume, and his voice boomed into the headset of the other passenger on the Blackhawk.

"Morning, Senator. Did you sleep well last night?"

Senator Hershell Maldray, who was about ten years younger and a hundred pounds heavier than the General, grabbed a cargo strap to steady himself as the Blackhawk leaned into a steep turn. Maldray's face was round and red and youthful, topped by a shock of prematurely gray hair. Less than fifty feet below them, the tops of pine trees skimmed by at better than one hundred fifty miles per hour. It had stopped raining. Scattered patches of fog struggled to break through a dense cloud cover.

"The accommodations were excellent, General. It's gratifying to see that tax dollars are being so well spent here at Fort Benning."

General King had come to accept the fact that he was a mandatory stop for Washington politicians who shamelessly craved photo-ops that could be exploited with constituents back home. This was because King was the highest-ranking black man in the United States Army, and every junketeering politician who made the stop at Fort Benning had a large percentage of minority voters he had to cater to. Though escorting wayward senators was a part of his job he could do without, he was good at it. But this was no ordinary politician. This was the majority leader of the United States Senate. This was a man who quite literally held the budgetary health of the Army and all of its units and installations and personnel in his hands. King knew he was a man who could make or break a general's career with the lift of an eyebrow, a nod or shake of the head. On this morning it was General King's job to keep Maldray's eyebrows firmly seated above his twinkling blue eyes and convince the majority leader that the separate commands at Fort Benning, and indeed Fort Benning itself, were worth saving in the latest round of cuts that would be recommended by the joint House-Senate congressional base-closure commission.

General King had an idea that this wouldn't be too hard. Senator Maldray was one of two Republican senators from the state of Georgia, and he had grown up in a military family that had been stationed for many years right here at Fort Benning. The state of Georgia had a large black population, and they turned out to vote.

Maldray had squeaked through his last election with just 50.2 percent of the vote, and he was facing another trial at the polls next year. Indeed, you could make the argument that Maldray needed King more than King needed Maldray, but the General didn't like to think in terms so nakedly political. He was an Army officer, and for thirty years he had endeavored to put as much distance between himself and politics as he possibly could.

He looked across the helicopter's troop-carrying bay at Maldray. The senator rooted around in a briefcase and pulled out a book with a large color photograph of himself on the cover.

"Have you seen my new book, General?" He handed the slim volume to General King. The title, *Decay and Renewal: America on the Rebound,* was in type half the size of the type used for his name.

"No, I don't believe I have," said General King.

Maldray pulled out a pen. "Here, I'll autograph it for you." He quickly jotted his name inside the cover and handed it to General King.

"Thank you, Senator. I'll have a look at it as soon as I get back to the office."

"Don't bother. It's actually a collection of recent speeches, and you probably got the sound bites from most of them from the news."

Smiling: "You're right. I probably did."

"You don't mind if we do some inside-the-Beltway talking this morning, do you, General?"

"No, sir. Of course not."

"You are no doubt aware that we're taking a hard look at budget priorities this year. Everything is on the table, including defense. We've got a bipartisan commission looking at a new round of base cuts right now."

"They shot Fort Jackson out from under me earlier this year, Senator. I hope you're not here to tell me they've got Benning in their crosshairs."

"No. Of course not. Fort Benning has an advantage that Fort Jackson didn't have. It's in Georgia." Maldray threw his head back and laughed long and hard at his own joke.

General King smiled thinly. "That's what Senator Alford told me last year about South Carolina."

"Senator Alford didn't have the benefit of my perspective, General. The landscape changes completely when viewed through the windows of the office of the majority leader."

"That's what Senator Alford told me about looking at things from the chair of the Armed Services Committee."

Maldray chuckled. "I'll have to talk to him about that when I get back to Washington."

The helicopter slowed as it passed over the rolling hills of the western part of the Fort Benning Military Reservation. King pointed out the door.

"I wanted to show you our new area for field exercises, Senator. We've got it set up where two brigades can go up against each other with mechanized infantry, armor, a live fire zone, the whole business."

Maldray glanced quickly out the window. "Interesting." He turned back to face the General. "There's something else we're taking a hard look at, General, and I wanted to get your thoughts on it."

"Shoot."

"The closure commission is going to look at force structure. We haven't announced this publicly yet. And we won't for a while. I wanted to get your thoughts before I turn them loose. Everything's going to get a tough going-over."

"I'll be glad to help in any way I can, Senator."

"This next round of budget cuts is going to take a larger bite out of Defense than it did last year. We both know that. The question is, where, and how much? It's my feeling that we could cut a couple of commands. We need the divisions, but I'm not sure we need the top-heavy bureaucratic structures that go with higher commands. We're going to run into opposition from the Sec Def on this. He's going to go crying to the White House and get the chief draft dodger on his side, and they're going to defend the status quo."

King looked out the window. This lunatic was trying to pull him into the dark alley between the Republican Congress and the Democratic White House, and that was an alley he wasn't going into without a fight.

Maldray glanced at the pilot and co-pilot over his shoulder, then leaned forward, closer to General King.

"There could be a promotion in this for you, General. When we reshuffle the command structure, there are going to be openings up and down the line. I'm thinking of a particular slot that will open up in about two months' time. I think you know I'm talking about the office of chief of staff of the United States Army."

King was still looking out the window when he said: "What unit did you serve in when you were in the Army, Senator?"

"I don't think I heard you."

"I asked what unit you served in, sir. Back when you were a soldier."

"I was never in the Army, General. I had a sensitive teaching position at the University of Georgia that made me ineligible for the draft."

"I see."

"Do you have a point, General King? Am I missing something here?"

"I was just curious which unit you served in, sir, because I thought if you had served in, say, the Fifth Army or the Third Army, you would probably have some loyalty to your former unit, because I know I would. I've got to tell you, Senator, I don't envy your position. It would be hard as hell for me to disassemble an entire Army command. You probably know that the Fifth Army took Anzio and Salerno and Rome and later conquered the rest of Italy and took the surrender of Kesslering's entire forces. They captured the German 18th Army Group in France, and drove straight into southern

Germany through the Strasbourg Gap. The only all-black unit to serve in ground combat was part of the Fifth Army. So was the famous 442nd Regimental Combat Team, the unit with the most casualties, and the most medals, of the entire war. It would be hard as hell for me, with all that history in front of me, looking at that flag with those battle streamers, to throw the whole damn thing in the shitcan and pretend that somehow dollars are more important than the lives that were shed to put those battle streamers up there on that flagstaff. It would be just hard as hell, Senator."

The helicopter banked steeply, and General King pointed out the window.

"That's Fifth Army Headquarters down there, Senator. It's not very big, only about a hundred in staff, maybe another sixty, seventy in enlisted support. You couldn't even put a down payment on an F-14 for what you're paying out yearly to the entire command. So if you want my feeling on this one, sir, I've got to put it to you like this: I understand the need for the cuts, and I'm all for saving the money, but there's a part of me who walks into that headquarters down there every morning, who wakes up and reads the *New York Times* and the *Wall Street Journal* and realizes down in the pit of my soul that a lot of what we're talking about here is just a big shell game, that the buck we save here"—he pointed at one side of the parade field—"just ends up shifting over there."

General King paused to let his words sink in. "I don't understand much about politics, sir, but I do know this much. It's not a zero-sum game. And there's one thing I know about the history of the Fifth Army, sir. The adding and subtracting that takes place within an army unit, I don't care if it's a squad or a platoon or a company or a battalion or a brigade or a division or a corps or an army, is done in human lives. That's my perspective, Senator. For what it's worth."

Maldray stared at General King for a long moment. The

helicopter was hovering, about to put down on the pad on the grassy parade between the headquarters. There was a jerk, and a loud *thump* as the wheels touched down.

"Thank you for your input, General. You have been a big help."

"Anytime, Senator."

Maldray looked out the window. Several television news crews were leaning into the wind from the chopper's blades, tugging at microphone wires, clinging to video cameras.

"Maybe we can get a shot with Fifth Army Headquarters in the background. Do you think we can do that, General?"

"I think that would be an excellent idea, Senator."

"Have you got a flag . . . a big one with the battle streamers, and maybe a gold eagle on top?"

"It's in my office, Senator."

"Good. We'll put the flag in the shot too."

Kara opened the Humvee's door and climbed inside. "Thanks for coming to pick me up, Sarge."

"No problem, ma'am." Sergeant Trevor Tevis, a skinny young man with an accent redolent of his native Alabama, threw the big vehicle into reverse. "Kind of a tight squeeze here, ma'am." He aimed the Humvee expertly between two trees, backed it around, put it in gear, and drove down the long gravel drive that led to the cottage she had found tucked into a stand of trees on the outskirts of Columbus.

"Nice place you've got there, Major Guidry. It looks real cozy."

"It's not much, but the rent is cheap and the privacy can't be beat."

"You didn't look much like one of those BOQ types when I seen you, ma'am."

"I'm not sure what you mean, Sergeant."

"You know, ma'am. Some of them over in the BOQ

look like if they ain't breakin' starch, they don't figure they're really puttin' on clothes."

"Green and mean, is that what you're talking about, Sarge?"

The Sergeant chuckled. "Yes, ma'am. You got it."

"Well, I'm not terribly green, but I'm as mean as they come."

Tevis laughed. He stopped at the end of the drive. A narrow two-lane blacktop ran through a thick stand of pines. "Where to, ma'am?"

"South Gate Road. I've got to pick up my Cherokee. I got stuck out there last night."

The sergeant turned left, and with a loud whirring of gears and humming of tires, the Humvee got up to speed.

"Be there in a short-short, ma'am. You just leave it to old TT. He'll take care of you."

"That's why I called you, Sarge."

Tevis grinned. "I 'preciate it, ma'am. It's always nice to know you're needed, you know what I mean?"

She was looking out the side window at the blur of dirty green flying past.

"I know exactly what you mean, Sarge."

The stainless steel doors *whooshed* open, and Major Hollaway walked into the main autopsy room at the Fort Benning morgue. Dr. Charles Evans was standing beneath a large articulated operating room light, pulling a sheet over the body on a gurney.

"Charlie. Thanks for calling me."

Evans pulled down a paper mask that had been covering his nose and mouth. He looked like he was right out of med school, but Hollaway knew that Evans' reputation in forensics medicine had him on military aircraft flying all over the United States and occasionally to Europe to consult on difficult cases.

"We've got trouble, Frank. It's just like I thought it was." Evans led the way into the morgue's refrigerated locker. He counted down the row of white enameled drawers and yanked one open. The ash white face of Lieutenant Sheila Worthy stared straight up at them, open-eyed. Evans pointed at the wound on her neck.

"I've been doing this awhile, Frank. I think you know that."

"You bet, Charlie. You're the best."

"I think I know a knife wound when I see one by now, Frank."

"Don't tell me."

Evans pulled on a fresh pair of operating gloves. With his forefingers he pulled gently at the sides of the wound.

"Frank, you see this entrance? Kind of irregular, don't you think?"

Hollaway leaned over. He had no idea what Evans was talking about. Evans knew this. It was his way, patient, instructional. It was also what made him a virtually bulletproof witness in a trial.

"What I'm talking about, Frank, look closely. You see here where the skin doesn't line up when I let the wound snap shut?"

He released his fingers. The sides of the wound eased together. Evans was right. It didn't line up. Evans looked over at Hollaway.

"With a puncture wound caused by a knife, you get an initial stretching of the skin as the point of the knife goes in. Let me show you."

Evans poked the little finger of his left hand into his own neck. The skin pulled tightly around the tip of his finger.

"It's like this with a knife. The point's not that sharp, and the motion isn't like the one we use with a scalpel, a slicing motion, like this . . ."

He drew his finger down his neck.

"You stab somebody, you stick it in and you pull it out. Simple as that."

"What are you saying, Charlie? Somebody killed this girl?"

"I'm not saying that exactly, Frank. We found enough water in her lungs to kill her, so she didn't die from this stab wound. But I've got the wound path mapped, and it was deep, but it missed the jugular and it missed the airway, so that's just what it was, a wound, and that's all."

"She would have lived if she hadn't drowned."

"In all probability, yes."

"But the wound contributed to her death, because it probably affected her ability to get free of the car when it flooded."

"You are reading my mind, Major."

"You know what my guess is, Charlie? She was outside of the car when the stabbing occurred. She ran from her attacker and jumped in the car, trying to get away. She was frantic. Maybe the attacker gave chase. That would explain why she blundered into deep water out there."

"That's it, Frank. That's the way it happened."

"You're certain this wound couldn't have been caused by something else? Say, a piece of glass, maybe?"

"Certain? You mean, like testifying certain?"

"That's what I'm asking you, Charlie."

"I know this much. I have yet to come across the piece of glass that could have made a puncture like this. We're talking about something three, maybe three and a half, four inches long, about three-quarters of an inch across. Thin. Sharp. Went in. Came out. Smooth motion through internal tissues. A classic knife-puncture wound, Frank. I'd stake my life on it."

"You don't have a life, Charlie."

"Okay. I'd stake *your* life on it."

Hollaway laughed. That was the thing about Charlie Evans. He made the grim details of forensics medicine bearable. Hell, he made it half fun.

*   *   *

"Jeez, this road was under some serious water last night, huh, Major?"

Sergeant Tevis pulled the Humvee up behind Kara's Cherokee. There was a dirty brown water mark about a quarter of the way up the driver's door. Kara got out. She looked past the Cherokee, out where Sheila Worthy's car had been. The flash-flood waters had receded. The car was gone.

"You'd better stick around while I see if this thing will start, Sarge."

"You got it, ma'am."

Kara opened the driver's door and climbed in. Water had seeped into the passenger compartment but stopped before it reached the seats. She put the key in the ignition and cranked it. The engine turned over a couple of times and caught. She gunned it. The engine settled into a comfortable idle. She got out, walked back to the Humvee.

"I got it going, but maybe you'd better follow me back to the office. It's supposed to be able to go right through wheel-deep water, but . . ."

Tevis laughed. "You know what they say about these civilian off-road vehicles, don't you, ma'am?"

"No, TT, I don't."

"They'll get you deep into them boonies, all right. Far enough so's when you get stuck, you got to walk back out to get somebody to come in there and pull you out."

She laughed. "Give me a minute."

"I'll be right here, ma'am."

Kara climbed back into the Cherokee. She was reaching to pull the shoulder belt around when she saw that the backseat was empty. Her overnight bag was gone.

So was Mace's.

Chapter Four

Kara stormed into Hollaway's office, her fists swinging at her sides. "All right, Frank, I want to know what the fuck is going on."

Hollaway looked up. "Geez, Kara . . ."

"Don't give me that 'Geez, Kara' crap, goddammit. I want to know what's going on, and I want to know now."

"I have no idea what you're talking about. Sit down."

He didn't have that cop-calm look about him, the twinkling eyes and easy smile they get when they know something you don't know, and they're getting off on it. She sat down.

"I'm sorry, Frank. This thing is getting me crazy, I guess . . ."

"What's wrong, Kara?"

"I went out there and picked up my car. Everything I had in it is missing."

"Somebody ripped off your car?"

"That's right."

"What'd they take?"

"Just the stuff I had in it."

"Which was . . ."

"I had a jacket and an overnight bag. I'd been down in Taylorsville, visiting friends."

"You want to make a report?"

Kara thought for a second. "Not now. Not a formal one, anyway."

"Why not? You're here. I'm the man to see about it."

"I'm too tired, Frank. I haven't gotten any sleep in thirty-six hours. I'll do it tomorrow."

He studied her for a moment. She was tired, that much was true. But there was something else. "What'd you storm in here for, Kara? You think I had my people out there going through your stuff?"

"It occurred to me. Who else knew where my car was?"

"You know I wouldn't seize any of your property without your permission."

"I've got to get some sleep, Frank. That's all there is to it. I'm not stressed out. I'm crazed."

"Tell you what. Let me take care of it for you. I'll get my people looking for your stuff. It'll turn up."

"Thanks, Frank. I appreciate it."

He stood up and they walked to the door. "There's something I've got to tell you, Kara."

"Not now, Frank. I've had enough for one day." She started out the door.

"You're going to want to know this sooner rather than later."

She turned around. "Okay."

"That wound in Lieutenant Worthy's neck? It's a knife wound."

"What are you telling me?"

"I just came from the morgue. A three- to four-inch knife. Evans is positive."

"So it's not an accident, it's a homicide? Duh? Earth to Hollaway. What did I tell you?"

Hollaway shrugged. "Should I rack it up to your feminine intuition?"

"Rack it up to life experience, Frank."

"I'll buy that. And I'll buy you a drink at the O-club sometime. I owe you one." He opened the door.

She walked into the hallway and paused. Then she turned slowly. He was still standing there.

"I haven't heard that in a long time, Frank. Thanks."

"What? That I want to buy you a drink?"

"That somebody owes me one."

"Oh. Well . . ."

"I'm going to hunt you down and drag that drink out of you. Mark my words."

He laughed. "You know where to find me."

She stood by the pay phone for several minutes, debating whether to call him, before she dialed. Finally she made the call and listened as it rang. Then his voice came on.

"Third platoon. Sergeant Nukanen speaking, sir."

"Mace. It's me."

He lowered his voice. "I thought we agreed you shouldn't call here. It's too dangerous."

"I know. But I had to call. Somebody took our bags."

"You're kidding me!"

"No. I went out there and picked up the car. Everything is gone."

"It was the MP's, that major," he whispered.

"No, it's not. I checked with Hollaway. He didn't know anything about it."

"And you *believe* him?"

"I've known him for years, Mace. He wouldn't lie to me."

"I don't trust him."

"Well, I do."

"Who took them, then?"

"I don't know, but I'm going to find out."

"Whoever's got them knows about us." He sounded shaky, scared.

She took a deep breath. "I know that."

"I'll get out of here and call you later."

"Mace. Be careful. Don't answer any questions if somebody starts asking. Get ahold of me first."

She heard voices in the background. He hung up before she could say good-bye.

* * *

She was still thinking about how scared Mace sounded driving back to the cottage. They had successfully hidden their relationship for months. This was the first mistake they'd made. How could they have forgotten to take their bags? Logic told her the storm had been raging, there had been a dead woman at their feet on the ground, a helicopter loudly pounding the air nearby, three medics running around . . . it was an easy enough mistake under those conditions. Still, their mistake could have grave consequences if the bags found their way into the wrong hands. Mace was right to be scared. So was she.

Her headlights found the drive, littered with pine needles. Huge puddles had formed in low spots in the yard. She unlocked the front door and flipped on the light. One of the cats jumped onto the kitchen counter and cried like an infant. She wondered where they learned that sound. Some kind of primal connector, back there in the far reaches of the ancient food chain, when maybe cats fed on humans instead of humans opening cans and feeding cats. She gave him a rough head rub.

"Wally. Wall-man. El-Wall-o. The big Wall-a-rino."

He purred.

The shingled cottage wasn't much to look at from the outside, but within it glowed a homey coziness that was a welcome relief from the garden apartment complex she had called home for the past three years. From the front door you walked into one big room with a fireplace on one side and a kitchen on the other. The walls were wainscotted in knotty pine, and the same oiled wood was used in a long counter that separated the kitchen from the rest of the room. The furniture was old but comfortable, a bequest from her grandmother when her mother had shipped her off to a nursing home. She walked over to the armoire and turned on the CD player and punched Play. The opening chords of a Replacements song filled the room, and she sang along with the smoky vocal.

Trailed by Wally, she skipped down a narrow hall to the single bedroom that had been tacked onto the back of the cottage in a lean-to fashion. Two more cats were curled up on the down comforter at the foot of a king-size bed.

"Weird-o. Peesheek. What's going on with you two lazybones cats?" Neither one of them so much as stirred a whisker. She rubbed Weird behind the ears, and he opened one eye. Peesheek stretched and nuzzled the back of her hand.

"Home at last, huh, you worthless monsters? You all want to eat?" All three cats responded to her entreaty by running to the door and thundering down the short hall and jumping up on the kitchen counter.

The phone rang.

"Major Guidry."

"That wouldn't be your boy Paulie Westerberg I hear in the background, would it, doll face? That luscious hunk—"

"Lannie! Where are you calling from?"

"Guess."

"An airplane."

"Close. My car. Take another guess."

"You're out of there! You beat the five-sided monster! You plastered the puzzle palace!"

"You damn right I did, girl! You know what I'm looking at right now? A thousand yellow flags flying over Bob's Big Time Used Cars on Victory Boulevard."

"You're *here*? At Benning?"

"Standing tall and proud, Captain Lannie Fulton Love is reporting for duty this very minute."

"I can't believe it! They *never* let you out of the Pentagon before your assignment's up. How'd you do it?"

"I marched in there to the colonel and I told her, either you call my branch and tell them you're letting me go, or I'm going to tell them about you and that bull dyke gallery owner you're living with down in Alexandria Old Town."

"You didn't."

"No, not really. Let's just say the colonel and me came to an understanding."

"What'd you used to call her?"

"Leslie Lipstick."

"That's right. Well, nothing like a little backhanded blackmail to set the accounts straight, is what I always say."

"You know what, Kara? If those assholes up there on the E-Ring knew what was going on down in the lower corridors of power in that building, there'd be so many fucking heart attacks, they'd run out of beds at Walter Reade."

"Code Blue! Code Blue!"

"Call the Crash Cart!"

"Get the paddles!"

"Clear! Whoooomp!"

Uproarious laughter.

"Do you know what job you're getting here, Lannie?"

"I've got a pretty good idea. You know the base closure commission?"

"Yeah."

"I'm going to be Fort Benning's liaison to the commission."

"Hey, that's not bad. Loads of TDY. Nobody looking over your shoulder. Who do you report to?"

"Some guy name of Roberts. Chief of staff at Third Army."

"I know him. He's not so bad. You might even like him." She paused a moment. "Where are you going to be staying? I've got a nice big sofa . . ."

"They're putting me up at the Ramada Suites off post till I get settled in."

"Hey, rolling out the red carpet, huh?"

"Demand the best, you get the best. And you know my rules: Only the very, very best for Lannie Fulton Love. Hey, passing through the post gates right now. Welcome to Fort Benning, Home of the Infantry. Yes, indeedy. Glad to be here. You know who's stationed here, Kara? Randy Taylor."

"I don't know him."

"He transferred into my company firstie year. You were long gone by then. He's a doll."

"Jeez, I can't believe it's been, like, almost fifteen years since I had you in my Beast Barracks squad."

"Best damn plebe ever put on Caydette Gray, am I right? Ooop. I'm pulling into Headquarters parking."

"Give me a call when you get settled in. Come over and we'll whip up one of our famous pastas."

"Take you up on it tomorrow. See you."

Click.

The cats were perched expectantly atop the counter as Kara skipped over to the CD player and hit the Repeat button. She grabbed a couple of cans of cat food from the cupboard.

"You hear that, rats? Lannie's coming to town!"

She was spooning food into their bowls when she heard a knock at the door. She looked out. There was a young officer standing on the porch. She opened the door. He was a second lieutenant, tall, good-looking. He took off his cap.

"Ma'am, my name is Lieutenant Barry Parks. There's something I need to talk to you about."

Oh, my God. Mace's platoon leader! Something's happened to him!

"Come in." She showed him to the kitchen and stood there waiting, trying not to show him how nervous she was.

"Sergeant Nukanen gave me your name. He said you'd given him a ride onto the post that night, and it was you and the sarge who found Sheila Worthy's body."

She relaxed. "Sit down, Lieutenant. Can I get you some coffee?"

"No, ma'am. I'm okay."

"Yes, Sergeant Nukanen and I found the body. It's

terrible what happened. Very sad. Were you a friend of hers?"

"Yes, ma'am. We were classmates in college. We were . . . close. Very close."

"I'm sorry for your loss, Lieutenant."

"Ma'am, Sergeant Nukanen told me you're a JAG officer."

"That's right."

"And you know the officer in charge of the investigation?"

"That's right. Major Hollaway."

"Ma'am, somebody killed her, and you've got to find out who did it. You've got to. She was . . ." He broke down, sobbing. When he had recovered, he said: "She was everything to me. Everything."

"Was she your girlfriend, Lieutenant?"

"Yes, ma'am. In college she was, anyway."

"But not any longer."

"No, ma'am. I asked her to go to the club with me for dinner, but she turned me down. She had another date."

"And you're thinking . . ."

"Yes, ma'am. If only she'd gone with me, she'd still be alive."

"But the decision was hers, not yours, Lieutenant. You shouldn't feel guilty."

"I keep thinking, if things had happened differently, if we'd gotten married, like we talked about . . ."

"There's nothing you could have done, Lieutenant."

"Ma'am, if there's anything I can do to help . . ."

"I'm not even part of the investigation, Lieutenant. But I'll tell Major Hollaway what you said."

He wiped a tear from his eye and looked up at Kara. "She was very, very special, ma'am. She came from an Army family. The Army was her life. I just know she was going to have a wonderful career . . . with me or without me."

"Can I ask you a question, Lieutenant? Her roommate told Major Hollaway and me that she had been seeing someone for quite some time. Do you know who he was?"

"No, ma'am. We didn't talk about . . . anybody else." He stood up to leave. "Ma'am, if there's anything I can do . . ."

"Thank you for coming, Lieutenant Parks."

She walked him to the door, and he stepped out into the cold.

So Sheila Worthy'd had more than one man in her life. A beautiful young lieutenant on a post full of hungry men . . . it was obvious she had raised some temperatures around Fort Benning. She had raised one of them high enough to get killed.

Chapter Five

The flight north out of Atlanta stopped in Raleigh-Durham and Richmond before it made a steep left turn over Mount Vernon and started its downwind leg. There, out the right window of the plane, was the dome of the Capitol, the Washington Monument, the Lincoln Memorial, and the twinkling lights of the nation's capital just beyond. The plane made a steep turn onto the final approach.

Back in coach, one of the passengers unbuckled his seat belt and slipped up a couple of seats and across the aisle, looking out the window as the plane passed over Georgetown and passed directly above the Potomac. The woman in the window seat turned around. She was wearing a tasteful blue suit and a single strand of pearls. She glanced quickly at his ring finger.

Bare.

"Beautiful, isn't it?" she ventured.

He smiled. "This flight stops twice, but I don't mind. The view is worth it coming into National."

"I'm Helen Young."

"Randy Taylor."

She looked at the ribbons above his left breast pocket on his military uniform, at the insignia on his epaulets. "Going home to visit relatives, Captain?"

"I'd have to fly the other way to see them. My folks live out in San Francisco."

"Army business, then."

"You could say that."

"Are you traveling space available?"

"Yeah. It's pretty easy to get a seat on one of these puddle jumpers."

The plane's wheels *screeched* as it touched down. She handed him her business card.

"I'm a travel agent. We have a little office just off Dupont Circle. We do quite a bit of military business. Feel free to give me a call anytime you need a ticket."

"Thanks."

The plane jerked to a stop. Grabbing their carry-ons, everyone crowded into the aisle, moving slowly to the front of the plane. Someone jostled her, and she bumped into him, her breasts pressing firmly against his back. Her shoulder bag fell to the floor. "Sorry."

He turned and picked up her bag, grinning. "That's what we get for sitting in the back."

She smiled shyly. "Do you, uh, need a ride? I've got my car. I'm going straight downtown."

"No, thank you. I'm not going in that direction. I'm being met, anyway."

Disappointed: "Oh."

He smiled warmly. "Thanks for the offer, though." They reached the plane door, headed through the jetway. Just inside the terminal he put his carry-on down and pulled on his overcoat. She walked up.

"Listen. I meant it . . . about calling the office. I've been in the Washington travel market for seven years. I know the best flights if you're going space-A."

"Thanks. I will." He picked up his carry-on and walked toward the door marked TAXIS-BUSES-GROUND TRANSPORTATION and stepped into the open door of a taxi. The driver glanced over his shoulder.

"Where to, sir?"

Intricately carved pumpkins were perched on every stoop of the narrow Georgetown street as Randy stepped out of a cab and watched its taillights disappear around the corner. He headed back the way they had come. He found P Street and turned left, walked another block, and turned right on a dead-end alley. He counted the gracious old brick town houses as he passed them . . . *one, two, three* . . .

He stopped under a short awning. There was a small brass plaque on the door reading LEXINGTON CLUB. He looked around. A taxi pulled into view at the end of the alley, and a man got out, paid the driver, and walked toward him. As he neared the awning, he extended his hand. He was a trim figure with cropped hair and an engaging smile.

"Randy."

"Ed, good to see you."

"I see you found it."

"No problem. The directions you gave were excellent."

"Come on. They're waiting."

He knocked on the unmarked door. A metal window slid open.

"Edwin Teese and Randolph Taylor."

The door opened and they went inside. The foyer was double-height, with a black and white tile floor, and the rooms just beyond paneled in mahogany. Leather armchairs abounded, and waiters in white jackets and black trousers floated through the rooms carrying silver trays. One of them stopped.

"Sir?"

"Martinis. Bombay. Two of them. Shaken, not stirred."

"Yes, sir."

Randy laughed. "You learned that from 007, I guess."

"No, from my father."

Randy took his hand and squeezed tightly. "I've missed you."

The older man looked into his eyes. "Me too."

They wandered into the next room. A clutch of older men stood around the fireplace. Several men wearing cardigans were sitting in leather armchairs, reading newspapers.

"How'd you find this place?"

"Believe me, they call you, you don't call them."

Randy looked at the painting hanging over the fireplace. "Did you see that? It's a Klee."

"There's a Mondrian in the dining room."

They walked through an arched doorway into another parlor.

Ed pointed across the room. "You recognize the senator, don't you?" A distinguished gentleman with dark hair was holding court in the corner, surrounded by several other men. He was wearing a velvet smoking jacket and forest green slippers with a gold crest on the toe.

"He's that right-winger from Mississippi."

"He may lean to the right on the floor of the Senate and at barbecues back home, but I'll guarantee you his left wing will get some exercise here tonight."

Randy laughed as Ed nodded at another man. "I see our Supreme Court justice is in attendance tonight."

As they passed, Randy caught a snatch of his conversation.

". . . I told him I didn't care what the judge in *Haley* versus *Felker* held, I fail to see how the state of Utah has a corner on the morals market!"

The man he was talking to laughed loudly.

They stopped as two men dressed in conservative pinstripe suits approached them. They were in their late fifties and smiled when they saw them.

The older of the two men shook hands. "Edwin. How are things over in Procurement?"

"Great. We're working on a new generation of anti-artillery radar for use in units down to platoon strength. How are things on the E-Ring, Jack? Is General Carson keeping you busy?"

"The damn flights coming into National are about to rattle the pictures off the wall, but other than that, fine."

Ed turned to Randy. "Jack Ranstead, I'd like you to meet Randy Taylor. He's the man I was telling you about."

They shook hands. "Nice to meet you, Randy."

Ed turned to the other man. "This is Terry Samuels. Jack's got three stars. He's the deputy chief of staff for Operations and Plans. Terry retired with two. He's over on Capitol Hill these days, working on Senator Maldray's staff as his Defense liaison."

"Glad to meet you, sir."

"Terry used to work for your boss," said Ed.

"You knew General Beckwith, sir?"

Terry Samuels was a heavy-set man with deep furrows in his brow. He looked Randy over.

"Did Ed tell you why he brought you here tonight?"

Randy glanced at Ed before he spoke. "He told me about the club. He didn't describe its membership. I must say I'm impressed."

Ed spoke up. "I wanted to wait until we got here." He turned to Randy. "Jack and Terry want to talk with you about your job."

"My job?"

General Ranstead stopped a waiter, whispered his order. The waiter left. "You've heard that Beckwith is on the short list for chief."

"I guess everybody has by now. It's been in the papers. We've got media people making requests for interviews almost daily."

"We want to stop him."

There was a long silence as Randy looked blankly at the two men across from him. He turned to Ed, a note of panic in his voice. "What are they talking about?"

Ed touched Randy's arm. "This is very important, and I think you'll understand once you've heard them out."

General Ranstead led them to a sitting area in the corner of the room, and they pulled chairs close together and sat down.

"Beckwith is a dangerous man, Randy. If he gets to be chief, everybody's going to suffer. Including you."

Terry Samuels leaned closer. "You read that shit he wrote on the op-ed page of the *Times,* didn't you?"

"His piece on don't ask, don't tell?"

"That's the one."

"I read it. I thought it took some guts."

General Ranstead's face turned red. "Guts? Who are you kidding, Captain? You don't think he was kissing ass, trying to wring whatever advantage he could from that so-called compromise? I've never seen such a naked, lily-livered performance in my life."

"I don't think you understand General Beckwith, sir. That wasn't his intent at all."

"Oh, I think it was," said General Ranstead. "What do you think you're doing here, son?"

"I told you. Ed said—"

"You're here because you're one of us, Captain. Look around you. This club is nothing but a high-class gay bar. There's more power in these few rooms than you could gather for a mom and apple pie rally on the Fourth of July on the lawn of the White House. And every last man you see is homosexual. You see those two men over there?"

He pointed across the room.

"The tall one is a congressman from Utah. The other one is on the National Security Council."

He turned around.

"No doubt you recognize the famous radio talk-show hostess with the mostess. He's talking to the president of a company with over twenty billion dollars in defense contracts. You know what they've got in common? They're both so deep in the closet, you could use their noses for tie racks. You know why? Because men like Beckwith want to keep them in the closet. Let me ask you something, Randy. Have you told Beckwith you're gay?"

Randy glanced nervously over at Ed.

"Of course not."

"What would happen to you if you did?"

Terry Samuels sat back in his chair and pulled out a cigar. "I'll answer that for you. He would court-martial you. That's what he did to Jimmy Prentiss. You heard about Jimmy? No, probably not. He was before your time. Look him up sometime in the Register of Graduates, USMA. He was on his way to the War College on the five percent list when he ran into Beckwith, who wasn't on the list but wanted to be. Beckwith got on the list, all right. He went to the War College, and Jimmy ended up in Leavenworth. He committed suicide there at the Disciplinary Barracks. Beckwith put the rope around his neck when he turned him in for being gay and filed court-martial charges against him."

"Jesus. I had no idea."

Terry Samuels finished lighting his cigar with a puff of smoke.

"Beckwith tried to get Jimmy to give up his lover. He told Jimmy if he turned him in, they'd drop the charges, but Jimmy sat there, and he looked at Beckwith and he told him to go fuck himself. That's why he ended up behind bars at Leavenworth. You know who his lover was, son?" He paused, looking across the room, exhaling a long puff of smoke. Without turning to face Randy he said: "Me."

Ed scooted his chair closer to Randy and dropped his voice. "Randy, you know how important this is. Beckwith doesn't know this place exists. He has no more of an inkling that these generals and congressmen and judges and corporate presidents are gay than he does about you. But imagine what would happen if he did."

Randy paused for a long moment. Finally he said, "I'd feel like I was betraying a trust."

General Ranstead chuckled. "You want to talk about trust? Beckwith would sell your ass to those dogs in the Civil Investigative Division in a split second if it served his purposes. And you know it."

Randy looked at Ed, then his gaze drifted to the two men who sat across from him.

"What do you want me to do?"

"We want to know everything you know about Beckwith. We want to know where he goes, who he talks to. That's the sum total of it. You keep us informed, and we'll do the rest."

"Can I ask you something?"

Terry Samuels exhaled another dense puff of smoke. "You sure can. Anything you want."

"Are you lovers?"

Terry Samuels looked over at the general. "I think you'd better answer that one, Jack."

General Ranstead leveled his gaze at the younger man. "Let me ask you something, son. How long have you and Ed been together?"

Randy glanced over at his lover. "Going on two years, sir."

"It'll be ten years for us next Friday." General Ranstead took Terry Samuels' hand. "The best years of my life."

Ed unlocked the door to his Arlington apartment and flipped on the light. Dedicated foraging in West Virginia junk and antique shops had transformed a high-rise apartment into an Empire–style Victorian manor house. There were Persian carpets, and the floor-to-ceiling windows overlooking downtown Washington had been trimmed in forest green velvet. He pulled the heavy drapes open and sank into an overstuffed chair. Randy stood behind him, gently massaging his neck muscles.

"How long have you known General Ranstead?"

"I don't know. Twenty years, maybe? We were stationed together at Leavenworth years ago."

"Is he the one you told me about? The guy who pinned on your stars when you were promoted to brigadier general?"

"Yeah, that's him."

"Pretty good guy, huh?"

"The best."

Randy leaned down and kissed the top of his lover's head. "Three gay generals sitting together in one room. If you'd told me I'd live to see this day when I was at the Point, I'd have said you're crazy."

"It's funny, isn't it?"

"What about the other guy? Terry?"

"I've known him almost as long. He's very, very bitter. They were closing in on him when he retired. He was never married. There were always rumors, I guess."

"That was an incredible story about his lover."

"Jimmy was a wonderful guy. Everyone loved him."

"You said General Samuels is on Senator Maldray's staff? I saw Senator Maldray with General King the other day at Fort Benning. He had media with him, local and national TV, the *Washington Post,* the *Times.* It looked to me like Maldray is backing King for chief."

"No, he's not. That was just to cover his ass with black voters in Georgia. He's backing Beckwith all the way. Terry heard it straight from the horse's mouth."

"Geez, it's all political, isn't it?"

"Everything's political in the United States Army."

"So you think I ought to do this? You think I should cooperate with them?"

Ed turned in the chair and looked up at Randy. "I do. I think it's really important that Beckwith is stopped."

"I don't know if I could live with myself. I'd feel like a *spy.* It goes against everything I was taught by my parents, everything I learned at West Point."

Ed stood up and walked around the chair and took Randy in his arms and kissed him. "Randy, I learned the same things you learned at the Point, but that doesn't stop us from loving each other, does it?"

Randy walked over to the window and stood there looking at the lights of the city.

"It's just so hard, Ed."

"I'm not going to lie to you, Randy. It *is* hard, and it's

not going to get any easier if your boss makes chief of staff."

"I know," said Randy.

"All we're asking is that you stand with us against this man's bigotry and intolerance."

"You've got to promise me one thing. You can use what I tell you against General Beckwith getting a promotion to chief of staff, but I don't want it used to destroy him and his career. I understand Terry Samuels' anger, but I'm not going to help him get his revenge. Understood?"

"Yes."

"Okay. I'll do it."

Chapter Six

The court-martial of Corporal Vernon Richards had already been called to order when Kara burst through the door of the court. She stopped in front of the military judge.

"I apologize for being late, Your Honor."

Kara slipped behind the defense table and opened her briefcase.

Colonel Simon Freeman peered disapprovingly over his glasses. He extracted a fat finger from beneath his black robes and wagged it in Kara's direction. "You have already cost this court a full day of trial, Major Guidry, and I have been tolerant of this delay because of the extraordinary circumstances in which you found yourself yesterday. If you're late again, I'm going to hand the keys to Major Sanders there, and have him cuff you to your table overnight while the rest of us go home, so you'll be certain to be here when I walk into this court-martial in the morning. Am I making myself clear, Major?"

Kara looked up from her briefcase. "Perfectly, Your Honor."

"Proceed, Major Sanders."

Major Howard Sanders glanced at Kara as he unwrapped his six-foot two-inch frame from his green government-issue chair and approached the battered lectern. As he faced the military judge, to his left, behind a metal railing, sat the members of the court-martial board: a lieutenant colonel, a major, two captains, a chief warrant officer, and two master sergeants. The lieutenant colonel was a black man, the major was a woman, and one of the master sergeants was also black.

The courtroom, a windowless pale green box, was unadorned by decoration save for an American flag hanging from the wall behind the judge, and was as empty as it was forlorn.

Behind Kara a metal chair scraped the worn linoleum floor as the court-martial's only spectator took her seat. Kara's eyes met those of Lateesha Richards, who was wearing a flower print dress and black scarf. Kara remembered the first time she had met Lateesha in the stockade parking lot on their way to see her son. A yellow cab had stopped, and a middle-aged black woman got out and paid the driver. "Major Guidry, I'm Vernon's mother. You've got to help my boy, ma'am, 'cause he's all I got."

Corporal Vernon Richards was the youngest of her three sons. The older boys had been bystanders who were cut down in a drive-by shooting when they were just eight and nine. Vernon watched it happen out the front window of their project apartment. When he grew up, Lateesha encouraged him to enlist in the Army because in the Army, at least, he'd be safe.

Now he stood next to Kara in Army prison garb— faded denim fatigues with a huge white P sewn onto the back of the jacket and down the side of his pant legs— charged with desertion. If he was found guilty, he would serve at least ten years in the Fort Leavenworth Disciplinary Barracks. The main portion of the evidence against him was uncontested. He had absented himself without leave for a period of forty-six days. It was right there on the morning reports day after day: Corporal Vernon Richards. AWOL.

Sanders had offered Kara a deal before trial. Plead to AWOL and take a six and six and a DD, and we'll wave the six in con and he's gone. Translation: If Vernon pled guilty to the lesser charge of AWOL instead of deser-

tion, he would be awarded six months' confinement to
the stockade, six months' reduction in pay, and a dishonorable discharge. The Army would drop the six
months' confinement, and he would be discharged
forthwith.

Kara had dutifully told Vernon about the Army's offer, and Vernon did not hesitate even a second before he
said, no deal. "I get myself a dishonorable, and what
am I gonna do back in New Orleans, ma'am? You know
from down there. Only job I'll ever get is washin' cars
down on Carrollton Avenue. They won't even hire me to
pick up garbage for the Sanitation."

Kara had explained that he was facing ten years plus
in Leavenworth, the evidence was heavily in the Army's
favor, and contesting the charges against him was going
to be difficult. Vernon was insistent. And so they stood
together in an empty courtroom located in a wood-
frame building next to the stockade facing a board of
senior officers and noncommissioned officers, hardly a
jury of Corporal Richards' peers. Kara had already tried
to challenge the captain and one of the sergeants off the
board, but her challenge had been rejected. She was
stuck with seven stern-faced military professionals in
whom the prohibition against desertion could be as-
sumed to have been inbred.

Major Sanders cleared his throat. "Your Honor, the
prosecution calls Captain John Eastlake to the stand."

Colonel Freeman nodded to a tall MP standing at the
back of the room. He opened the door and escorted
Captain Eastlake, a slight figure in his green Class A
uniform, to the front of the court. The MP held a Bible.
Eastlake placed his left hand atop the Bible and faced
the prosecutor.

"Do you swear to tell the truth, the whole truth, and
nothing but the truth, so help you God?" Sanders asked.

"I do," said Eastlake.

"Be seated, Captain." Sanders riffled through the papers on the lectern and looked up.

"You are Corporal Richards' company commander, Captain?"

"Yes, sir, I am."

Sanders walked over to the witness and handed him a sheaf of papers. "These are your morning reports for the period of January 15 to March 3 of this year, are they not?"

Eastlake looked through a few of the pages. "Yes, sir."

"Your Honor, I'd like to submit these morning reports as prosecution exhibits one through forty-six." He handed the reports to Colonel Freeman, who glanced at them and handed them back.

"Prosecution exhibits one through forty-six are admitted into evidence. Proceed."

Sanders turned to the witness. "Can you tell this court what distinguishes these reports from others you have filled out for your company, Captain?"

"They reflect the AWOL status of Corporal Richards, sir."

"After the thirtieth report of AWOL, Richards was carried on your company morning report as a deserter, is that correct?"

"Yes, sir."

"The signature on the bottom of each morning report is yours, Captain?"

"I think my XO signed four or five of them while I was on leave over a long weekend, sir."

"But you are the initiating officer, and you are ultimately responsible for the accuracy of the morning reports in your company?"

"Yes, sir."

"And these morning reports are accurate as to Corporal Richards' AWOL status to the best of your knowledge?"

"Yes, sir."

"He was AWOL for a total of forty-six days, and carried as a deserter for sixteen of those days, until his arrest by the military police in New Orleans on March the third of this year?"

"Yes, sir."

Sanders sat down. "Your witness, Major."

Kara stood behind the defense table. "Captain Eastlake, are you aware of Department of the Army policy regarding family accommodation?"

Sanders looked up. "Objection. Not relevant."

Colonel Freeman looked over at Kara. "Major?"

"Sir, this question goes to the heart of the defense case. Its relevancy will be revealed in due time."

"Objection sustained. Proceed."

"How long have you been a company commander, Captain Eastlake?"

"For just under a year, ma'am."

"That means your first officer efficiency report rating is coming up, is that right?"

"Yes, ma'am."

"You are rated on the number of AWOL's you carry in any given year, is that correct?"

Sanders stood. "Objection. Captain Eastlake's career isn't at issue here."

Kara glared at Sanders. "I'm trying to show—"

Colonel Freeman boomed: "Objection sustained. Stick to the testimony at hand, Major."

"No further questions." She started to sit down, then stood. "The defense reserves the right to recall this witness at a later time."

"Granted. Major Sanders, does the prosecution have another witness?"

"Sir, the prosecution rests."

"Major Guidry, is the defense ready with its case?"

"Sir, the defense requests a brief recess."

"Very well. This court-martial will reconvene at 1400 hours after lunch." Freeman banged his gavel, and the members of the court stood and filed from the room.

Corporal Richards stood as two MP's approached

from the back of the court. "Don't worry, ma'am. Everything's gonna be okay."

"You just remember what I told you before, Vernon. Don't say a word to anyone while you're in the holding cell over lunch."

"Yes, ma'am." The MP's led him away. Lateesha Richards was standing behind Kara, clutching a Bible to her breast.

"The Lord is watchin' over us right now, Major Guidry. I can feel him."

Kara closed her briefcase and picked up her cap. "I certainly hope so, Mrs. Richards."

She was sitting in the Cherokee with the windows rolled down, playing the radio at full volume. A shadow fell across the dash. She looked out the driver's window. An MP was tapping his nightstick on the roof. The music was so loud, she couldn't hear it. She turned off the radio.

"You're violating the commanding general's order on noise abatement, ma'am."

"What?"

"He's got some kind of big quality-of-life thing going on, ma'am. Supposed to be no loud music playing in cars or in homes or in public spaces."

Kara looked at the MP's impossibly young face. He was smiling sheepishly. He didn't get it any more than she did. "Thank you, Corporal. I'll remember that."

"Yes, ma'am. My pleasure, ma'am." He tucked his nightstick into his belt loop and walked away.

Kara turned the radio on again and reached into the bag tucked between the seats.

Cheetos and a Coke. Lunch.

She glanced in her rearview mirror. An airport taxi pulled up. The trunk popped open. A civilian in a seersucker suit grabbed his suitcase and looked around.

Sweet Jesus, he made it!

* * *

"All rise."

A door opened, and the members of the board filed in and took their seats. Colonel Freeman looked down at Kara.

"Is the defense ready?"

"We are, Your Honor. The defense calls Mrs. Lateesha Richards."

Clutching her Bible, Lateesha walked around the defense desk to the front of the court. An MP walked up to Lateesha carrying another Bible, but Freeman gave him a nod and he stepped away. Lateesha raised her right hand.

Major Sanders stood. "Do you swear to tell the truth, the whole truth, and nothing but the truth, so help you God?"

"Yes, sir. I do."

"Be seated, Mrs. Richards."

Lateesha sat down in the witness chair and looked nervously at Kara, who had moved behind the lectern.

"Are you nervous, Mrs. Richards?" asked Kara.

"Yes, ma'am. I'm so scared my hands is shakin'."

"Well, don't be. I'm going to ask you some questions, and then Major Sanders is going to ask some, is that all right?"

"Yes, ma'am."

"Where do you live, Mrs. Richards?"

"New Orleans, ma'am."

"Where in New Orleans?"

"On Franklin Street, in the St. Thomas Projects, ma'am."

"Is that a nice place to live, Mrs. Richards?"

"No, ma'am. It's like a piece of hell on earth, is what it is."

"It's an area with a heavy crime rate, isn't it?"

"Yes, ma'am."

"A lot of drug dealers and guns?"

"Yes, ma'am. More than you can count."

"Is it true, Mrs. Richards, that your first two sons

were killed as bystanders in a drive-by shooting in the St. Thomas Projects?"

"Yes, ma'am. It's true."

"How old were they?"

"Eight and nine, ma'am. They was just babies."

"Do you have any neighbors, Mrs. Richards?"

Major Sanders stood. "Objection. I fail to see how the living circumstances of the defendant's mother bears upon these proceedings."

Kara turned to Sanders coldly. "It's my turn, Major. The defense has great latitude in the presentation of its case—"

Freeman banged his gavel. "You will address the court, not each other, is that clear, Major Guidry?"

"Yes, sir."

"Objection overruled. Proceed."

"I'll ask the question again. Do you have any neighbors, Mrs. Richards?"

"No, ma'am. They moved out."

"Because your neighbors moved out, you live alone in the only occupied apartment in a four-building quad in the St. Thomas Projects?"

"Yes, ma'am. I'm all alone there. Been that way for two years now."

"Your son came home for a visit last Christmas, didn't he?"

"Yes, ma'am. First time he been home since after he finished his trainin'."

"But Christmas wasn't the only reason for his visit, was it, Mrs. Richards?"

"No, ma'am."

"Can you tell this court why you wanted Vernon to come home?"

"Gang bangers come by and they told me to get out. They was takin' over that part of the projects, and I was the onliest one left down there by the river end."

"Did they threaten you, Mrs. Richards?"

"Yes, ma'am. The big one, the one they call Snooper,

he come right into my house and he smashed my windows, and he went in and smashed up the toilet, and when he was done, he come out and he told me I wasn't out by Christmas, he was gonna kill me."

"When Vernon came home, what did he do?"

"He helped me fix up the windows, and he put in a new toilet, and he—"

"I understand he helped to fix up the apartment, Mrs. Richards. What else did he do?"

"He carried me down to the police station, and we filed a report, and then he carried me over to the Legal Aid on Magazine Street, and the Legal Aid, they took me into court, and the judge, he gave me a piece of paper—"

"He issued a restraining order, commanding the person known to you as Snooper and his gang members to stay at least one hundred yards away from you and your apartment, is that right?"

"That's right."

"And what else did Vernon do?"

"He went over across the projects and he seen this Snooper and he told him to stay away from me."

"I have one last question for you, Mrs. Richards. Where was your son during the forty-six days he was AWOL from the Army?"

"Why, he was with me at the St. Thomas Projects, ma'am."

"The whole time?"

"Every minute of every day."

"No further questions."

Sanders stood at his desk. "Is it your testimony, Mrs. Richards, that you knew your son was AWOL, that he had broken the law, and you did nothing to notify the proper authorities as to his whereabouts?"

"I told Vernon, I said, Vernon, you know you're makin' those Army people plenty mad at you—"

"Your Honor . . ."

Freeman looked down at Lateesha. "Answer the question, Mrs. Richards."

Lateesha looked over at Kara.

"Could you have the question read back to her, sir?" asked Kara.

Freeman nodded to the court stenographer.

"The question was: 'Is it your testimony, Mrs. Richards, that you knew your son was AWOL, that he had broken the law, and you did nothing to notify the proper authorities as to his whereabouts?' "

"No, sir. I didn't tell nobody, 'cause I knew—"

"That will be all, Mrs. Richards. Thank you."

Kara jumped to her feet. "Finish your answer, Mrs. Richards. Why didn't you notify the authorities?"

" 'Cause I was afraid, 'cause this Snooper done put the word out in the projects that he didn't listen to no courts, and he wanted me gone and he was gonna see to it hisself I was gone."

"What did you understand him to mean, Mrs. Richards?"

"Snooper was all over the projects sayin' he was gonna take me out and he was gonna take Vernon out, too. He had a gun, Major Guidry. A big gun."

"Thank you, Mrs. Richards. You may step down."

Lateesha, still clutching her Bible, walked back around the defense table and sat down.

"Will you state your full name and occupation, sir?"

The man in the witness chair tugged the lapel of his ill-fitting seersucker suit and cleared his throat.

"Detective Philip Ignatius Mancuso. I am acting deputy homicide inspector for the fourth district, New Orleans Police Department."

"Detective Mancuso, did you respond to a call in the St. Thomas Projects on March the second of this year?"

"Yes, I did."

"Who made that call, Detective?"

"The defendant."

"He called you from Mrs. Richards' apartment, is that correct?"

"Yes."

"Can you tell this court what you found when you arrived at the Richards' apartment?"

"Two bodies."

"Did you determine the identities of the bodies you found?"

"One of 'em was a known crack wholesaler they call Snooper. The other was his enforcer, a guy we suspected of committing about twelve murders, but we could never get anyone to talk about him. His street name was Buckshot. I've got their given names right here—"

"That won't be necessary, Detective. Where were the bodies when you found them?"

"This Buckshot, he was inside the apartment, facedown on the floor of the living room. Snooper, he was lyin' in the door, face up."

"Were they armed?"

"Oh, yeah. They were both carrying Tec-9's with forty-round magazines."

"How were they killed, Detective?"

"They were both shot in the face. Snooper, he had a big hole right in the middle of his forehead. Buckshot, his was just over the right eye, took out his whole eyebrow right up to his hairline."

"Do you know who shot them, Detective?"

"The defendant shot them."

Kara paused for effect. The members of the court-martial board were shifting in their chairs. Colonel Freeman took his half glasses off. He stared at the witness, open-mouthed.

"Do you know the circumstances under which the defendant shot these two St. Thomas Projects gang members, Detective?"

"Yes, I do. It was about eleven o'clock, and the one they call Buckshot, he kicked down the door, and he was coming into the house shooting. Mrs. Richards, she was in the bathtub, with the curtain drawn. The defendant, he was over in the kitchen, down behind the counter. He had a twenty-gauge over-and-under shotgun he picked up across the river, at Guns n' Stuff, loaded with deer-hunting slugs. He shot Buckshot first, then he swiveled and took out Snooper."

"You interviewed the defendant at the scene?"

"Yeah. He told me what happened."

"Did you take him in for questioning?"

"No. We just picked up the bodies. He wrote out a statement for me and signed it right there on the kitchen counter."

"Is that normal police procedure in New Orleans, Detective? I mean, you had a man who admitted to you that he had killed the two persons you found dead at the scene, and all you did was take a statement from him?"

"Sure. We knew Mrs. Richards had a restraining order against these punks. He was defending life and limb. It was self-defense, pure and simple. I didn't want to complicate his life any further."

"But the incident that night did complicate his life, isn't that right, Detective?"

"I guess so. The *Times Picayune* got it off the police blotter and reported it, and he was picked up by the MP's the next day."

"How would you describe your feelings that night, Detective, when you walked in and found Mrs. Richards and the defendant in that apartment in the St. Thomas Projects, and the two bodies on the floor?"

"I been in this business for nineteen years, Major Guidry. I've been around, if you know what I mean. I thought I was looking at just about the bravest young man I had ever laid my eyes on. All I could do was stand there and admire this young man who had defended his mother's life like that. When I found out the next day that he had gone AWOL from the service because she was in danger, well, I thought about what the nuns had taught me down at St. Francis middle school years ago. They used to tell us that the highest state you could reach as a human being was selflessness. Corporal Richards there"—he pointed at Vernon—"I walked in that apartment in the Projects, and I knew it immediately. What he did was selfless. The Army should be giving him a medal, not subjecting him to . . . this."

Kara walked back to the defense table from the lectern. Without turning to look at Sanders, she said: "Your witness, Major."

"Your Honor, the prosecution has no questions for this witness."

"You're excused, Detective," said Colonel Freeman.

As Detective Mancuso walked past Vernon, he stopped and squeezed his shoulder. Kara stood.

"Your Honor, the defense recalls Captain Eastlake to the stand."

The doors opened, and Eastlake took the stand. Sanders reminded him he was still under oath.

Kara didn't bother with the lectern. She stood behind the defense table, glaring at Eastlake. "Good afternoon, Captain."

"Good afternoon, ma'am."

"You recall where we left off this morning? I was asking you if you were aware of Department of the Army policy on family accommodation. I'll ask you again. Are you cognizant of the policy, Captain?"

"Yes, I am."

"Doesn't the Department of the Army policy say that as company commander, you should take steps to accommodate the needs and responsibilities of service men and women in times of family stress and emergency, Captain?"

"Yes, ma'am, it does."

"Isn't it true that Corporal Richards asked you for an emergency leave in order to secure his mother's safety? Isn't it also true that he told you his mother's life had been threatened, and it was absolutely necessary that he go home and protect her?"

Eastlake squirmed nervously in his chair. "Corporal Richards approached me, yes. But as I told him at the time, the company was going on field maneuvers for two weeks and all leaves were canceled."

"Even emergency leaves, Captain Eastlake? Was that in keeping with DA policy?"

"I'm not sure—"

"I'll read from the policy memo for you, Captain." Kara pulled out a sheet of paper and began to read. " 'Emergency leaves will be granted in times of family emergencies, according to the judgment of the company commander, except for alerts for deployment in national emergencies, foreign or domestic.' Does that sound familiar, Captain Eastlake?"

"Yes, ma'am."

"What would an alert for deployment be, Captain? Would something like Desert Storm qualify as such an alert?"

"Yes, ma'am."

"Were we going to war in the Middle East on January 13 of this year, Captain?"

Sanders jumped to his feet. "Objection. Badgering the witness."

Freeman glared down from the bench. "Sustained. Watch your step, Major."

"Did you follow both the letter and the spirit of the policy, Captain, when you denied Corporal Richards his request for emergency leave?"

"We were scheduled for—"

"That's not what I asked you." She turned to the judge. "I would like the witness instructed to answer the question, Your Honor."

"You are so instructed, Captain. Answer it."

"No. I didn't."

"So when Corporal Richards went AWOL because he knew his mother's life to be in danger, he did so because you had refused to allow him to go to her aid under circumstances that would have been authorized under the law. Isn't that true?"

Eastlake glanced at Sanders, who had his face buried in the notes he was taking.

"I guess you could make that interpretation, but—"

"That is all I have, Captain."

She sat down. Sanders stood.

"Captain Eastlake, did you have any way of knowing whether or not what you were being told by the defendant was true?"

"No, sir. I did not."

"So you made your judgment based on your best estimation of the situation at the time. Is that right?"

"Yes, sir."

"And at the time you made your judgment regarding Corporal Richards, you felt you were acting within the guidelines set forth by Department of the Army. Correct?"

"Yes, sir. That is correct."

"Thank you, Captain. That is all."

Kara stood. "Redirect, Your Honor."

"Proceed."

She walked around the defense table and handed Eastlake a piece of paper. "Have you seen this before, Captain?"

Eastlake studied the paper for a moment and looked up. "Yes."

"Describe for the record what is on the sheet of paper I just handed you."

"It's a court order from a judge in New Orleans. I think it's a restraining order."

"Corporal Richards showed you this restraining order when he asked you for an emergency leave, did he not, Captain?"

"Yes."

"So in fact you did have evidence that Corporal Richards' mother's life was in jeopardy, didn't you?"

"There is no mention on this form about Mrs. Richards' life being in jeopardy."

"For what reason do you think judges issue restraining orders, Captain?"

Eastlake squirmed. "I had no way of knowing how this restraining order came about."

"Corporal Richards told you how it came about, Captain. He told you his mother's life had been threatened, and that was the reason he had sought the restraining order. Isn't that true, Captain?"

"He showed me the restraining order. I determined that the Army's needs were preeminent in this case. That is my testimony."

Kara turned and looked at the members of the court-martial board. "Your Honor, the defense rests."

Major Sanders looked up at Eastlake, who was still in the witness chair. "The witness is excused." As Eastlake stood and walked out of the court, the members of the court-martial board followed him with their eyes. The door closed, and they looked at the military judge.

Colonel Freeman rustled some papers on his desk and looked at his watch. "Are both the prosecution and defense prepared for closing statements?"

Kara looked over at Sanders. "Sir, the defense is prepared."

"The prosecution is prepared, sir."

"Proceed."

Sanders took the lectern and faced the members of the board. "We've heard a lot of testimony today about events that took place over in New Orleans, but the only evidence in this case that pertains to the charges as they are set forth before you is to be found on the morning reports of Company B, First Battalion. Those reports reflect, without dispute, that Corporal Vernon Richards absented himself without authorization for a period of forty-six days. Because his period of AWOL was greater than thirty days, he stands before you charged with desertion. The facts in this case are uncontested. Therefore I ask you to find him guilty as charged. Thank you."

Sanders took his seat.

Freeman looked over his glasses at the defense table. Kara touched Vernon on the arm and walked to the lectern.

"Were the facts in this case so simple, none of us would be here today. As we have heard the facts in testimony presented today, the facts are these. Corporal Vernon Richards became aware that his mother's life was in jeopardy. He asked his company commander for an emergency leave in order to travel to New Orleans and protect her. Captain Eastlake, confronted with evidence of the truthfulness of Corporal Richards' concerns, and in apparent violation of Department of the Army policy regarding family accommodation, denied him leave. Two days later, Corporal Richards left the post at Fort Benning and traveled to New Orleans, where he found that indeed his mother's life was in peril. Detective Mancuso gave you all the evidence you need of this fact. Corporal Richards killed two men defending his mother's life. I ask you to take these extraordinary circumstances into consideration when you deliberate today, gentlemen. Military law under the Uniform Code of Military Justice is not an inflexible canon of commands that must be exercised without regard to the human beings in uniform who are subject to its strictures. On the contrary, the very structure of command in the military gives individual commanders great latitude in exercising judgment when it comes to every sort of matter involving members of their commands. This is especially true when it involves the personal lives of soldiers. You have heard testimony today that Corporal Richards was not afforded a fair hearing when he asked the Army to recognize the special circumstances his family was facing. For this reason I ask that you find Corporal Vernon Richards not guilty."

Colonel Freeman turned to the members of the court.

"You have already received instructions from the court regarding your duties in this matter. You will retire in order to reach a verdict."

The members of the court filed out. Everyone stood as Freeman left. Vernon reached around behind him and took his mother's hand.

"What's gonna happen now, Major Guidry?" Lateesha asked.

"We wait," answered Kara.

The MP's came to take Vernon away. Just as he disappeared through the door, a buzzer sounded in the court. Colonel Freeman came through the door from the judge's chambers.

"All rise," called an MP.

The members of the court filed in. Kara stood.

"Your Honor, the defendant is not present."

Freeman pointed at an MP standing at the door leading to the holding pens. "Bring him back in here."

The door opened, and Vernon returned to the courtroom. The MP's removed his cuffs, and he took his place behind the defense table.

Freeman turned to the lieutenant colonel who was serving as president of the court-martial board. "Have you reached a verdict?"

"We have, Your Honor."

Kara reached for her client's hand, gave it a tight squeeze.

"What is your verdict on the charges and specifications pertaining to the defendant in this case?"

"On the charge and specification of desertion, not guilty, Your Honor."

"Members of the court, I would like to thank you for your diligence in this matter. You are dismissed." They began to file out of the courtroom as Freeman turned to the defense table.

"Young man, your heroism is undeniable. But your judgment needs some work. I'm going to make a suggestion to you. The next time you are confronted with a seemingly impossible situation such as the one you faced recently, and let us pray that such a day never comes to pass, do me a favor, will you?"

Vernon looked at him uncertainly. "Yes, sir."

"Call the JAG office. Ask to speak to Major Guidry."

Smiles broke out on Kara's and Vernon's faces. Lateesha rushed forward and hugged her son.

"Corporal Richards, you are returned to duty with full back pay and allowances. Your records will be expunged, and nothing will reflect negatively against the continuance of your career in the United States Army."

As Freeman banged his gavel, the sound disappeared in the empty courtroom, which was filled with sobs of joy from Lateesha Richards. Major Sanders walked across the divide between the prosecution and defense tables.

"You know, Kara, in a civilian court of law they would have required you to disclose that detective to me, and we could have made a deal."

"You offered me a deal, and we turned it down, remember, Howard?"

"I mean, a *real* deal, Kara."

"You want to see the *real* deal, Howard? There's the real deal, right there."

She stepped aside and pointed at Lateesha and Vernon, who were still in each other's tight embrace, rocking slowly from side to side, lost in the eternal dance of love between mother and son.

Chapter Seven

Major Hollaway pulled up next to Kara outside the court as she was unlocking her car. He rolled down his window, and before he could speak, she said:

"You're just the man I want to see. I had a visitor the other night. Lieutenant Barry Parks. He dated Sheila Worthy in college, and he went out with her at Fort Benning too. He was pretty broken up by her death."

"Oh, yeah? Maybe I ought to talk to him. He could be the guy she was going to see that night."

"I don't think so. If they dated in college and were dating here on the post, why would he want to meet her out by the firing range? Doesn't add up. Had to be somebody else."

"I see what you mean."

"You haven't come up with anything on my bags, have you?"

"Not yet. We're still looking. They'll turn up. Listen. I've got something I want to show you."

Exhausted from the trial, Kara ran her fingers through her hair. "Where are we going?"

"I thought you'd like to have a look at Sheila Worthy's car."

"You found a knife."

"Not quite."

A few minutes later, he pulled into the MP motor pool and cut the engine. The car was up on a hydraulic lift on a concrete slab next to the motor pool office. It was heavily damaged, fenders dented, roof caved in. All the windows were missing, along with the hood, three wheels, and most of the right front fender.

"The flood flipped it over and carried it for more than a mile. We found it downstream, on its side up against an uprooted oak tree."

A motor sergeant in greasy overalls walked out of the office.

"Sergeant Kennedy, this is Major Guidry. She's the one I was telling you about."

Kennedy was wiping his hands on a shop rag. "Nice to meet you, ma'am." He threw a lever, and the lift hissed as the car was lowered to the ground.

"Not much to look at, ma'am."

Every surface of the interior was plastered with leaves, sand, mud, and grass. The driver's door had been pried open. "I've had my forensics guys going over this thing all day. We haven't come up with a single print. Not even Sheila Worthy's. Going down that river was like putting the car through a washing machine."

"How about hair and fibers?"

"Big victory. We found one of her hairs under the floor mat."

"No fibers?"

"Not unless you want to include those from the carpet."

"So what'd you bring me down here for, Frank? I'm not one of your investigators. I've got a job to do, and it's not out here in the goddamned MP motor pool." She started walking away.

Hollaway walked around to the passenger side, pried open the door, and knelt on the rocker panel. "I don't guess you want to see what we did find."

She returned and leaned over his shoulder. He pointed at two tiny pin holes in thin mud that had dried on the fabric of the passenger seat. "I'll give you two guesses what we found right there."

"I give up."

Hollaway pulled a plastic bag out of his pocket and handed it to Kara. It contained an officer's U.S. insignia.

"So? She was a lieutenant. It's part of the Class A uniform."

"How many lieutenants do you know who own solid gold insignias, Kara?"

"You've inspected hers, I trust."

"Brass."

She turned the insignia over. Tiny letters were engraved on the back.

"N.S. Meyer."

"Just like yours are, I hazard a guess."

"Good guess. But like you said, mine aren't gold either."

"Do you think the N.S. Meyer company has a record of all the officers who have bought sets of solid gold insignia over the years?"

"If I was a betting girl, I'd put my paycheck on it."

"So would I."

"C'mon, Frank. Out with it. You checked with N.S. Meyer, and . . ."

"And we're waiting for the list. They're going to fax it to us first thing in the morning."

"They're in New York. Everybody who graduates from West Point buys insignia from them. They have a big uniform show first class year, and they offer a good discount."

"I've already thought about that. I checked records over at personnel. You know how many West Pointers are currently stationed at Fort Benning? Five hundred and twenty-two."

"How many of those are men?"

"We can't rule out the possibility the person she was having an affair with was a woman."

"I rather doubt it, Frank. You heard her roommate."

"If Sheila was hiding her sexuality, everything she told her could have applied to a woman as easily as it applied to a man."

"You can't be serious, Frank. This girl wasn't sleeping with some dyke colonel."

"What makes you so sure?"

"Have I been wrong so far?"

"There's always a first time, Kara."

"I doubt it. What's next?"

"The N.S. Meyer list will narrow down our list of potential suspects."

"And what then? You can't go around asking everyone on that list to see their insignia and count their solid gold U.S.'s."

"Of course not."

"So you're stuck with a list of suspects and a bunch of evidentiary rules that preclude your doing anything about them. What else is new?"

"Not exactly. I thought we might take a page out of one of those cop shows on TV."

A slow smile formed on Kara's face. "If the word got out you had a piece of evidence like a distinctive uniform insignia, somebody might start doing a slow squirm."

"You're reading my mind, Major Guidry. You know what I like about you, Kara? Nobody can tell you anything. You already know it."

"You know what I like about you, Frank? You always keep your promises. And it seems I recall that you owe me a drink."

Her name was Roberta. The general had called her Robbie since they began dating halfway through his cow year at the Academy. She was a Vassar girl, and it was a time before the war in Vietnam when cross-pollination between West Point and Vassar, just across the river in Poughkeepsie, was still possible. She came from a wealthy family down South. Her father had the good fortune to foresee that a changeover was coming from nylon stockings to panty hose, and he built a half dozen heavily leveraged panty hose mills when everybody else was still cranking out hose. The guys down at the country club called him a pantywaist. He laughed all the way to the bank when he paid off the loans in eighteen months and started racking up profits that had never stopped. Then he bought the bank.

Robbie inherited a fifth of the family business when her father died, which on top of her generous trust fund had made life in the Army for the Beckwiths more comfortable than most. They had given lavish and frequent parties that many among his compatriots said had greased the tracks of his steep yet rapid upward climb through the ranks. Now they lived in the commanding general's quarters at Fort Benning, a wood-frame Victorian monster on a tree-lined avenue at the center of the old post. The Army provided a generous entertainment allowance, a cook, and a housekeeper, not to mention a squad of gardeners who spent several days a week tweaking and trimming the two acres of grounds surrounding the house. Robbie supplemented the Army staff with a butler and an upstairs maid, but still there were times, such as the night of the big shindig at the officers club, when a fit of Southern belle overcame her, and it was during those moments of stress and indecision that the general's aide was pressed into service. Robbie Beckwith didn't see eye to eye with many of the General's military men, but his aide was another matter. Randy Taylor had become the son she'd never had, and she depended on him in ways the General never knew about.

The life of a commanding general's wife could be a lonely one. Military protocol dictated when you could, and could not, associate with other officers' wives, and most of those occasions were formal in nature, such as Robbie's position as honorary president of the Officers Wives Club. There were monthly luncheons, of course, and more frequent afternoon teas to welcome the wives of newly assigned officers. Nevertheless, she didn't have any close friends at Fort Benning, and her relationship with Randy had filled a gap that had existed in her life for years. She needed a soul mate, and in Randy she had found one.

She had made with Bill Beckwith what her mother would have called a "good marriage." They had two daughters. One, Virginia, was attending a boarding school in Rhode Island, studying hard, trying to get her grades up so she would be accepted at Princeton. The other daughter, Cathy, was a senior at the University of North Carolina. The girls were happy and well adjusted, and every time Robbie picked up one of them at the airport, she felt like dropping to her knees in prayerful thanks for the happiness they had brought her over the years.

Everything in her life, in fact, was better than she had expected when she first learned they were going to Fort Benning. Even her relationship with the General was on an upswing. Of course, the demands of the job on his time were arduous, but they managed to have dinner together at least twice a week, and depending on his schedule, which included frequent travel to view Third Army training and an average of one trip a week north to the Pentagon, they took a weekend off at least once a month. One weekend in August they had spent at a luxurious condo complex down in Florida. The condos were unattached single-family homes. They had played a couple of rounds of golf, and spent the evenings on the condo's generous porch watching the sun go down over a delicious expanse of watery lowland, populated by waterfowl and deer. She had talked to him about buying one of the larger homes in the complex, even the very condo they had rented for the weekend, but the General had pooh-poohed the idea. That was when he told her he wasn't going to retire anytime soon. He was going to be the next chief of staff, and that meant a presidential appointment of at least three years, possibly six. They were moving to Washington, D.C.

It was a prospect that gave her chills. They had spent

more than their fair share of time inside the Beltway when he served on the National Security Council, which had been followed by a position as deputy director of operations at the Pentagon, an important job for a young general on his way up. She had thrived in the Washington social whirlwind, even though the politics could make her blood boil. The prospect of being the wife of the chief of staff of the United States Army made her whole lifetime with the General worthwhile.

She had known when she married him at the West Point chapel that his ambition was like cold fury inside him, and now that he was so close to realizing his dreams, the fury had taken on a life of its own. He was distant and difficult, but he had been that way to one degree or another for years. All of her life with him, Robbie Beckwith existed in a kind of half world, waiting for those moments when the perks and poses of power got too much for him to bear, and he turned to her for the sustenance a marriage was supposed to bring.

Now, watching him come through the door, she knew this was going to be one of those nights. He opened the side door and walked in, his face ashen with exhaustion.

"Did you see what King did today? He took Maldray up in a Blackhawk and gave him the grand tour and dropped him off just in time to catch his flight back to Washington, and I didn't even get so much as a howdy-do."

Robbie took his overcoat and hung it in the closet. "He was just down here visiting King to shore up his left flank for the election. It was all over the news tonight. You shouldn't get so upset. He didn't snub you."

"I know Maldray didn't snub me; it was that scheming King! Maldray and I go way back. Hell, I knew him when he was still a congressman from the peanut hills of west Georgia. I testified before the Armed Services Committee a dozen times when he was on it. King knows Maldray and I are close. He wanted to kiss Maldray's ass in private. The Republican moderates are pushing King for chief, and he was trying to get Maldray to at least stay neutral on the appointment."

"You know Maldray is backing you, Bill. He told you himself when you were in Washington last week."

"Yeah, but I trust him about as far as I can throw him, and the way he eats, that isn't far." He opened the kitchen door and looked down the long center hallway leading to the front door. "Where is the butler? I need a drink."

"He's worked seven nights straight. I gave him the night off. Here. I'll fix your drink. What are you having?"

"Black Label. A double. On the rocks."

Robbie opened a bottle of Black Label and poured a generous glassful. She grabbed a handful of ice from the ice maker and dropped it in the glass and handed it to the General.

"Where's the cook? You give her the night off too?"

"No. She's at the commissary. We ran out of butter."

Beckwith drank deeply from the scotch. "I've got the pass in review for the Sec Def tomorrow morning. I'm going to tell him what Maldray told me about the Defense budget last week. That'll cut King cold."

"I wouldn't if I were you, Bill. The Secretary knows Maldray is backing you, and so does General King. You'll be running a risk of cutting down General King unnecessarily in front of the Secretary."

"So? What do I care what King thinks?"

"This much. If he makes chief instead of you, he'll see to it that you end your career at the Kenworthy ammo depot counting 105 shells."

"He's never going to make chief, not this year, not ever. I'm going to beat him if I have to pull every trick in the book to do it."

"I'm sure you will, dear. But there's no sense in burning your bridges. If you make chief, he'll be a good man to have in your corner. He's got debts that are owed to him on every Army post in the world, and you could be the one for whom he collects them."

Beckwith sat at the kitchen table and loosened his tie. "I don't trust Maldray. I know King is playing the race card with him. If Maldray stabs me in the back and backs King to be chief, he'll get fifty percent of the black vote next year. He'll coast back into office, and if he runs for president next time around, and a whole lot of people say he's going to, he'll make sure King is re-upped as chief and use his association with the Great Black Hope to drag the black vote into the Republican column. And the thing is, it'll work."

"You're making your chances look dimmer and dimmer by the minute, Bill. You and I both know you're going to be the next chief, even giving away the race thing to Bernie King."

"I'm not going to take Maldray's support for granted, Robbie. I'm going to make sure Maldray knows about the changes I've made down here. He and Greenwich over in the House are busy cutting the budget to the bone. I'm going to make sure he knows how many federal dollars I've saved down here at Benning." He paced up and down in front of the refrigerator for a moment, then turned to Robbie, smiling widely. "You know what we ought to do? We ought to give a party at the Association of the United States Army Convention up in Washington. We'll invite Maldray and Greenwich and everybody on the armed services committees. We'll invite the CEO of every Defense contractor there is."

"That's a brilliant idea! How many people are we talking about?"

"I don't know . . . AUSA's a big convention. Three, four hundred?"

"That's going to be expensive. Those hotels up there overcharge for everything right down to cocktail napkins."

"Whatever it costs, it'll be worth it. I want those bastards in Washington to know I'm a player. People don't notice you unless you give them some flash and pomp and circumstance." Beckwith walked over to her and put his scotch on the counter and took her in his arms.

"I want to rock and roll at that convention. We're going into the AUSA with real firepower. Bernie King's going to be wandering around the Colt Industries display playing in the popgun booth, and we're going to be hosting a party for the *really* big guns."

He gave her a kiss on the forehead and rubbed the back of her neck. She closed her eyes. Her mother would have told her that a good marriage means you think about your husband before you think about yourself. She had spent thirty years doing exactly that. They had been a team, a good one, but the interests of her husband had always come first. Now that they were about to ascend to the pinnacle of Army power, she knew that her interests and his were coequal. He couldn't engineer his way onto the E-Ring of the Pentagon without her. This meant that for the first time in their long relationship, she had the power.

She remembered what her mother had told her in the fitting room the first time she tried on her wedding dress at Henri Bendel on Fifty-seventh Street in New York City. She was surrounded by women with mouths full of pins, tugging at her waist, nipping the cut of her bodice, measuring the hem. The wedding department at Bendel's was the most feminine place she had ever been, before or since. Her mother was sitting on a pale peach damask loveseat across the room, sipping white wine. She could still see her mother's white gloved hands wrapped delicately around the glass as she moved it to her lips. Her voice was husky from cigarettes and whiskey, and as she spoke her eyes darted from one seamstress to another, making sure they were doing up her daughter right.

Just remember this, dear. Women don't have choices. They have duties.

And who was she to argue at that stage in life? But thirty years of climbing the rungs of Army power had taught her a thing or two. She had a choice now, and she relished the moment. If she didn't pitch in and help him, he would never make chief, and he knew it.

"I'll call Betty Forrest. She knows all the party planners. We'll give a party like no one has ever seen. They'll be talking about you in Washington for weeks when we're through with them. Your name will be the only name on their lips. Bernie King won't stand a chance when we're through."

He kissed her, on the lips this time.

"Chief of Staff William Beckwith. I like the sound of it, don't you, hon?"

Oh yeah, she liked it. She liked it *a lot*.

"Let's have another drink," she said. It was an instruction, not an invitation. "I want to start on the guest list."

Chapter Eight

Lieutenant Colonel Barbara Lambert's office was three doors down and around the corner. She had twenty years in the service, and she was on the list for colonel. That's all you needed to know about the staff judge advocate, Kara thought as she knocked on Lambert's door. She heard her voice from the other side.

"Come in."

As usual, Lieutenant Colonel Lambert was sitting behind her desk. She was a tiny woman, thin to the point of emaciation, with a prominent nose and overly rouged cheeks. People around the office said her husband was her polar opposite, very short and as wide as he was tall, but Kara had never seen him. The clerks called her the Sitting Judge Advocate, because she got up from her chair so infrequently. No one in the office had ever seen her leave her desk long enough to go to the bathroom. It was like the job title and the big leather chair behind the big oak desk that went with it were inseparable in her mind.

Kara didn't bother reporting formally. Protocol was comparatively loose in the office of the SJA. The assumption seemed to be that if you spent your time on matters legal rather than military, the job would get done more efficiently. Kara liked Lieutenant Colonel Lambert. She was brusque with everyone, but her manner was so evenhanded, no one took it personally. Lambert had let it be known around the office that her fondest desire was to pick up her promotion to colonel and finish out her career up in Washington running the Contract Appeals Division of the Army Legal Services Agency, an obscure but powerful backwater in the capital swamp. Kara hoped she got what she wanted. Anyone who had put up with what Lieutenant Colonel Lambert had for twenty years deserved to have at least one wish come true.

Kara sat down in a chair across the desk. Lambert's brow furrowed, and as usual she didn't waste words. "I got a report from Colonel Freeman this morning about your performance at the court-martial of Corporal Richards. It seems you left quite an impression, Major."

Kara smiled. "Thank you, ma'am."

"Colonel Freeman described your case as, and here I quote, 'aggressively and expertly presented.' " She looked up from the page. "He also called me this morning. He said the prosecution didn't have a chance against you."

Lambert ran her fingers through her cropped hair. "I like your style, Kara. That's why I'm moving you over to the prosecutor's desk. I want you to put your talents to use sending a few of the bad actors on this post to jail. This reassignment is a strong vote of confidence in you, Major. Even though you've only been a JAG for less than a year, you're already turning some heads."

"Well, I just put on the best case I could, ma'am."

"So consider yourself a prosecutor, Major Guidry."

"May I ask you a question, ma'am?"

"Shoot."

"Was this your idea or someone else's?"

A smile formed slowly on Lieutenant Colonel Lambert's features.

"You're thinking that the commanding general might have had something to do with this, aren't you?"

"It crossed my mind, ma'am. He's made it clear he wants more convictions."

"You can relax, Kara. This was entirely my decision. If the commanding general had been involved in this decision, somewhere down the line some smart defense attorney might have charged that command influence was used in changing your assignment from defense to prosecution. That's not going to happen. I'm the one who wants you prosecuting cases, and the first one I'm going to assign you to is the Sheila Worthy murder."

"It's now formally a murder case, ma'am?"

"Frank Hollaway was in here last night. He recommended that we treat it as a murder and investigate it as such. The stab wound might not have killed her, but it was a contributing factor. That makes it second-degree murder. You'll be working hand in hand with Frank. I assume you know each other."

"Yes, ma'am. Very well."

"Pay close attention to him. You can learn a lot from him."

"Yes, ma'am. He's good at what he does."

Lieutenant Colonel Lambert leaned back in her chair. "Do you mind telling me where you learned to put on a case like that? I mean, Colonel Freeman was impressed. He said you just tore Sanders up. You went to West Point, didn't you?"

"Yes, ma'am."

"But you didn't go right into the JAG Corps out of the Point."

"No, ma'am. I flew helicopters after I graduated from West Point. Resupply choppers, mostly. Later I checked out in Blackhawks and flew them for several years. I had sufficient time in grade and more than enough seat time to qualify for a squadron command when my turn came. Then Aviation Branch cut me off at the knees. They could swallow, just barely, a woman behind the stick of a Blackhawk, but they couldn't stomach a female squadron commander. I wanted to resign from the Army over that issue, but an old friend of yours,

Colonel Masters, talked me out of it. She got me in the JAG law school program, and I ended up here. Colonel Masters herself made sure I got this assignment to your SJA office, because she thought that you would be more receptive to a female JAG officer with an off-kilter career pattern, who wasn't starting off as a captain the way everyone else does."

"All I'm interested in is performance, Major Guidry. I don't care if my lawyers wear a skirt or pants as long as they perform. Somebody out there killed that young woman, Major. I want the killer tracked down and brought to justice."

Kara stood up. "We'll find her killer, ma'am."

General Beckwith was standing at the window in his office when Retreat sounded. Everyone down on the parade field below him turned and saluted the flag as it was lowered by a squad of MP's. He watched them fold the flag and form up and march away. Then he turned and bellowed: "Randy! Where's my damn drink!"

Randy Taylor came through the door carrying the General's martini. "Got it for you right here, sir."

The General took a generous sip and sat down on the leather sofa between the bookshelves. He put his feet up on the coffee table and lit a cigar and exhaled a thick plume of smoke. Randy stood nervously to the side, waiting for the General to invite him to sit down. If the truth were told, he had done his best to avoid moments like this one since his return from Washington. He dreaded what was about to happen. The General was going to engage him in small talk for a few moments, and then he was going to ask him for a favor of the kind he would be obliged to report to General Ranstead.

The General cleared his throat. "I forgot to ask how your trip to Washington went, Randy. Did you get that business taken care of at DESPER?"

"Yes, sir. It took most of the day, but I was able to

make the last flight out of National, so it turned out okay."

"Excellent. Excellent. It's nice that we've got a comparatively short hop to Washington. I'd hate to be out there at Fort Lewis and be facing six goddamn hours in the air every time I thought about going back to the Pentagon for a meeting."

"So would I, sir."

"Have a seat, Randy. Is everything ready for the reception for the Sec Def tonight?"

"Yes, sir. I talked to Peters over at the O-Club. He's got a wonderful spread laid on, sir. He was able to get fresh shrimp out of Panama City this morning, and they've done a ten-rib standing rib roast, and he's got a good selection of cheeses he picked up in Atlanta this morning. I was over there at noon. He had everything almost ready then."

"Excellent. Peters is quality people. I'm glad we've got him on the team."

"Yes, sir. He came out of the Cornell hotel school, you know, sir."

"I didn't know that."

"Yes, sir. He's worked in the Bahamas, and he was the assistant manager at the Hotel Thayer up at West Point before he came down here." Randy was stringing out the small talk as long as he could, hoping against hope the phone would ring, or the chief of staff would interrupt them.

"I'll be damned." Beckwith pulled contentedly on his cigar for a moment. "You picked up my uniform from the cleaners?"

"Yes, sir. It's ready."

"Damn fine work, Randy. Damn fine." He puffed contentedly for another moment, then turned slowly to Randy.

Oh-oh. Here it comes.

"Are you, uh, escorting anyone to the reception tonight?"

"No, sir. With my aide duties—"

"Right. Right." Beckwith sipped his martini. "You know what I'm going to do, Randy? I'm going to release you from duty tonight. I've got a special assignment for you. I want you to escort Captain Love to the reception, Randy. She's brand-new on the staff. Have you met her?"

"We're classmates from West Point, sir."

"That's right. I forgot!" He took a pull on his cigar. "What I meant to ask was, have you had a chance to chat with her since she became my new liaison to the base closure commission?"

"No, sir, I haven't. I was in Washington, and . . ."

"That's right. Well, I want her to meet the Sec Def and his staff and make a good impression. She's going to be doing a lot of business up there in the coming months. You think you could do that for me?"

"Yes, sir. I guess so, if it's all right with Captain Love."

"Oh, it's fine with her. I already mentioned it to her."

"Sir, uh, do you know where she's staying?"

"Downtown at the Ramada Suites. You can pick her up there. Why don't you use one of the staff cars? Make it easier for you."

"Yes, sir."

"Randy, I want you to make sure she meets the Sec Def. I know you can do that for me, can't you?"

"Yes, sir. Sure."

Beckwith clapped Randy on the shoulder. "I knew I could count on you, Randy. You're the best goddamn aide in the United States Army, you know that?"

Randy swallowed hard. "I think that's a bit of an exaggeration, sir."

"Negative. You're the best. None better. Now get with it, son. You've got a beautiful young woman waiting for you. Get."

Downstairs, the staff car was waiting, as if the General had known all along what Randy's answer would be. He climbed in the backseat.

He's up to something, Randy thought as the driver pulled away from the curb.

But then, of course, so am I.

Chapter Nine

She was reaching for the skirt to her dress blues when she heard him. He didn't make much noise, but she knew he was there. She turned, half expecting him to take her into his arms and throw her on the bed, but he didn't.

He was standing in the bedroom door, thumbs hooked in his belt. "You're going out tonight."

"I told you about it yesterday."

He stood there looking at her, and she thought something truly stupid. She thought, Those are the biggest lashes on a man I have ever seen, and it's only right now that I noticed them.

"Oh, yeah. You've got that thing with the Secretary of Defense."

"That's right."

"But if you stay home, you'll have a thing with the sergeant of platoons. So who's it going to be? Me or the Sec Def?"

"Why don't you wait here? I'll be back in two hours."

"I could have hung out in the barracks, shot some pool."

"What are we going to do, Mace?"

"Stay home. Make love. Eat. Drink. Be merry."

"No. I mean, in the greater scheme of things . . . how long can we keep this up? We've already made one mistake. Somebody's going to figure it out, and then it's going to be all over for both of us."

He sat on the edge of the bed.

"How'd you get out here tonight?" she asked.

"Caught a bus."

"Were there any other soldiers on it?"

"Don't worry. I got off a half mile down the road and cut through the woods. Nobody saw me coming down your drive."

She wrapped her arms around him. "I hate this. It's so . . . unnatural."

"That isn't the word I'd pick to describe it. Fucked up, is what it is."

"We'll be okay. We've just got to be really, really careful."

"Don't worry. I'm like a stealth bomber when it comes to you. I come in under their radar."

She laughed. "What kind of a day did you have?"

"Shitty. Lieutenant Parks had us polishing boots and brass, getting ready for the Sec Def parade; then it rained and they called it off."

"That reminds me," said Kara. "Parks came by the house the other night."

"I bet he told you he used to date Sheila Worthy."

"How'd you know that?"

"Platoon sergeants know everything about their lieutenants. It's part of the job."

"Lieutenant Colonel Lambert called me in and put me on the case. I'm going to be the prosecutor this time."

"You'd better watch your step. A dead female lieutenant, daughter of a colonel . . . you're going to be sticking your face through the canvas on that one."

"What do you mean by that?"

"It's an old carny expression. There's always a booth on the carnival midway where the mayor or the school principal sticks his face through a hole in the canvas, and all the kids throw water balloons at him for a quarter. You just stuck your face through the canvas. Everybody's going to be throwing water balloons at you on this one, from the commanding general on down."

"Hollaway is talking about questioning Parks."

"You don't consider him a suspect, do you?"

"Not yet. We're going to talk to anybody she dated, and he's on the list. He's going to have to account for his whereabouts the night she was killed."

"You think she knew the guy who killed her."

"That's right."

"Parks is a pretty good guy. He's got a little time in grade, so he's not green around the gills like most of the platoon leaders I've had. He's got a temper, though. Sometimes the littlest thing can really set him off."

"Like what?"

"Like yesterday, when we were getting ready for the parade, one of the troops spilled a can of Brasso. It made a big stain on the floor. The kid cleaned it up, but Parks comes through the platoon and sees the stain, and he lit into that kid like he'd just lost his weapon or something. He's a real stickler for neatness. It's hell getting that platoon ready for Saturday inspections with him hanging over your shoulder."

"Have you ever heard him talk about women? Like, you know, guy talk."

"Almost everything between him and the platoon is strictly military. But I used to hear him talking on the phone. He was really gone on her. I know something happened between them, because he stopped calling her and he seemed real depressed there for a while."

"Interesting."

"I've had other lieutenants have a girl walk out on them. It's not a pretty sight." He leaned back on her bed and crooked his finger at her, grinning. "C'mere. We've got time."

She laughed. "The way you are, you bet we do."

"You're asking for it." He grabbed her hand and pulled her to him and licked her navel.

"I was just teasing, Mace."

"You should have thought about that before."

"I haven't got much time."

"Then tell me that you love me before you go."

She looked down at him. She took his face in her hands and kissed him. Looking in his eyes, she said: "It's not that easy, Mace. It's going to take some time."

"Why?"

"You never told me, for one."

"I love you. You know that."

"See what I mean? It's easier for guys."

"I thought we were the ones who were supposed to be so afraid of commitment."

She stood there looking at him. He was right. It was supposed to be easier for girls.

"I just need some time, I guess."

"How much time?"

"I don't know. I have *got* to finish getting ready and go."

"Oh. Excuse me. This big-time party you've got is more important than what's going on with you and me."

She put on her dress shirt. "Don't do that, Mace."

"Why not? It seems like every time there's something that pulls us together, there's something that pulls us apart."

"This is work. I don't yell at you when you tell me you've got to work all night getting ready to go to the field, do I?"

He looked at her and his big lashes worked up and down and he dropped his head. "I'm sorry. I don't want to do anything that's going to hurt us."

"There's beer and food in the fridge. Stay. Fix yourself something to eat. I'll be back before you know it."

He grinned. "Hell, I was just going to knock off a piece and head back to the barracks, but now I think I'll stick around."

She laughed and kissed him on the lips and he held her close and she felt her shoulders start to let go and she started to droop into his arms until she remembered she was in her dress blues and she had to go. She pulled gently away.

"I'm going to be late."

"If I was an officer," Mace said to her back, "I'd walk in there with you, and the two of us in our blues, we'd make their eyes bleed."

She stopped at the front door. "You'll be here, won't you? When I get back?"

"Sure."

"I'm sorry, Mace. It's just that—"

"I'm worried, Major. Every swingin' dick on this post is going to be after you, the way you look tonight."

"Well, you keep that dick of yours in a non-swinging mode for two hours, and we'll discuss this entire matter when I get back. Deal?"

"Deal."

Bradley fighting vehicles from the 24th Infantry lined the drive to the officers club, headlights on, a squad standing at attention in full field gear next to each track. Each squad member had three flashlights, filtered red, white, and blue, attached to his web gear in a horizontal row. Their fresh young faces shone brightly in the headlights of the Bradleys across from them.

Beckwith, thought Kara as she drove past the Bradleys. *He's pulling out all the stops tonight.*

She found a spot for the Cherokee and wound her way through the crowded parking lot to the front of the club. Two Humvees were parked on either side of the entrance. Each was fitted with a Xenon spotlight. Their twin beams crossed above the door. Inside, infantry blue bunting was swagged in huge billowing loops, held aloft by crossed M-16 rifles mounted on the walls. A young lieutenant directed her into the ballroom, where the receiving line had formed against one wall. She waited her turn, and passed through the line. General Beckwith and his wife stood to one side of the Sec Def, General King and his wife to the other. It was the first time she had met Mrs. Beckwith, an attractive woman wearing what appeared to be a well-practiced if weary smile. Kara said hello to each of the dignitaries and moved quickly down the line. When she reached the end, she headed directly for the bar, where she found Lannie seated at the far end.

"Kara!"

"Lannie!"

Captain Lannie Fulton Love had huge brown eyes that darted from side to side like a hawk's. She seemed to turn every piece of military clothing she owned into an object of femininity, and her dress blues were no different. She was poured into her tight-fitting jacket, her skirt was hemmed about two inches above regulation, and she was wearing non-military heels.

Kara sat down, and they exchanged reacquaintance noises. Then Lannie said:

"I want you to meet Randy. You probably just told him your name. He's General Beckwith's aide."

"The cute one," observed Kara.

"Gorgeous." Lannie whispered, "He's my date tonight." Lannie made a show of looking around the room. "Where's your date?"

"I haven't got one."

"Whatever happened to that delicious helicopter jockey you were so crazy about?"

"He took a walk when I got into it with Aviation Branch over getting a squadron."

"A gigantic tower of strength during your time of need."

"Like a redwood. He toppled like one too when the pressure got to him."

"Typical."

"I'm afraid so."

"What's Randy like?"

"Smart as hell. He graduated, like, third in our class. And just as sweet as the day is long."

"You're not fucking him, I take it."

"Not my type."

They laughed. "So who is your type, Lannie? I've never been able to figure you out."

Lannie smiled coyly. "Oh, I don't know . . ."

"You're seeing someone, you devil."

"I didn't say that."

"No, but your eyes did." Kara whispered: "Who is it? Can you tell me?"

"Not right now. It's too early. I want to take my time with this one."

"That sounds *very* serious."

Lannie shrugged. "We'll see."

Kara signaled the bartender for another round. As he pushed the glasses across the bar to her, a hand laid a ten on the bar next to them. "Those are on me."

"Thank you." Kara turned. "Frank, do you know Lannie Fulton Love? Lannie, this is Major Frank Hollaway. He's the deputy provost marshal."

"Very nice to meet you," said Lannie.

"Same here," said Hollaway. The bartender poured a glass full of beer and handed it to him.

"Did you get that list from N.S. Meyer?" Kara asked.

"Sure did."

"You guys are going to talk shop, I think I'll move along," said Lannie. "The receiving line is breaking up. I'm going to get Randy."

"Bring him back here," said Kara.

"Will do," said Lannie.

Kara turned to Hollaway. "So? Who's on it?"

"Let's just put it this way. They're all right here in this room tonight. Every suspect we've got."

"How many are there?"

"Twenty-two. Sixteen men and six women."

"That narrows it down, doesn't it?"

"Neatly."

"Anyone stick out prominently on the list? Maybe somebody she worked with?"

"Six are in Third Army Headquarters. Two are women, a major and a first lieutenant. Among the men there's a colonel, a major, a brand-new second lieutenant, and . . ." Hollaway looked behind him, then whispered: "General

Beckwith himself. He bought a new set of gold insignia earlier this year. Ordered them by mail."

"Well? What do you think, Frank? Any ideas?"

"It could be any one of them, Kara, although the chance that it's one of the women is slim. I've talked to a few of Lieutenant Worthy's friends. One of them was in ROTC with her. She liked guys."

"What'd I tell you, Frank?"

"You were right. What can I tell you?"

"Right *again,* you mean. You'll never guess what happened to me today."

"Lambert called you in and put you on the case."

"She told you."

"Hell, I recommended you."

"Thanks, Frank. I owe you one."

"This is a big one, Kara. Commanding generals don't like it when somebody starts killing female lieutenants. It's the kind of thing that gets in the papers and makes them look bad."

"Yeah, I know." She looked past Hollaway down the bar. General Beckwith walked up in the middle of a covey of colonels and majors. He signaled the bartender, looked up and down the bar. "The drinks are on me."

Kara raised her glass. "To the Corps, sir!"

Beckwith looked down the bar and smiled. "To the Corps!" He moved down the bar. They touched glasses. Beckwith nodded to Hollaway. "Good evening, Major."

"Evening, sir."

He turned to Kara. "I understand Lieutenant Colonel Lambert put you on the investigation of Lieutenant Worthy's death."

"Yes, sir," said Kara. "Major Hollaway and I are working on it together.

"How's it coming?"

"It's a homicide now, sir," said Hollaway.

Beckwith looked surprised. "A homicide? I thought she drowned."

"She did, sir. After someone stabbed her in the neck."

"Have you informed the parents?"

"Yes, sir."

Beckwith's eyes wandered. The Secretary of Defense had moved into the clutch of officers down the bar. "You'll have to excuse me."

He moved down the bar. The bartender was handing the Secretary a drink. "Put that on my tab, bartender," Beckwith called loudly. His eyes found Lannie in the crowd, and he reached for her hand. "Mr. Secretary, I've got someone I'd like you to meet."

The crowd surrounding the Secretary pressed close. Kara and Hollaway grabbed their drinks and drifted away.

"I didn't know that you knew the General," said Hollaway.

"He was my tac at West Point."

"What was he like?"

Kara thought for a minute. "Just like he is now. Garrulous. Confident. An expert player of the game."

The crowd was pushing them past a table full of wives when a hand reached out and touched Kara's arm. She looked down into the eyes of Mrs. Beckwith.

"Kara, isn't it?"

"Yes, ma'am."

"Bill was talking about you the other day. Please. Sit down."

Kara glanced at Hollaway. He gave a little wave and wandered away. She sat down. Mrs. Beckwith introduced her around the table. They were colonels' wives except for Mrs. King, who sat across from them. Mrs. Beckwith half turned away from the rest of the table, sipped her drink. "I wonder if you'd come by the house for coffee one morning. There's something I would like to talk to you about."

Kara tried hard not to show her surprise. "I'd be glad to. When would you like me to come?"

"Tomorrow? Around nine? Would that fit into your schedule?"

"I'll make room."

Mrs. Beckwith patted Kara's hand as her eyes found her husband, floating past in a cloud of colonels. "Good. I'll see you then." She stood, and the waters parted as she walked regally to her husband's side.

Kara glanced across the table. Mrs. King had seen and heard the whole thing.

Mace was gone back to the barracks by the time she returned home. He had left a note that said he had checked in with his platoon. One of his troops had gotten sick, and he had to go over to the hospital to check up on him.

It was late, and she was alone, and it was the worst time of the day for her. She wished she had someone to call. She thought about her mother in California, who was probably still awake, but she didn't feel like talking to her mother. She thought about calling Lannie, but she was probably still partying.

When she sat right down and really thought it through, she didn't have anybody to call because she didn't have many friendships that went much beyond the rather insignificant connective tissue of everyday semi-professional, semi-personal chat. It was another of her regrets, that deeper kinds of friendships came so hard to her. She wondered who to blame. Her mother? Her father? Herself? The zeitgeist of modern female life?

The truth was, she didn't much like talking to other women. She didn't like hearing about their trials and tribulations. She didn't like the tendency some women had to whine with each other. That's why she found herself alone on this night and many others.

Except for Mace. She wasn't truly alone as long as he was somewhere across the post, looking after his troops. She cursed herself for not having simply uttered the words *I love you* earlier that evening.

What in God's name was wrong with her? There she was, with this beautiful man in her bedroom holding her around the waist, looking into her eyes, and all he wanted were three little words, and she couldn't say them. What did she have to lose? Her pride? He was the most delicious male creature she had ever come across, and she was leaving him dangling out there like she could care less which way the wind blows him? She needed her goddamned head examined, is what.

She took off her dress blue jacket and poured herself a glass of red wine. Across the room on the kitchen counter, the answering machine red light was blinking. She walked into the kitchen and pressed Play. It beeped twice, then a familiar voice said:

"You know who this is. Meet me tomorrow afternoon at 1900. There's a place out on the Macon Road, about ten miles outside of town where Route 80 crosses 96. It's called Jason's. You'll see it on your right."

Beckwith.

She felt a knot in the pit of her stomach. At nine the next morning she was due to have coffee with Mrs. Beckwith, a little get-together about which she was certain the General was unaware. At seven that evening he wanted to meet her in a place well away from prying military eyes. There was a familiarity to these developments that unnerved her.

But then again, she had spent a lot of time being unnerved lately, enough to cause her to wonder what she was doing wrong.

Or doing right.

Chapter Ten

The Army had finished building the King house just months before they moved in. One of the crazy things about the downsizing that had closed the previous headquarters of the Fifth Army at Fort Jackson was a military fact of life: When you move generals around, you've got to have general-type places for them to live. Fort Benning had one set of commanding general's quarters, currently occupied by General Beckwith. The arrival of the Fifth Army Headquarters and its commander meant a new set of general's quarters would have to be built all the way across the post from General Beckwith (the Army at least had the good sense to see to it that generals, who were by nature competitive beasts, didn't have to look at each other across the back fence), and they built a house that was just as large as the one assigned to General Beckwith—even larger, if you counted the partially finished third floor and the servants' quarters over the detached garage. It was situated on a small hill surrounded by trees overlooking the Chattahoochee. By leaving old-growth trees in place and doing an instant landscaping of the grounds with grass sod and full-grown shrubs, they had managed to make the place look like it had been there forever. It was a neo-Georgian brick mansion with a row of six columns in front. When Dahlia King first laid eyes on it, she thought, Isn't this perfect? This place looks like some kind of Civil War mansion. But her husband had the last word. The house had been built so close to the

Chattahoochee, to get the view of the river, that there were no other military buildings or houses nearby.

"This must be the *new* Negro neighborhood," he had said as they made the drive up to the house for the first time. He laughed so hard, tears came to his eyes.

Mrs. Bernard King's given name was Dahlia Toussaint, and she had been born in the New Orleans Seventh Ward, which lay north and east of the city's French Quarter between Franklin Avenue and Elysian Fields. The Seventh Ward was the city's unofficial or official Creole neighborhood, depending on who was doing the talking, and the voices talking in the city of New Orleans were loud, because the issues raised by the Seventh Ward and its ways were about shades of color and they were contentious indeed.

You couldn't live in the Seventh Ward unless your skin was light, ran one line of talk. You can't live here unless you have worked long enough and hard enough to afford to live here, ran the line of talk of those who occupied the neat, freshly painted shotguns and Creole cottages that made up most of the dozen-square-block area, along with the usual scattering of po-boy shops and bars and sno-ball stands that inhabited every New Orleans neighborhood.

The truth probably lay somewhere in between, and to the wife of the commander of the Fifth Army, it hardly mattered anyway, except when her mother came to visit, which because her mother was only an hour away on Delta Airlines had become more frequent than either Dahlia, or her mother, for that matter, probably wished.

Dahlia's mother's name was Eunice Toussaint, and she was something of a grande dame in the Seventh Ward, given the fact that she had started out hiring blues bands and frying chicken and icing down kegs of beer and charging money for the house parties she had given years before Dahlia was born. She had ended up being one of the powers behind SOUL, the ward's political organization that had helped elect the first black mayor of New Orleans twenty years ago and had kept a light-skinned black man from the Seventh Ward in office ever since.

Eunice was a tall, light-skinned woman with an un-lined face and wavy black hair, and so was Dahlia. She remembered thinking when she was growing up that her mother was the prettiest woman she had ever laid her eyes on, and even though the years had slowed Eunice's step and caused her bones to creek with arthritis, she was still as beautiful as she had been when Dahlia was a little girl in the blue plaid skirt and white blouse of St. Anthony's, following her mother as she made her rounds at election time getting out the vote.

Dahlia King had had a good life in the Army. Her mother had had a good life in the Seventh Ward. What Dahlia wished now was that her mother would leave her alone and stop talking about getting Bernie to retire and bring him back to New Orleans and talk him into run-ning for mayor, like he was some kind of Colin Powell or something. Of course, there was a certain logic to it, because her husband had come from the Seventh Ward too. Or from its edges, just on the other side of Elysian Fields Avenue on Tonti Street, to be precise. And though he was darker than Dahlia, the years he had spent in the Army and the rank he had achieved had softened the distinctions of color that had relegated Bernie into one crowd and Dahlia into another in high school at St. An-thony's. Power could change people's perceptions of you, she had learned over the years. And no one had been more instrumental in teaching her about power than her own mother.

Now that her husband was on the short list for chief of staff, the mayoralty of the city of New Orleans paled in comparison to being the most powerful military fig-ure on the entire planet. Bernie had served thirty years in the United States Army, and she liked to think that she had served her thirty years right alongside him, even though she didn't wear the uniform and his rank wasn't hers. But she had learned something important from her mother years and years ago.

They will treat you right if you act right. And they will treat you with respect if you demand respect, her mother had drilled into her when she was a little girl having a little girl's problems and heartaches in middle school at St. Anthony's.

She and her husband had endeavored to act right in their lives, and for thirty years they had demanded respect, and in the Army, at least, they had gotten it, finally, after a rocky start when he was a junior officer and most black men in the Army wore sergeant's stripes, not the gold bars of a lieutenant as Bernie had.

Now he was a four-star general, and she was the four-star general's wife, and she found herself right where her mother had always told her she would end up: in politics. And to add insult to injury, her mother was in their house, and she was busy telling Dahlia I told you so along with trying to run every other aspect of her life, just as she had tried to do from a distance as Dahlia and her husband moved from one Army post to another around the world over the years.

Dahlia poured another cup of coffee and carried it into the den, where her mother was sitting on the sofa near the window. "I don't care what you think, Momma. I'm going to help that young man. He was found innocent by the court-martial, and he needs some help, and I'm going to make sure he gets it, you hear me?"

"Dahlia, he's not our kind. It won't go over good back home."

"My home is right here, Momma. Why can't you understand that?"

"You own this house? Tell me. You own it for real?"

"You know better than that."

"Then what have I been telling you."

"Momma, just because the Army owns this house and

we're living in it during this duty assignment doesn't mean it's not ours. It is."

"Show me the papers, Dahlia. Then I will believe you."

"There are no papers, Mother. It's the Army. It's not like it is in the Seventh Ward."

"What have I been saying? In the Army you own nothing. All you've got is what they let you have for a year here, a year there. What kind of life is that? You get Bernie to retire and come back to New Orleans, and you'll have the biggest house on St. Charles Avenue, if that's what you want, after we elect him mayor."

"He's not going to run for mayor of New Orleans, Mother. He's going to be the next chief of staff of the Army if I have anything to say about it. And I do."

"Dahlia, those men up in Washington, they don't like black men, and they like pushy black women even less. You better be careful what you say."

"I am careful, Mother. Now I want to stop talking about my husband, and I want you to tell me that you will help me get Vernon Richards' mother out of that damn St. Thomas project and into a decent apartment somewhere. You know you can do it if you put your mind to it."

"He killed those two men, Dahlia."

"They came after his mother! They were going to kill her!"

"That's why I don't want to have anything to do with those projects. They are bad."

"The projects may be bad, but the people in them aren't. I have talked to Mrs. Richards. She is a good person, Mother. She has a steady job working uptown."

"You mean cleaning houses."

"Yes, I mean cleaning houses. What's wrong with that? It seems to me I had an Aunt Brunelle who cleaned houses, and she still does, as far as I know."

"She comes from your father's side."

"She is my aunt, and she cleans houses, and there is nothing wrong with that."

Her mother turned her head defiantly, and Dahlia knew she was about to give in, because that's what she did, acted up before she gave up. "I don't know," she said flatly.

"Mother, how many times have I asked you for a favor?"

"You're not asking for a favor. You're asking for my soul."

"Mother, you should be ashamed of yourself for saying that. I'm asking for one favor. Help Mrs. Richards find a new place to live. Get her into that program the church runs."

"St. Anthony's is not her church."

"It could be."

"She's probably Baptist."

"I happen to know that she is a good Catholic woman, as if that mattered."

She lifted her chin. Now it was coming for sure. *Surrender.* "I'll see what I can do."

Dahlia crossed the room and took her mother's chin in her hands and kissed her on both cheeks. "I knew I could count on you."

"I'll help that woman get out of that project on one condition."

"What's that?"

"You bring your husband home for Thanksgiving. And you get those children of yours to come too."

"I promise you Bernie and I will be there. But I'll have to talk to Charles and Patricia. I don't know what their plans are."

"Well, they can just change their plans if they have to."

"Mother, Patricia is a television reporter all the way up in Hartford. If they've got her scheduled over Thanksgiving, she can't just walk off the job. And Charles, he's over in Fort Sill going to the Artillery School, and I don't know how much time they're giving the students off. But I promise you I'll check with them and tell them you want everyone to come. I'm sure they'll try to make it if they can."

"We're going to have a party on Friday night, and our congressman is going to be there. You remember him. He lived right around the corner, on Law Street. Johnny Calhoun. He went to St. Anthony's, same as you and Bernard."

"Johnny Calhoun was playing with sticks in the gutter when I left home, Mother."

"And he's in the United States Congress today, thank you very much. And it won't hurt Bernie in the least to meet Johnny and some of the others who'll be there. It's going to be a wonderful party."

"The Senate confirms appointments of general officers, Mother. Not the House."

"Johnny's got friends over in the Senate. It won't hurt."

"No, I guess it won't. But I don't want Bernie to get the feeling this whole thing is about him, Mother. Promise me that party isn't going to turn into some kind of campaign function."

"I promise."

"Now, Mother, I'm going to call Corporal Richards' lawyer, and I'm going to get her to put Mrs. Richards in touch with you when you get home, and when she calls, I want you to be as nice as you can to her, you hear me?"

"You don't have to worry about me. I know how to act after all these years. You just keep in mind who it was who taught you manners, young lady."

"I'm not young anymore, Mother, but I love you for saying so, and I love you for everything you taught me." She kissed the top of her mother's head. Eunice looked up at her and smiled.

"See, I can still get you to do just exactly what I want."

"What do you mean by that?"

"All you had to do was give me a little kiss."

Dahlia kissed her on the forehead, and she held her mother and stared out the window. There was no one in the world she loved more than her mother at that moment.

No one.

Chapter Eleven

Two men were mowing the grass, and a third was trimming the hedge in the front yard of General Beckwith's quarters when Kara pulled into the gravel drive. She drove a little farther around a bend in the drive, and she saw two more men, one pushing a wheelbarrow full of dirt and the other running a leaf blower. A massive pile of leaves had accumulated next to the drive. In her rearview mirror Kara saw a truck pull in behind her and stop next to the leaf pile and begin vacuuming it up. She drove through a covered portico and parked next to a green Volvo station wagon in the rear of the house. Mrs. Beckwith was standing on the back patio, wearing tan pants and a gray sweatshirt with ARMY on the front. She was holding a gardener's hoe.

"Major Guidry. Why don't you go on inside? I'll be right behind you."

Mrs. Beckwith stopped at the door and took off her gardening gloves and boots before she followed Kara into the house.

"Turn right. Let's go into the kitchen."

Kara walked past the stairs and through a pantry that opened onto a large, well-equipped kitchen. Mrs. Beckwith began to wash her hands.

"I hope you don't mind my informality. Morning is really the only time I get completely to myself."

"No, ma'am. Not at all. Having a garden like yours must be wonderful."

"It is. This garden is my joy." She dried her hands on

a dish towel and smiled. "I'm Roberta, but everyone calls me Robbie." She chuckled. "That is, when they're not calling me Mrs. General behind my back."

They shook hands. "Would you like some coffee?"

"Very much. I didn't get a chance to make any this morning, and I refuse to drink the stuff they serve at the Seven-11."

"I don't blame you. It's truly godawful." She poured two cups and led the way to a breakfast room overlooking the back garden. They sat down, and Mrs. Beckwith looked out at the graceful curve of the driveway bordering the garden.

"They just put new bluestone gravel on the drive. It's beautiful, don't you think?"

"I was admiring it as I drove in."

"Cream and sugar?"

"Black is fine."

Mrs. Beckwith stirred a spoonful of sugar into her cup. "I guess you're wondering why I asked you over here this morning."

"You've got my curiosity aroused, I'll admit that much."

"I know my husband saw you at the hospital the night that young woman died in the flood. He told me you were the one who found her, you and a Staff Sergeant Nukanen, I believe."

"Yes, that's right."

"I've heard, not from my husband, that you're involved in the investigation."

"Major Hollaway is in charge of the investigation. I've been assigned as prosecutor."

"I know something about the young woman who died."

Kara studied her for a moment. She was an attractive woman with light blue eyes and honey-colored hair with streaks of gray. She sipped her coffee calmly, as if she had conversations like this every morning.

"Mrs. Beckwith, I need to know what this is about. I

feel like I'm about to get mouse-trapped here, and I've got obligations as prosecutor on this case that might turn anything you have to say to me into evidence."

Mrs. Beckwith took a deep breath and turned slowly and looked at Kara with a level gaze. "What this is about is the last twenty-six years of my life. That's when Bill started having affairs. Twenty-six years ago."

Kara could have said something, but she remained silent. Mrs. Beckwith looked out into the garden. Her face remained impassive.

"I know all about Bill and his affairs. We haven't slept in the same bedroom in years."

Oh-oh. Here it comes.

"Bill was seeing the young woman you found. You're a good lawyer, and I've heard Major Hollaway is a fine military policeman, and I knew that sooner or later you were going to find out."

Kara breathed an interior sigh of relief. She had thought Mrs. Beckwith was going to bring up West Point.

Mrs. Beckwith sipped her coffee, apparently waiting for her to say something, but Kara had learned that sometimes the best way to get someone to talk was to shut up and listen.

"He was supposed to see her that night, after his speech to the Officers' Wives Club. They were going to meet out by the firing range, but the storm came up, and he didn't go."

She stared out the window for a moment, then turned to Kara. Her face seemed to have fallen, sorrow relaxing the little muscles around her mouth and eyes.

"He left the Officers' Wives Club dinner and went over to the post child-care center, where several children had been injured. Then he came home, and he was here at home until he got the call from the hospital."

"What time did he get home, Mrs. Beckwith?"

"Just at ten o'clock."

Kara waited for a moment for Mrs. Beckwith to say something else, but she was finished.

"Why are you telling me this, Mrs. Beckwith? This is information that could prove very damaging to your husband."

"Because I knew when you discovered Bill was having an affair with the dead girl, it would make him a suspect, and that would have ended his career."

"It might still make him a suspect, ma'am."

"I know that Bill called you last night, and that you're going to see him later today. His motives are the same as mine. If he admits his affair to you before you find out about it on your own, you will be less likely to consider him as a suspect."

"Then why didn't you wait for him to admit it himself?"

"Because I know you wouldn't believe him. That's why you had to hear it from me first. You must believe me. He was nowhere near that young woman the night she died. He was at the club, he was at the child-care center, and he was here at home."

"You're making a very serious admission about your husband, Mrs. Beckwith. I'm going to have to report your statement to Major Hollaway and make this a part of the official record."

"I guess you know all about serious admissions regarding my husband."

All she had to do was glance up from her coffee at Mrs. Beckwith. She knew.

"I think I can count on you to keep this confidential. If you go to Hollaway and tell him what I've told you, or indeed what Bill is going to tell you, Hollaway is going to want to know why this very senior officer and his wife opened up to you and not to him. I think we both know the reason, and I think we both know you don't want that reason to get out."

"That happened a long time ago, Mrs. Beckwith. You were separated at the time."

"That's what you thought. I think if you went looking for the court papers making that separation legal, you would have a hard time finding them, because they do not exist."

"If that's true, how was I supposed to know?"

"You weren't. But that hardly absolves you."

"It's still a long time in the past. The statute of limitations on the crime of adultery has long since run out."

"You've heard the joke about the Army's memory, haven't you, Kara? It's not in a big computer somewhere. It's in the promotion boards. That's where truths are hidden. Or come out."

Kara pushed her coffee cup away and stood.

"You've thought this out very carefully, haven't you, Mrs. Beckwith." It was a statement, not a question.

"And you have listened very carefully, haven't you?"

"I'm wondering, why take the good time out of your day to defend him like this, given what he's done to you."

"I'm not defending my husband. I'm defending myself." She looked around the kitchen, gestured toward the garden. "All of this . . . it's my life too. Don't you see?"

Kara looked into her eyes. They pleaded from the same bottomless pool of hurt that her mother's used to plead, on the nights her father didn't come home. She would come into Kara's room and stroke her back and say softly, to herself more than to Kara . . . *it's okay . . . everything's going to be okay* . . . and Kara would turn over in the dark and she could see her mother's eyes in the light streaming through the window from the streetlight outside, and though she never saw tears, she knew her mother was crying inside.

Kara picked up her purse and got ready to leave.

"I understand, Mrs. Beckwith. I understand only too well."

* * *

The General had taken off early for some reason, so Randy Taylor wrapped things up at Headquarters and jumped in his car and drove off post. He changed clothes at his apartment downtown and headed north toward Atlanta, which was only about an hour away.

Fort Benning had few advantages as an Army post, but its proximity to Atlanta was definitely one of them. Randy had spent a tour at Fort Carson, which was about an hour from Denver, and Carson was the only post that compared to Benning in this way. The year he'd spent at Fort Rucker, Alabama, a long, long way from a city, had been like being stranded on a desert island. Fort Rucker was surrounded by a wilderness of hole-in-the-wall country and western bars and cinder-block strip clubs and used-car lots and fast-food joints and not much else.

He pulled into downtown Atlanta just after dark and had no trouble finding the Peachtree Hotel, because he had been there many times before. He parked in the garage and took an elevator to the twenty-second floor and knocked on Suite 2255. Ed Teese came to the door, a cordless phone pressed to his ear. He was still wearing his Class A trousers and shirt. He waved Randy inside and kept talking.

"I understand that. Right. I'll get right on it. I'll talk to Senator Maldray about it first thing tomorrow."

He pressed Off and reached for his address book. Randy sat down on the sofa.

"I'm sorry about this. I've got to make one more call."

"That's okay. I've got all night."

Ed smiled. "That's nice to hear." He dialed the phone and waited for the ring. "Major Andrews, I need you to do a favor for me."

Randy wandered into the bedroom. Ed's uniform jacket was hanging neatly on a jacket stand, the stars on his epaulets gleaming in the dim light. His freshly shined shoes were at the foot of the bed, which had been turned down, his pajamas neatly folded atop the pillow.

In the bathroom a single toothbrush was laid out next to a travel-size tube of toothpaste lying next to a razor. There was one of everything, and each item was in its place. He sat down on the edge of the bed and thought about all the hotel rooms he'd been in, just like this one.

You live alone, and when you leave, you travel alone, and you take a shower alone, and you brush your teeth alone, and you go to sleep alone, and when you get up in the morning, you get dressed alone and drive to work alone.

Life in the closet. It must be the same all over the world.

He heard Ed cradle the phone, and then he was standing in the bedroom door. He had a five o'clock shadow that hardened his features and emphasized the crinkles at the corners of his mouth when he smiled. He looked older than when Randy had seen him in Washington only days ago.

"So how is life at the Home of the Infantry?"

Randy stood up. "It could be better." He took Ed's hands and kissed him. "It could be a lot better if you got down here to Atlanta more often."

"I do my best. We've got two factories producing components for the new laser range finders, and I get down here on quality-control inspections every chance I get."

"How long are you staying?"

"Overnight. I've got to be back for a meeting tomorrow at 1400. Somebody from Fort Leavenworth is coming to meet us with the report on Training and Doctrine from the TRADOC Analysis Center at the Command and General Staff College."

"Sounds fascinating."

Ed laughed. "You'll be out there at the Command and General Staff College soon enough, so don't make fun."

"Ed, I'm thinking about getting out."

"What?"

"This isn't the first time I've thought about resigning

my commission. It's been on my mind for most of the last year."

Ed led him into the suite's living room. They sat on the sofa. Ed muted CNN, which had been burbling softly in the background. "This is all my fault. I should have never taken you to meet Terry and Jack. We should have never asked you to watch Beckwith for us."

"That doesn't have anything to do with it. I'm just tired of living this goddamned lie. The other night Beckwith had me escort a hot new captain I know he's screwing. So there I am at this big reception for the Sec Def, and I've got to take her around and introduce her to all these assholes and make believe we're both having such a wonderful time. It made me sick."

"Who is she?"

"Just another gorgeous girl Beckwith found up in the Pentagon and arranged to ship down here. She's his new liaison to the base closure commission. Captain Lannie Fulton Love. Isn't that just perfect?"

"I know her. She used to work down the hall from me in the Pentagon. Beckwith's got taste, at least. She was one of the prettiest girls in the Department of the Army."

"Oh, he's got an eye, all right. You should see the bevy of young things he's cycled through Headquarters. It's been like the invasion of the Dallas Cowboy cheer-leaders around there."

Ed laughed. "He's really that open about it?"

"I don't think the staff suspects anything. He and the missus put on a big show around the post. They're at the club, lovey-dovey at a table in the corner. They make a show of taking a walk through the main post on Sundays after chapel. You can't miss them."

"You're sure he's seeing this girl?"

"It's been going on for months. Remember when he was flying up to Washington about once a week? He had me calling all over, looking for an excuse for him to jump on a plane for Washington. Every time I saw the word Infantry on a Pentagon schedule, I picked up the phone and called Delta."

"I remember."

"He called in every debt he had at DESPER to get her reassigned. He used the base closure thing to justify the transfer."

"I had no idea." Ed walked over to a kitchenette in the corner and opened the refrigerator. "Do you want a beer or a glass of wine?"

"I'll take a beer, if they're cold."

Ed handed him a can of Budweiser. "Freezing."

Randy snapped open the beer and took a sip and tapped his finger on the side of the can nervously. "All I am is a pimp and a beard for the almighty General Beckwith. I can't take it anymore."

Ed put his beer down. "You've got to hang in there. This isn't going to go on much longer. When he misfires in his shot at chief, he's out. They'll retire him with a big ceremony on the parade field, and a week later he'll be out in Desert Hot Springs working on his golf swing."

"I don't see how you're going to stop him, Ed. He's got a lock on it. All the guys who were on the NSC staff with him are pushing him at the White House. On the E-Ring at the Pentagon, his guys are bumping into each other running around whispering his name."

"We're going to stop him with Bernie King."

"General King?"

"Bernie is running hard. He's got the strong support of the vice-president and all of the Democrats on the Armed Services Committee. With the kind of stuff you just told me about Beckwith, we're going to put him away and Bernie's going to be chief. This president can't afford to appoint an adulterer to be chief of staff. No way."

"Beckwith hates King."

"Now you know why. Beckwith can read the tea leaves. Bernie just jumped onto the list."

"Well, none of this solves my problem. I can't stand it anymore, Ed. You guys were right. If Beckwith ever found out I'm gay, he'd run me out so fast, I wouldn't know what hit me, the two-faced, hypocritical bastard."

"Look. You just keep doing what you're doing, and this whole mess will be over before you know it."

"What about us? You're playing big-stakes poker with this guy, Ed. And he's got spies everywhere. If he finds out about you and me—"

Ed interrupted him. "He won't."

"He won't bother with destroying your career, Ed. He'll go after you big-time. He'll court-martial you. You could end up in jail."

"Look, Randy. I've been at this a long time. You don't get to be a brigadier general *and* be a gay man unless you have learned a thing or two about how the game is played. I know Beckwith is a ruthless SOB. But he's not the only ruthless SOB. We've got a few on our team too."

"You're talking about Jack and Terry."

"And me. I'm not playing around here, Randy. If this man gets to be chief of staff, it's going to be over my dead body. I'll do whatever it takes to bring him down."

"You're not going to sacrifice your career over him."

"Whatever it takes, Randy. It's that important to me."

Randy looked at his friend with a renewed respect. It was true that if Bernie King made chief of staff, the Army would be a better place for everyone. Even gay men and women.

Ed picked up the phone. "What do you want for dinner? I'll call room service."

"I'd rather go out."

Ed's face fell. "I don't think that's such a good idea."

"Oh, come on. I know a place on the west side. They've got wonderful soul food, nobody will know us—"

"We can't take that chance. There's too much at stake."

"You see what I mean? I'm so sick of this."

Ed put the phone down and took Randy's hand. "Don't you think I know how tough it is? I've been living like this for twenty-five years. If Beckwith makes chief of staff, it's going to get a lot worse. He'll ignore don't-ask, don't-tell; he'll run purges."

"I know. I know. It's just that . . ." His voice trailed off. "It's hard."

"I know it is." He picked up the phone. "I'm having a big Caesar salad and a filet, and I'm ordering a bottle of Ravenswood zinfandel."

"I'll have the same thing. Make it two bottles of zin."

Ed turned around, smiling. "That's the spirit."

Chapter Twelve

The place was a juke joint tucked into a grove of trees off a state road about twenty miles east of Columbus. Kara parked the car next to a battered Camaro and went inside. Her eyes adjusted to the dim light and found him sitting in a booth in the corner, nursing a scotch and water. She walked up and put her purse on the table.

"I don't know about you, but this feels familiar, doesn't it, General?"

Beckwith looked up. "Sit down, please. I haven't got much time."

Kara slipped into the booth opposite him. A gum-cracking waitress in tight jeans and a plaid shirt tied at the waist sashayed over to the booth. "Will ya'll be needin' a menu? Or are ya'll just drinkin'?"

"I'll have a glass of wine. White, please."

"Well, we've got yer Almaden and yer Gallo and yer Reuniti and yer Franzini—"

"I was thinking of a nice glass of chardonnay."

"Oh, that would be yer Franzini. We've got that in a box, ma'am. I'll get it for ya." She started to walk away. Kara stopped her.

"I was looking for something a little better than that."

"Yer box wine is yer better wine, ma'am."

Kara took a deep breath and smiled. "Just bring me a beer. Any beer."

The waitress walked away. Kara looked across the table at Beckwith. "Your wife told me all about you and

Lieutenant Worthy, so if you're in a hurry, you can skip that part."

Beckwith's eyes widened. "You talked to my wife?"

"This morning. We had coffee in the breakfast nook, overlooking the garden. Very peaceful."

"What did she say, exactly?"

"She said you were supposed to meet Sheila out by the firing range, but you never made it."

"I had no idea."

"No idea about what, General? That your wife knew you were having an affair? Or that she and I had a little talk?"

Beckwith glared at her. "Don't you get insubordinate with me, Major."

Kara glared right back. "General, I didn't ask to be put in this spot between the two of you. I'm not a marriage counselor, and I'm sure as hell not a priest taking confession."

The waitress appeared with a tall bottle of Bud. "Will there be anything else?" Kara shook her head. Beckwith stared at his drink. "My name is Enid. People call me Ennie. Ya'll just yell if ya need me."

After the waitress walked behind the bar, Beckwith looked up from his drink.

"Why don't you start by telling me where you were the night Sheila was killed?"

"I don't have to answer your goddamned questions."

"All right, then, I'll just take what your wife told me to Hollaway and let him take it from there."

"I was nowhere near Sheila Worthy that night."

"So your wife says."

"If you know what's good for you, you'll keep your mouth shut."

"You know I can't do that. I've been assigned to this case as prosecutor, and I've got an ironclad obligation to pursue all leads. If I don't, I could be charged with obstruction of justice."

"That's not going to happen."

"Really? That's supposed to make me feel better?" She took a long pull on the bottle of Bud. "You can't guarantee that, General."

"Yes, I can. As the commanding general, I'm the court-martial convening authority. I'm the one who would have to approve charges against you. No one can overrule the commanding general."

"That assumes you're going to remain commanding general, doesn't it?"

Beckwith looked at her, his eyes full of fire. "Are you threatening me?"

"I'm just telling you the way things look from my perspective, sir."

"Look, Major, we can do this the easy way, or we can do it the hard way. Your choice."

"The easy way is, I believe you and your wife that you were with her, not Sheila. That would mean I'm taking the word of two people who have a lot to lose and everything to gain if I believe them. That would mean I'm in the pocket of two people whose marriage is a sham, who are virtually living a lie every day of their lives." She took another sip of beer. "And the hard way would be?"

Beckwith took a Polaroid photograph from his inside jacket pocket and handed it to her. "Recognize these?"

"Where'd you get this?"

Beckwith held his finger to his lips. "Sssshhh." He unfolded a sheet of paper and handed it to her. "This is an inventory of the contents of the two overnight bags in the photograph. The bags were seized as evidence during the investigation of Worthy's death and are under my control." He pushed the paper across the table. "You'll take special notice of items four, five, sixteen, and seventeen. Item four is a motel receipt for a double room, paid for with an American Express card. Item five is your American Express card receipt. Item sixteen is a list of the contents of Sergeant Nukanen's bag, which was found in your car. Item seventeen is a female diaphragm showing signs of recent use."

Kara looked up from the paper. "You fucking bastard."

"You're spending your nights screwing this hotshot NCO, and you're going to sit here and tell *me* that *I'm* the one who's living a lie? You've got a lot of nerve, Major."

"It's a long way from fraternization to adultery, General. And an even longer way from there to murder."

He had a sadistic little smirk that told her just how much he was enjoying this. "And I guess you're the one who can tell me just how far that is."

"You're damn right I am." Kara glared at him. "I'll tell you what, General Beckwith. You go right ahead and do what you have to do, and I'll do what I have to do, and we'll see who comes out ahead. You may ruin my career, but I swear to God, you're the one who's got some explaining to do, and no amount of backing and filling is going to get you promoted to chief of staff."

Beckwith shrugged. "I take it you haven't discussed this with Sergeant Nukanen. You'll probably end up with a reprimand of some sort that will prevent your promotion to lieutenant colonel, thus effectively ending your career on a sour but hardly disastrous note. But I happen to know what Sergeant Nukanen's brigade commander does with fraternizing NCO's in his command. He'll run Nukanen through a special court-martial, reduce him in grade to private, throw him in the stockade for six months, and give him a less than honorable discharge from the service. You'll go on and get a position with some big city law firm, but Sergeant Nukanen? He'll have trouble getting work pounding condominium roofing nails in a hundred-degree sun down on the Gulf Coast."

"You're threatening to railroad him. That's illegal. I'll stop you."

Beckwith sipped his drink calmly. He looked up at her with an indulgent smile. "Your trouble is, you haven't been in the Army long enough to learn how the system works, Guidry. We're not running a democracy here. Politicians are always saying, this is a nation of laws, not men. Well, this is an Army of men, not laws. There are men working for me who owe me not just their loyalty but their lives, and they will do what I say, even if they personally disagree with me. Therefore, if I say Sergeant Nukanen's career is finished, he's finished. You don't have a say in the matter, Guidry. I do. That's the difference between a general and a major."

Kara leaned against the plastic back of the booth. "You'd do anything to make chief of staff, wouldn't you?"

"I'll do whatever it takes."

"Is it worth it?"

He smiled. "You're damn right it is."

"Well, you're not worth it, General. But Mace is. So you've got your deal. I'll sit on the poop about you and Sheila. But you know something? You're never going to make chief of staff. And you know why? Guys like you, guys who can't keep it in their pants, one way or another the word gets out. Somebody's going to find you out. Some other general, up at the Pentagon. And they'll take you down, and I'll be watching, and I'll be laughing my head off."

"You're learning."

Kara drained the last of her bottle of beer and stood up. "There's only one thing I can't figure about you, General. You want to know what it is?"

Beckwith finished his drink and looked up.

"What I can't figure is, how do you do it? How do you get these young women like Sheila Worthy to keep fucking you? It must be the stars on your shoulder, General. Because it's sure as hell not your dick."

Beckwith's face turned red and he made a move, but Kara held up her finger, wagging it at him. She turned to walk away, stopped, and made a show of snapping her finger, like she just remembered something. When she turned to face him, she had a big smile on her face.

"Almost forgot. Good afternoon, sir." She snapped a quick salute and walked over and threw a twenty on the bar and pointed at Beckwith. "Ennie? Bring my friend another drink. Make it a double. He's going to need it."

She drove home the long way, a county road around the edge of the military reservation, taking a short cut through the east gate. Driving through Fort Benning felt like passing through the years of her life. There was the medical dispensary where her mother had taken her for flu shots. And down the street—she went ahead and made the corner—was the grade school where she had passed first and second grades. She drove through the housing area of one-story duplexes where they had lived when her father was an instructor at the Infantry School. The trees were taller, and the grass seemed thicker, less trampled by little feet than she remembered, but the dull brick side-by-side duplexes looked just the same, and so did the kids who scampered in the backyards, chasing footballs and playing soccer and building the dirt-berm forts that all kids, even girls, seemed to build on Army posts the world over.

She felt dislocated, driving through the neighborhood where her father had been a captain, and now here she was, a major. These days she wouldn't have qualified for on-post housing because she wasn't married, and she didn't have kids. She didn't fit into the Army's all-encompassing plan the way most officers her age did—insert a kid into slot A, fold second kid, tab B, insert third kid into slot D—and so she was free of the deadly economic noose the military encouraged you to loop around your own neck—get a bunch of kids and a couple of car payments and a load of life insurance and take your chances with the storms of duty reassignments and hardship tours and low pay and bad housing and hope for the best, hope they're not going to oust you in the next RIF, or worse still, eliminate the very ground you're standing on, downsize your unit and the post where you're stationed right out of existence. The world had gone round and round and round since she was a little girl playing in the backyard of one of those duplexes so many years ago. But General Beckwith had reminded her, as if she had needed reminding, that what goes around in the Army doesn't necessarily come around. The military axiom was the same as it was in Caesar's day. The guy with the most men and the biggest guns wins.

She pulled up to a stop sign. She thought she recognized the street, so she turned left. Lee Circle looped around, and there, in the corner of a cul-de-sac, the little postwar duplex was just the way she remembered it, a bit forlorn after all these years, tucked away back there at the edge of a stand of trees. In the backyard she could see the old concrete clothesline poles and a sandbox made of railroad ties. She stopped. There were lights on in the living room. She heard a child's cry. A light snapped on in the bedroom . . .

He would come home late, still wearing his fatigues, his voice slurred from drinking. The sound of their voices leaked through the thin walls of the duplex, even though she could tell her mother was struggling to keep her voice down.

Don't you lie to me. I can smell her on you.
SLAP.

The sound of his jump boots pounding the wood floors, a door slammed, her mother sobbing softly in the kitchen.

Kara backed out of the cul-de-sac and drove out of Lee Circle the way she had come. On the corner was the child-care center where her parents would leave her on nights they went to battalion cocktail parties when she was just five, and then six. The lights were on, and she could see fresh repairs on the part of the roof that had blown off in the storm. Someone was moving around inside. On a whim she pulled into the parking lot and cut the engine.

She recognized her when she walked in. Her hair was gray now, her body stooped, but her blue eyes blazed just the way she remembered them. "Mrs. Bennett?"

The old woman lifted her head and squinted through thick glasses. "I'm sorry, we're closed. I'm just straightening up some things."

"Mrs. Bennett, it's me, Kara Guidry. Do you remember me?"

Mrs. Bennett put her hands on her hips, and a smile formed at the corners of her mouth. "Little Kara with the pigtails and the missing front teeth? My Lord, young lady, it has been about a hundred years!"

They embraced. "Closer to thirty, Mrs. Bennett. I was driving by, and I saw you through the window. I hope I'm not interrupting you."

"Heavens, no. You know, you're the second one of my young charges who has stopped by here this week. There was a young boy, he came along a few years after you left, little Tommy Butler. Well, turns out he's working for a bank downtown, saw the article in the paper and came by the next day, helped clean up. Are you just passing through?"

"No, I'm stationed here. I'm a JAG officer now. A major."

"My goodness! Who would have guessed!"

Kara laughed. "I read about the damage you suffered in the storm."

"Oh, it was a mess around here, all right. Took us this long just to get things cleaned up."

"I heard some of the children were injured."

"Just two, cut by flying glass. We were very, very lucky."

"I remember one night when I was here, there was a tornado, and my folks came to get me. You had us huddled together under the tables against the wall."

"I remember. That was back when we used to put pallets down for you kids and you'd sleep on the floors."

"You don't do that anymore?"

"The children sleep on big gym mats now, but they bring their own blankets, just like you used to."

"They said part of the roof blew off. Do you remember what time of night it happened?"

"Oh, I think it was about nine-thirty. Yes, that was it. I remember because I was watching a movie on HBO, and it had just come on."

"The paper said the General came by. That must have created a big stir around here."

"It certainly did! We don't get to see the General very often, although Mrs. Beckwith is here once a month. She volunteers at the thrift shop."

"Oh, really? I didn't know that."

"She is such a wonderful lady. You'd never guess she was a general's wife. Have you met her?"

"Yes, briefly. She is very nice." Kara looked around. "You said something about a thrift shop."

Mrs. Bennett opened a door and flipped on a light. Kara walked into a large room full of rolling racks hung with children's clothes, winter coats, dresses, men's suits, a typical thrift shop except for the racks of uniforms hanging along one wall. "It's really more of a consignment shop. People bring things by, and we put a price on them, and take ten percent when they sell. We get a lot of uniforms from soldiers who are being discharged. More now than we used to, with the downsizing and all."

Kara walked over to a glass display case. One side held a selection of watches and costume jewelry. The other side, much larger, held military insignia— captain's bars, major's oak leaves, colonel's insignia. In one corner was a large pile of old U.S. insignia. Mrs. Bennett pointed at two stars in the front. "Mrs. Beckwith brought these. They were General Beckwith's

brigadier stars. I think it's the first time we've ever had
general's stars in here."

"Not much of a market for those, I don't guess."

Mrs. Bennett laughed. "I keep thinking somebody
will buy them as a kind of souvenir, but there they are,
haven't sold in months."

"You said the roof blew off about nine-thirty. Do you
remember what time it was when the General got
here?"

"It was sometime afterward. The MP's got here first,
and the fire department came, and the ambulance, and
then the General drove up."

"So it was, like, nine forty-five or so?"

"About that." Mrs. Bennett peered at Kara over her
glasses. "You sound awfully curious about what happened that night. Is there something I should know?"

"I guess I'm just curious by nature."

Mrs. Bennett chuckled. "You certainly were curious
when you were a little girl. I remember you used to tug
on my skirts and ask questions all day." She sing-
songed: "Mrs. Bennett, where do clouds come from?
Mrs. Bennett, why is the sun so hot? Mrs. Bennett, why
does it rain?"

Kara laughed. "You've got some memory, Mrs. Bennett, that's for sure."

"I never forget a name or a face. I can't help it. It's
just the way I am."

Mrs. Bennett turned off the light, and they walked
back into the child-care center. "Do you have children
of your own, Kara?"

Kara looked out the window. "No, I never married."

"Oh, you'll find a man if you keep looking. A nice
girl like you deserves a husband and a family."

"You're still married to Mr. Bennett, I guess."

"Forty years next June."

"That's amazing, you and Mr. Bennett together all
these years."

"He's a good husband, except this time of year, when

football season turns him into a hermit. He bought one of those new dishes, and he can watch about fifteen games every weekend if he wants, and he hasn't missed many, I'll tell you that much."

"Well, if football is a vice, it's a minor one."

Mrs. Bennett laughed. "I'll have to remember that."

Kara glanced at her watch. "I'd better be going."

"Stop by again, Kara. I'm here every day until five." She pressed Kara to her ample bosom, patting her back affectionately.

Kara unlocked the front door and flipped on the light. She whistled for the cats. "Weird! Wall-monster! Peesh! You lazy good-for-nothing cats wake up and get in here!"

The message light on the answering machine was blinking. She punched Play.

"Hi, babe, it's Lannie. Pick up. You there? Call me, will you, babe? We have *got* to get together. I've got this new bar I found I've got to take you to, you hear? Okay. Call Lannie, hear? Bye."

The machine beeped twice.

"Guidry? Hollaway. I've got something scheduled for tomorrow. Give me a call first thing in the morning."

Two more beeps. A pickup. Silence.

Two more beeps. A final long beep, signaling the end of messages.

She hit the reverse button on the answering machine and walked into the kitchen and grabbed a can of cat food from the pantry and tapped on the edge of the can with a knife. "Weird! Peesh! Wall-monster!" Nothing. She snapped the can into the electric can opener, and looked for them as the can opener *whirred* loudly.

Nothing.

This was very strange. The cats were three of the laziest felines on the face of the earth, but when they heard the can opener, they came running. She flipped on the hall light and walked into the bedroom. She turned on the lamp next to the bed. Then something caught her eye.

The curtain in the window across from the bed was blowing softly into the room, and a cold breeze blew through the open window.

She opened her closet and knelt down and swept her shoes into a pile in the corner. With her fingernail she pried open a floor board in the back. When she stood up, she was holding a .45-caliber pistol. There was a sharp metallic *snap* as she drew back the slide and let it go, chambering a round.

The screen was gone, and the window was wide open. She found the latch on the floor, popped out, pieces of wood still attached to its screws.

Picking up the phone, she dialed quickly. "Mace! You've got to get over here! Someone broke into the house!"

She hung up the phone and looked out the window into the darkness.

"Peesh! Weird! Wally!"

Nothing.

Chapter Thirteen

She found the cats huddled together under the back porch. When she knelt and urged them to come out, they pulled farther away, hiding behind a pile of old lumber. Going back upstairs, she got the can of cat food and stood in the open door and tapped on it with the knife. Weird stuck his nose out first. She tapped again, and he came running. The others followed quickly behind. She closed the back door and turned the latch.

She was in the kitchen feeding the cats when she heard Mace at the door. She opened the door, and he took her in his arms. She felt the outlines of a weapon under his jacket.

"What'd they get?"

"I haven't had time to check. The cats were missing when I got home. I've been looking all over for them."

"Are they okay?"

"Cold, and a little scared, but they're all right."

Mace pulled a Colt Magnum from his belt and laid it on the kitchen counter. He looked around the room. "TV's still here. They didn't take the stereo. Did you check your jewelry?"

"You know me. I don't have anything valuable."

"Let's have a look."

Kara led the way to her bedroom and pulled out the drawer in her dressing table. A jumble of costume pieces—earrings, necklaces, a couple of her mother's old cameo pins—slid to the front of the drawer. She pawed through it. "I don't see anything missing."

Mace was standing at the window, fingering the broken latch. He opened the window and looked outside, running his hand along the edge of the screen. "They cut the screen with a razor." He turned around. "Did you call the Columbus police?"

Kara was standing by the bed. "I don't want to call the police yet, Mace."

"Why not? Somebody broke into your house. It's what you do."

Kara walked back into the living room. Mace followed. She was standing by her desk. Her Toshiba notebook computer was open on the desk. "My computer was closed when I left this morning. That's how I turn it off. Now it's open. Somebody's been messing with this computer, Mace."

She sat down and turned it on. Quickly the computer powered into Windows. She clicked the mouse a couple of times and pointed at a small bar graph in the top right corner of the screen. "That's the battery power indicator. It was indicating full power when I turned it off last night. It's down to three-quarters. Somebody was on this machine for a half hour, Mace. They went through my files."

"People don't break into people's houses to sit down and go through their computer files."

"They do if they think there's something on the hard disk that can hurt them." She walked over to the sofa and sat down. "There's something I haven't told you." Mace was standing across from her, arms folded across his chest. "I saw General Beckwith tonight. I used to know him at West Point. He was my tactical officer."

"What does that have to do with somebody breaking into your house?"

"Plenty. He was the only person who knew I'd be gone from the house tonight. He called me last night and asked me to meet him about twenty minutes outside of town. He knew where I was going to be at seven o'clock, how long it would take me to get there and get back home. He knew I lived alone and the house would be empty the whole time I was gone. He set up the whole thing."

"Maybe somebody broke in during the day, while you were at work. It's so private back here in these woods, nobody would have seen them."

"It didn't happen during the day. I came home before I left to meet Beckwith. The windows were closed. The cats were inside when I left."

"You think the commanding general had something to do with this? Why?"

"He was having an affair with Sheila Worthy. He was supposed to meet her out there by the firing range the night she was killed. He claims he didn't make it. He and his wife both swear he was at home at the time she died."

"Do you believe him?"

"No. Beckwith admitted his affair with Sheila because if I found it out myself, I'd put it in my report, and that would make him a suspect. I know he's lying. Here."

She pulled out the Polaroid and handed it to him. "He's got our bags, Mace. He found the motel receipt from Panama City. He'll go to any lengths to get me to keep my mouth shut about him and Sheila. If it gets out he was having an affair with the dead girl, he can forget about chief of staff. His career will be over."

"Do you really think he killed her? Maybe he's telling the truth. Maybe he was supposed to meet her out there, but he never made it."

"That's a possibility, but I think he's lying about the whole thing. I think he killed her and he's blackmailing me to keep it covered up."

"Did they get anything off the computer?"

She reached for her purse and pulled out two 3.5-inch floppies. "I keep all my stuff from the office on these. I take them home from the office, and I don't load them until I'm ready to work."

"So the whole time you were talking to Beckwith, you had what he was looking for with you."

"Right in my purse."

"What are you going to do?"

"I don't have any choice, Mace. If I take what I know to Hollaway, he'll go to the provost marshal before he files a report, and the provost marshal will go to Beckwith, and we'll be finished. Both of our careers will be over. He threatened specifically to see to it that you get a special court-martial for fraternization. You'd end up with a bad discharge."

"Jesus."

"I'm going to keep my mouth shut for now, but I'll stay on Beckwith until he makes a mistake, and when he does, I'm going to get him. He killed her, Mace. If I have anything to say about it, and I do, he's going to Leavenworth."

"You're making a big mistake, Kara. Guys like Beckwith, they step on people like you and me. The Army's not going to get in his way. He's everything they want in a general. Look at him. He's on the goddamned list for chief of staff."

"They don't like generals with dead mistresses at the Pentagon. He knows it, and he wants the top job so bad—"

Mace interrupted: "He'd kill for it."

The phone rang. Kara started to reach for the receiver, but Mace grabbed her hand. "Let the machine get it."

The machine picked up with her message. "Kara Guidry. Please leave a message. Thanks." *Beep. Beep.*

Silence. A hang-up.

"I got one of those earlier."

"They're checking on you."

"Let 'em check."

"If General Beckwith knows about us, somebody else is going to find out, and they're going to catch us, Kara. You know they will."

"Fuck Beckwith. Two can play this blackmail game. He knows if he or any of his people so much as make a peep about us, I'm going to file a report on him and Sheila Worthy. He's not going to take that chance. He's got too much at stake."

"Maybe he's got so much at stake, he's not going to depend on you keeping your mouth shut. If he killed Sheila Worthy . . ."

"I've thought of that."

"Well?"

"Let me tell you something, Mace. Beckwith isn't going to get away with murder. If that means I've got to watch my backside, then I'll do it. But I'm not running away from this. No way."

Mace pulled her to him, tucking her head under his chin. "You love this shit, don't you?"

"Like you can't even believe."

"You know something? I think most people live their lives like they're watching a movie. The stuff that's happening around them is way up there on a screen, and they're just reacting. But there's no distance between you and what's up on the screen. You're *in* the movie."

"Isn't that the heart of war? Either you engage the enemy, or you get the hell off the battlefield."

"Where'd you learn that?"

"From my father."

"I thought you didn't get along with your father."

"I didn't."

"Sometimes learning is a painful experience," Mace said gently.

"All of the time it is."

Mace kissed the crown of her head. "You want me to stay?"

She looked at her watch. "It's late."

"So that's a definite maybe."

She leaned against his shoulder, and as she did, she felt the muscles in her neck let go, flooding her face with warmth. "You know something?"

"What?"

"I know what you're thinking."

"Oh, yeah? What am I thinking?"

"You're thinking, what can I do to make this better? What can I do to take away the sting?"

There was a long moment while she rested her head against his shoulder and he looked down at her, his brow furrowed. She was watching his face, and what she read there, she wanted to tell her mother. She wanted to tell her that this guy at Fort Benning, this staff sergeant she had found in a canoe on a river in north Georgia, she wanted to tell her mother that this guy was like a house, with four sides and a floor and a roof and all-weather siding; he was there when the wind howled and the rain blew, and what he wanted to do was, he wanted to protect you, and she wanted to tell her mother, that was the greatest feeling in the whole damn world.

Finally he smiled. "What I'm thinking is, let's go to bed."

"See? I was right."

He took her by the hand, and when they got to the bedroom, he lifted her off the floor and he put her on the bed and he pulled her blouse over her head and he buried himself in her breasts and she inhaled the aroma that seeped from his body as they came together. He raised his head and when he looked into her eyes, she thought, if this is love, then what the hell am I afraid of?

Chapter Fourteen

"So what's up?" Kara slid onto the worn sofa and tossed her cap on the coffee table. Hollaway's office would have looked right at home in a machine shop. File folders were stacked against the walls like cordwood; even his diplomas on the walls were crooked. Coffee stains abounded. It was a wonder anything got done amongst such chaos.

Hollaway was chewing on an unlit cigar. He took it out of his mouth and grinned. "We're closing in on Sheila's killer."

"How do you figure?"

"I've given our suspect list a haircut. There were twenty-two who bought gold U.S. insignias from the N.S. Meyer company. We're down to five, and out of the five, two I don't like, and three I do like, and out of those three, two I really like. You and I are going to see number one this morning. Later we're going to pay a call on number two. I think we're going to bust this puppy." He stood up. "You want a cup of coffee?"

"Sure." Hollaway poured her a cup from a carafe on his desk and handed it to her, spilling some on the floor. He didn't seem to notice. "So tell me how you narrowed down our list."

"We had twenty-two. I threw out the six women—"

Kara interrupted sarcastically. "Thank you very much."

Hollaway grimaced. "That left us with the sixteen men. I called around and checked schedules. Ten of them weren't even on post the night Sheila was killed. Four were on TDY, three had taken leave, and three of them were out in the field on maneuvers. All ten of them had morning reports to establish their where-abouts. That left six suspects. I threw one of them out right away."

"Who might that be?"

"Beckwith. I just don't see the commanding general as a murder suspect. He doesn't come up on the screen."

Kara took a sip of coffee and stared out the window. She felt like saying to hell with it and telling him what she knew, but then she thought about last night, lying in bed next to Mace, and how safe he made her feel, and she thought, there's no way I can do anything to hurt this guy. No way at all.

"You look lost in your thoughts, Kara. You disagree with me about Beckwith?"

She took a deep breath. "No. Go on."

"Okay, that left us with five. Two I discount out of hand. I just don't see these two guys coming out of left field and killing a girl they couldn't have known. Both of them are second lieutenants over in the Infantry Offi-cer Basic Course. They've been on post for less than a month. You know the way IOBC is. They don't have time to wash their socks, much less run out to the firing range in the middle of a storm and kill a lieutenant they didn't know."

"What's the statistic? Ninety percent of people who are murdered know their killer?"

"That's right. The guy who killed Sheila knew her. I take that as a given. So that leaves us with three. One of them is another guy I don't like as a suspect. He's been here at Benning for two months. He was gone on TDY for thirty days out of sixty. He's got a steady girlfriend up in Atlanta. There's just nothing I can find that would connect him to Sheila."

"So that brings us to your favorites."

"Yeah. We've got a Headquarters guy, he's single,

and he dated Sheila several times. The second guy is the kid who came to your house. Parks. I ran his records, tracked down their college stuff. There's a picture of the two of them in the yearbook. They were voted 'most likely to make general,' or something like that. He was in a fraternity, and she was in the sister sorority to the frat. I talked to the colonel in charge of the ROTC program. He told me Parks took Sheila to the Artillery Ball. He went off to Infantry Basic Course, and she went into the Adjutant General's Corps."

"And they started dating again when they got stationed together here at Fort Benning."

"Something like that."

"Who's the other guy?"

"You're going to love this. Beckwith's aide."

"Randy Taylor? We met him at the reception for the Sec Def. He was with a friend of mine, Lannie."

"I was there. Remember?"

"He dated Sheila Worthy?"

"Three or four times. Dinner at the O-Club, a movie, that sort of thing."

"That doesn't sound serious."

"Not on her part, from what I can tell. There wasn't much talk about them around Headquarters. But Parks and Sheila were definitely serious. I talked to Sheila's roommate again. She told me Sheila said he was the love of her life in college."

"And he turns up on the N.S. Meyer list."

"Like a big dog. Bought his gold insignia just before he graduated from college. Gold second lieutenant's bars. Gold Infantry crossed rifles. Gold U.S.'s."

"So when are you going to question him?"

"When are *we* going to question him, you mean. Today. After lunch, if that's good with your schedule."

"I already talked to him once, Frank. Maybe you ought to take a stab at it alone."

"I want you there, Kara. He came to you in the first place. You established a rapport."

"Okay, I'll meet you."

"He's over in the 2nd of the 29th. You know where it is?"

Kara took a deep breath. *Mace's unit.* She exhaled. "I'll find it."

"We're going to get the guy who killed Sheila, Kara. This is the Army. He can't run and he can't hide, and we'll track him down and nail his ass."

Kara was walking toward the door. She didn't turn around. "Yeah, we sure will, Frank. See you later."

She parked the Cherokee in a dirt lot next to the 2nd Battalion headquarters building. Hollaway was standing two cars down, waiting for her.

"Hey, Frank. Ready?"

"Sure."

They started walking toward the mess hall, a wood-frame building across the street from the headquarters.

"Parks know we're coming?" asked Kara.

"I called him this morning. He's meeting us in the mess hall."

"Did you tell him we're considering him a suspect?"

"Not yet. We don't have a probable cause to conduct a search of his personal effects. All we've got is his name on the N.S. Meyer list."

"Yeah, and he already came to my house volunteering to help out, Frank. He's not exactly stinking to high heaven."

"He could have been trying to throw you off his scent by *appearing* to be cooperative."

"That's a possibility."

Hollaway opened the mess hall door. It was an enormous room with a serving line that separated the kitchen area from the tables. A huge coffee urn dominated the center of the room. The only concession to modernity was a salad bar that had been set up along the far wall. Lieutenant Parks was in the kitchen talking to two of the cooks. His face paled when he saw them.

"Major Guidry. I didn't know you were coming."

"I've been assigned to the investigation, Lieutenant Parks. This is Major Frank Hollaway."

Parks led them to a table in the corner. Hollaway sat down and opened his briefcase. He took out a yellow legal pad and a pen. He pointed at Kara. "Major Guidry is the JAG officer on the investigation of Lieutenant Worthy's murder. I handle the police duties. We have some questions for you."

Parks swallowed nervously. "Yes, sir."

Hollaway leaned back in his chair. "We're trying to put together an idea of how Sheila led her life. We're talking to everyone who knew her, Lieutenant Parks."

Kara watched Parks closely. His accent came from somewhere in the Midwest. Wisconsin, she guessed. He looked like an athlete. His whole life was ahead of him. Sheila's death had been the first bump on his road.

Hollaway made a note. "You attended Beloit, up in Wisconsin, didn't you, Lieutenant?"

"Yes, sir."

"You told me you dated Lieutenant Worthy in college," said Kara. It was always best to go over material you already had the answers to, see if he started trying to hide things right off the bat.

"Yes, ma'am."

"Did you date her steadily?"

Parks paused for a moment before he answered. "We were pretty serious there for a while."

"What happened?"

"You go your separate ways when you graduate, ma'am. I guess that's what happened to us."

Kara leaned forward and got his attention. "You told me you had talked about marriage, Lieutenant. That's the kind of detail we're looking for here. You might say something you think is insignificant, but it might turn out otherwise."

Parks' voice was flat. "Oh. I see what you mean."

"We were talking about your relationship in college."

"We thought about getting married, but we knew we'd both have to go off to our basic courses first, so we decided to wait."

Hollaway made another note. "Did you stay in touch? When you went off to your separate assignments, I mean."

"Yes, sir. On the internet. We e-mailed each other."

Kara asked: "Were you both dating other people during that time?"

He looked down at his hands. "I was. I don't know about Sheila. We never talked about it."

"Did you start dating Lieutenant Worthy soon after you both ended up at Benning?" asked Hollaway.

"Not right away."

Hollaway was scribbling on the yellow legal pad. He glanced at Kara, nodded, letting her know to take the lead.

"Why was that, Lieutenant Parks?"

"I knew she was seeing someone else."

"I thought you said you hadn't talked about dating other people."

"We didn't, ma'am. But I could tell."

"How was that?"

"Lots of things."

"Like what, Lieutenant? If she was dating other people, that might be important."

"I used to call her at night, and somebody was always clicking in on her call waiting."

"That could have been a friend. Or friends."

"She always took the other call. If it was just one of her friends, she would have stayed on the line with me some of the time, anyway."

"I see."

Hollaway looked up from the yellow pad. "Do you know who else she was seeing, Lieutenant Parks?"

"No, sir."

"Did you ask her?"

"It wasn't like that. She had her life. I had mine."

"But she was definitely seeing other men," said Kara.

"I think she was seeing only one man."

"What makes you think that?"

"I knew her for a long time, ma'am."

Hollaway pushed his chair back. "I think I'll have a cup of coffee." He walked over to the urn and filled a cup. Parks was watching him. Standing at the coffee urn, Hollaway asked: "You and Lieutenant Worthy dated here at Fort Benning, is that right?"

"Yes, sir."

"How many times?"

"I don't know, sir. A bunch."

"Ten? Twenty?"

"We were seeing each other once or twice a week."

Kara watched him closely. "Were you intimate?"

His face darkened. "This is getting pretty personal, ma'am."

"Murder is a very personal business, Lieutenant." She glanced at her notes. "Where were you when you learned that Lieutenant Worthy had been killed, Lieutenant?"

"It was the next day. I heard at work, ma'am."

"How did you find out?"

"One of the men came back from sick call. He said everybody at the hospital was talking about it."

Kara watched him closely. "You told me you asked her out the night she died, but she had another date. Did you end up going to the club alone that night?"

"No, ma'am. I went home."

"Where do you live?"

"Off post. I've got an apartment over in a new complex out on Magnolia."

"Can anyone vouch for you being there?"

"I live alone, ma'am." He paused for a moment, looking down at his hands. "I want to understand something here. Am I a suspect?"

"Not at the present time, Lieutenant."

" 'Not at the present time'? Then there's a chance I could be a suspect?"

Hollaway stepped in. "Anybody on this post could be a suspect, Lieutenant. That's the way you go about a murder investigation. When you start you don't rule anybody out."

"Do I need a lawyer? Is it like that?"

"We'd tell you if you were a target of the investigation, and you would be advised to get a lawyer immediately. We're way short of that stage with you, or anybody else for that matter."

Parks' eyes were flinty. "I don't think I should answer any more questions."

"We can compel you to answer, Lieutenant Parks," said Kara.

"Then maybe you'd better go ahead and do that, Major Guidry."

Hollaway stepped in. "That's all we have for now, Lieutenant."

Kara stood. "You're acting like you've got something to hide, Lieutenant."

Parks' face was a blank mask. "I don't have anything to hide."

Hollaway touched her arm, and they walked away. Outside, Hollaway stopped to tie his shoe. "Well? What did you think?"

"I think killing is his job, and he has no alibi."

"That could describe three-quarters of the men on this post," said Hollaway.

"You're right about that."

"So do you think he did it?"

"I don't know. Maybe I was a little rough on him. Maybe I scared him off."

"And maybe he *does* have something to hide."

Chapter Fifteen

The thing about having a friend like Lannie Fulton Love was talk.

Talk, talk, talk. All you did was talk. It had been better when Lannie was up at the Pentagon. You could chat endlessly on the internet via e-mail: messages left, messages received, hours spent at the keyboard doodling into the ether. The great thing was, you could pick up your e-mail when you wanted, and reply at your leisure. But now she was right next door, and the phone rang constantly. The phone was ringing right now, in fact. She picked up.

"Hi, Lannie."

"How'd you know it was me?"

"Who else calls at nine o'clock at night?"

"Are you still up?"

"Yeah."

"I'm coming over. Is that okay?"

"Sure. Where are you?"

"I'm making that turn, you know, by the Seven-11."

"The Quik Stop."

"That's the one. Be there in a minute. Bye."

Kara hung up. Peesh the cat jumped from the top of the sofa to her shoulder and purred in her ear. "What do you think this crazy girl is up to now, Peesh? You're a woman. You must have an idea." Peesh wrapped herself around Kara's neck and rode up there as she walked into the kitchen and poured herself a glass of wine. Out the window, headlights appeared on the drive. She heard Lannie gun the engine and shut it off. Her car door slammed. She ran up the stairs and pressed her face and fingers to the window next to the front door. Kara laughed. She looked like a Cabbage Patch doll. She opened the front door, and Lannie breezed in carrying a paper bag, heading for the kitchen. She opened the bag and pulled out a bottle of Dom Perignon.

"What's the occasion?"

"No occasion. I just felt like splurging."

"On captain's pay?"

"Hey, a girl's got to let it loose every once in a while, don't you think?" She unwrapped the foil and untwisted the wire holding the cork in place. Holding the cork with a kitchen towel, she turned the bottle slowly until the cork slipped out of the narrow neck with a soft hiss.

"You look like you've done that before."

Lannie grinned. "Once or twice. You want a glass?"

"Sure." Kara got two champagne glasses from the cupboard, and Lannie filled them with the bubbly wine. They each took a sip and Lannie licked her lips. "Just goes to prove, you get what you pay for."

"So what's new in your life in the last six hours?"

"Six hours?"

"We talked at fifteen hundred, remember?"

"I've been getting ready for the AUSA convention in Washington. The base closure commission is having a hearing up there on the Thursday the convention starts. Every three-star and four-star in the Army's going to be there. Very astute of them. Putting us on the spot in front of the brass."

"Who's giving the testimony?"

"The General. I'm spending all my time getting his briefing ready."

"You had better make it good."

"Don't I know it? This feels like finals at Woo Poo.

I'm telling you." She drained her glass and refilled it. "You going to the AUSA convention?"

"Yeah, I guess I'll show my face. I want to see what the new model Apache looks like. They're supposed to have a mock-up of the cockpit on display."

"You'll probably run into some of your pals from Aviation there."

"I'm sure I will."

"What'd they used to call their cockpit seats?"

"Studbuckets."

"Assholes."

"You're telling me?"

"You're well out of that mess of hormonally impaired gorillas."

"I was good at what I did, Lannie. My scores were in the top five percent of the entire branch."

"Yeah, I remember. They spend all that money training you and then just blow it off. It's a crime. What they're doing to women in the Army is giving lip service a bad name."

Kara laughed out loud. "I couldn't put it better if I tried!"

Lannie was giggling into her glass. She slugged back the rest of her champagne and reached for the bottle. "You want some more?"

"Sure."

Lannie refilled their glasses. One of the cats walked along the counter, and she gave its neck a rough rubbing. "Which one is this?"

"Wally. He's the prince of the family."

"And the other one is his monarch?"

"King Weird. Last of the Galahads."

"He's the cat you found when you were living on that river during law school, right?"

"It was more of a creek, but they called it the Gap River. Yeah. He was about four inches long and wet and scared, and I took him inside and dried him off with a towel and gave him some milk, and he curled right up in my lap and went to sleep. It was love at first sight. Did that ever happen to you?"

"Yes. This year."

"So you *do* have a guy. Tell me about him. How'd you meet him?"

"You're not going to believe this. E-mail."

"Come on. That doesn't happen."

"It did this time. I answered a post on a bulletin board. He e-mailed me back. This was, like six months ago. We got to know each other; he was in Atlanta, I was in Washington. Then I moved down here, and so I e-mailed him I was coming, and we made a date to hook up one night, and I was real nervous, 'cause he could have turned out to be a real dog, but I walked in this club up in Atlanta, and he was at the bar, and Kara, this guy is gorgeous. I couldn't believe it."

"So you're still seeing him."

"He's right at the top of my list."

"You've got to introduce me to him. If he's as gorgeous as you say, I've *got* to meet him."

Suddenly Lannie's face fell. "Yeah. Right. Problem is, he travels all the time on business, and I'm going to be pretty busy until the AUSA convention is over. The General is taking this whole thing real seriously. He and the missus are giving a big party. I've got my hands full, between the base closure commission hearing and the party and all the rest of it . . ."

"Maybe after the convention."

"Yeah, everything will be slowing down by then." She brightened. "So you never told me if you've got a guy. Do you?"

Kara took a sip of champagne. She thought briefly of telling Lannie about Mace, but decided it was too dangerous. She had a big mouth, and even though her boss, General Beckwith, already knew about her and Mace, there was no sense baiting him. She might make a mistake and let it slip she knew, and he might take it the wrong way and use that as an excuse to go after them. No way she could take that chance.

Lannie grinned. "You do. I can tell."

"Nope. Not yet. I just moved down here a few months ago. Give me some time. I'll find somebody ready, willing, and able."

Lannie laughed. "I think this champagne is going to my head. I'm getting the giggles."

"It feels good, doesn't it? Getting a little drunk. Letting go. Being happy."

Kara looked into her friend's eyes. There was pain behind the sparkle and the laughter. She hoped Lannie wasn't using champagne and talk as emotional camouflage. She had before. For all the goofy charm and energy the girl exuded like natural carbonation, there was a place inside Lannie that Kara had never touched. Maybe nobody had. Maybe not even Lannie.

Lannie sighed. "Don't you wish it wasn't so man-dependent, happiness? I mean, Lord knows, if we didn't need them so damn much, life would be so much easier."

Kara laughed. "Sometimes I wish I was one of my cats. All you've got to do is scratch their bellies, and those cats are happy as a clam sunk down in about a foot of muck."

They laughed. Lannie said: "I wonder if guys know we talk about them like this?"

"Guys are worse. Much worse." Kara took a sip from her glass, and Lannie poured the rest of the bottle and gazed at the bubbles popping at the surface of her glass.

"It's different with guys, Kara. I've known guys who could be happy as hell with a twenty-seven-inch TV, a cot, and a fridge for beer and a phone to call for take-out."

"What kind of life is that, anyway?"

"It was my life up in Washington, you want the truth."

"Mine too, in law school."

"But this is a new season, right, Kara?" She raised her glass. "Here's to guys who wouldn't know a studbucket if it bit them on the ass!"

Kara laughed. "I'll drink to that."

Chapter Sixteen

Kara was early, so the nurse's aide showed her to the waiting room. There were a couple of young male NCO's standing along the wall, but everyone else in the room was in civilian clothes and female—wives and daughters mostly, although two or three of them could have been young enlisted women. Kara took a seat on one of the amazingly uncomfortable plastic chairs. It was then that she noticed that at least half of the women were pregnant. The young woman next to her was reading *People*. Kara whispered to her: "Is this the waiting room for Ob-Gyn?"

She looked up from the magazine. "No, ma'am, they're up on the third floor. This is outpatient services."

The nurse's aide appeared in the door. "Major Guidry? Captain Evans will see you now."

Kara followed the aide down a long corridor and through a set of automatic stainless steel doors. Evans was pulling off a pair of latex gloves. He tossed them into a metal trash can and extended his hand. "Charlie Evans."

"Kara Guidry. It's very nice to meet you."

"Same here." He led her into a small office just off the main autopsy room and pulled up a chair for her at his desk. "Slow week. One training death. A fatal car accident. A death from pneumonia, believe it or not."

"I didn't know anybody died from pneumonia anymore."

"It happens. People think they've got a cold and ignore it and keep working, and it's too late by the time the doc gets to them. I see one or two cases a year like that. Pneumonia is an extremely virulent infection. What can I help you with?"

"I wanted to talk to you about Sheila Worthy."

"Of course. Frank Hollaway called yesterday. You found the body, right?"

"Yeah."

"And they gave *you* the prosecution?"

"Yeah. Surprised me too."

Evans swiveled his chair around and started rummaging through a file drawer. He was wearing steel rim spectacles that gave him a professorial air. He swiveled back around and opened the file. "Tell me what you want to know."

"I'm looking for a time of death."

"That's a tough one."

"I thought that'd be your answer."

"Let's start with what we know. What time did you find the body?"

"We got to the car about 2330. I guess it took us about twenty minutes to get her on shore."

"My records show the EMT's got there at 2354."

"That sounds about right."

"She was pronounced dead in the emergency room seventeen minutes after midnight."

"I'm trying to get some idea of what time she actually died."

"Sergeant Nukanen reported that she appeared to be dead when he reached her. That would have been sometime between 2330 and 2350, according to your calculations."

"Closer to 2350."

"Well then, we know from Sergeant Nukanen she was dead at, say, 2345. She must have died sometime before that. The problem is, with a drowning it's very difficult to tell."

"Why is that?"

"With other kinds of fatal trauma, say, death by gunshot, or death by stabbing, or death by blunt-force blow to the head, you can make certain calculations. You can measure blood loss. You can measure the amount of blood that collects and congeals around the point of impact from a blow to the head. You can also make an estimate based on body temperature. After the heart stops beating, the body begins to cool. Of course, in the case of drowning, if the body is submerged, it is cooling even before the heart stops, and after the heart stops, the cooling is more rapid. The temperature of the water affects how fast the body loses heat." Evans took off his glasses and cleaned them with the edge of his jacket. "In every case all you're really getting is a rough estimation, usually in hours, not minutes. It's an inexact science."

"What about the wound in her neck? She wasn't bleeding when we got to her."

"That's because her heart had stopped pumping blood."

"Did she lose much blood?"

"Hardly any at all. It was a very small wound, and it did not sever an artery. The wound to her neck was not the cause of death. Drowning was."

"So the closest we can come is . . . ?"

"If you put me on the stand, I would have to say she could have died anytime between 2100 and when Sergeant Nukanen reached her at 2345 or so. That's about it."

"The time of death could have been as early as 2100? Are you sure of that?"

"As certain as I can be. If she had drowned any earlier, her body temperature would have dropped lower than it was when we measured it in the emergency room. Twenty-one hundred is a solid lower limit for the time of death. I'll swear to that."

"What else can you tell me about the knife wound, Doctor?"

"It was fairly deep, but it didn't do too much damage. Certainly not enough to kill her. Hollaway and I surmised that the stabbing took place away from her car. She rushed back to the car and drove away, trying to escape her attacker. She was panicked, and she drove straight into the flash flood and stalled the car. I'm pretty sure her attacker was standing right there and watched the water engulf her."

"Do you have any idea what kind of knife was used in the attack?"

"It was single-edged, sharp. If I were to guess, the knife went in up to the hilt, so the blade wasn't much longer than three, three and a half inches."

"That sounds a lot like a kitchen paring knife to me."

"Or a pocket knife, maybe even a switchblade. Hard to tell."

"Aren't switchblades a lot longer? Five inches or more?"

"Most of them. But I've seen smaller switchblades. Then there's always the chance the knife didn't go in up to the hilt."

"Quite a few imponderables."

"About as many as there are in every murder case I've been in on. Is this your first?"

Kara felt her face flush and wondered if he noticed. "Yeah."

"Welcome to the club."

"It's not something I was looking forward to."

"None of us do. Not even Frank, and he's got one of the sunnier dispositions around, for a cop."

"Yeah, Frank is great. It's a pleasure to work with him."

"Anything else I can help you with, Major?"

"You didn't find any sign of sexual activity?"

"None."

"Did you do a pregnancy test, Doctor?"

A smile formed slowly on Evans' face. "You know something? I didn't."

"Can you still do one?"

"Sure."

Kara stood. "I'm very interested in those results, Doctor. When can you get them to me?"

He checked his watch. "Too late today. First thing in the morning."

She was standing at the door. "Thanks, Doc. It was nice meeting you."

"Same here." He paused at the door, wiping his glasses on the hem of his jacket again. "What made you think of the pregnancy test, if you don't mind my asking?"

Kara gave a teasingly exaggerated shrug. "I don't know. Feminine intuition?"

She could still hear Captain Evans laughing as she turned the corner and went through the automatic doors.

Kara ran her finger down the list of names on the buzzer of the main gate leading into the complex. She hit the keypad with his code, and the gate swung open. She had convinced Hollaway that Randy Taylor should be handled one on one. It was already getting dark by the time she found his apartment.

Randy answered the door wearing jeans and a cable-knit sweater. "Come in. I just put on some coffee. Would you like a cup?"

Kara was right behind him. "Sure, if you're offering."

Randy handed her a steaming mug and sat down across from her. He was in a garden apartment complex out near the airport. Kara studied the room. It was furnished with the typical strange mix of styles you came across in Army houses: a few inherited antiques, some pieces from an assignment in southern Germany, a couple of prints from a TDY in Japan, some Central American ceramic figures picked up after Jungle Warfare School in Panama.

"Did you get those wood carvings in Germany?" She

pointed across the room at several reliefs of quaint village streets hanging on the wall.

"Yeah, in Oberammergau. Do you like them?"

"Yes. I wanted to get down there to Bavaria when I was overseas, but they kept us pretty busy." She sipped her coffee. "Thank you for seeing me on such short notice."

"I want to help out in any way I can. Sheila was a friend. A good one."

Kara put down her cup. "You and Sheila dated for a while, is that right?"

"Yeah."

"How many times did you go out?"

"Six, seven. Something like that. We met going through in-post processing the day we both arrived for our duty assignments. We didn't know anybody at Fort Benning, and I guess we kind of fell in together."

"When was that?"

"About a year ago." Randy shifted nervously in his chair. "Can I ask what this is about? I mean, why I'm being questioned?"

"We're talking to everyone who knew Sheila, trying to fill in some blanks. Quite frankly, there are more than a few of them. It appears that she kept pretty much to herself."

"She was quiet and a little shy, and I think she was intimidated by having a Headquarters job. Everybody around her was a major or a colonel. It can be a little scary until you get used to it."

"Can you tell me why you two broke up?"

"We didn't break up. There was nothing *to* break up. We were just friends."

"I'm sorry if this is getting personal, but investigations like this have to cover ground that's sometimes uncomfortable."

"I understand."

"After you stopped seeing Sheila, did she start seeing anyone else?"

"I saw her in the O-Club a couple of times with a guy. I can't remember his name . . ."

"Barry Parks?"

"That was him."

"Did she ever talk about him with you?"

"She told me he was someone she had known in college."

"And that's all?"

"She was a very private person. I guess you're finding that out."

"Did Sheila have any close friends? Was there anyone else she talked about?"

"Her roommate. Becky Carrington."

"Lieutenant Carrington told us she thought Sheila was having an affair with a married man. Do you know anything about that?"

He hesitated, and his eyes flicked quickly away before he answered. *He knew.*

"Like I said, she kept pretty much to herself."

"Randy, I have to ask you where you were on the night Sheila died."

"You don't think I—"

Kara interrupted. "We're asking everyone who knew her. There's a chance someone may have seen her car. She had to pass straight through the middle of the post to get out there on the South Gate Road that night."

"I was with the General at the O-Club. He gave a speech to the Officers' Wives Club."

"What time was that?"

"I got there about 1900 and left about 2130."

"Where did you go?"

"I went home."

"We think Sheila might have been driving out to the firing range about 2130. You didn't see her, did you?"

"No."

Kara stood up. "That's all I've got for now. I want to thank you for your cooperation, Randy. I know it's difficult, losing a friend."

"She was a sweet, sweet girl. I'd give anything if . . ." His voice trailed away.

"If what?"

"Nothing. Nothing. It's just sad she's gone."

Mace was coming into the barracks when he heard Lieutenant Parks' voice.

"Sergeant Nukanen, have you got a minute?" He found Parks sitting behind his desk. "Close the door, Sarge. Have a seat."

There was something about the look in Parks' eyes . . . Mace had seen it before, with another lieutenant just before he had a breakdown, and they had medicalled him out of the service. Parks looked cornered, like a man with few options and no exit.

"Have you got the men ready, Sarge?"

"Yes, sir. They're loaded up and ready to go."

"Great." Parks fished in his drawer and came out with a sheet of paper. "I wanted to make sure you were up on platoon operations for the coming year." He pushed it across the desk to Mace. It was a training schedule for the next six months. "Stick this in your files. It'll give you a head start on what the captain has planned for us."

"Yes, sir," said Mace. He didn't know where this was headed. It was very unlike Parks to include him on company planning. All he expected Mace to do was show up every morning and run the platoon on a daily basis. Long-range stuff was for officers.

Parks handed him a set of keys. "This is a copy of my keys for the arms room and the platoon files." He pointed at a locked file cabinet in the corner. "I keep meaning to give you a set. This morning I remembered when I was over at the PX and had them made up. I wanted you to have your own keys in case I, uh, I'm on vacation or on TDY and forget to give you mine."

"Thank you, sir."

"We've, uh, had a pretty good year together, Sarge. You and the platoon and me, I mean."

"Yes, sir, we have."

"I wanted you to know how proud I am of both you and the platoon. This has been the best year I've had in the Army. They say there's nothing like command, and they're right."

"The men are proud of you too, sir. Everybody knows you're the best platoon leader in the battalion."

"That's very nice of you to say, Sarge." He stood up, checking his watch. "I don't want to keep you. I know you've got a lot to do."

"Yes, sir."

Parks offered his hand, and they shook hands. "Keep up the good work, Sarge. The Army needs men like you."

"Thank you, sir."

She could hear the phone ringing when she got out of her car. As she raced up the porch stairs and unlocked the door, her answering machine picked up. She ran to the receiver, panting, out of breath. "Hello?"

"That's a real unfamiliar sound you're making there. For a desk jockey, I mean."

She paused, catching her breath. "You should talk."

"Listen, something weird happened this afternoon. Lieutenant Parks called me in and gave me the training plans for the next six months, and my own set of keys to all the locked areas in the platoon."

"So?"

"It was like he was preparing for him not being around much longer, Kara."

"What do you mean?"

"I mean, I think he's going to split."

Kara whistled. "Where is he now?"

"They came down tonight with a big readiness alert for tonight. He's in there getting the platoon ready to go."

"He's got his field gear on and everything?"

"Yeah. I'm not saying he's going to split tonight. I just think he's considering it."

"What kind of alert are you guys on?"

"I don't know. When they've done it before, they get us all loaded up, and then they call it off."

"I'm going to find out what's going on."

"You'd better make it quick. There isn't much time."

"Where are you?"

"Outside the motor pool at a pay phone."

She quickly wrote down a number and hung up and dialed the phone. "Captain Love, please. Yes, I'll wait." In a moment, Lannie came on the line.

"Lannie, it's me."

"Hey, babe. What's shaking?"

"That's what I called to ask you. I heard there's some kind of alert going on. You know anything about it?"

"Where'd you hear that?"

"I've got my sources."

Lannie laughed. "So who is he?"

"C'mon, Lannie. What do you know?"

"You heard right. It came down from Department of the Army. Big-time. People are bouncing off the walls up here."

"The downsizing commission's behind it."

"Right again. We've got to get the 24th in the field by 0600. They're going out to the Harmony Church training area. They're going up against the 29th Infantry in a combat competition. It's real hush-hush. The whole thing's supposed to look like a regular alert till they hit the field; then they're going to pull the trigger and give them ops orders and turn 'em loose. Not even the General knew it was coming. He's going out of his mind."

"Are you going?"

"Does the snow fall in Manitoba on the black bears in the woods? I'll call you and let you know what's going on."

"That'd be great, Lannie. Thanks."

"Gotta go, Kara." She hung up.

Kara dialed the number Mace gave her. He answered.

"It's some kind of a combat contest. They're going to run you guys out to the field, and just when you think you're going to turn around and go back, they're going to give you an ops order. You're going up against the 24th."

"No shit. You're sure about this?"

"Yeah. Do me a favor, will you? Keep an eye on Parks. I don't think he's going anywhere as long as you guys are in the field."

"Will do."

She heard another truck engine start, and a voice yelled, "Sarge! You're wanted up front!"

"I'll call you when I get back."

"Mace . . . wait."

"Gotta go."

"Mace, I—"

He hung up.

She walked into the kitchen and put on water for a cup of coffee. Spooning some instant into a cup, she poured the boiling water and opened her briefcase, spreading her notes on the kitchen table. It was time to assemble the facts of the Sheila Worthy murder as she knew them, and to note what she didn't know.

She flipped through a yellow legal pad to a blank page. At the top she wrote, "Sheila Worthy time line." She shuffled through her notes, checking the times she had recorded.

2100—Sheila leaves Camelia Apts. Witness: Lt. Carrington.

2130—Beckwith leaves Officers Club. Witness: Capt. Taylor.

2145—Beckwith arrives at child-care center. Witness: Mrs. Bennett.

2200—Beckwith arrives at home. Witness: Mrs. Beckwith.

2330—Sheila's car spotted in river. Witness: Kara and Mace.

2350—Sheila removed from car. Witness: Kara and Mace.

2358—Helicopter lands, Sheila taken to hospital. Witness: Kara and Mace.

0017—Sheila pronounced dead at hospital. Witness: Maj. Hollaway.

0030—Beckwith enters hospital. Witness: Me.

Kara stared at the page. Mrs. Beckwith had said her husband got home at 2200, but Mrs. Bennett had said he arrived at the child-care center around 2145. With children injured and the roof blown off, he must have stayed longer than fifteen minutes. She made a note to check how long it took to drive from the child-care center to General Beckwith's quarters.

She tapped the page with her pen. She was sure Mrs. Beckwith was lying about what time her husband got home. He was alone in his staff car that night. There had to be some kind of records kept on usage of the staff car. She knew drivers signed the cars out from the motor pool. She wondered if mileage was noted on the sign-out sheets. She wondered if anyone saw the general that night in his staff car.

There was work to be done. Kara made a vow. She would fill in every gap in the time line the night Sheila was killed. The truth was in the details. Somewhere on that time line were the moments when Sheila was stabbed in the neck and panicked and drove into the river. If she filled in the gaps, she knew she'd find those moments and she'd find the killer.

Chapter Seventeen

The sun was shining brightly out the window of the Chief of Staff's office when General Ranstead walked in carrying a thick briefing book and a roll of maps. The office was huge, on the southeast side of the Pentagon building, overlooking the Capitol in the distance. The chief, General Paul Carson, was sitting at the head of a conference table at one end of the office. His aide was talking on the phone, and several colonels were sitting along the sides of the table.

"Have you got the plan, Jack?"

"Yes, sir." Handing the map to one of the colonels, he took the seat at the far end of the table and put the briefing book down on the table. "I did it just like you said, sir. We sprang an alert on them and you'll deliver the ops order in the field. They never knew what hit them."

"Great. That's exactly what I wanted."

"I've got only one question, sir. I've run this ops order out in two directions, like you said. Operation Hellfire is a standard assault-and-defend exercise. Third Army would defend the objective, and Fifth Army would have the job of taking them out. Operation Native Son is the peacekeeping exercise. Units of the Third Army would be the peacekeepers, and Fifth Army units would be the partisans. The problem I have is this, sir. We haven't run one of these peacekeeping exercises before. I'm wondering if it's fair to Generals Beckwith and King to spring a brand-new exercise on them with such short notice."

General Carson chuckled. "That's the whole point. It's *not* fair. I don't want these guys doing a song and dance they've soft-shoed through a hundred times before. I want them hanging out there, wondering what in the hell hit them. One of them is going to be sitting in this chair in a couple of months. I want to see if either one or both of them panics when we hit them with the plan."

"Well, sir, if anything's going to panic them, this is."

"Excellent. I spoke to the Secretary about it yesterday. He's going on-site. The President has asked him to be his eyes and ears on this thing. He's feeling a lot of heat from the Hill on this appointment. Did you see *Meet the Press* on Sunday morning?"

"No, sir. I was down on the Rappahannock, fishing."

"Lucky you. Maldray was on there pushing Beckwith, and that Democrat from Wisconsin . . . what's his name?"

"Fuegel."

"Right. Fuegel was on there pushing King. The Secretary told me the President feels this whole thing has gotten way too political. He wants a military spin put on the selection of the next chief of staff. You know how the Republicans are always chipping away at him on Defense issues. Well, he knows he's vulnerable, and the last thing he wants is to be seen as making a political appointment to a sensitive military position such as this one."

"Things have changed since you were appointed, haven't they, sir?"

"I don't recall this kind of naked politicking six years ago."

"No, sir. But Maldray ruffled his feathers when you were reappointed three years ago."

"That's right. He did."

General Ranstead smiled as he opened the briefing book. "All right then, sir. You say the President wants a military spin? I think Operation Native Son is just what the doctor ordered."

"Run it down for me, Jack."

"Sir, what we've done is put a modern twist on a classic situation. King's 29th Infantry Regiment will hold this ground here." General Ranstead leaned over the table and tapped the map with a metal pointer. "His people will be the fierce partisan guerillas in the fictional country of Blucania. They've held the territory for three years and used their positions to terrorize the surrounding citizenry, which opposed them in the bitter civil war that has been going on for more than six years. Somewhere far from their position, in the capital city of Cernivitzia, a peace treaty has been signed that has yielded their territory as part of an overall regional settlement of the conflict. Beckwith and his partisans aren't happy about it. They don't want to make peace. They want to hang onto your turf and continue to make war on your sworn enemies."

He tapped another spot on the map. "General Beckwith's 24th Infantry will be NATO peacekeepers. It will be their job to dislodge General King and his Blucanian partisans from their hard-won and fiercely held territory. Here's where it gets interesting, sir. The earth has shifted under the feet of the modern American fighting man. They're giving us situations like Haiti and Somalia and Bosnia, and it's no longer our job to go in there and kill everything that moves and call it a victory. These situations are political, and the role the Army is being asked to play has become increasingly subtle. Success isn't measured in dead bodies counted, or tons of ordnance rained down on target. That's where the scoring of the exercise comes in. We're going to try something new. We'll use the laser scoring system we've used in countless other field exercises, but we're going to total the scores in a completely different way. Beckwith's partisan fighters have been hardened in the civil war, but we're going to tell them they are facing a vastly superior force of peacekeepers. It has been made clear to the peacekeepers that any kind of serious resistance to the peacekeeping efforts will be met with massive retaliation. Therefore, King's methodology of resistance will have to be closer to escape and evasion than to conventional warfare. It'll be his job to make it as difficult as possible for General Beckwith's troops to move him out of his positions without resorting to conventional warfare. The fact is, if King's partisans start shooting up the woods, the peacekeepers are going to rain down holy hell on their heads, and they will sustain unacceptable losses. So General King's task is going to be keeping his troops under control. If his partisans start slaughtering peacekeepers, they're going to be cleared to use their superior firepower, and he's lost the game."

General Carson stood up and studied the map. "What about Beckwith? What's his dilemma?"

"General Beckwith's job is to displace the partisans from the area as nonviolently as possible. He will be empowered to respond to partisan attacks with massive retaliation, but he'll score higher if his peacekeepers surround and subdue the partisans. In this exercise we will score a partisan unit as successfully displaced if General Beckwith's troops surround the unit and score a capture. On the other hand, we'll score General King's partisans as successfully holding their ground if they can avoid being surrounded and captured. Killing the enemy isn't the point in this exercise. Surrounding and subduing him is. We're going to score this thing just like an election. We're giving them forty-eight hours. If the majority of the partisans haven't been captured at the end of that time, King wins. If Beckwith's peacekeepers have surrounded the majority of the partisans, he wins." General Ranstead looked up. "What do you think, sir?"

"How are we going to score a capture, Jack?"

General Ranstead took a magic marker and outlined a

Chapter Eighteen

"Frank, have you got a minute?"

Hollaway looked up blankly from his desk. "Sure. Come on in." Kara flopped onto his sprung-seat sofa. Hollaway put away the paperwork he had been studying. "You had lunch yet? We could go over to the PX and pick up a couple of biscuits. Everyone on post is out in the field on alert. We'll have the whole place to ourselves."

"No, thanks." She dug into her briefcase. "I've been going through Sheila Worthy's personal effects, Frank."

"Right. How's it going?"

"Did you know she had a cell phone?"

Hollaway looked half-startled. "We didn't find one in her car."

"It must have been one of those hand-held jobs, got washed away in the flood."

"That makes sense."

"I got Southeastern Air-Tone to pull her bill, Frank. There are two very interesting calls she made the day she died." Kara handed him several pages, stapled together. He flipped through the bill.

"You've identified these calls?"

"I ran a reverse on every one of them. Her office, her apartment, the local 76 station, making an appointment for an oil change. Then we come to the two calls I highlighted in yellow."

"What are they?"

"They're calls to the secure switchboard on post, Frank."

"What does that mean?"

"She called the switch, and they patched her through on a secure line to someone else."

"I know they've got a secure-patch system here, but—?"

"Frank, she was calling someone with access to a secure line. Look at the time of the calls."

"2240, 2242."

"Evans said she died sometime between 2100 and when we found her at 2345. She was in her car, Frank, talking on her cell phone. These were the last calls she would ever make, and she was calling the guy she was going to meet out there. How many people do you figure have phones that tie in to the secure lines on this post, Frank?"

"I don't know, but I could find out."

She passed another page across his desk. "I already did. Twelve. Six of them general officers. King. His deputy, Michaels. Beckwith, his deputy, Simons. Seger, commander of the Infantry School. His deputy, Lanford. Then there's your boss, Colonel Desadiro. And the garrison commander, Colonel Porche. There are four other secure lines in each MP substation around the post."

"Maybe she dialed a wrong number."

"She called the secure switch twice. She knew where she was calling."

Hollaway studied the page. "Yeah."

"Sheila made these calls only minutes before she died. None of these men are named Parks or Taylor. We've got a new set of suspects, Frank."

"No, we don't. If she made these calls to a secure phone just before she died, how could one of these men be out there close enough to kill her?"

Kara paused. He had a point. Hollaway rubbed his chin. "Maybe she was calling one of the MP substations. Maybe she saw something, an accident or a downed tree, and she was reporting it."

"If all she was doing was reporting an accident, why would she call the secure switch, Frank? Why didn't she just dial 911?"

"Good point."

"This thing could drop the killer right in our laps if we could figure out where those calls went."

"I know." Hollaway paused, leaning back in his chair. "You don't actually think one of these guys killed her, do you? I mean, these are the six or eight most powerful men on this post."

"We've got to go where the investigation takes us. I think we've got to canvass every person with a phone tied into the secure switch."

"Do you really expect that the killer is just going to up and admit he received her call? I mean, that would be tantamount to an admission of guilt."

"Then we've got to do it some other way. Maybe there's a computer tied in there we don't know about. Maybe we can trace these two calls past the switchboard."

"I just have a hard time looking at this list with six generals on it, thinking one of them might be the killer."

"Let's keep this between us for the time being, huh, Frank? I mean, if we're wrong, and it gets out we're looking at these guys as suspects, that would be the end of both of our careers."

"You're right about that."

Kara stood, straightening her skirt. "Frank, we're going to get this guy. You know that, don't you?"

"I sure hope so."

Chapter Nineteen

"Hey, Sarge! The captain's lookin' for ya! He's gonna have my ass if I don't—"

"I'm coming, Radley. Where is he?"

"He's up front in the lead vehicle, Sarge. Somethin's up. I don't know what it is, but the captain, he's real eager I get you up there."

Radley, a skinny little guy from Elizabethtown, Kentucky, was Mace's right-hand man in the platoon. He'd been in the Army for a couple of enlistments and had found a home as an E-4 squad leader. His enormous dark brown eyes gave him an uncanny ability to see in the dark, making him especially useful in night maneuvers. He could make out terrain features at great distances on nights when cloud cover obscured the moon and stars.

Mace and Corporal Radley made their way along the line of Humvees and trucks idling at the side of the road. The company's vehicles were the last ones in the long battalion convoy. They found Lieutenant Parks and Captain Long sitting in the right front seat of the company-command Humvee talking on the radio. When the captain saw Mace, he signed off and handed the receiver to his RTO.

"You have any idea what's up, Sarge? What do you hear from the men?"

"I hear we're going on some kind of big-time field exercise, up against the 24th."

"No kidding? Where'd you hear that?"

"Around, sir. It's just a rumor."

"You heard anything, Lieutenant?"

"No, sir. The orderly just called me and told me to get my stuff and report the same as everybody else."

"You guys better get back to your platoon. We're about to move out."

"Yes, sir." Lieutenant Parks fell in next to Mace.

"What'd you hear, Sarge?"

Mace glanced at Parks. The chin strap on his helmet was snapped tightly, and his face looked impossibly young and eager. "I heard it's some kind of downsizing thing, sir."

"That means the brass is going to be everywhere."

"Yes, sir. I'd imagine."

They reached the platoon vehicles, a command Humvee and a couple of trucks. The men were lying around on the ground, resting against their field packs. Mace felt a tug at his jacket sleeve. He turned as Radley whispered: "Sarge, the captain's on the radio. He's giving the order to move out. The whole battalion's on the move."

Ahead of them, engines roared to life and taillights came on.

"Get the men on the vehicles, Sergeant."

"Yes, sir." He turned to the platoon. "Mount up. Let's go."

The platoon picked up their gear and started getting into the trucks. Mace walked up to the Humvee and climbed in the back. Lieutenant Parks climbed in the front seat.

"Looks like it's going to be a long night, Sarge."

"Yes, sir."

Lieutenant Parks stared out the windshield. "Well, I hope they're ready. Whatever this thing is, it's going to be rough."

"They are, sir."

The Humvee's engine started, and Radley put it in

gear. Ahead of them, a set of brake lights was fast disappearing. Radley stepped on the gas. Behind them, the trucks lurched forward. The platoon radio spat static, and the captain's voice came on.

"Where the hell are you guys, Parks? Get your asses up here with the rest of the company."

Parks picked up the mike. "On our way, Six."

Mace looked out the top of the Humvee through the open machine gun mount. Overhead, storm clouds had obscured the moon. It was dark and getting darker, and there was another storm on the way. He could feel it in his bones.

Lannie ran under the whirling blades of the Blackhawk and climbed in. She took the seat next to General Beckwith and buckled up. The big bird shuddered, tilted forward, and rose skyward from the pad. She put on an intercom headset and adjusted the volume.

Beckwith's voice crackled in her ears. "What'd you find out, Captain?"

"The Chief of Staff lifted off at 1900 from Andrews, sir."

"Dammit!"

"It's just like you thought, sir. We're going up against General King's 29th Infantry Regiment."

"King's people up in Washington stage-managed this. I can smell it. Pendleton called me yesterday and said something was up. He saw that goddamn Ranstead going in and out of Carson's office all day. He couldn't get anyone to tell him what they were up to. My guess is, we just found out."

"Do you remember my friend Carla Gonzales?"

"You were at the Point with her."

"She's working in the Chief's office now. General Carson moved her out of DESPER and installed her in his PAO shop. I talked to her a few minutes ago. General King is meeting the Chief out at Lawson Airfield as soon as he gets in."

"If he took off at 1900, he's already here."

"I'm afraid so."

The chopper banked steeply. Below them, the lights of a convoy snaked through the dark woods along a dirt road. Lannie pointed out the window. "There they are. Our guys are right on time."

Beckwith leaned across her to get a better look, resting his hand on her leg. She twisted the intercom mike away from her mouth and whispered loudly enough for him to hear her over the sound of the chopper's engines: "Watch it. I'm ticklish there."

He leaned into her ear. "Elsewhere too."

She laughed. Her headset crackled. It was the pilot. He sounded like he was about eighteen.

"Aahhh, we're going to touch down in zero-two, sir."

"Roger that."

The chopper came in over the trees and hovered above a wide meadow crowded with Bradleys and Humvees. When they touched down, Beckwith pulled open the door and stepped out. Lannie followed close behind. Just as they suspected, General King was standing with General Carson next to a Humvee flying a four-star flag. Carson was stocky, maybe five-seven. He had deep-set eyes and a jaw that wore a permanent five o'clock shadow. Lannie knew that the word on him in the Pentagon was unanimous: General Carson was a soldier's soldier. He had commanded a company in Vietnam and later did a stint as Army liaison to the Congress, but in between he had taken every command job he could find. He had been superintendent of West Point at the time Beckwith was commandant. The word at West Point had been that they hated each other.

Lannie didn't recognize the other general standing with them. From the look on Beckwith's face, he knew who he was. Beckwith saluted smartly. Carson extended his hand.

"Good to see you, Bill. You know Jack Ranstead, don't you?"

"Yes, sir." Beckwith had a thin smile on his lips as he turned to the other general. "Long time no see, Jack. How have you been?"

General Ranstead was tall and slender and wore a look of perpetual relaxation. His face cracked a wide, engaging smile.

"Never better."

"You enjoying the E-Ring, Jack?" asked General Beckwith.

General Ranstead chuckled. "I'm finding my way around."

Carson laughed and the others joined him. General Beckwith turned to General King. "Evening, Bernie. Looks like the Chief's got something special up his sleeve tonight."

"That's what I hear," said General King. "Your guys ready?"

"They're fueled up and raring to go."

"I'll see if my troopers can't give you a run for your money, Bill."

"We'll be ready for you."

General Carson cleared his throat. "Each of you were alerted four hours ago. Two hours ago you received your ops orders by fax. Are there any questions?"

General Beckwith stepped forward. "Sir, I've got a question. How are you going to score a capture?"

"Good question, Bill. That's where Jack Ranstead comes in. He's going to oversee scoring the exercise. His boys will accompany each of your units down to company level. They'll make the determinations as to whether or not a unit has been captured in the field."

General Carson lit up a large cigar and blew a puff of smoke into the air. "This operation is being conducted in conjunction with a live-fire exercise." He pointed to an area of the map that had been outlined brightly with a red magic marker. "Inside the red-lined area to the west of the area of operations will be a live-fire zone, simulating continuing conflict in the region. We've got it marked pretty clearly out there, but it's going to be the job of each of you to make sure your units down to the individual soldier are keenly aware of the live-fire zone. Your men are to stay two hundred meters clear of its outer boundaries. We don't want any accidents out here. They're going to be bringing in air strikes and hitting that ground with every kind of artillery they can throw on it. Anybody entering that live-fire zone is going to walk right into a shitstorm of ordnance."

Both generals nodded gravely.

General Carson held up a yellow plastic flag about the size of an automobile license plate. "You'll find these flags every fifty meters along the edge of the live-fire zone. They mark the boundary of a two hundred-meter warning area. Your men will keep well outside the warning area, and under no circumstances will they cross into the live-fire zone. Understood?"

Beckwith said, "Yes sir. Understood."

"Got you, sir," said General King. Carson handed each man a manila folder.

"You've got two hours to take your positions. Bernie, your men hit the line of departure at zero-two-hundred." Carson checked his watch. "The clock is ticking, gentlemen. You are free to move out."

Both generals saluted. General King and Command Sergeant Major Conklin headed toward a Humvee parked across the dirt road. General Beckwith and Lannie walked in the opposite direction. A Humvee flying red four-star flags drove up. Beckwith got in.

"It's just like Carson to set up a unit competition that discourages actual combat. Ranstead's behind this thing. I want you to stay right here and keep an eye on him. I don't trust him. He's up to something, and I want to know what it is."

"Got it, sir."

"I'll have Randy check in with you. Have you got your cell phone?"

"Yes, sir."

"Good. Stay off the regimental net. Use your cell phone. Find someplace to charge your extra battery, 'cause you're going to need it. I want to be updated twice a day. If Ranstead gets a cold, I want to know how many times he sneezes."

"Roger, sir."

Beckwith closed the Humvee's door. Lannie snapped a salute as the vehicle accelerated. She walked back toward the Chief of Staff, who was still bent over the map.

Ranstead. Ranstead. Where have I heard that name before?

The rain had let up, but during the day a cold front had pushed through, driving the temperature down into the thirties by nightfall. Mace wrapped himself tighter in his poncho liner and looked through a peephole he had whacked out of the patch of briars he was using for an observation post. He was lying flat on the ground next to Lieutenant Parks. The thicket was so dense, they had to dig their way under one side and squirm beneath the twisted, thorny branches until they reached an open spot in the middle where they covered themselves with leaves and dirt. Mace knew that from the outside they were invisible. He squinted into the misty darkness. There was something moving out there.

Over on the right. Yeah.

He nudged the lieutenant and picked up the mike: "Radley. You see 'em?"

"Yeah, Sarge. 'Bout three squads, comin' up the hill."

"Spread the word. Cover up tight. Total silence."

"Right, Sarge. Will do."

The platoon was spread out behind them, scattered through the dense woods, dug into one- and two-man holes with thickly woven weeds and branches pulled in over them. Mace had learned the technique of camouflage and concealment from an old platoon sergeant when he first got in the Army. The sergeant had learned it during the war in Vietnam. The VC called them spider holes. You dug in and constructed a sturdy lid for the hole that looked just like the forest floor. If you did it well enough, as the VC certainly had during the war, an entire company could walk quite literally over your positions and never see you. Why maneuver and scoot around avoiding the enemy when you could fix it so he didn't even know you were there? That morning when they were finished digging in, Mace had crawled out of his thicket and walked back through the stretch of forest where he knew the platoon was. There wasn't the slightest evidence that the woods had been disturbed by man.

Lieutenant Parks had been dubious about the plan until Mace pointed out that once an enemy unit had walked past them, it was very unlikely they would turn around and cover the same ground again. This gave the platoon a choice of staying in their holes and maintaining concealment until the exercise was over, or maneuvering against the enemy from his rear. Either way they enjoyed the element of surprise. As a tactical matter, you couldn't have it much better than that.

The figures were closer now. You could make out their helmets and packs and weapons. They were moving slowly, probably because they couldn't see any better than Mace could. You could hear them whispering softly to one another. They knew they were close to the partisan lines. Mace pegged the third guy in line as the lieutenant. He kept nervously stopping and turning around to check and recheck that everyone was following along behind. Finally he stopped directly in front of the thicket where Mace and Lieutenant Parks were concealed. He took out a penlight and checked a map. His platoon sergeant tilted his helmet back and took a swig from his canteen.

"They've got to be around here somewhere, Sarge. The captain said intelligence had the partisans strung

out all the way across the front to this creek here, and
we just crossed the creek a few minutes ago."

"Maybe they done moved off already, sir. They got
plenty of room to maneuver to the north."

"Yeah. Let's keep going. Tell the men to look closely
for signs of the enemy's position. Our recon patrols saw
smoke earlier this afternoon. They had to have built a
fire around here somewhere."

He turned off the penlight and folded the map. As
they brushed past the briar patch, the lieutenant caught
his web gear in the thorns. He cursed under his breath,
pulled it loose, and kept moving. When they were well
past Mace's position, he shifted around and looked out
the back of the thicket.

"Radley, they've got to be right on top of you," he
whispered into the mike.

There were two quick bursts of static through his ear-
piece as Radley confirmed yes by keying his mike. In a
moment Radley's voice came on, in a whisper.

"They're gone, Sarge. Back down the other side of
the hill. We're home free."

Mace tugged Lieutenant Parks' sleeve. "They're past
our position, sir."

"Worked like a charm, Sarge. I've got to hand it to
you."

Just then the company radio crackled, and Parks
grabbed the receiver. It was Captain Long. "Rattlesnake
three, this is Rattlesnake six, over."

"This is three, go ahead."

"Rattlesnake six. The whole damn battalion is getting
overrun. Peacekeepers are coming up on our position
now. Get your platoon out of there, or you'll be scored
as captured. If you can avoid the peacekeepers, they
won't score the whole battalion as captured. Think you
can do that, three?"

"Roger, six. Understand. We'll beat 'em. Three out."
Parks turned to Mace. "Saddle them up, Sarge. We're
out of here."

"What happened, sir?"

"They overran the rest of the battalion. We've got to get out of here and keep on the move till the end of the exercise, or Fifth Army's going to lose this thing."

Lannie unzipped her sleeping bag and slipped away from her cot, careful not to wake the others in the tent. She waited until she got outside to put on her field jacket, zipping it tightly against the cold, turning up her collar, trying to sink deeper into its warm reaches. She rounded the corner of the tent, heading for the latrine. The wind hit her full force, making her eyes water. As she turned her head, wiping her eyes on her sleeve, she bumped into something and looked up.

"Randy! You scared me!"

"Sorry."

"I thought you were staying behind at Headquarters, holding down the fort."

"I was. The General called and told me to get over here and see what's going on. He's been trying to reach you on your cell phone."

Lannie took her phone from her jacket pocket. It had gone dead. "Must be the cold. I charged the battery this afternoon."

"Why don't you show me around? I'll call him and tell him I checked everything out."

"There's not that much to see."

"I've got to be able to tell him something, Lannie."

"Okay. I'll take you through the control shack." She led him down the row of tents, and they entered the shack through the front door. It was warm inside, and the place was buzzing with activity. Lieutenants wearing headsets were furiously entering radio reports from the field into their laptops. A female major was standing at a huge map mounted on the wall. It was covered with red- and blue-flagged pins. One of the lieutenants raised his hand, and the major walked over. He pointed at something on his laptop. She leaned forward, reading.

Then she walked back over to the map and moved one of the red pins a few inches.

Lannie walked up behind her. "Major Hammett, this is Captain Randy Taylor. He's General Beckwith's aide."

Major Hammett turned around. She had prematurely gray hair, and her eyes were rimmed red from lack of sleep. "What can I do for you, Captain?"

"I thought I'd come over and see what was going on, ma'am. I don't want to get in your way."

Major Hammett picked up a pointer. "The red flags denote peacekeeper companies belonging to the 24th Infantry, Captain. The blue flags are partisan companies in the 29th. As you can see, your peacekeepers are closing on partisan positions, but the partisans have been doing a pretty good job of staying out of their way. We've had a couple of reports of partisan units captured, here and here." She pointed at two orange flags that had been pinned next to red flags. Another lieutenant rushed up and whispered in the major's ear. "Your peacekeepers just captured most of the partisans' Second Battalion, Captain. They're chasing down one last element of the battalion right now."

She pinned a large yellow flag next to a small concentration of red flags. "That's a real blow to the Fifth Army. I'd have to say your guys have been behind up until now, but if you're able to capture the rest of that battalion, that's going to put you way ahead in the scoring."

The imposing figure of General Ranstead appeared in the door. "Did I hear you say the partisans lost a battalion?"

"Yes, sir," said Major Hammett. "Just happened, sir."

General Ranstead walked into the shack's main room. Randy and Lannie snapped to attention. Major Hammett stepped forward.

"Sir, Captain Love and Captain Taylor work for General Beckwith. Captain Taylor is his aide."

General Ranstead nodded at Lannie. "Captain Love." He paused, looking at Randy. "Captain. Nice to meet you." The general held Randy's eyes for an instant, then turned quickly to the map as Major Hammett pointed out the position of the captured battalion. When she was through, the general walked quickly back into the rear office and closed the door behind him.

"Anything else I can do for you?" asked Major Hammett.

Lannie looked at Randy. He was staring at the door to the general's office. He hadn't heard a word the major said.

"No, thank you, ma'am. I think we've seen enough." She grabbed Randy's arm and pulled him away. He stumbled through the door into a cold wind. Lannie pulled on her gloves as Randy stared straight ahead at the observation tower, his BDU jacket unzipped, a blank look on his face.

"Let's get out of the cold."

Randy just stood there, shivering.

"What's the matter? You look like you just saw a ghost."

"Nothing. It's nothing."

"Did you used to work for Ranstead? He was sure looking at you funny, like he recognized you from somewhere."

"No. I've never met him before," Randy lied.

"C'mon." She pointed. "Let's get a cup of coffee."

A diesel heater glowed in the corner of the empty mess tent. Randy grabbed a couple of cups and filled them with coffee. They sat down at a picnic table near the heater.

"You sure you don't know him? There was a moment there when I thought you two were going to start going over old times."

"I've heard of him. I think I read something about him in the *Army Times*."

"Yeah. There was a big article about him a couple of

weeks ago. Did you see the way he zipped out of his office when he heard that battalion was captured?"

"Yeah."

"Every one of those scorekeepers works for him. He could throw this thing either way, and I'm betting against him giving the Third Army a break."

Randy broke his spell and turned to her. "Why do you say that?"

"Something Beckwith said about him. He doesn't trust General Ranstead."

"General Beckwith doesn't trust anybody."

Lannie laughed. "That's true." She drained the last of her cup and stood up. "I'm going to try to get some sleep. Are you going back to Headquarters? I'll get you a ride."

"I've got my POV."

"Well, this thing will be history in another fifteen hours. I guess I'll see you around the campus when we get back."

"Yeah. Thanks for your help."

"No problem. Watch yourself on these back roads. It's getting slick out there."

"I will."

Lannie pulled the mess tent door closed behind her. Randy checked the chow line to see if there was anything to eat, but even the cooks had turned in for the night, so he scooted a folding chair closer to the heater and sat there sipping his coffee. Lannie suspected he and General Ranstead knew each other. She would probably tell Beckwith. That meant he would have to come up with a good excuse for the awkward moment between them. He racked his brain. Maybe they had shared a military flight once, a couple of years back. Both he and Ranstead had been in Haiti at the same time. So, yeah, maybe he caught a hop on a C-130 out of Haiti, and who was on the flight but Ranstead? The *Army Times* article reported that Ranstead had flown back and forth to Haiti on inspection tours for the Chief of Staff. It was plausible.

Lieutenant Parks stopped at the top of a shallow saddle between two hills. Mace crept forward. Parks removed a pair of binoculars from a case clipped to his web gear and peered into the darkness. He swept the binoculars back and forth and handed them to Mace.

"You see a way out of this, Sarge?"

"I'll have a look, sir."

Mace trained the glasses down the hill. To the east was a swampy area that was bound to be a real mess after the rain. To the west the going was easier, but there was another problem in that direction. The boundary of the live-fire zone was less than a mile from their present position, leaving them only a narrow corridor through which they could move. The surprise appearance of a peacekeeper company made Mace wonder if other enemy units had been moved into their area. He knew the chance of the peacekeepers setting up a position in the swamp was a slim one, so he handed the glasses back to Parks.

"Sir, I think we can avoid them if we head east, but I'm not real sure."

"Maybe we ought to stay put for the time being. It's going to be light in a few hours. Just before dawn I want to double back and try to make it to the positions we occupied last night. If we can get there by first light, we can hole up and wait this thing out. I'm sure the peacekeepers have moved on and our old position will be safe."

"Yes, sir."

"Tell the men. I'll wait here."

Mace crept back to Radley and spread the word. When he returned to the front of the patrol, he found Lieutenant Parks huddled under a tree, wrapped in his poncho.

"Sometimes the Army can be a real shitty place, you know that, Sarge?"

"Yes, sir. Like tonight."

There was a long pause. In the distance he could hear the distinctive *caaaaruuump* of 155mm artillery impacting the live-fire zone.

His words came in a whisper. "You know, they think I killed Sheila."

Mace remained silent, waiting.

"They think because we were lovers, I killed her. Can you believe that?"

"No, sir."

"I didn't kill her, Sarge. You've got to believe that." He paused for a moment. "You believe me, don't you?"

"Yes, sir."

"I'm worried. They were asking me about where I was. I told them I was at home, but I wasn't."

Mace tried to find his face, but it was too dark.

"I followed her that night. I knew she was going to meet him, because she told me. So I followed her, but I lost her in the storm. She went around a corner and when I turned the corner, she was gone. You believe me, don't you, Sarge?"

"Yes, sir."

"They all but told me to get a lawyer."

A barrage of artillery hit the live-fire zone, shaking the ground they were sitting on.

"I'm afraid they're going to start asking around at the apartment complex where I live, and find out I wasn't at home that night like I said. I think they're going to charge me, Sarge. But I didn't do it. I didn't!" He reached out and grabbed Mace's arm. "I didn't kill her! I loved her!"

Another huge barrage hit the live-fire zone. Mace waited for him to release the grip on his arm, but he didn't let go. He just sat there whispering, "I loved her, I loved her, I loved her. . . ."

Chapter Twenty

Mace had dropped off to sleep and awoke when he heard them. He quickly signaled the platoon to lay low.

A force of maybe fifty men was moving through the trees downstream from them. He pulled out his binoculars and adjusted the eyepiece. More troops, a larger enemy force this time, was moving slowly toward them along the far side of the stream.

Lieutenant Parks crawled up next to him. "How long have we got to the end of the exercise, Sarge?"

"Maybe six hours, sir."

"You see any way around these guys?"

"Yes, sir. We could make our way east. We'd have to go through the swamp, but I think we'd still make it."

"We'll never get through the swamp before daybreak, Sarge. I want you to head us west."

"Sir, I don't know about that. We're awfully close to the live-fire zone, and going west is going to take us straight into it."

Parks reached in his pocket and pulled out a copy of the ops order. "They call off the live fire at 0400. It's 0415 right now. We can get around these guys by going through the edge of the live-fire zone. It's over, Sergeant. Look. Right here in the ops order. 0400." He handed the sheet of paper to Mace.

Mace studied Parks. He looked cornered, desperate. "I don't like it, sir. I've been on a bunch of these field exercises. I've seen guys get killed messing around close to the live-fire."

Parks' lips drew tightly across his teeth in a brittle smile. "I'll tell you what, Sergeant. We're going to skirt the edge of the live-fire zone, and you're going to follow me or I will bring you up on charges when we get back to the barracks."

The guy had a death wish. Mace was certain of it. He made a vow not to lead the platoon into the live-fire zone. If this zoned-out lieutenant wanted to cash his check, so be it. But he wasn't going to take the platoon with him. He let Parks move out ahead a good distance before he gave the order for the rest of the platoon to follow. They were just starting down a hill when he saw the distinctive yellow flags marking the outside edge of the live-fire zone. Lieutenant Parks brushed past the first flag and kept going.

He heard some Apaches and looked up. They were gaining altitude, a whole formation of them, a deafening whine of turbine engines and beating rotors. Then they were directly overhead, and one after another they unleashed pods of 3.5-inch rockets that streaked through the night, impacting with fiery explosions that lit up the sky.

He heard the distant sounds of an artillery barrage being fired. Overhead, the 105 rounds whistled through the dark sky and exploded in the distance. There was another series of explosions as more artillery was fired. This time the whistling of the incoming rounds was sharper.

It was going to come in short!

He tore downhill, slipped, tumbled down the slope, regained his feet, and kept running. He saw the lieutenant stop and turn. There was a huge explosion as several of the rounds hit maybe two hundred yards away. Mace started screaming, *Get out of there! Get away!* There was another whistle of artillery, and suddenly a blinding flash of light. A huge pine exploded, knocking him to the ground. He shook his head, trying to focus his eyes. The acrid aroma of cordite filled the air. He looked through the smoke, trying to find the lieutenant.

He was gone.

Mace looked down at his arm. There was a long gash from elbow to wrist, and blood flowed freely. He looked up and saw Radley's face, and he heard his voice as if he was a mile away.

"You're gonna be all right, Sarge . . ."

Then darkness closed in around him and he felt cold. Very, very cold.

Chapter Twenty-one

The phone rang just as Kara was going out the door to work. She had decided to let the machine get it when she heard the voice of a young man, insistent, frantic: "Major Guidry? Are you there? Pick up, please, ma'am!"

She rushed to the phone. "This is Major Guidry. Who's calling?"

"Ma'am, this is Corporal Radley. I'm one of Sergeant Nukanen's squad leaders. The sarge has been wounded, ma'am. He told me, anything ever happen to him, I'm supposed to let you know, ma'am."

She felt her lungs heave as she took air in short, shallow breaths. She paused for a moment, trying to catch her breath. "What happened? Can you tell me?"

"It was out in the field this mornin', ma'am. Lieutenant Parks, he was takin' us pretty close to the live-fire zone. Then he just took off runnin', and the sarge, he went after him, and this artillery barrage come in, and Lieutenant Parks, he's dead, ma'am, and the sarge, he got shook up pretty bad, but I heard one of the dudes come to get him in the chopper, and he said the sarge's gonna be okay, ma'am."

Quickly: "Where is he?"

"They choppered him straight to the hospital, ma'am."

"Thank you, Corporal. Thank you very much."

"No problem, ma'am. Uh, ma'am, I think you oughta

know the sarge is a pretty tough old bird. He's gonna pull through okay."

"I know he is. Thanks again." She hung up the phone and found herself staring out the window at the wind-whipped branches of the trees, remembering. She'd had pride as a plebe at West Point, that they had never made her cry. She saw herself standing in the colonel's office, her face flushed and hot, as he told her she'd never get a Blackhawk squadron command because she was a woman. Even when she got home, sad, confused, enraged, emotions whirling within her, she never cried. And she remembered her father's funeral at the National Cemetery at Fort Leavenworth, standing beneath the tall oaks in the hot shade of August, watching them lower his casket into the ground. She hadn't cried there either.

Now she knew that her tears when she heard that Mace had been wounded meant she loved him the way she had never loved anyone before.

He was lying on his side, and he was moving. When he opened his eyes, he saw pale green walls rushing past. He got it now. He was in a hospital on a gurney. He looked up at the sweating face of the young corpsman pushing him. He could see that the corpsman was talking to someone, but his ears were ringing, like his head was hollow and somebody was blowing a whistle in there.

The gurney made a turn and he saw curtains being yanked back and he came to a stop under a huge white light. People were yelling. He felt someone pressing on his good arm, pressing, pressing. Faintly he heard a male voice:

"I've got a live one."

He felt a needle and then he felt the warm rush of whole blood flowing into his vein.

A big guy was giving loud, sharp orders. He could barely hear him.

"Suture."

It was funny. They were sewing up his arm, and he couldn't feel it. The ringing was turning into a hollow echo. Everybody sounded like they were yelling at him from the bottom of an empty quarry.

"Suture."

The man's face. He could tell the big man was yelling, but his voice sounded far, far away. "Sergeant, can you hear me?"

He nodded.

"You remember me? I'm Captain Taggert."

Taggert. Taggert. Yeah, he remembered. The night they found the body. Nice guy. Doctor.

"I want you to know you took a pretty rough pounding out there this morning, but you're going to be A-okay, you hear me?"

He nodded.

"That's the spirit. Hang in there."

The big guy's face disappeared.

A new voice. A woman. Young.

"Pressure's coming up."

The big guy: "Let's put a drip in. He needs fluids. Give him some morphine."

Somebody started pressing on his thigh, and he felt another needle go in.

A man's voice: "We've got the stitches in him. He's stable. Let's move him."

They were moving him again. He was on his back watching fluorescent lights rush past in a blur. They pushed him into a small room, and hands lifted him from the gurney and slid him onto a mattress that felt like the softest place in the whole world. He heard a faint beeping, and slept.

He woke up as the door opened and Captain Taggert walked in, a stethoscope dangling around his neck. He flipped open a metal chart folder, scanned it briefly, and looked up, smiling. "How are you feeling, Sergeant?"

"Kind of fuzzy. Everything seems real far away."

"You might have a slight concussion. We're going to keep you here awhile and check you out. What do you think about that?"

"Okay, sir." He tried to sit up, but was overcome by a wave of dizziness and nausea and flopped back against his pillows.

"Room swimming a little bit?"

"Yes, sir."

"You lie there and rest awhile, Sergeant. It'll pass. We're going to get you fixed up, you don't worry about that."

The door opened, and Captain Long walked in. "How is he, Doc?"

Taggert squeezed his hand and turned away. "They don't make 'em much tougher than this one."

"Can I ask him some questions?"

"A few. Don't take too long. He's got a concussion, and I want him to rest."

Captain Long came around to the other side of the bed. "How are you feeling, Sarge?"

"Kind of here and then there, sir."

"Yeah. I know what you mean. Sergeant, we'll be doing a full investigation later, but right now I've got some preliminary questions. You feel up to it?"

"Yes, sir."

"Can you tell me what happened out there?"

"I'm not real sure exactly what happened, sir."

"Well, just do your best, Sergeant."

"Yes, sir. What happened . . . it's still kind of fuzzy to me, sir. Parks . . . he was going into the live-fire zone, because he thought all the live-ammo stuff was over. I saw him at the bottom of the hill, then all this ordnance started coming in, and I heard this one round coming in short, and I tried to get to him, but . . ." His voice trailed away.

"That's okay, Sarge. You just rest. You're going to be okay."

He closed his eyes and he thought he could hear them whispering at the door, and then he passed out again.

It was dark outside when he awoke. He wondered what time it was. Late, probably. The chugging, factory-like sounds of the hospital had died down to a whisper. He sat up. The nausea was gone. He swung his legs over the edge of the bed and stood there holding on with his good hand. His other arm was bandaged, in a sling. He wondered if he could make it to the bathroom. He took an unsteady step. Another. He let go of the bed's foot-board. A couple more steps, and he was there. He was running water to wash his face and hands when he heard the door open. He dried his hands and walked into the room. Kara was standing with her back against the door. She was wearing jeans and an old jacket and a scarf.

"You shouldn't have come. What if somebody sees you?"

"Nobody saw me. It's quiet as a church out there." She slipped the scarf from her head and kissed him. "I was so worried. Your corporal called me this morning. This has been the longest day of my life, waiting to get in here. How are you feeling?"

"Better. My head still hurts pretty badly. The arm's okay, though. The doc says the wound isn't deep, and it'll heal right away."

"What happened?"

"It was a short round, I guess. Parks had us right on the edge of the live-fire zone. The live-fire exercise was supposed to stop at 0400, but for some reason they kept firing."

"Oh, God, Mace, I was so worried!"

"I thought about trying to get word to you, but they don't even have a phone in here." He pointed at the empty bedside table.

"When do you think they'll let you out?"

"I don't know. A day or so." A wave of dizziness came over him, and he stumbled backward. She caught him around the waist and helped him to the bed.

"I'll get you some water."

He heard the faucet running in the bathroom. She opened a drawer at the bedside and found a straw. He rolled over on his side, trying to reach the straw.

"Oh Jesus, that hurts."

"Wait. I'll help you." She shoved an extra pillow behind his back. With some effort, he leaned forward and she slipped the straw between his lips. The water was cold, the best thing that had ever passed his lips. He leaned back against the pillows and closed his eyes.

She rested her hand on his. "Do you feel better?"

He nodded.

"I'm going to go. I just wanted to make sure you're okay."

He opened his eyes. She leaned over and kissed him lightly on the forehead. As she was putting her scarf on, there were voices in the hall outside the room. He pointed at the bathroom. "Quick!"

She closed the door just as General King walked into the room with Captain Taggert. Mace sat up stiffly in bed.

General King held up his hand. "At ease, at ease, Sergeant Nukanen. How are you feeling?"

"Better, sir."

The General sat down on the edge of the bed. "Your company commander has interviewed the members of your platoon about the accident, Sergeant. That was a fine thing you did out there. I'm going to recommend you for the Soldier's Medal, for heroism not in conflict with an enemy."

Mace didn't know what to say. He swallowed, and the words "Thank you, sir" escaped from his mouth. He glanced at the bathroom. You could see light at the bottom of the door. Captain Taggert idly studied his watch as he took Mace's pulse.

"Pulse is good. How's the head?"

"I've still got some dizziness, sir."

"Bed rest will fix that right up."

General King stood, pulling on his gloves. "It was a tragic accident. Tragic. I'm glad you're okay, Sergeant Nukanen."

"Thank you, sir."

"We'll let you get some sleep now. I'll stop by your platoon some morning after they let you out of here. Maybe you could fix me up with a cup of coffee."

"Yes, sir. Be glad to, sir."

General King and Captain Taggert walked out of the room, closing the door behind them.

Mace whispered: "It's okay. They're gone."

Kara took his hand. "That was close."

"Too close. You'd better wait a minute before you go. They might have stopped down the hall."

She pressed his hand between hers, gently stroking his fingers. "Mace, I . . . I . . ."

"Ssshh." He saw a tear slowly making its way down her cheek. "I'll call you when they let me out of here."

She kissed him lightly on the lips and walked across the room and cracked the door. The hallway was darkened and empty. She slipped out the door.

The conference room was on neutral ground, in the Infantry School headquarters, which by a quirk of the Army bureaucracy was under the command of neither General King nor General Beckwith. Everyone snapped to attention as General Carson strode into the room, followed closely by General Ranstead and Major Hammett. General Carson opened his briefing book and looked up. "At ease."

Everyone sat down. Lannie, who was sitting next to General Beckwith and directly across the table from General King, opened a notebook and wrote "Post-Operation Briefing" across the top of the page.

"I'm going to make this short and sweet," said General Carson, slipping on a pair of reading glasses. "It was very, very close, but General Beckwith, you won."

Beckwith smiled widely. King was impassive.

"Bill, your boys did an excellent job out there. The capture of Bernie's Second Battalion was a stroke of pure genius."

He turned to General King. "Bernie, with the exception of the Second Battalion, your partisans did an excellent job of escape and evasion. You would have scored much lower except for the fact that overall, you captured more of Bill's troops than he captured of yours. But the loss of an entire battalion determined it."

General King cleared his throat. "Sir, can I ask how you figured I lost an entire battalion? The assessment of my commanders doesn't square with that."

"I'm aware of the discrepancy, Bernie. That's why right from the beginning, I decided that in the event of discrepancies, we would go with the figures of the neutral party, which are those of the scorekeepers. Any more questions?" He looked quickly around the room. "Excellent." He closed the briefing book and stood up. "You will each be provided with copies of the scoring assessment. It'll be sent to the office of the Secretary of the Army this afternoon for further disposition."

With that, General Carson and his entourage walked briskly from the room.

General Beckwith waited until the door of his staff car had been closed before he exulted. "Did you see Ranstead's face when Carson announced the winner! Jesus, that was sweet!" He leaned back, smiling. "I'm calling Senator Maldray this afternoon. I want to make sure he knows we won."

Lannie touched him lightly on the arm. "Sir, you are the next chief of staff of the Army. It's a done deal now."

Beckwith's face darkened. "I wouldn't be too sure, with a Democrat in the White House. It could still go either way. That's why I want Maldray and his Republican troops lined up. They still control the Senate. If the

President is afraid the Senate won't confirm his nominee, he's going to appoint the man who *will* be confirmed, and I want to make sure he understands from Maldray that person is me."

Chapter Twenty-two

They were at speed on the interstate through the sandy, wintery Mississippi flatlands of the Gulf Coast. Kara was driving. Mace had talked his way out of the hospital. Thanksgiving in New Orleans was less than two hours away. The doc had changed his bandages just before they left, and Mace absentmindedly rubbed his arm.

She passed a slow-moving car and looked over. "Still hurt?"

"It itches."

"Taggert said it would take awhile before your arm is back to normal. He wants you to keep squeezing the tennis ball. Where is it, anyway? Did we forget it?"

"Here it is." He reached for the ball down on the floor and squeezed, wincing at the pain.

"Your arm is going to get better and better. You'll see."

"It's funny. I get a piece of shrapnel in me, and it's from a shell made right here in Mississippi."

"Only you would know that."

"Come on. How could you not? It's stenciled on the ammo boxes in big black letters. Made in Picayune, Mississippi. By patriots, no doubt."

She smiled. "I'm sure."

"It feels good to be out of there."

"I hate hospitals."

"I meant Fort Benning."

"Yeah. Me too." She watched him out of the corner

of her eye. "Did you hear about how they scored the exercise?"

"No."

"Beckwith won."

"Well, I guess he's the next chief of staff."

"I'm not so sure. Beckwith's still running scared. He called Hollaway and pressured him to close the case. Hollaway had turned in an interim report naming Parks as our number one suspect. The provost marshal forwarded the report to Beckwith, and now he wants us to hang the thing on Parks and be done with it."

"You still think Beckwith did it."

"All I know is, he's pressuring us to use Parks' death to close out the case."

"Maybe you ought to just do it."

"Do what?"

"Close the case."

She glanced over at him incredulously. "Do you really mean that?"

"Parks was acting really weird out there in the field, Kara."

"What do you mean?"

"I think he committed suicide. That last night, he was sitting there in the dark, hanging onto my arm, muttering, 'I loved her, I loved her,' over and over."

"You're saying he ran deliberately into the live-fire zone?"

"I *know* he did that. I was right there. There's another strange thing he told me. He said he followed Sheila that night."

"He told me he was at home," Kara said.

"I know. He was afraid you were going to find out he lied."

"Do you think he killed her?"

"I don't know. He could have. He was ready to get us all killed out there. He wanted to take the whole damn platoon through the live-fire zone."

"That sounds crazy."

"I told you, he was acting very strangely."

She drove in silence for a moment. They were coming up on Biloxi. The interstate was lined with gaudy billboards for casinos. Turn signals were blinking all over the place as traffic swerved over and piled into the exit lane.

She pulled around an eighteen-wheeler and stepped on the gas. "This place sure has changed."

"That's what happens when you repeal a hundred years of prohibition."

"What do liquor laws have to do with this crap?"

"It's the old slippery slope. The rednecks got so crazed behind the liquor, they voted in a bunch of yahoos who let the floating casinos in, screaming about lowering taxes and taking in all those gambling revenues. Now they're in real trouble. The rednecks are gambling away their paychecks every month, and nobody's got any money left to buy ammunition for hunting season. The ducks are the big winners. Population is up by record numbers. Deer are breeding on people's front lawns up in Jackson. The rabbits are hanging out at the Seven-11, nibbling Doritos and sipping Cokes."

She laughed out loud. "You sound like you're feeling better."

"I'm just trying to make conversation. I'm beat to shit."

"There's a pillow in the backseat. Why don't you lean your seat back and take a little nap? We'll be there in an hour or so."

"I think I will."

"You ought to, with what you've been through."

He closed his eyes. The wind whistled sweetly, and the Cherokee's tires sang along, and he was asleep before the last exit to Biloxi disappeared behind them.

General Beckwith closed the door to his study and switched on his desk lamp. The number was around somewhere. He rummaged through his top drawer and found it clipped to his homework from the office. He dialed the phone. It answered on the third ring.

"Major Hollaway."

"Major, this is General Beckwith. How are you?"

"Fine, sir."

"I hate to bother you at home like this, but I was in meetings all afternoon. Did you get a chance to speak with Major Guidry before she left for Thanksgiving weekend?"

"Yes, sir."

"What did she say?"

"She believes closing the case at this juncture is a bit premature, sir. The evidence we've got on Lieutenant Parks is far from conclusive at this point, sir, and I agree with her."

There was a long pause before Beckwith spoke.

"Major Hollaway, I thought we had an understanding."

"We did, sir. I told you I'd speak to Major Guidry, and I did."

"I mean getting this case closed and out of the way. I'm not sure you understand the downside if this thing gets strung out. We're coming up to a meeting of the base closure commission, Major. The fate of Fort Benning itself will be on the line in that hearing room. Do you understand me?"

"Yes, sir."

"An open murder investigation is one problem I don't need when I go before that commission, do you understand me, Hollaway?"

"Yes, sir."

"Listen to me, Major. We can treat this thing as a formality. If you take what you've got on Parks today and close the case, there's always the possibility that you could reopen the case later, after the base closure commission hearing is over. Do you get what I mean?"

After you're in the chief of staff's office in the Pentagon is what you really mean, thought Hollaway.

"Yes, sir, I understand."

"So you'll reconsider your decision?"

"Yes, sir. I'll speak with Major Guidry the moment she gets back from her weekend leave, sir."

"Excellent. I appreciate your cooperation, Major. You'll report back to me next week, then."

"Yes, sir."

"All right. I'll look forward to your call. Good evening, Major Hollaway."

"Good evening, sir."

Outside, the sky over the French Quarter had turned a strange ocher color, flooding the room with yellowish light. The room was small, but there was a balcony overlooking a pool in the courtyard. She threw open the French doors. From the bed she could see the old brick buildings of the Quarter cloaked in a low-hanging fog, and above the fog, the tops of ships passing on the Mississippi only two blocks away. The river's aroma mingled with the smell of fried shrimp from the restaurant next door, filling the New Orleans air with the essence of the bayou that had been there nearly three hundred years before. Her mother used to say you could land-fill all the dirt you wanted raising a city out of a swamp, but you couldn't take the swamp out of the city. Not in Louisiana you couldn't, anyway.

Mace stepped out of the bathroom with a towel around his waist, his face flushed from a hot shower. She took his hand and traced her finger along the scar on his arm, red and still swollen. There were a couple of small scars on his chest and stomach, where splinters of wood had penetrated his BDU's and left their marks. He sat down on the edge of the bed and ran the towel between his toes.

"Remind me and I'll teach you a thing or two about picking hotel rooms, lady. I spit with more water pressure than that shower has."

She unsnapped the front of her bra, cupping her

breasts with her hands. "I've got a thing or two to teach you, mister."

He pulled her on top of him and she shrugged off her bra and he held her around the waist and kissed her breasts, lingering, caressing her nipples with his tongue. He looked into her eyes.

"You were saying I could learn something from these breasts of yours. Like what?"

"They could teach you lots."

"Where'd they get so smart?"

"Experience."

He laughed and rolled over. "Geez. I keep forgetting I've got to watch that arm."

"Did you hurt yourself?"

"No."

"Let me see."

He held out his arm, and she started kissing at the elbow and worked her way down toward the wrist. "Feel better?"

"Much."

She slipped out of her panties and stretched out on the bed naked, arms above her head. "Your turn."

He started kneading the soles of her feet, kissing her toes. "There must be, like, a whole book's worth of knowledge in this big toe here."

"More like an encyclopedia."

"And how about this leg?" He was kissing her ankles, working his way up to her knees. "I bet it's seen some action, knows some stuff."

"Like you don't even know."

He had his hands on her knees and he was licking her calves. He spread her legs and kissed the insides of her thighs. The top of his head brushed against her pubic bone. "What about here?"

She looked down at him. "Where?"

"This sweet little spot right here." His lips found her vagina, his tongue darting inside. He sucked softly. She drifted into a reverie of sweet longing and bliss as the moments passed. He looked up. "What's this nooky got to teach me?"

"About life. About love." She reached under his arms and pulled him on top of her. She felt him inside her. "See? You're learning."

He laughed, burying his face wetly in her neck.

She raised her knees and locked her ankles around his back and felt him going deeper. He was kissing her neck and her breasts and she felt his rough chin on her breastbone and she kicked her feet higher and he rose up and arched his back and she felt him go deeper. In her dreams she felt him inside her and she felt him inside her getting dressed in the morning and she felt him inside her sipping coffee and she felt him inside her in meetings and she felt him inside her driving home in the evening and she felt him inside her feeding the cats and she felt him inside her when she slid between the sheets at night and she never ever wanted that feeling to go away not ever ever ever ever ever ever.

Eddie's Restaurant was a nondescript wooden building on a residential block in the city's Seventh Ward. There were Cadillacs and Lincolns double-parked the length of the block. A couple of chauffeurs stood in a knot down the street having a smoke.

Their cabbie pulled to a stop. "Big night. You got reservations?"

"No."

"You be okay. Eddie's never turned away a payin' customer I heard of."

Mace paid the cabbie and they stepped out into the chilly night air. The door swung open and a clutch of well-dressed men and women exited laughing. They pushed into the narrow foyer. There was a bar on the right, lit by what looked like a permanent display of Christmas lights. A large woman in an apron filled the inner doorway.

"You got a reservation?"

"No, but we drove here today from Atlanta and we were hoping—"

"Atlanta? Darlin', you must be hungry. Come on in." She led them to the back room and took down Kara's name on a clipboard. "We having a buffet tonight, it bein' Thanksgivin' and all. Ya'll just help yourselves and see me on the way out."

"Thank you."

She left them in the door and turned to greet a new couple coming in. Eddie's was a typical New Orleans neighborhood joint, studiously plain, its walls covered with travel posters for distant and exotic lands interspersed with photos of local political figures. A well-heeled Seventh Ward crowd filled the place to capacity. The women had big hair and even bigger earrings, and the men were resplendent in dark double-breasted suits that shone in the dim light. A few tables in the back room had been shoved together for a buffet piled with Creole delicacies—deep-fried turkey, boiled crawfish, fried shrimp, red beans and rice, fried chicken, and of course, oyster dressing, an aromatic mash of oysters chopped with the Creole trilogy of peppers, onions, and celery, all of it dusted with a nearly fatal dose of cayenne pepper.

Kara walked into the room inhaling the intoxicating aromas of her birthplace. Her mother's parents had lived in Gentilly, a neighborhood not far away. Her father had been on a hardship tour in Korea when she was born, so her mother traveled home to New Orleans to have her first and, as it turned out, only child. They spent practically every Christmas with her grandparents, and when she got older, she flew by herself from wherever her father was stationed to spend the deathly hot, humid summers wandering the streets of New Orleans, eating sno-cones and boiled crabs and beignets and drinking bitter French Market coffee with chicory. She felt as grounded within the four walls of Eddie's as an Army brat could possibly feel. If New Orleans wasn't exactly her hometown, it was her Lourdes, a spiritual place where spices replenished her soul.

She walked quickly to the buffet table and picked up a plate. It was piled half-full when Mace appeared awkwardly next to her in line. He spooned a fat mirliton onto his empty plate.

"What's this?"

"Mirliton. It's like a stuffed squash. The mirliton's just a shell to hold the andouille sausage stuffing. It's great."

"Weird."

"Wait until you taste it."

Mace spooned a bit of stuffing into his mouth with his finger. He grinned. "Hey. This is *good*."

"You're telling me? I grew up on those things."

They moved down the line. Mace was piling food onto his plate eagerly now. He popped a fried shrimp into his mouth. "Man, where did you find this place? This is the best food I've ever eaten."

"You haven't even started. Wait till you get to the oyster dressing."

They reached the end of the buffet and carried their plates back into the front room and sat down at a table along the wall. Kara had a bite of oyster dressing, savoring the elegant blend of sea and spice on her tongue.

"You must taste this," she said, pointing at a spoonful of mush at the edge of his plate. Mace gingerly took a bite.

"Jesus! It's like . . . I don't know what it's like. I've never had anything like it before."

"And you won't have it again either, unless you come back to Eddie's. That's the best oyster dressing in the world. Period. No question about it."

Mace forked in another mouthful. "My tongue's on fire."

Kara grinned. "So I noticed."

He laughed. "Ready for round two?"

"Anytime you are, Sarge."

"What are we doing tomorrow?"

"Corporal Richards' mother is taking us to a party at the Fairmont, remember?"

"Right."

Just then a tall, elegantly dressed black man stopped at the table. "Little Kara? That you?"

She leapt to her feet and threw her hands around his neck. "Oh, my God! I can't believe it!" She broke the embrace and turned to Mace. "Mace, I want you to meet Franklin Washington. He used to own the sno-cone stand at the end of my grandmother's block."

"Still do. Best sno-cones in the whole city."

"Franklin, this is Mace Nukanen."

They shook hands. Kara pulled out a chair. "Sit down, Franklin. Tell me what's going on. I haven't been back in town in years."

"Same old same old. Nothin' ever changes in New Orleans. There's people still sittin' on the same bar stools they was sittin' on last time you was here."

"That's New Orleans, all right."

"There's some new folks bought your grandparents' place. They got a little girl, 'bout this high. Reminds me so much of you. Watchin' that little girl growin' up is like goin' back in time."

"I'll have to bring Mace by tomorrow for one of your sno-cones, Franklin."

"We closed this time of year. Gettin' cold, you know. Ain't sno-cone weather in November."

"What was I thinking? Of course."

"So you been goin' 'round to some of the old spots?"

"We just got in town, Franklin. This is our first stop."

"When ya'll finish, you come get in my cab and I'll drive you by the old place. I'm still drivin' nights. Gotta pay that rent."

"Oh, Franklin, that's okay. We don't want to impose."

"My treat, Little Kara."

Kara looked at Mace. He was chewing on a piece of fried chicken. "Okay by me," he said between bites.

"That'd be great."

"I'll be in the bar. Ya'll just come and get me when you're ready." He stood up and patted her shoulder with a massive, weathered hand and pushed his way through the crowd.

"I have such fond memories of those days, Mace. God! It's like it happened yesterday. I used to get a quarter from my grandmother and walk down to Franklin's stand, and he'd fix me the biggest, reddest cherry sno-cone, and I'd sit on a tall stool under his awning and watch the people walking by. Franklin, he knew everybody. I mean, he had half the parents in the city stopping there and buying sno-cones for their kids, and he knew every one of them. When I got older, in the seventies, I found out he was one of the sharpest black political organizers in the city. He was in a political club called SOUL, and they got out the vote on election day, and people said they controlled the whole Seventh Ward. Franklin was sitting there running that sno-cone stand all day every day, and nights he drove his cab all over town delivering poll cards and fliers and lawn signs. I learned more about politics sitting on that stool at that sno-cone stand than I learned in four years of West Point political science classes."

"He's an amazing-looking guy."

"Not a line in his face. I'll bet he's seventy if he's a day."

They trolled the buffet table for seconds and polished them off and paid up. Franklin was standing in the bar talking with several men. He spied Kara in the hall and excused himself.

"Ya'll ready to go?"

Kara took his arm. "Are you sure we're not interrupting you and your friends?"

He laughed. "I spend half my day listen' to those fools flappin' they jaws. Let's beat this joint."

In the cab, Franklin wound his way over to St. Claude

Avenue and went west to Rampart Street, the north edge
of the Quarter. "They put the gamblin' up there in Louis
Armstrong Park, but it closed down now."

"Must be a lack of fools in the neighborhood,"
cracked Mace.

"Naw, they plenty of fools 'round here. The gamblin'
folks, they just forgot you cain't separate a fool from his
money if he ain't got no money."

He turned right on Canal Street and headed north. As
the taxi passed under the massive live oaks that lined
the avenue, Kara felt like they were closing in on a kind
of glowing center where she had formed attachments to
a past she never really knew. All of her life she had felt
like she was slipping away, slipping away, further and
further from a place inside her that she was afraid to
know. But since she had met Mace, and since she had
fallen in love with him, that sense of falling and root-
lessness had given way to a warm spot that had grown
inside of her. She squeezed his hand. She knew where
the warmth came from.

Franklin stopped the cab across the street from the
house and cut the engine. It was a center-hallway cottage with a wide front porch and the deep overhangs of
Creole architecture. "There it is," he said.

Kara rolled down her window. "There used to be a
porch swing, remember, Franklin?"

"Yes, ma'am. I do."

"And we used to play in the yard under the magnolia
tree, and Grandma was always yelling at us, 'Keep off
that monkey grass, you little hellions!' I can still hear
her."

"So can I," said Franklin. "I could hear that woman
all the way down to the sno-cone stand."

"You said there are nice people living there now?"

"Yes, there are. The man, he works for the post office, and the lady, she's got a job at the school in the
front office. They real nice, both of 'em."

"That makes me feel good. There are a lot of memories inside those walls."

Mace put his arm around her. "Maybe we can get a house like that someday."

She kissed him. "I know we can."

Franklin started the engine and pulled away. "Sound to me like you two 'bout headed down the aisle."

Kara nuzzled against Mace's shoulder. She had to admit that for the first time in her life, the thought had crossed her mind.

At the Fairmont the next night, they took an escalator up to the ballroom. There was a table at the door staffed by a bevy of young women in short black dresses. Kara handed one of them the tickets, and they went inside.

The ballroom was decorated in black, gold, and purple, the colors of Mardi Gras. There were huge flower arrangements on the tables, and up on the bandstand Dr. John's sixteen-piece band was chugging through a Delta blues.

They picked up drinks from the bar and cruised the room. Dr. John segued into a rolling Bourbon Street shuffle, and they put their drinks down and shoved their way onto the crowded dance floor.

The song ended, and Dr. John stood up from his piano bench and growled that the band was taking a break. The crowd on the dance floor broke up, and they went looking for the table where they'd left their drinks.

"I was sure they were right over here," said Mace.

"No. They're over on the other side of the room."

They were crossing the dance floor for a second time when Kara saw him. She wheeled around, grabbing Mace by the arm.

"Whoa. I don't want him to see me."

"Who?"

"Look over my shoulder. That's General Beckwith's aide over there, sitting at that table against the wall."

"He's sitting with General King!"

"I know he is. The other guy, I've seen him some-where before. I just can't place him. Wait a minute. His name is Teese. He's a general."

Mace took her hand, and they melted into a crowd and found the exit and went into the hall. "Mace, what do you think the aide to General Beckwith is doing sit-ting at a table with his boss's arch enemy?"

"I don't know, but I don't want anything to do with this scene. We should go back to the hotel. General King came to my room when I was in the hospital. He'd recognize me if he saw me. They catch us together here, and it's all over."

"Oh, come on. This party is packed with people. All we have to do is keep our distance. They'll never see us."

"I don't want to take that chance. Let's go." He took her arm and started for the escalator. She stopped and he wheeled around. "Come on. This is too dangerous. We didn't come all the way to New Orleans to end up at a party where generals are hanging around."

"I want to stay, Mace."

"What!"

"You go on back to the room. I'm staying. I've got to find out what's going on."

"You're crazy."

"They're cooking up something over there, and I want to know what it is. I'm going to find Mrs. Richards, see if she knows anything."

"What if that captain sees you?"

"I'll tell him I'm from New Orleans. This is my hometown. Why wouldn't I be at a function like this?"

"I don't know what's up with this scene, but I don't like it. I think you ought to come back to the room with me."

"I'm staying, Mace."

Angrily: "Suit yourself." He started down the escala-tor without her.

Back in the ballroom, the band struck up a shuffle and the General and his wife got up to dance, leaving

Randy and the older man alone. Kara took up a position in a crowd at the bar across the room from their table. The band finished the song, and the General and his wife made their way back to the table.

There was a roll of drums from the bandstand, and an announcer's voice filled the room. "Ladies and gentlemen, the mayor of the city of New Orleans!"

A sharp-dressed young black man flashed a wide smile and took the microphone. "My papa used to say there were three honorable professions for a young man in this world. The priesthood, politics, and the Army." The crowd howled with laughter. "As I look around this ballroom, I can see we have the usual representatives of the former two professions with us tonight, and it is my great pleasure to introduce to this crowd our honored guest and most distinguished representative of the latter profession, that of Arms, General Bernard King!"

A spotlight searched the room and found General King's table. Dr. John's band struck up "The Caissons Go Rolling Along" as General King stood up to thunderous applause. The crowd around his table parted, and he made his way to the bandstand. The mayor handed him the mike.

"I'm sure you all know that Dahlia and I grew up here in New Orleans, and we were educated here in New Orleans at St. Anthony's, and that we return home for Mardi Gras when we can, so we can march with the Zulu parade—"

More applause, much more, at the mention of the only black Mardi Gras Krewe. The General let the applause die down before continuing.

"But I'm not sure that you know we have decided to buy a house and retire here when that time comes—"

More applause, people on their feet, stomping, banging on the tables.

"New Orleans is our hometown, but this city means much more than that to Dahlia and me. It is the place that nurtured us when we were children and made us

the people we are today. It will be our home in our twi-
light years, and I hope we can bring back to this city the
rich, enduring values we took from here as we went out
into the world. But first, before we return home for
good, it looks like my country will call me to duty one
last time."

At this the crowd leapt to its feet and cheered.

"And I want the people of New Orleans to know that
if this final call to duty comes, I will answer it and carry
with me to Washington, D.C., the principles and spiritu-
ality that were imparted to me as a boy, right here in this
town. Thank you, Mr. Mayor. Thank you, ladies and
gentlemen, and good night."

The spotlight followed General King as he descended
the steps of the bandstand and waded through the ador-
ing crowd. At the table, his wife and mother-in-law
stood clapping until he finally reached them. Dahlia
threw her arms around him, and Eunice Toussaint
beamed.

Kara was standing against the wall, far across the
ballroom.

*So that's what this party is all about. The city of New
Orleans is doing its part to launch their favorite son
into the office of chief of staff.*

Chapter Twenty-three

He was waiting up for her when she returned from the party. Sitting in a chair by the open doors to the balcony, he turned his head when he heard the door close.

"Have fun?"

"Mace, you don't understand—"

"I understand you're obsessed with General Beckwith, and it's going to ruin both of our careers. That's what I understand."

She sat down on the bed across from him. "Nobody saw me. I was very careful."

"That's not what I'm talking about."

"You're acting like I committed some kind of crime."

"Kara, the problem is, we came all the way to New Orleans to get away from the Army, so we can be together, and we walk into that party tonight, and the whole thing we left back at Benning is staring us right in the face. And what do you do? You want to take your chances they won't see us together, and all because you think something's up with Beckwith. Well, let me tell you something. I can't afford to take chances like that. The Army is the only job I've got. I've got less than ten years to get my twenty, and I'm not doing anything to jeopardize my retirement."

"I'm not asking you to."

"Not in so many words. But you said yourself Beckwith called you up and threatened you and me, and you see his aide at the party, and what do you do? You stick your nose in his business."

"Mace, he's spying on Beckwith for General King. I just know he is."

"Oh, really? And who told you that? What if it's the other way around, and he's spying on General King for Beckwith? You ever think of that?"

"I don't think it's very likely. That's why I'm going to see Captain Taylor in the morning. I found out where he's staying. Mrs. Richards said—"

He leapt to his feet. "Now you've got her involved! I can't believe you, Kara! The whole fucking town is going to know what you're up to by tomorrow!"

"I'm going by myself. He'll never know I'm here with you."

"You better believe you're going by yourself." He walked over to the closet and started pulling his clothes off the hangers.

"What are you doing?"

"I'm leaving." He threw his overnight bag on the bed and stuffed the clothes inside.

"Mace, I don't want you to leave."

"You don't? Then why don't you just do what Beckwith said? Why don't you close the case and get out of his way? This guy is going to be the next chief of staff, Kara! He'll step on you and he'll step on me when he gets up there in the Pentagon! Who do you think is going to stop him? I know it doesn't matter to you, because you've got a law degree, and you'll end up in some big law firm pulling down twice what you're making in the Army. But what about me? I get kicked out of the Army, and what am I going to do? Huh?"

"You're not going to get kicked out of the Army, Mace. I'm not going to do anything that would possibly hurt you. Beckwith isn't going to do anything to us. You're forgetting that I know he was having an affair with Sheila. We've each got something on the other. He can make big noises, but he doesn't have the balls to turn us in."

Mace came out of the bathroom with his toilet kit and stuck it in the overnight bag and zipped it shut. Picking up the bag, he walked to the door and turned around.

"That's not good enough, Kara. You're an officer, and you might be able to talk about going up against the next chief of staff of the Army, but I'm a noncom, and I don't play in those leagues."

He opened the door to leave, stopped, and turned around. "The thing that gets me is that you haven't listened to me. You haven't heard a thing I've said."

"I have!" she cried.

"Then why don't you go along with Hollaway and close the case? You've got both of our asses in a sling on this thing. That means me too, Kara. Not just you."

"What do you want me to do, Mace? Just forget I've got credible evidence that General Beckwith may have killed Sheila Worthy? You want me to throw away the obligation I've got to follow the law?"

"I want you to think about us, and all you want to think about is your goddamned job." With that, he walked out, slamming the door behind him.

She sat there on the bed for what seemed like a long time after he left, his words still ringing in her ears. He was the best thing that had ever happened to her, and now he was gone, vanished into the night. What if he was right? Was it true that she was taking too many chances with their careers, especially his? She knew this much: He loved the Army in a way she did not. He loved being a platoon sergeant. He loved his men. The Army truly was more than a job for him. It was a home, and a life, and a fulfillment of his dreams.

She thought about packing her bags and going after him. He couldn't get a flight back to Atlanta until the morning, and if she drove all night, she could be back at Fort Benning by the time he arrived. She could apologize, and maybe, just maybe, they could go on from there.

She stood up and walked toward the closet, but something stopped her: a girl's laughter, on a side street below. She remembered that sound—the carefree noises you make when you're twenty-two, twenty-three, and life is a series of discoveries and thrills, and if you have a care in the world, it's tucked away in your back pocket with your dreams.

Sheila Worthy had laughed like that, not so very long ago. She was a brand-new lieutenant, and she had a life ahead of her full of surprises and delights and wishes and hopes and dreams she never realized.

She walked over to the balcony doors and stood there listening as the girl's heels tip-tapped down the street, her laughter tinkling in the night air. When you're twenty-two years old, you have more than twice that much time left on the earth, days and weeks and months and years you can fill any way you wish.

All of that had been taken from Sheila.

She would try to make Mace understand when she got back to Fort Benning. In the meantime she had a job to do. The Army had given her the prosecution in the case of the murder of Lieutenant Sheila Worthy, and she would not neglect her duty.

Chapter Twenty-four

The Hotel Maison de Ville was on Toulouse Street, just south of Bourbon. They said Tennessee Williams completed *A Streetcar Named Desire* in one of its slave-quarter cottages, but the story was probably apocryphal, like most stories about New Orleans, especially those about the French Quarter. Every summer when Kara had visited her grandparents in New Orleans, she had taken frequent jaunts through the Quarter, and its denizens had provided her with a colorful maze of fascinating legends and tales about the old section of the city. There was the one about the young man down on Urusulines Street who murdered his wealthy mother and kept this secret for years, because both of them were considered "shut-ins" and no one found it at all unusual that she hadn't been seen in a while. They found her remains lying in bed where he had done the deed, the legend went. Then there was the fable of the photographer who lived down at the far end of Royal Street who was said to be able to photograph the dead. He took his cameras to the St. Louis Cemetery No. 1, across Rampart Street from the Quarter, and set up his tripod. If the atmospheric conditions were right, the fable went, the photographs he took of crypts revealed a ghost-like image of the person who lay within.

She walked into the tiny lobby of the hotel. A languorous young man looked up from the desk with a weak smile. "Are you checking in?"

"No. I'm looking for my friend. Do you have a Randy Taylor registered?"

"Yes, we do. He's in bungalow number five. I'll ring his room now. You can take the call on the house phone, right over there." He pointed at an antique instrument perched on a mahogany table. Kara picked up the receiver from its brass cradle. Randy answered.

"Hello?"

"Randy, it's Kara Guidry."

"Oh . . . Kara . . . what are you doing here?"

"I saw you across the room at the mayor's party last night. I was wondering if you'd like to have lunch."

There was a long pause before he answered. "I don't know . . ."

"We've got to talk, Randy. I know you were sitting with General King and that general from the Pentagon, Teese."

"Kara, what is this about?"

She covered the receiver and turned her back on the desk man. "I think your interests and my interests coincide when it comes to your boss."

This time there was no hesitation. "I'll be right out."

Kara hung up the phone. The sleepyhead at the desk pointed at some open French doors. "You can wait in the garden. His bungalow is just across the way."

She took a seat on a wrought iron bench under a banana tree. The door of a low-slung cottage opened, and Randy walked out.

"Where shall we go?" asked Kara.

"Someplace quiet, I hope," said Randy.

"I know just the place." She led the way through the lobby, and they turned down Toulouse Street toward the river. The street was lined with crappy little souvenir shops and stands that dispensed margaritas and pina coladas from frozen-drink machines.

"This place has turned into Disneyland for adults," said Kara. "They blew out all the old shops so they could service the casino crowd. Play the slots, drink a frozen Hurricane or two, buy a T-shirt for the kids, and go home."

When they reached G & E's Courtyard Grill on Decatur Street, across from the French Market, the owner escorted them to a canopied table in the garden near an open wood-fired rotisserie. They were the only ones there.

"If you don't get the fried soft-shell crab salad here, you are really missing out," said Kara, picking up the menu.

Randy glanced at his, and folded it shut. "I'll take your suggestion. You seem to know what you're doing around here."

The waiter took their orders and left. Randy squinted into the winter sun, which had crept around the edge of the canopy. "So. You called this little get-together. What's on your mind?"

Kara signaled the waiter. "You never took our drink orders. I'm having a Sazerac. Want to join me?"

"I'll have a Ramos gin fizz," said Randy.

"They invented that drink down the street at Tujaque's," said Kara.

Randy said, "I know."

Kara leaned forward in her chair. "New Orleans is about food and drink and music, so let's make this short and to the point, and I'll let you get on with the serious business of enjoying yourself. Deal?"

Randy nodded.

The waiter brought the drinks. Kara gave hers a stir and lifted the glass to her lips. The taste, somewhere north of an old-fashioned and south of a Manhattan, made her throat tighten and her cheeks burn. "I could use some help here, Randy. I think Beckwith killed Sheila Worthy. What do you think?"

A gust of wind caught the canopy, and it flapped loudly. Randy stared at her, speechless. He took a sip of his gin fizz. "That's a very serious charge. I wouldn't go repeating it around Fort Benning."

"Don't worry, I won't," said Kara, taking a sip of her drink. "I know you're working with General Teese to prevent Beckwith from getting appointed chief of staff. A mule with blinders could have seen that last night. I want to know why."

"Look, I'm not in favor of General Beckwith becoming chief of staff, but I certainly don't think he's a murderer."

"You know something, Randy? I think you withheld a few things when I questioned you. You knew Beckwith was having an affair with Sheila, and you kept your mouth shut. You knew he was supposed to see her that night, and you kept your mouth shut. You knew he was alone in his staff car that night, and you kept your mouth shut about that too. I don't think you told me the truth then, and I don't think you're telling me the truth now."

"That's your privilege, isn't it?"

"Yeah, it sure is my privilege, and because I've been put on the investigation of Sheila's murder, I can act on it. How'd you like it if I arranged an Article 32 hearing and put you under oath, and asked you what you were doing here in New Orleans with generals King and Teese talking about Beckwith? Make you a little nervous, would it?"

"You wouldn't dare."

"That's the wrong answer, Randy."

"You can't prove I'm working for King."

"I may not be able to prove it with hard evidence, but I would say that the fact you were sitting at that table last night with generals King and Teese was way more than coincidence. The fact of the matter is, you and I are loaded down with what the law calls guilty knowledge. I know you're working for King, and you know I think Beckwith is a murderer. We're in the same boat, Randy, and we may as well each pick up an oar and start rowing in the same direction, or we're going to go round and round and round."

He took a sip of his gin fizz and licked the foam from his lips. "I don't know why I should cooperate with you. You've got your agenda and I've got mine, and I don't see how they're at all the same."

"You'll cooperate because it serves your interests."

Randy looked uncertainly around the garden. A tourist couple carrying a brace of shopping bags came in and were seated over next to the old slave quarter building that housed the kitchen. The rest of the courtyard was still empty. "You're putting me on the spot, Kara."

"You don't have to think Beckwith's a killer to help me out here. What I want to know is, what's going on with you and generals Teese and King?"

"I'm sworn to secrecy on that. I'm sorry."

"Well, your secret's out, and if you don't want it to go further, you'd better start elaborating."

Randy took another long pull on his gin fizz. The waiter brought their orders. Kara started eagerly tearing the claws from her soft-shell crab. Randy stared at his plate, poked at the food with his fork, and looked up.

"It isn't that I don't get along with General Beckwith. In most ways I do."

"Do you want another drink?" asked Kara. "I'm going to have one."

"Sure."

Kara signaled the waiter to bring another round. "You were saying?"

Randy took a deep breath. "There is a list of forty generals who have pledged to publicly resign if Beckwith is made chief."

Kara whistled.

"The feeling among the younger generals is that Beckwith is way too political. He owes his career to his political connections, and the way they're downsizing the Army, that's not a good thing. Their thinking is, how's he going to fight for us, the men in the military, when he's so deeply indebted to the politicians who are taking the Army apart, unit by unit?"

"And how about you? Do you agree with them?"

"Yes, I do."

"But that's not all of it."

"Let's put it this way. I agree with the logic of their thinking, and I agree with them on the character issue. He's not the right man for the job, but he looks inevitable at this point."

"So General Teese approached you because you're the closest person to Beckwith."

"General Teese is a friend. I worked for him a few years ago, back at the Infantry School. I trust him, and I value his judgment. He is one of the generals who have pledged to resign, but he doesn't think it's a particularly good idea. He thinks if there's a mass resignation of junior generals, the Army will come out looking like a bunch of ragtag martinets in a banana republic."

"He wants to force Beckwith out of the race before a mass resignation becomes necessary."

"Exactly."

"So you're spying on Beckwith for him."

"In a manner of speaking."

"Have you told him about Sheila? That she and Beckwith were having an affair?"

"Yes, and I've told him about Lannie too."

Kara dropped her fork. Randy smiled.

"I see your friend hasn't let you in on her little secret. She's been seeing Beckwith since way before Sheila came into the picture. It's been going on since she was up in the Pentagon. Apparently, he's told her that he's leaving his wife as soon as they promote him, and she's going to become Mrs. Chief of Staff. Lannie has a lot riding on Beckwith, and she's in love with him. Deeply."

Kara picked up her fork and looked idly at her salad for a moment. "It was right in front of me, and I didn't see it," she mused. "Out of the blue she shows up at Benning, no letter saying she's getting transferred, no advance warning. And who does she work for? Not just work for, but report *directly to*? None other than the dark prince himself. How could I have been so dumb?"

"They've done a pretty good job of keeping it secret. I don't think his wife even knows."

"She knew about Sheila."

"How did you find that out?"

"Mrs. Beckwith told me. She knew Beckwith was supposed to see her that night, but the storm came up, and he never made it. She's his alibi. She said he was at home with her."

"I was aware she knew about Sheila, but I'm almost positive she doesn't know about Lannie. For about a year the only time Beckwith saw her was when he went up to Washington for meetings. I was surprised when he got her shipped down to Benning, to tell you the truth. He must be very confident that his wife has no suspicions."

"You must know her pretty well. What's Mrs. Beckwith like?"

"Long-suffering. Worldly wise. Socially adept. A typical general's wife in many ways, but completely atypical in others. She doesn't wear her ambitions on her sleeve the way many of them do."

"But she's got them, all right. In spades."

"Oh, you can be certain she does. Her trick is, she has been able to conceal her ambitious side, so she's got a lot of sympathy from the other wives. Even generals' wives are on her side."

"And she's playing that sympathy for all she's worth, trying to get him appointed chief, I'll bet."

"That's a bet you'd win in a walk."

"Whew. What a piece of work that marriage is."

"She's organizing a big party the first night of the AUSA convention. She's calling in every chit she has amassed in three decades of Army life. It's going to be the richest mix of active-duty and retired Army officers and politicians and captains of industry this country has ever seen, and General and Mrs. Beckwith are going to be the red-hot center of it all."

"Are you helping out?"

"Up to my bloody neck . . . excuse the expression." He smiled nervously. He was digging into his soft-shell crab in earnest now. He swallowed a large bite and pushed his plate away. "If I eat another bite, I'm going to pop."

Kara signaled the waiter for the check. "Tell me more about Lannie and Beckwith."

"I've been bearding her for him a long time now. It's like we're buddies. I know all her secrets."

"Who is she seeing up in Atlanta?"

"No one. That's a cover for Beckwith."

"She suggested that we get together and double-date sometime. Why would she do that?"

"She probably figures you'll never take her up on it. Or if you did, she'd find a way to wiggle out of it. That's what you do when you're having an affair with a married man. You wiggle in, around, and out of stuff. She's good at it. *Very* good at it."

"Well, she fooled me."

The waiter brought the check, and Kara handed him a credit card. Randy reached for his wallet, but she waved him off. "My treat."

"Well, thank you. This was delicious."

"I'm sorry if I came on a little strong there at first," said Kara. "I think he's a very dangerous man. I guess I tend to go a little overboard." They walked through the front part of the restaurant and stepped outside. It was about seventy-five and sunny. New Orleans winter weather.

"I still don't think he killed her, Kara. I've known him awhile now, and I don't think it's in him."

They were walking up Decatur Street, passing under wrought iron balconies laced with bougainvillea and purple trumpet vines, many of them still in bloom. They stopped at the corner of Toulouse, where Randy would make the turn to go back to the Maison de Ville.

"I almost forgot," said Kara. "Where was Beckwith stationed before Benning?"

"At the Pentagon, and before that at the White House."

"When was his last command time?"

"He had a brigade at Fort Polk about five, six years ago. He couldn't wait to get out of there, the way I heard it."

"Thanks, Randy," said Kara.

They shook hands, and Randy walked north on Toulouse. Kara walked over to the levee and sat on the grass and watched the Mississippi flow past. The current was surprisingly strong. When she was a girl, her grandmother had always been telling her of people who fell in and drowned, but she hadn't paid any attention. Now she watched a huge piling from a rotted pier flow rapidly past and get caught in the swirling wake of a tug and get sucked under. It *was* a dangerous river.

She turned around and looked at the spire of the St. Louis Cathedral, rising above the rooftops of the Quarter like a piece of noble sculpture. In the summertime, when she was a girl, it would get really hot in the afternoons, and she and her friends would open the big doors to the cathedral and go inside, where it was dark and quiet and cool.

The town was like a church to her, a place you come to renew yourself and worship the past. She could hear the rushing burble of the river, the enormous diesel engines of the tugboats, the faint echo of street musicians playing boogie-woogie on the street behind her in the Quarter.

I wonder if he killed any other young women along the way.

The door to his room at the Maison de Ville opened as Randy reached for his key. Ed pulled him inside.

"What in the hell is *she* doing here?"

"She was at the party last night. She saw us with General King. She had already figured it out, so I told her everything."

"Jesus!"

Randy sat down. "Now that our secret's out, to Major Guidry anyway, I, for one, feel relieved."

Ed sat down across from him. "She doesn't know we're staying here together, does she?"

"No."

"So tell me what she said."

"She was at the party with a friend of hers from New Orleans. It was pure happenstance. But she's no dummy. She took one look at our table and knew immediately what was up."

"What did she tell you?"

"She thinks Beckwith killed Sheila Worthy. She wants my help."

Ed stood up and paced the room for a moment. "What kind of time table is she on?"

"A tight one. Beckwith is putting pressure on her and the MP in charge of the investigation to close the case. She knows if she doesn't get enough evidence to charge him by the time the President appoints him chief of staff, it's all over. They'll never bring murder charges against the chief of staff of the Army."

"She's right. Is there any chance she'll have her evidence before the AUSA convention next week?"

"I don't think so."

"If Beckwith pulls off his act at the convention, he's a shoe-in. We're screwed if that happens. We've got to come up with something to counter his moves at the convention." He sat down on the bed.

"You mean you do. I'm out of it, Ed. This finishes me off."

"Do you really want to see a man like him become chief of staff?"

"You know something? I don't care anymore. If you

and General Ranstead are going to pull anything at the convention, you're going to do it without me. I've given you the guest list. I've told you what he's going to do. I told you Maldray has something planned. What more do you want from me?"

"Randy, I understand if you're scared. I would be too—"

"You don't understand, Ed. You're a general. I'm a captain. Beckwith has probably figured out that you're opposed to him becoming chief. Between you and him it's just Army politics. You're another faction in the Pentagon. But with me, it's not politics, it's betrayal."

"He's not going to find out what you've done for us."

"You're not listening to me. I feel like the lowest piece of crud on earth. Don't you even care about how I feel?"

"Of course I do."

"Then you'll tell General Ranstead I'm out of it."

"If that's what you want."

"That's what I want."

Ed took Randy's hand. "I'm sorry I got you involved, Randy. I don't want to do anything to hurt you. You believe me, don't you?"

"Yeah."

"You don't have to worry about a thing from now on. I'll tell Jack, and we'll protect you."

"You know what he'd do to me if he found out," said Randy.

Ed touched the younger man's cheek. "I know only too well."

Chapter Twenty-five

Fort Polk was near the Texas state line, about three hours from New Orleans. The sun was coming up over the prairie of western Louisiana as Kara made the turn off Route 171. It had been a long drive, and a longer night. Her second long night without Mace.

It was the news about Lannie and Beckwith that had startled and frightened her and sent her on her way to Fort Polk. If she came back from Polk with evidence that another young woman had been killed during the time Beckwith was stationed there, that would make Beckwith a suspect in Sheila's murder, even for Frank Hollaway. There was a lot at stake, and getting the information she needed wasn't going to be easy. She couldn't let on about the target of her investigation. She would have to play her hand very, very carefully.

The MP at the gate saluted the blue officer sticker on the Cherokee's front bumper. She returned the salute and pulled to a stop next to the guard post.

"Corporal, can you give me directions to the provost marshal's office?"

"Yes, ma'am. You just follow this street here about two miles, and when you come to your first red light, you turn left, and it's right there next to the stockade. You can't miss it, ma'am."

"Thank you, Corporal."

The MP snapped to attention and saluted smartly. "Pleasure, ma'am."

Kara returned the salute and pulled away from the

guard shack. She made the turn at the light, and the provost marshal's office loomed on her right, a large brick building in a cluster of old wood-frame retreads from World War II.

A single MP sergeant was at the desk inside. "May I help you, ma'am?"

Kara showed him her military ID. "I'm Major Guidry. I'm a JAG from Fort Benning, and I'm investigating a series of murders of female soldiers that have happened over the past few years. I was wondering. Could you point the way to the duty officer's shack?"

The MP's eyes shifted nervously. "Ma'am, the duty officer has, uh, gone for breakfast, ma'am. Maybe I can help you."

"I'm sure you can, Sergeant," Kara said, picking up immediately on the fact that the MP duty officer was ghosting, probably asleep at home in bed with his wife instead of on duty, as he should have been. "I'd like to see your homicide records for, let's see . . . the last six years. Would that be possible?"

"Yes, ma'am." The MP sergeant studied her for a moment. "Ma'am, this wouldn't be an emergency request, would it, coming like it does on a Saturday and all?"

"Yes, it would, Sergeant. You're very astute."

"In that case, follow me, ma'am." He led the way down a long corridor and turned down the stairs. Two flights down, he opened a door and flicked on the overhead lights. One wall of the small room was lined with black five-drawer file cabinets. He walked down the row, tapping the top drawers with his finger. Finally he stopped.

"You can start with this one, ma'am. This top drawer here is the current year, and the other drawers go back four more years, and if you want to go back further than that, you just start with the top drawer of the next cabinet. They're all marked."

"Thank you, Sergeant. You've been very helpful."

"Ma'am, there's a copying machine in the next room,

but if you're going to be needing originals, you're going to have to sign them out with me at the desk, and then take them to the colonel and get him to countersign the requisition."

"Right. Why don't I just check with you before I go anywhere with this stuff?"

"Yes, ma'am. That'd be a good idea. That way I can make sure all the forms are filled out okay." He stopped at the door. "Ma'am, you just give a holler if you need anything."

"Okay, Sergeant."

He closed the door and she was alone. Randy had said Beckwith was stationed at Polk five or six years ago. She opened a file drawer. She would start with six years ago, and go one year earlier and one year later, in case his memory was off. She started flipping through the files. The first year had been a slow one for crimes at Fort Polk. Only twelve incidents listed on the index to the burglary file, probably because Polk was a locked-down post, where you needed a sticker to get through the gate.

She pulled another file, major felonies, assault and battery, armed robbery. She kept flipping through the file drawer. *Homicides.* She carried both files to the table and opened the homicide file. First page: a husband charged with killing his wife. Next page: a racial thing, two Latino enlisted men jumped a white guy. There was an eight-by-ten of the suspects.

She kept looking. Female. Nineteen. Rape-murder. She turned the page. Civilian authorities arrested her ex-boyfriend. She closed the homicide file and opened major felonies. She was halfway through this file when she stopped at an assault and battery. Female Second Lieutenant Patti O'Brien, badly beaten. She reports it as a robbery, says somebody jumped her from behind and clobbered her with a club and stole her purse. The investigators think she's lying. They believe she knows her attacker but won't identify him. Local address in the file is an apartment in downtown Leesville.

She looked for a home address for O'Brien. Nothing. She made a note to check with Fort Polk personnel later. She opened the next drawer in the file cabinet and thumbed through its contents for a moment, found the homicide file and carried it back to the table and started reading.

It was right there on top. First Lieutenant Sheryl Jansen, stabbed in the neck. Body found off post in the woods. No prints. Minimal physical evidence. One arrest, a townie. He came up with an alibi and it stuck. She made a note about the unsolved murder and opened the next major felony file. She was flipping through the file when a loose page fell to the ground. She picked it up. It was a misplaced page from the Patti O'Brien assault with a cross-reference notation at the bottom of the page.

Now, *this* was interesting. If she could find the cross-reference . . .

She checked each of the cabinets along the wall. There were two more cabinets across the room, but they turned out to be empty. She opened a door and switched on a light. A dusty copying machine was set on a table in the corner. A piece of dirty olive drab canvas was draped over something next to it. She yanked the canvas away, exposing a stack of battered Stor-All cardboard boxes. She sat on the floor and started going through the boxes.

An hour passed before she got to the bottom box. She opened it and pulled the first file. The cross-references matched. She carried the file to the table in the next room. She flipped through the file, found the index: "Interrogations in the matter of the murder of First Lieutenant Sheryl Jansen."

Bingo.

The first person listed on the index was Second Lieutenant Patti O'Brien, interrogated at 1501 First Street,

Apartment 6, Leesville. She looked at her notes on the Jansen murder. Jansen's address was 1501 First Street, Apartment 6. They had been roommates. She went through the thick file one page at a time and reached the end. O'Brien's interrogation was listed on the index, but the transcript was missing. She drummed her fingers on the table for a moment.

Someone had gone through the files on the Jansen murder and had deliberately misplaced key elements of the investigation. The Jansen interrogation transcripts hadn't been in the original homicide file in the first place. The transcript of the interrogation of Patti O'Brien was missing. Somebody had made one hell of an attempt to conceal the fact that Patti O'Brien had been questioned in the matter of her roommate's murder.

She decided to read the transcripts of the other interrogations. The first person they had talked to was the guy who found Jansen's body. He was out hunting, tripped, and fell on it. The body was covered with leaves, hidden behind a large log.

She read further. The next two interrogations were of Jansen's co-workers. They had been the last ones to see her alive. They all met for a drink at the O-Club earlier the night she was killed. The last interrogation was Lieutenant Colonel Harry Roberts.

Kara looked up. He was Beckwith's chief of staff at Fort Benning!

She scanned the page. Back then Roberts had been a brigade XO. And the brigade CO was . . . Beckwith!

She started reading the interrogation of Colonel Roberts. Right there in his answer to the first question was the T word. Lieutenant Jansen was a "troublemaker," according to Roberts. She had received a very low OER. Always late with paperwork. Late to work. Too many sick days. A whiner and complainer.

She turned the page and kept reading. There were questions about Lieutenant O'Brien. She and Jansen had both worked for him. What kind of an officer was Lieutenant O'Brien? Fine officer.

She closed the file. One question about Jansen, and Roberts is running at the mouth, putting down the victim, and one question about O'Brien, and they get a monosyllable of praise.

The door opened. A young officer wearing an MP arm band walked in. "I'm Captain Talmadge. I'm the military police duty officer. Sergeant Kenny informed me that you arrived early this morning and asked to see some old case files?"

Kara stood up. "That's right, Captain. I'm Major Guidry, from Fort Benning." They shook hands. "I'm looking into a series of murders of young females that we believe have been committed on military installations over the past five or six years."

"You think there's a serial killer? In the Army?"

"Maybe. We don't know. That's why I'm here."

"Usually we get a request through channels when we're being asked to share investigatory data."

"I'll tell you the truth, Captain. I hadn't planned on stopping here at Polk at all. I was driving back to Benning from Fort Sam Houston, and a huge storm hit just outside Shreveport, so I turned south to get around it, and I looked at the map, and what's dead in my path but Fort Polk. That was when I decided to stop off and see what you all have in your case files."

The captain nodded. "I see. Well, I'm going to have to check this out up the chain of command. You understand. Protocol, ma'am."

"Of course."

"I'll get back to you as soon as I can."

"Thank you, Captain."

He took one last look around the room and left. Kara grabbed the file she had been reading. She knew he'd be back with questions about her investigation and military forms to fill out, and the best plan was to get the files copied before the paperwork started. She threw the switch on the copying machine, and it hummed to life.

At the main gate she returned the guard's salute and stepped on the gas. She passed through the Leesville suburbs and drove straight into cattle country, musing about what she had discovered from a spec-4 at post personnel: There was no permanent home address in the system for O'Brien, but she had been commissioned through ROTC, so maybe she could find it in her college files.

She ran down the chronology the files had coughed up: Lieutenant Jansen had been killed in January. Lieutenant O'Brien was assaulted in February. In March, O'Brien was given a waiver of her service obligation from ROTC and allowed to resign with a compassionate discharge. Now, what could have brought that on?

The answer was Beckwith. He had cashiered her out of the service to shut down the investigation of Jansen's murder. It would have been easy enough for him to do. They'd had a competent, thorough investigation of Jansen's murder. They tried as hard as they could to get O'Brien to open up about Jansen, and she wouldn't. They tried to get her to tell them who beat her up, but she wouldn't cooperate there either, and a month later she's out of the Army and headed to parts unknown. All that work they did ended up in a bunch of investigation files, and some of those files were "misplaced," and at least one of them had disappeared. Beckwith wouldn't have even needed the cooperation of the MP's to do that. He could have done it himself.

The fact that there were missing files in a murder investigation was troubling but hardly surprising. In a typical conspiracy of military circumstances, this gets moved, that gets lost. General So-and-So gets transferred. Beckwith goes to the Pentagon. The provost marshal retires. The great thing about the Army from the point of view of a criminal is that everybody moves around so much, there is almost no institutional memory. There was no one around at Polk to remember all the details of what had happened during a three-month period five years ago. Nobody.

And now Beckwith was doing the same thing at Benning, putting pressure on Hollaway to close the case with the accidental death of a suspect, Parks.

It started to rain, and she switched on the wipers. She squinted, trying to make out the white lines running down the middle of the road ahead. If she drove straight through to Georgia, she could hit the phone first thing Monday morning and try to track down Patti O'Brien. She hadn't cooperated with military investigators at the time of the murder, and there was a chance she would be just as reluctant now. But five years was a long time. There had to be a spot in O'Brien's heart she could reach. She had to have known her roommate was having an affair with Beckwith, and Kara was certain that she would want the man who killed her friend brought to justice.

That man had to be Beckwith. There were too many coincidences. Two dead female lieutenants, both of them stabbed in the neck, both killed out in the boonies. If O'Brien would testify that Jansen had been having an affair with Beckwith, that would establish the pattern she needed to charge him with Sheila's murder.

And then there was Lannie. She thought about stopping to call her but thought better of it. She gets a call from her best friend telling her that her lover is a murderer . . . there was no way that was going to work.

There was nothing left to do but press her foot to the gas pedal and head for Benning.

Chapter Twenty-six

Mace found Hollaway's office and knocked on the door.

"Have a seat, Sergeant," said Hollaway.

Mace sat down stiffly.

"I've got a few questions for you about Parks' death."

Mace could feel the major's eyes drilling straight through him. He didn't like this one bit.

"What kind of a platoon leader was Lieutenant Parks?"

"A pretty good one, sir. I've had worse. A lot worse."

"You had been out in the field with Parks previously?"

"Yes, sir."

"Did he act any differently than he used to that night?"

"Yes, sir."

Hollaway looked up from the notes he was taking. "In what way?"

"He was real nervous, sir. And he kept talking about Lieutenant Worthy."

"What did he say?"

"He was talking about how much he loved her, sir."

"Anything else?"

"Yes, sir. He said he followed her the night she was killed, but that he lost her in the storm. I think he felt like, if he hadn't lost track of her, he could have stopped her from being murdered."

Hollaway took his time noting what Mace had said.

"I think there's a possibility that Lieutenant Parks committed suicide, Sergeant. What do you think?"

"He was pretty upset, sir."

"Upset as in, depressed?"

"I'd say so, sir."

"Would you say that he ran into the live-fire zone deliberately?"

"Yes, sir. I warned him we were too close. You could see the yellow flags marking the zone. He just took off running and didn't stop."

"And you went after him. Did you call out to him?"

"Yes, sir."

"And that didn't stop him?"

"No, sir. He just kept going."

Hollaway stood up. "You've been very helpful, Sergeant. Thank you for coming."

Mace saluted and left. He was turning the corner to go down the stairs when he ran into her. Rain water was dripping into her eyes from the visor of her cap as she looked into his eyes.

"Excuse me, ma'am," said Mace, brushing past her.

Kara watched him go down the stairs, wondering what he had been doing in her building.

Hollaway, she said to herself as she unlocked the door to her office. She took off her wet raincoat and was hanging it up when a spec-6 stuck his head in the door. "Major Guidry? Colonel Lambert wants to see you."

Oh-oh. Here it comes. That MP captain from Fort Polk has already called her.

"Tell her I'll be right there."

"Yes, ma'am. I'll do that."

She took off her cap and raincoat and hung them on the coat rack and got out a spare pair of military heels she kept in her bottom desk drawer. She slumped into her chair and tried vainly to dry her stocking feet with Kleenex. Those bastards at Fort Polk. There was one thing military law enforcement people had in common with criminals. Turf. They both jealously protected it, and now they were going to make her pay for waltzing into Fort Polk and violating their turf.

Colonel Lambert was glued to her desk chair, as usual, when Kara reported.

"Have a seat, Major," said Colonel Lambert. She finished signing some kind of official document and looked up. Her face was wooden, impassive.

Kara steeled herself. She was tossing explanations around in her mind like tennis balls when Colonel Lambert smiled.

"Did you have a nice holiday?"

"Yes, I did." She prayed her surprise didn't show.

"It's a nice time of year, Thanksgiving. Did you visit relatives?"

"Mother lives out in California, and it's a rough haul, ma'am, even on a long weekend. I just couldn't hack the airlines this year."

"Nor could I. They had a nice spread at the O-Club, though. Were you there? I didn't see you."

"No, ma'am. I drove over to New Orleans and saw some friends."

"That must have been wonderful. I'll bet the food was to die for."

"Unbelievable."

Colonel Lambert rocked back in her chair. "How is the investigation going?"

"I'm patching together a time line of her last day, leading up to her murder. It's coming along. I've still got a few blanks to fill in."

"I talked to Frank Hollaway at the Thanksgiving buffet at the O-Club. He seemed to think Parks was a pretty strong suspect."

"I know he does."

"Frank said he didn't have an alibi."

"Neither did Captain Taylor, but I don't find that at all surprising."

"Why is that?"

"Well, ma'am, you're single. So am I. Would you

have had an alibi the night Lieutenant Worthy was killed, if you'd had to come up with one? I couldn't have. I was at home alone. I live outside town on a quiet private lane off a county road. Nobody ever sees me coming or going. Where do you live, ma'am?"

Colonel Lambert hesitated before she answered. "I live in post housing, but I see what you mean." She picked up a stack of papers on her desk and tapped them neatly into alignment. "But I'm not sure that's good enough. Major Hollaway thinks he's got enough on Parks to hold a postmortem hearing and close out the case."

Kara thought quickly. There had to be a way to stall it. "I think we need some more time, ma'am. I don't think we have enough evidence."

"Well, I've gone over the evidence with Major Hollaway, and I agree with him on this. I want you to get together with him and prepare the evidence. I'm going to order the hearing. I want the Sheila Worthy case put behind us, Major. This isn't good for the Army, and it's certainly not good for Fort Benning."

It was obvious that Beckwith had come down hard on Lieutenant Colonel Lambert as well as Hollaway. It was like he was with them in the room.

"Ma'am, there's a killer out there, and we'll bring him to justice."

"We don't have much time, Major. I want this case closed before the base closure commission has its final meeting next month."

So that's the angle Beckwith's playing.

"I want to be updated regularly on your progress. I want this case closed, do you understand me?"

"Yes, ma'am." *So she can take the OER Beckwith will write for her up to Washington when she goes fishing for that promotion and new job,* Kara thought as she closed Colonel Lambert's door behind her.

She found Hollaway standing at her office window.

"Quite a storm out there," he said, turning around when he heard her walk in.

"I'm so tired of the rain, I'd take an assignment to Fort Huachuka, Arizona," said Kara. "I'd sell my soul to the devil. I'd pay cash to the clerk who cut my orders."

"And then the sun and the heat would fry your brain, and you'd want out of there too," laughed Hollaway.

"That's the Army brat in me. Take a reassignment anywhere, anytime, just for the change of scenery." She perched on the edge of the desk. "I just came from Lambert's office."

"I can't get over the way she reminds me of Kathy Bates," said Hollaway. "I mean, I'm sitting in there with her, and the whole time I'm thinking I'm James Caan, and she's got this huge sledgehammer in her hand."

Kara laughed. "You don't sound like you find her particularly thrilling to work with."

"General Beckwith called me over the weekend. At home. The pressure's on."

"The pressure of wanting an appointment to chief of staff, you mean."

"You're probably right. Are you ready to go to the hearing and present the stuff we've got on Parks?"

She took a deep breath. "I've got to tell you, Frank, I don't think so. It's the lack of physical evidence against him. I mean, all we've got is that damn U.S. insignia and the fact he had been Sheila's lover. If that car hadn't gotten swamped, and we could have dusted it for prints and had your forensics guys go over it, I bet we wouldn't be sitting here today commiserating with each other. We'd have caught the guy by now, and we'd be downtown at the Horseshoe Bar and Grill ordering huge steaks and the best bottle of wine they've got."

"I just interviewed Parks' platoon sergeant. He thinks Parks may have committed suicide. He told me he was yelling at him, and Parks simply ignored him. He said the yellow markers for the live-fire zone were clearly visible, and the artillery was impacting very, very close to where they were standing, and Parks just kept going straight into it. Maybe he figured it was just a matter of time before we pulled together enough circumstantial evidence to call him in."

"Would you have cashed your check like that, Frank, if you were the killer? I mean, you're sitting there, and you know for sure that the flood destroyed all physical evidence, and you know you haven't got a record that would make you a suspect, and you've been interviewed by the two investigators in charge and they didn't lay a glove on you. Would you have committed suicide under those conditions? I don't think so."

"I still think there's a strong probability he killed her and then he killed himself, Kara. I think we should take what we've got to the postmortem hearing and be done with it."

"Look, I understand the pressure we're under. But isn't everyone a little eager to put this thing in a box and shove it in a closet? I mean, we don't want to do a rush to judgment here. There's the dead girl to think of. Sheila Worthy was the daughter of an officer. I can guarantee you that if we try to sweep this case under the rug, Colonel Worthy is going to be all over us."

"You need something solid to take to Lambert if you want to delay the hearing, Kara."

She opened her briefcase and laid the Xeroxed files from Fort Polk on her desk.

"I drove to Fort Polk over the weekend, Frank. I found some evidence over there that I think bears on this case."

Hollaway looked surprised. "Fort Polk? What does that hellhole have to do with Sheila Worthy's murder?"

"A friend of mine tipped me off," she lied. "There was a very similar murder at Polk about five years ago. A young female lieutenant by the name of Jansen was stabbed in the neck in a densely wooded area. They never solved the crime. It's still an open case. That's why I don't think we should rush into closing the Sheila Worthy case."

Hollaway whistled. "You know what this means, don't you?"

"I know Parks wasn't even in the service five years ago. He couldn't have stabbed Jansen at Fort Polk, and I don't think he stabbed Worthy at Fort Benning."

"We're going to have to run a cross-check on our suspects lists. See who was stationed out at Fort Polk back then, if anyone."

"You think you can handle that, Frank?"

"Yeah. Sure. I'll get right on it."

"While you're at it, see if you can't track down an address for this woman." She handed him the file on Lieutenant O'Brien.

"How does she fit in?" he asked, looking up from the material.

"She was the dead girl's roommate. We need to talk to her."

"I'll see what I can do."

"We're getting close, Frank. We're going to break this case."

"You sound pretty confident for someone who's got no suspects, no physical evidence, no circumstantial evidence, no motive, no nothing."

She grinned and shooed him out of her office. She was not at all certain that they were going to break the case, but she wasn't going to let him know that.

It was still raining when she got home. She fed the cats and started a fire in the fireplace and poured herself a glass of wine. The cottage was a cozy place on a cold winter night. The only thing missing was Mace. She picked up the phone and started to dial his number and then hung up. It was hard, but it was better to wait. Maybe he would call her. Maybe she'd run into him downtown.

Maybe he wouldn't call. Maybe she'd never hear from him or see him again.

She drained the last of the wine. He had made her feel like a teenager when they were together. Now they were apart, and she still felt like a teenager, sitting by the phone, waiting for it to ring, knowing it probably wouldn't. Why couldn't life be easier? Why was it that when you got in your thirties, every day you went under another assault of shitty realities? Was it just women, or did men feel the same way, that life was hard and getting harder?

She got up and whistled for the cats. How much was choice and how much was chance? Did it matter?

She was in bed, about to turn out the light, when she saw the photograph of herself and Lannie on her dresser. It had been taken a few years ago at the beach in Ocean City, Maryland. She had driven up from law school in Charlottesville, and Lannie had driven over from Washington. It had been a wonderful weekend. They lazed around on the beach all day and stayed up late drinking wine and talking and laughing. The last day they were there, one of those photo guys came by, and they paid him five bucks and he took their picture. Now, as she turned off the light, their smiling faces looked so young and eager and alive.

She dreaded it, but she was going to have to talk to Lannie. At least this much in her life wouldn't be left to chance. She had to tell her friend what she knew about Beckwith, even if it meant breaking her heart.

Chapter Twenty-seven

They were in Mrs. Beckwith's Lexus on Victory Boulevard, and she was driving.

"I can't tell you how much I appreciate this, Randy. You know the Army. We requested the painting they're doing at the quarters six weeks ago, and they have to get around to doing it this week. Did you ever see so many drop cloths and ladders in your life?"

Randy laughed. "Well, you've got a big house, ma'am."

"Too big. I don't know what I'd do without you, Randy. You're a sweetheart to help me."

She parked in the lot outside Randy's apartment, and they went inside.

"Where can I put these boxes, Randy?"

"Over there, ma'am." He switched on the lights. She put the boxes down and collapsed on the sofa.

"I'll get the rest of them out of the trunk, ma'am."

"I am positively exhausted. I do not understand why every bit of the responsibility to get this party ready has fallen upon you and me. I spoke to Bill about it last night, and I asked him if there weren't some discretionary funds available to hire a party planner, but he said no, we'd have to do it ourselves. Not fair, is it?"

"Doesn't seem so, ma'am."

Randy unlocked the trunk and got the rest of the invitation boxes and went back inside.

"I have *got* to get these invitations done. I'll tell you

what. I'll make excuses to Bill if you'll stay here and help me this afternoon. I've got my list right here, and I'm going to separate them out by category. We've got active-duty Army, we've got retired, we've got corporate officers, we've got members of Congress . . . it's going to take us the rest of the day."

"Sure. I'll be glad to, ma'am."

"You're a saint, Randy. I swear that you are."

He grinned. "I don't think I've ever been called a saint before."

She laughed. "Always a first time."

Randy helped her arrange the piles of invitations on the dining room table. There wasn't enough room. "I'm going to take these and go in the kitchen and spread them out on the dinette, ma'am. We'll have more room that way."

"Good idea."

In the kitchen, he started addressing envelopes. He turned on the radio and thought about the call he'd gotten from Ed. He read an article over the phone that had been in the papers that morning in Washington. Senator Maldray had made a speech at a fund-raiser in Virginia, attacking affirmative action. At the end of the speech he had laid into General King without mentioning him by name: Certain people in the armed services have risen to positions of power and responsibility and are now using those positions to protect the affirmative-action policies that got them there. What kind of message are we sending to our young soldiers and sailors, Maldray had asked, if we tell them that the color of your skin matters to promotion boards and presidential appointments?

Ed said that everyone in Washington knew the speech was a direct warning to the President that he meant to oppose General King in the Senate if the President dared to appoint him chief of staff. It was looking more and more like Beckwith had the job sewed up, Ed had said. Randy was glad his brief involvement in the military's political process was over. Ed said if Beckwith made it, he was going to resign from the service. Randy thought that maybe he would too. He hadn't really made up his mind. But whatever he did, at least he knew the most powerful military man in the world wouldn't consider him his sworn enemy. And neither would his wife.

Kara drove through the gate to Lannie's condo complex and looked at the cars parked outside the condos as she searched for Lannie's unit. None of them had military stickers. The complex was way north of Columbus, in the suburbs surrounding Atlanta. Under other circumstances she would have thought Lannie had made a strange choice of a place to live, giving herself an hour's drive to work when there were plenty of nice places right outside Fort Benning. But she knew what Lannie was doing, putting miles between herself and the military. For south Georgia, anyway, they didn't make a better trysting spot than this one. She found Lannie's condo in a distant corner of the complex. It was an end unit, with covered parking for two cars and its own separate entrance behind a wall. She cut the engine and turned off the headlights and got out.

She had been dreading this moment all day. Lannie wasn't going to buy her warnings about Beckwith. She was probably in love with him. She rang the doorbell.

The door opened. Lannie's surprise was obvious. "Kara! What are you doing here?"

"I was in the neighborhood and thought I'd drop by," she joked. She handed Lannie a bottle of good French Bordeaux. "I needed somebody to drink this with, and your name came up."

Lannie laughed. "I had no idea you knew where I lived."

"It wasn't easy to find. You're kind of out of the way here, aren't you?"

Lannie led the way to the kitchen and got out a corkscrew and opened the bottle of wine. "I got tired of living around a nest of other single officers when I was up in Washington. Everywhere you looked, all you saw were people with shiny shoes and uniforms carrying briefcases full of Pentagon homework. I figured when I got down here, I was going to find myself a place where I could get away from all that, and I did." She reached into a cabinet and got a couple of wineglasses and poured. "To good wine, fast cars, and faster women."

"I'll drink to that," said Kara. "So. You're closer to your guy in Atlanta up here too. Must be nice."

Lannie didn't miss a beat. "You noticed, huh? Atlanta's only a few miles up the road."

They pulled up stools and sat at a counter separating the kitchen from the living room.

It's now or never, she thought.

"Lannie, there isn't any guy in Atlanta you met on the internet."

Lannie feigned surprise. "What in God's name are you talking about?"

"I'm talking about General Beckwith."

Lannie relaxed with a little smile. "I see you figured out my little secret."

Kara was grim-faced. "Yes, I did."

"Neat, huh?" Lannie swilled down the last of her glass excitedly and poured another. "Oh, Kara, he is the *most* sexy man I have ever been with!"

Kara took a sip of wine. This was going to be even harder than she thought.

"You don't seem very excited for me, girlfriend," said Lannie, picking up on Kara's mood.

"I'm not."

"Oh, what are you going to say now? He's *married*, and I shouldn't be going out with a *married man*? Even you must have made a pass or two at a married guy over the years. Everybody does it, Kara."

"Yeah, everyone ends up going out with a married man at least once in her life. But not everybody falls for a liar and a murderer."

Lannie sat there for a moment, staring into her wine-glass with a hurt look. "What are you talking about?"

Kara leaned closer to her friend. "Beckwith killed Sheila Worthy, Lannie. I can prove it."

"You don't believe that."

Kara sat silently for a moment. "Lannie, I know this is hard for you, but you've got to hear me out."

Lannie stood up, her back to Kara. "*Hard* for me? My best friend walks into my apartment and tells me the man I love is a murderer, and it's *hard* for me?" She turned around. Her eyes had filled with tears. "I knew you could be jealous, Kara. I've heard you talking about some of the other women we've known. We even made a joke out of it, remember? I used to call you Miss Green Gills, when you went off on somebody who had lucked into meeting a gorgeous guy."

"Lannie, if there's one thing I do not feel at this moment, it's jealousy. I'm worried about your safety. I came here to warn you—"

Lannie held up a hand, stopping her. "Warn me? All you're doing is hurting me."

"I'm not trying to. I'm trying to tell you what I know so you *won't* end up getting hurt. Or worse."

Lannie took a couple of steps away from the counter and turned. "How can you do this to me? I thought we were *friends*."

"We are friends. That's why I came here."

"You can't be serious, Kara. Is this some kind of sick joke you're playing? If it is, it isn't funny."

"I came here as a friend, Lannie. He killed Sheila Worthy, and he probably killed another girl out at Fort Polk five years ago. I don't want you to be next."

"This is incredible! I don't believe what I'm hearing!"

"Lannie, he was having an affair with Sheila Worthy.

His wife told me he had a date to meet her out by the firing range the night she died, and even he admitted it to me later. Both of them claim he was home at the time Sheila was killed, but I think she's lying to protect him."

"I don't believe you."

"You have *got* to believe me, Lannie."

"What did you think I'd say? Did you think you'd shock me, and I would throw a jealous fit and tell him to go to hell? I *love* him, Kara. I love him like I've never loved anybody in my entire life."

Kara stared into her glass of wine. "I knew this was going to be difficult when I got in the car to drive out here, but we've been friends a long time, Lannie, and I don't want anything to happen to you. I'm sitting here, as your friend, and I'm telling you that this man you've fallen for is a killer. If I didn't know what I know about him right now, I'd say, hey, more power to you. Go for it. But it's not like that. He's a very dangerous man, Lannie, and I don't want you to end up dead like Sheila Worthy."

Lannie picked up her glass and drained it. "Bill Beckwith is the most honest, open human being I have ever met. I cannot believe that you think he killed that girl. I cannot believe it! I don't know what's gotten into you, Kara, but you have come into my house and you have hurt me very, very deeply. I don't know what I ever did to you to deserve this kind of betrayal. What have I ever done to make you act like this?"

Kara hung her head. "Nothing, Lannie."

"I know. I've never done anything to you. That's why I'm going to ask you to leave, please. Now."

Kara stood up. "Lannie, I—"

Lannie pointed at the door. "Please. Spare me. I've heard enough for one night."

Kara grabbed her purse and walked to the door. She hesitated for a moment, then she heard Lannie sob behind her and walked out. It was one of the most difficult things she had ever done in her life. Now it was over, and she felt empty, expunged of emotion, limp with sadness. As she got into the Cherokee, she saw a light blink on in what was probably the master bedroom. Kara knew she wanted to call Beckwith, but Lannie faced the lonely reality of every woman who loves a married man. She couldn't call him at night, because he was at home with his wife, and no matter what happened, you did not violate the sanctity of the married man's home. But she faced something else too, something not faced by any of the other fools who played by an adulterer's rules.

Danger.

Kara put the Cherokee in gear and drove away. For a moment there, she had wondered if Lannie wasn't at least just a little right when she accused her of being jealous. She thought back to when she was a cadet and he was a major, and the night they stole that was filled with their passion. It seemed so long ago. Had a youthful indiscretion turned into an adult obsession? Mace certainly thought so. Now she had opened herself up to Lannie, and she probably did too. But she knew she wasn't dealing with a memory. She was dealing with a killer.

She turned onto the highway and headed south. The next few days would be crucial. If she could come up with the girl from Fort Polk, the pieces of the puzzle would start to come together, and the picture they would form would be that of a handsome, cunning murderer wearing general's stars. She could push the case forward and get him charged and remove him from Lannie's, and the Army's, life forever.

There was an old Volkswagen GTI parked in front of her house when she drove up. Frank Hollaway was standing on the front porch.

"I've got something for you." He reached into his

pocket and pulled out a neatly folded piece of paper and handed it to her.

"What's this?"

"An address for the girl from Polk, Patti O'Brien. It's in Chicago."

Kara studied the page. "I know right where this is. It's on the near North Side, just off Lakeside Drive. How'd you get it?"

"I ran a check through Finance and this popped up. Seems she had some leave time coming when she got out."

"They usually count up your days and pay you in cash when you're going through out-processing."

"Not when it's a Sunday, they don't."

"She processed out on a *Sunday*?"

"Yep. Finance at Polk wasn't open except for a duty NCO, and they don't give the duty NCO the keys to the cash cage, so she had to leave a forwarding address."

"Bingo!"

"Are you going to call her?"

"I'll try in the morning. No phone number?"

"Nope. Just the address."

"Well, this is a big help. Thanks, Frank."

"Anytime."

"You want to come in for a cup of coffee?"

"I'm bushed. I'll talk to you tomorrow at the office."

"Okay. Thanks again, Frank."

"No problem." He got into his car and headed down the drive.

Inside, she took off her overcoat and was hanging it up when she saw the red light blinking on her answering machine. She pressed Play.

"Uh, uh, I was just calling to, uh, tell you I hope there are no hard feelings. I guess I was a little rough on you that night in New Orleans. I'm sorry. I hope every-thing's okay with you. Bye."

She played the message over again, listening for some kind of signal in his voice, a tone that would let her know what he was thinking, if he still loved her. He sounded hesitant, nervous, like he'd been thinking about making the call all day and was glad when it turned out he got her machine.

At least it was *something*.

Chapter Twenty-eight

There wasn't enough time to meet at the condo, so they settled on a motel they had used before out on old U.S. 80, across the river and west of Phenix City. It was one of those places the interstates had passed by, and so apparently had everyone else, because the parking lot was empty when Lannie pulled in just before noon. She looked around for his car but didn't see it. She gave the desk guy the phony name they used, and he gave her a key to a room on the back side of the motel. She unlocked the door and found him waiting inside.

"Where's your car?" she asked, removing her cap.

"I'm not going to park outside this dump in broad daylight. It's down the street." He pulled her toward him, and they kissed. "Where have you been? You told me you'd be here by noon."

"It is noon, Bill."

Nervously he checked his watch. "What's this about, anyway? I don't like being yanked off post in the middle of the day. I had to cancel a lunch with the mayor of Columbus."

"I had to see you. Kara Guidry came to see me last night."

"She told you I was seeing Sheila Worthy, didn't she?"

"Yes."

"If she keeps up with this kind of slander, I'll bring charges against her. I'll put her behind bars."

"You don't have to worry about her, Bill. She's just a jealous, angry woman."

Beckwith stood up, his face suddenly red. "She's going to take her goddamn lies to Bernie King, and he'll put rumors out all over Washington, and if that happens, it's all over. Everything that we've worked for will go down in flames."

"You don't have anything to worry about, darling. You're twice the man King is. He's a loser, Bill, and you're a winner. Did you hear about Senator Maldray's speech? That put King in his place."

A lean, satisfied smile crossed Beckwith's face, and some of the color drained from his cheeks. She sat down and he stroked her hair. "I should have brought you on board a long time ago."

"What have I always told you, Bill?"

"If I leave things to you, my worries are over."

"Exactly. And aren't we right on schedule, like I told you we'd be this time last year? Aren't you one of two generals under final consideration for chief of staff?"

"I'd rather be one of one."

"But then, that wouldn't be a horse race, would it? That wouldn't be the United States Army we have come to know and love." They laughed.

"That's the problem with the Army today. Chickenshit indecisiveness. Nobody will make a damn decision."

"But decisions come easily to you, darling. That will be a change for the Army. Finally we'll have a leader who knows where he wants to take us." She pulled him close to her, reaching for his belt buckle. It came undone with a soft *click.*

He checked his watch. "I've got a meeting at 1330."

"That gives us fifteen minutes. I love pressure, don't you, darling? It's *so sexy.*" She unzipped his uniform trousers and stroked him. "You want it, don't you?"

"Yes."

Slowly she lowered her head, whispering softly: "Tell me what it's going to be like when you're chief, darling. Tell me what you're going to do to them. Tell me again."

"Ranstead? I've got plans for Ranstead. I'm going to put him on a slow boat for the Solomon Islands. He's going to find himself watching the sun set over a garrison of fifty men standing guard over an old ammo dump . . . oh . . ."

Kara called Chicago information and asked for a Patti or Patricia O'Brien, but they had no one listed by either of those names. Hollaway walked in just as she was dialing the Chicago Police Department.

"I stopped by to tell you I got a report on a sample I sent out to a lab awhile back." He handed her a manila envelope. "It's a new thing . . . newish, actually. There's a guy up at Georgia Tech in the Department of Geology who's kind of a crime buff, and he has established kind of a database on dirt."

"Dirt?"

"Well, that's an inelegant shorthand for it. What he does is, you send him a sample and a location, and he analyzes it and gives you a report that amounts to an exclusivity check. Either that, or you can do it the other way around. Send him a sample without a location, and he has a look at it, and he comes back with a report on the likelihood of where it came from."

"That sounds wild."

"I took a couple of samples from the area where you initially found Sheila's car and sent them in."

She opened the report and started reading.

"He got a very interesting result. The statistical likelihood that those samples came from anywhere other than the area immediately surrounding the firing range at Fort Benning is practically zero. It's like that low area over near the river was part of an ocean floor eons ago or something, and there are specific things you find there that make it very, very unique."

"That *is* interesting, Frank. What you mean is, if we

were to take soil samples somewhere else, say, from the bottom of somebody's shoe, and he checked them against the sample you sent him, he could give you a statistical probability on whether or not they came from the same place."

"Yeah. He's testified as a forensics witness in several trials. No acquittals so far."

"Can I keep this?"

"That's your copy. I've got the original in the evidence file. And something else came in. I got the autopsy results on Lieutenant Parks. He was taking an antidepressant. One of those new ones. The level in his blood established that he'd been taking it for some time."

"Well, that goes some distance to back up your suicide theory, doesn't it?"

"I reported this to Colonel Lambert. She has ordered the postmortem hearing on Parks."

"Well, I guess we'd better get to work."

"Yeah. I'll summarize my investigation and get it on your desk in the next couple of days."

"Okay, Frank. That'll be great."

She waited until he was out of sight down the hall. Then she closed her office door and picked up the phone and called Detective Brenda Fogel of the Chicago Police Department. They had been classmates at West Point. Brenda had been an MP who resigned after six years and moved back to Chicago and went to work for the Police Department. She had risen to deputy chief of the Homicide squad. Kara asked her to run a check on Patti O'Brien. Fogel said she's put a squad car on it and get back to her.

Robbie Beckwith had showered and was in her pajamas by the time the General got home. He clomped in through the kitchen door and started banging around the kitchen, looking for a glass, probably. He still didn't know where anything was, never had, not in any of the quarters they'd lived in. She put on her robe and went downstairs.

"Where are the goddamned glasses around here, Robbie?"

"Where they've always been, Bill. Right in front of your face." She pointed at a cabinet. He got himself a glass and plopped some ice cubes in it and filled it half full of scotch.

"Bad day at the office?"

"Not particularly."

"I'm getting lots of RSVP's. It looks like ninety percent of the people we invited are coming."

"Maldray?"

"He's coming, but his wife is in the Caribbean, so he'll be stag."

"General Carson?"

"Him too."

He walked right past her into the den and sat down heavily in his armchair. He picked up the remote and flipped on CNN. She followed after a measured interval. A few swigs of scotch and a minute or two of news worked miracles on him. She poured herself a glass of wine and straightened the glasses he had shoved aside when he reached into the cabinet. Finally she sat down on the sofa. Her voice was soft, unobtrusive, a little dark, like the lighting in the den.

"I heard something interesting today."

"Really? What?"

"Dahlia King stage-managed some kind of party for her husband over the Thanksgiving weekend in New Orleans. Very political. The whole Louisiana congressional delegation was there, along with some big-wigs from Texas and Mississippi and Oklahoma and Arkansas."

"That's just politicians cruising for black votes."

"That may be true, but their voyage took them to the shores of Bernie King's empire, and the way I heard it, they were impressed. He gave a speech that brought down the house."

"Asshole thinks he's Jesse fucking Jackson."

"We've got to pull off something like that at the party, Bill. Public speaking is such an important part of the chief of staff's job. You'll have a captive audience. I've got just the subject for you. You'll hit a home run."

His eyes brightened. "What are thinking I should talk about?"

"Army family values."

The words hung in the air between them like a puff of smoke from the barrel of a gun.

"I'm serious. You can talk about the worldwide Army family. You can throw in stuff like 'brothers in arms.' You can celebrate the crime-free family environment found on each and every Army post. You can even brag about being 'married to the Army.' It's win-win, Bill. You'll have them in the aisles, cheering at the top of their lungs. You'll make mincemeat of King, and the delicious thing is, he'll have to sit right there and listen to you, and he won't have a chance to address the same crowd. It will be a knock-out punch. He'll never recover. Every one of those 'honorable gentlemen' will go back to Washington with 'Army Family Values' ringing in their ears. 'Army Family Values' will be a political gold mine, and who will hold the deed? You will. How will they possibly deny you the chief's office after we're finished with them?"

"They won't. It's brilliant. Perfectly *brilliant*. How did you come up with it?"

"You always said I had an instinct for the jugular. I just followed my instincts."

"I'm going to start working on the speech immediately."

She reached under the newspaper on the sofa next to her and produced a booklet jacketed in infantry blue.

"I've already written it for you. Here." She handed him the booklet. "Start memorizing. It would be better if you didn't read it."

He opened the booklet to the first page and started reading. His face relaxed into a smile. "I like the first line." He cleared his throat, and his voice dropped a half octave. " 'There are no values more dear to the hearts of those of us in this room than Army Family Values.' " He looked across the room at her. "You've done it, Robbie." He held up the booklet and shook it. "This is our ticket to Washington."

"Get to work. By the time Friday comes, I want you so familiar with that speech it's oozing out of your ears. We're going to take your mediocre talents as a public speaker and give them a shot in the ass. You are going to know that speech word for word, paragraph for paragraph, page by page. It's going to scroll across the insides of your eyelids as you sleep. And you are not going to screw it up, you hear me? I mean it, Bill. You are not going to touch a drop until you've delivered the speech. What you do after that is your business."

A look of what passed for love came across his features. "I knew I could count on you coming through for me."

"If only, Bill. If only."

Detective Fogel had called back late in the afternoon with the disappointing news that the O'Brien family had moved from 403 West Roscoe. The building engineer didn't know where they went. Detective Fogel said she'd keep looking, and Kara thanked her.

Driving home, she was deeply disappointed. She was running out of time. She knew Lieutenant Colonel Lambert had ordered the hearing on Parks, and Sheila's murder was going to get hung around the neck of the dead lieutenant like a necklace, just to curry favor with Beckwith. She had heard Beckwith was going to make a big splash in Washington. People were saying after the AUSA convention, he was a lock for chief of staff. The day they announced his appointment to chief was the day she could forget the whole thing. The Army would rather let a murderer go free than suffer the embarrassment of trying the highest-ranking general officer they had.

The phone was ringing as she walked in. She rushed over and grabbed it, hoping it was Mace.

It was Hollaway. "How'd it go? Did you find O'Brien?"

"It was a roller coaster all day. I thought I had her located in Chicago, and it came up a dry hole."

"I'm almost finished with my summary for the hearing. I'll drop it by your office tomorrow."

"Great, Frank. See you."

She hung up and flipped through her mail. There was a neatly addressed envelope with no return address on the bottom of the pile. An invitation to Beckwith's party was inside, along with a note: "Figured you wouldn't want to miss this one. Randy."

Chapter Twenty-nine

From the sound and light booth in the balcony above the ballroom, the stage looked like it was draped with enough red, white, and blue bunting to wrap the Reichstag. The backdrop, where Patton's huge American flag would have hung if General Beckwith was shooting a movie instead of giving a party for himself, was a gigantic, very expensive logo: AUSA in letters twenty feet high.

In front of the AUSA logo, looking rather small because he did not enjoy on a hotel ballroom stage the size-enhancing qualities of a Panavision lens, stood General William Telford Beckwith. There was no microphone, though of course Randy had miked him with a clip-on under his tie. Softly, into his headset, Randy called for the Super-Trooper spot to open up and get him head to toe. He whispered to the light guy, seated next to him at the control panel.

"Sweeten the reds and blues. That Super-Trooper is making his face look like a bowl of milk." The light guy pumped up the reds and blues, and suddenly Beckwith looked healthy, ruddy even.

The sound checks had been done to an empty room. Now the place was filled with more than a thousand happy lobbyists, politicians, and Army brass. Randy prayed he'd set the levels right. He poised his finger above the main volume slide on the sound panel and watched the meters. He glanced at the stage. The General stood there above the faces in the crowd, and he furrowed his brow and opened his mouth and let loose with it.

It went just the way Mrs. Beckwith had written. Army. Family. Values. The heart and soul of us all. Randy half expected Beckwith to burp forth with the motto of West Point, and then, unscripted, there it came too: Duty, Honor, Country. He was hitting *all* of the notes, and they were going over big. Very big.

Then he asked the "ladies" to stand and saluted "Army wives." This brought the house down. Randy softened the lights as he lowered his voice and intoned the final words of his speech:

"We may be, as the saying goes, 'married to the Army,' but in no sense does that fact diminish our commitment to our sacred vows. It is in the arms of those we love that we have gotten the strength to take our knowledge and courage to the beaches of Anzio, the mountains of the Central Highlands, the trenches at Verdun, the snowy, barren hills of Korea, the desert sands of Kuwait. Indeed, we owe our lives to Army Family Values. Thank you, and good night."

At first, from the sound and light booth, there was a sense that the room had been sucked dry of oxygen. They were utterly silent, and then they burst into frenzied applause. General Beckwith stood there, bathed by the Super-Trooper, and he drank it in. Finally, just as the applause was dying down, Randy whispered into his headset for the Super-Trooper to take it down, slowly, slowly, slowly, and he reached over and tapped the light guy, and he pushed the slides on the light board and the stage went dark. Randy waited a beat, then nodded to the light guy, and he brought the stage lights back up. As they had rehearsed, Beckwith was gone.

Randy looked for him and whispered to the Super-Trooper. The spot picked him up moving through the crowd, shaking hands and grinning like a Southern sheriff working the room down at the Legion hall. Randy marveled at the ease with which he took their

adulation. You would have thought you were watching a
political rally instead of a gathering of the military in-
dustrial complex. He felt a hand on his shoulder.

"Excellent, Randy. Well done. Your service tonight
will be remembered where it counts, I am sure." Mrs.
Beckwith turned and walked out of the booth.

"Who the fuck was that?" asked one of the union
guys who stood around the booth doing nothing, collecting a paycheck so Randy could have the freedom to
run the show with his own workers and without union
interference.

"The General's wife."

"That's a hard case, I ever seen one," said another of
the union guys.

"She's got a lot on her mind," said Randy.

"Yeah. Him," said the union guy, pointing into the
crowd where the Super-Trooper still followed General
Beckwith.

The union guys wandered off. Randy picked up his
script of the speech and was about to leave when he was
met by a woman in an elegant black shift with her hair
done up in a twist.

"Good job, Randy. You had him looking so much like
Patton, all he's got to do is slap a soldier, and he's got
the job."

"Kara!" Randy whispered hoarsely under his breath.

"Didn't recognize me?" She struck a little pose.

"You look stunning."

"Why, thank you, Randy."

"I guess you got your invitation."

"Yesterday. Thanks."

"Don't let him see you," Randy said, nodding toward
Beckwith, still followed by the spotlight in the crowd
below them. "He doesn't know I sent you an invitation,
and he'd have my ass if he found out."

"Don't worry. I just came for the free food and
drinks. I'll stay out of his way."

"The missus too. She's not a happy camper."

"I noticed. You look tired, Randy. Long day?"

"I've been at this since four this morning, and we've still got hours to go."

"Big parties are a pain. Are you staying here at the Sheraton?"

"Yeah."

"Me too. Give me a call in the morning. Maybe we can meet for a late breakfast. I want to fill you in on what I found out at Fort Polk."

"Great. I'll do it."

Kara made her way downstairs from the booth and worked along the edge of the crowded ballroom until she found the bar. She ordered a scotch, and the bartender poured Black Label. She turned around just as Frank Hollaway walked up.

"This party must be costing General Beckwith a fortune," she said.

"It's like the stock market, Kara. You can't win if you don't pony up the bucks and play." He signaled the bartender. "I'll have what she's having."

A four-piece combo was playing bad jazz in one corner of the ballroom.

"You want to dance?"

"Why, Frank! You old charmer!"

They put their drinks down and joined a small number of dancers near the band.

"Where'd you learn to dance?" asked Kara. "You're good."

"My mother."

"She must be some character."

"Yeah, she is. She used to take me over to a friend's house, and they'd play old 45's on a little record player that was, like, from the fifties. My dad didn't like to dance and neither did her friend's husband, so they used to crank up that record player after I got home from school, and they'd take turns dancing with me. The excuse was, they were teaching me, but it was really 'cause they wanted to dance."

"That's kind of sweet."

"I thought it was strange at the time, but I'm glad they taught me now."

Hollaway spun her around, and she saw Lannie, and Lannie saw her. Lannie was wearing her dress blues, and she marched over, scowling.

"What are you doing here?"

They stopped dancing. Frank had a look at the anger on Lannie's face and stepped away. "I'll meet you at the bar, Kara."

"Okay, Frank." She turned to Lannie. "I was invited."

"I'm surprised you came, Kara," Lannie said sarcastically. "Aren't you afraid? He's such a dangerous man, showing up here like this, uninvited, you might get hurt. Or worse."

"I'm not trying to pick a fight with you, Lannie."

"I'm going to ask you to leave. If you don't, I'll call hotel security and have you removed."

"You're making a mistake—"

Lannie interrupted: "Are you going to leave, or am I going to have to call security?"

"The power is going to your head, Lannie. It shows, and take it from me, you don't wear it well at all." She turned and walked away.

General Teese stopped General King and Dahlia on their way out of the ballroom. "Did you ever hear such a load of crap in your life?"

General King shrugged. "What did you expect?"

"I talked to Maldray's PR guy this afternoon. He's going to warn the Senator. I don't want him making any more veiled attacks on you, General."

"You know what? I think we ought to just leave this thing alone. I'm sick of the whole game."

"But, General, I've made a plan for this week. You're going to address the Armed Services Committee. That's bound to make the papers. And that's just what we're starting with."

"I'll go before the committee, but I don't want you doing anything with that trash about his sex life. If that's what it takes to get a presidential appointment these days, I don't want any part of it."

General Teese grimaced. "All right, sir. I'll honor your wishes. But I'll tell you this much. If Beckwith had any dirt on you, he'd be spreading it around this party like cheese on a cracker."

"I guess that's the difference between me and him, Ed. We'll see if that counts for anything in the current political climate in this town."

General King saw someone down the hall and waved. "Gotta go. Call me about the committee hearing."

"Will do, sir."

General and Mrs. King made their way down the hall. General Teese turned into the hotel cocktail lounge and found General Ranstead in the corner.

"Did you talk to him?" asked Ranstead.

"Yeah. It sounds like he's given up. He told me to hold off on tipping the press about Beckwith and the girl."

"What are we going to do? I don't know who wrote that speech, but if that doesn't land him on the front page of the *Washington Post* in the morning, I don't know what will."

"Yeah, we're fighting a losing battle. I get the feeling that putting King in front of the Armed Services Committee is just nibbling at the edges of the process. Nothing he has to say is going to change their minds one iota."

"Then we've got a problem, Ed. Beckwith's got the momentum. The only thing that's going to stop him is if the President thinks his appointment will hurt him with the rank and file. You know how he is about currying favor with the troops. I don't see how we make that case at this point."

"Why don't you let me think about it over the weekend? I'll come up with something by Monday. We can always call our friend in the White House."

"You mean Nichols? He's on the domestic-policy side. He doesn't have anything to do with military affairs."

"No, but he knows everybody in the White House who does," said Teese.

"Look, I don't want to make that move unless we have to. If Nichols starts running around the White House bad-mouthing Beckwith, everybody wearing pants on those halls is going to know it's a gay thing, and we're dead in the water. The President will appoint Beckwith just to prove he's not in the pocket of the homosexual lobby."

"I'll admit it's a desperation move, but it might be all we've got left."

"If it is, we're dead." General Ranstead looked at his watch. "Jesus. It's late. I've got to get going."

"Are you going to be around tomorrow?"

"No. General Carson wants me to fly down to Fort Hood and make an appearance at a parade he can't attend."

"I'll talk to you on Monday, then."

"Good deal."

Lannie made sure Mrs. Beckwith had left the party before she walked up to the General, and even then she made it official.

"Sir, I've got your schedule for tomorrow. Would you like me to leave it at the desk for you?"

"One moment, Captain," Beckwith said to her, just as officiously.

The General excused himself from the group of colonels he had been talking to and turned to Lannie. "So what did you think?"

"I thought you were brilliant, sir," she said. "The way you delivered it, it was five times as good as it was on the page, sir."

He lowered his voice. "I wish there was some way we could be alone."

"So do I," she whispered.

"Why don't you go upstairs right now, and I'll see if I can sneak out of here in a few minutes?"

"Do you really think you should?"

"I'm not promising anything, but I'll try."

He straightened up, and his voice took on its official tone. "All right then, Captain. Very well. Leave my schedule at the desk. I'll pick it up later."

"Very good, sir. Good evening."

The General returned to the clutch of colonels. Lannie stood there for a moment, watching him. He was born to do this, she thought. He'll make the greatest chief of staff the Army has ever seen.

Chapter Thirty

Randy stepped off the elevator and looked in both directions down the empty hall. It was late, and everyone had long since gone to bed. He had his key ready when he reached the door and quickly walked inside. Ed was in bed with the covers pulled up to his waist. "Tired?"

"Exhausted. I thought this day would never end."

"Everyone was talking about Beckwith's speech. I must say, I was surprised. Who wrote it?"

"His wife, believe it or not. He's been rehearsing it all week." Randy unbuttoned his dress blues jacket and shrugged it off. He untied his shoes and slipped them off, rubbing his feet. "I've been on my feet all day. I need a drink."

Ed held a bottle of aged bourbon. "How about some of this?"

Randy whistled through his teeth as he took the bottle. "Where'd you get this stuff?"

"Down the street. It's very rare. See? Each bottle is numbered. Cost me half a month's pay."

Randy laughed. He opened the ice bucket. "Christ. There's no ice." As he reached for his shoes, he noticed the red message light on the phone was blinking. "Did someone call?"

"The light was on when I got here," said Ed.

"I'd better see who it was." He pressed the button for messages. An operator answered. "This is Captain Taylor in Room 910. You have a message for me?" He listened for a moment and hung up. "Lannie left a message at the desk. She wants me to stop by her room."

"It's late. Can't she wait until morning?"

"I'd better go. Beckwith will have my hide if he left something for me with her and I don't pick it up."

He tied his shoes and was about to walk out of the room when Ed handed him the ice bucket. "May as well get ice on your way."

"Sure. Be back in a minute."

He took the stairs down to Lannie's floor. He looked at the sign for room numbers and turned right. Halfway down the hall he found her door cracked open. He pushed the door and looked in. Lannie was lying on the bed in a black lace teddy.

Then he saw the blood. He ran into the room.

Her eyes were wide open, staring at the ceiling. There was a knife embedded in her neck, and blood had formed a pool on the bed. Randy grabbed the knife and pulled it out. He threw it on the bed and grabbed her shoulders, shaking her.

"Lannie! Lannie! Can you hear me?"

There was no response. He climbed on top of her and started pressing on her chest, administering CPR. He listened again for a heartbeat. He was reaching for the phone when he heard a loud *click* behind him. He turned his head and stared straight into the barrel of a Glock 9mm.

"Don't move. Don't even think about moving. Hands behind your back."

The man with the gun snapped a pair of cuffs around Randy's wrists and pulled him roughly off the dead woman.

"I was going to call the operator . . ."

"Sure you were, fella. Turn around."

"This has been a big mistake . . ."

"You're the one made a mistake, mister. Turn around. What's your name?"

"Captain Randy Taylor." As he turned, he caught a

look at himself in the mirror across the room over the dresser. His face was spattered with her blood. The front of his dress blues jacket was covered with it. He turned sideways and saw that his hands too were bloody.

"Oh, my God . . ."

The detective held the gun with one hand and a radio in the other. "Base, this is Reilly. I've got one down in Room 824. Suspect in custody."

The radio crackled with static. "Roger. Don't touch anything. We'll have DCPD there in a few minutes."

"Roger. Out." He shoved the radio in his pocket and motioned with the muzzle of his weapon for Randy to move. "In the hall. We've got a crime scene to protect here."

"But I didn't kill her!"

"We know that, mister. I just cuffed you for practice."

He pushed Randy toward the door with the barrel of his weapon. Outside the open glass doors to the balcony, he could hear sirens echoing in the night.

Chapter Thirty-one

It was still dark when the bedside phone rang, waking her from a deep sleep.

She rubbed her eyes, trying to think of who would be calling her in a Washington, D.C., hotel in the middle of the night.

She picked up.

"Kara, wake up. It's Frank Hollaway."

She noticed a hollow, echoing noise in the background. "Frank, jeez, what time is it?"

"Just after five. I'm down at D.C. central lockup. There's been another murder, Kara." He paused for a second. "You awake yet?"

"Who is it?"

There was a long pause before he answered: "You'd better get down here, Kara."

She felt the words catch in her throat before they croaked out: "Who is it, Frank?"

"D.C. Police made an arrest. We've got him downtown. I need you down here. They're going to let us in to question him in a half an hour."

She took a couple of deep breaths. Her nightmare had come true. "It's Lannie, isn't it?"

"I'm sorry, Kara."

She felt herself starting to sob, but cleared her throat, trying to pull herself together. "Who'd they arrest?"

"Captain Randy Taylor."

"I'm getting dressed right now. I'll be there in twenty minutes." She hung up the phone and switched on the light. She stepped into her uniform skirt and shoved her feet into her shoes. She hit the door at a run.

Randy was standing at the bars of the holding cell wearing an orange prison jumpsuit. Behind him unfolded a sea of human detitrus. There was a guy with both eyes bleeding, lying on his back on the floor, screaming at the top of his lungs: "I'm a Catholic in a Jewish jail! Help me! Help me! I confess my sins!" Another prisoner, an elderly black man, was dancing a slow soft-shoe by himself in the corner, singing "Mr. Bojangles." The smell of urine and vomit was overwhelming. A young cop approached and proceeded to unlock the door. Inside, Randy recognized Kara and Frank Hollaway.

"Taylor! Randolph Taylor!"

Randy stepped to the door.

"Assume the position." Randy turned around and held his hands behind him. The cop cuffed him and grabbed him by the collar. "This way."

Kara and Hollaway fell in behind the guard as he led them down a long row of holding cells and unlocked a green metal door. A pair of D.C. detectives were waiting inside.

"We'll give you ten minutes with him," said the tall one.

"That doesn't seem like much time," said Kara.

"You're out of your jurisdiction, miss. We're doing you a favor as it is."

The detectives walked out, and the door closed behind them with a loud *clank*. There was a gray metal table and two chairs, all screwed to the floor. Randy sat down uncomfortably. Kara took a notebook from her purse and sat across from him. Hollaway stood behind her.

"We haven't got much time, Randy. We need to know what happened."

"Kara, this is so unbelievable."

"I know it is. I'm going to read you your rights, Randy. You have a right to an attorney. You don't have to make a statement to us, but if you do, it could be used against you."

"I didn't do it! I swear to you! I didn't do it!"

Hollaway stepped around to one side of the table. "Do you understand your rights?"

"Yes, sir."

"One of the detectives told me you waived your right to an attorney when they questioned you."

"I didn't do it! I don't have anything to hide!"

"All right, then. Start at the beginning. Be precise."

Randy leaned forward, looking anxiously into Kara's eyes. "You have got to believe me."

"We're here to listen, Randy. I'm sure your cooperation at this point will be helpful to you later."

"Okay. I worked late at the party, and got back to my room about three a.m. The message light was on, so I called the desk, and Lannie had left a message to come down to her room."

"You were on what floor?"

"Nine."

"So you went down to . . ."

"Eight. I was going for ice anyway, so I grabbed my ice bucket, and I went down the stairs, and I walked up to her door, and there she was on her bed, covered with blood. It was awful. There was a knife sticking out of her neck! I ran into the room, and I listened to see if she was breathing, and I thought I heard something, so I got up on top of her, and I was pressing on her chest, you know, doing CPR, trying to massage her heart, and that was when they walked in."

"You said 'they.' Who is 'they'?"

"I guess he was a house detective. I heard him talking on his radio. His name is Reilly."

"You said you saw the knife sticking out of her neck. What kind of knife?"

"A knife. I don't know."

"Did you touch the knife?"

"I pulled it out the minute I got to her. I thought she was still alive."

Kara glanced over at Hollaway.

"Did anyone see you in the hallway?"

"I don't think so."

Kara and Hollaway stepped away from the table. "You heard enough, Frank?"

"Let me take a stab at a confession."

"You're not going to get one."

"Let me try," said Hollaway.

They walked back to the table. Both of them remained standing.

Randy looked up at Hollaway plaintively. "You believe me, don't you?"

"Captain Taylor, it's going to be in your interest if you tell us what really happened in that room. We'll take it to the D.C. prosecutor, and they'll take it into consideration during sentencing."

"But I didn't do it!"

"You killed her, Captain. The D.C. detectives told me you were covered in her blood, and there was a cut on your right hand, showing signs of a struggle."

"That must have happened when I pulled the knife out of her neck! I swear! I didn't do it!"

Kara touched Hollaway on the arm. "I've heard enough."

They walked over and tapped on the door. A key turned, and the door swung open. Behind them, Randy beseeched: "Please, you've got to believe me! I was trying to save her life!"

The door closed behind them. "Frank, have you seen the crime scene?"

"Yeah, briefly."

"I'm going to go back to the hotel and have a look."

The tall detective walked up. "You get anything out of him?"

"The same stuff he told you," said Hollaway.

"He ain't going to come clean. We'll lock him down till the arraignment."

"Detective, do you think you could arrange it so I could go over the crime scene?" asked Kara.

"Sure. Just tell the uniformed officer that Detective Howard authorized you. They got questions, tell 'em to call me."

"Thank you, Detective."

"What time will the arraignment be?" asked Hollaway.

"About ten. You know where the General Courts Building is?"

"We'll find it," said Kara.

"First floor. Ask for Part One." The detectives walked away.

"How do we get out of here?" asked Kara.

"This way," said Hollaway. They started walking down the row of holding cells. "I'm heading over to the courthouse. The DA said I could use their office. I've got to call Lieutenant Colonel Lambert."

"I'll meet you at the arraignment, then," said Kara.

They reached a barred door, and a buzzer sounded and the door slid slowly open. They passed through another door and were outside. It was starting to get light as Kara hailed a cab and headed across town.

Lannie's room was guarded by two uniformed C.D. police officers. Kara showed them her military ID and dropped the name of Detective Howard, and they lifted the yellow crime tape and let her inside.

The blood on the bed had started to dry. Fingerprinting dust still covered the phone and the bedside table. Lannie's uniform was hung neatly on a hook on the open closet door. Her shoes were on the other side of the bed, and the pair of hose she must have worn were in the waste basket next to the bed. A single black high-heeled mule was at the foot of the bed. The other was on top of the bed, partially hidden by the bloody sheet.

For several long moments Kara stood at the foot of

the bed and stared at the blood her friend had shed. Then she went into the bathroom and sifted through Lannie's makeup bag and toiletry kit: all the regular stuff, lipstick, compact, foundation, hairbrush. There was not one but two toothbrushes.

She walked back into the room. There was something she was missing. She tried to recall the details of what Randy had told them.

That was it! He had been carrying an ice bucket!

She looked around the room and found an ice bucket on the desk. It was strange. Usually in hotel rooms you found the ice bucket on a little tray with three or four glasses in wax paper covers. This one was just sitting there, alone.

She walked back into the bathroom. Another ice bucket was on the counter, sitting on a tray with the requisite paper-clad glasses.

There were two of them! Randy wasn't lying! Not about carrying the ice bucket with him, anyway.

Her mind raced as she stooped under the yellow crime tape and headed down the hall. Beckwith had set him up. He had framed his own aide for murder.

Part One was a courtroom with peeling paint and battered benches and an American flag hanging behind the bench that looked like it had been put up when there were still forty-eight states. Kara found Hollaway sitting behind the prosecution table. She slipped into the chair next to him, and he introduced her to the assistant DA, a young woman who looked to be in her mid-twenties. The DA excused herself and turned around and started going through her pile of cases. Hollaway leaned close to whisper:

"Lambert wants us to try to get him extradited to our jurisdiction."

"What?"

"Beckwith ordered it. He's taking the position that Captain Love was a soldier in his command, and so was

Captain Taylor, and he wants the Army to court-martial Taylor for murder."

"That son of a bitch is grandstanding for the D.C. press. This isn't about jurisdiction. It's about his campaign for chief of staff!"

"Whatever it is, Lambert told me to act on Beckwith's order. She wants you to make a motion to extradite Taylor to Fort Benning. You are to file the necessary brief if the judge requires it. Lambert said D.C. is a federal jurisdiction and so is Fort Benning, so we stand a good chance of getting the case transferred and charging him down there. The District of Columbia DA has agreed to let him go. Apparently anything we can do to reduce their caseload is acceptable to the DA. The District is broke and getting broker."

"I can't believe Beckwith is trying this, Frank."

"Look, Kara, would you rather see Taylor be put through this godawful system here in D.C.? He'll get a fair trial at Benning. If he stays here, he'll spend two years behind bars with no parole just waiting to come to trial."

"You've got a point there."

"Just play along and follow orders, Kara. Beckwith's going to be watching every move we make. If we don't follow his orders down the line on this thing, he's going to chop heads when we get back."

"Do you know what I found in Lannie's hotel room?"

Just then the bailiff called loudly, "All rise!" and everyone stood as the judge walked in and took the bench. The bailiff called the case, and they brought Randy in through a side door. His hands were cuffed in front, he was in leg irons, and he looked frightened. They removed the cuffs and irons, and he sat down next to a Legal Aid lawyer who had been assigned to his case.

The judge was a short man with thinning hair that had been sprayed and combed so it brushed his ears. He read from the charge sheet without looking up.

"The District of Columbia against Captain Randolph Taylor. Gentlemen?"

"Felicia Dobber for the District, Your Honor. The District has agreed to let counsel for the Army take part in these proceedings."

Kara stood. "Major Kara Guidry, United States Army Judge Advocate General, Your Honor."

The Legal Aid lawyer stood. "Vincent Eastman for the defense, Your Honor."

The assistant DA spoke up. "Your Honor, normally the district attorney would present evidence and testimony at this time, asking for an indictment, but this case is out of the ordinary. We have been asked to defer jurisdiction in this matter to the Army. If the court agrees, Captain Taylor will be transferred under military police guard to the stockade at Fort Benning, where he will be tried for the murder of Captain Lannie Fulton Love. Because Fort Benning is a federal jurisdiction, the district attorney has agreed to this arrangement, and we seek an order by this court releasing Captain Taylor from District of Columbia custody and transferring him to military custody at this time."

"This is a very unusual request, Ms. Dobber."

"Your Honor, yes, it is. But it's one the DA has agreed to because of the burgeoning caseload we face here, of which I am sure Your Honor is more than aware."

"Indeed." He turned to the defense lawyer. "Does the defense have a response?"

"We do, Your Honor. The defense will contest this request. We would request that this defendant be afforded the normal procedures any other accused person is entitled to in the District of Columbia. We ask that a grand jury be empaneled, that evidence is presented to the grand jury, and that the defendant have an opportunity to testify before the grand jury before charges are brought."

The judge turned to the prosecution table. "Ms. Dobber?"

The assistant DA shuffled through her papers. "There is a Supreme Court decision—I am not certain of the title . . ."

"*Solorio* versus *United States,* Your Honor, is the case Ms. Dobber is referring to." Kara stood and took the podium. "The Supreme Court held in *Solorio* that military courts have jurisdiction over crimes committed by active-duty service members, no matter whether those crimes were committed during duty hours, on post or off post, because military courts are in fact just another form of federal court, Your Honor. In other words, both the District and the Army have jurisdiction in this matter. This request may not be a typical one, Your Honor, but according to the law, it is a legal one and up to the discretion of this court."

"And the defense objects? Is that what I am to understand?"

The Legal Aid lawyer stood. "Yes, Your Honor."

"Very well. Submit briefs to this court no later than forty-eight hours from now, and the court will take the matter under advisement. Defendant will be remanded to the custody of the district attorney in the meantime." He struck his gavel. "Next case!"

Two burly uniformed policemen came to take Randy away. They put the cuffs on him, and his lawyer whispered something in his ear. With policemen on both sides, Randy was escorted through the side door. Holl-away lingered behind the prosecution table as Kara consulted with the assistant DA. Finally she joined him and they walked out of the courtroom.

Outside, they stopped at the curb, waiting for a cab.

"Pretty impressive in there, counselor."

"Just doing my job, Frank."

"Are you going back today?"

"I think I'll stick around and use the Georgetown Law Library and file my brief before I go back to Benning."

"Sounds like a good idea. I'm going to see my sister

in Maryland this afternoon, then I'll head back tomorrow. We can link up and search Taylor's apartment day after tomorrow."

"Good enough." A cab pulled up. She paused, wondering whether she should tell him about the second ice bucket in Lannie's room. Then she thought better of it and got in the cab.

Chapter Thirty-two

They got a key from the complex manager and let themselves into Randy's apartment. The place was stuffy, and all the shades had been pulled. Kara went around turning on lights and opening the shades. They had a brief look around the living room, finding nothing out of the ordinary.

"This is creepy," said Kara.

"It's always a little weird going through people's houses. I've found some strange stuff in my day."

"Like what?"

"I had a case where a colonel got killed in a car accident one time, and he was single, and there were no survivors, so they gave it to us. I found a closet full of women's clothes. Size about eighteen. High heels big as diving boards."

Kara laughed. "Takes all kinds." She opened the door to Randy's bedroom and switched on an overhead light. Inside the closet, battle dress uniforms were hung neatly in a row next to his Class A's. Hollaway pulled one of his Class A jackets off its hanger.

"Unless my memory's playing tricks on me, Taylor was on the N.S. Meyer list, right?"

"Yeah."

Hollaway fingered the U.S. insignia on the jacket lapel. "These aren't gold."

"It's probably his extra uniform jacket."

Hollaway pulled the other Class A jacket from the

closet. He removed the U.S. insignia. "These aren't gold either."

Hollaway opened the top drawer of Randy's dresser and removed a wooden tray holding uniform insignia and ribbons and started going through it. "Look at this." He handed her a single U.S. insignia. Kara turned it over. It was gold, and it came from N.S. Meyer.

"Did you find its mate?"

"No."

"Frank, this is too weird."

"Let's keep looking." He got down on his hands and knees and started throwing shoes out of the bottom of the closet. He went through a gym bag full of old clothes that was stuck in a back corner; then he got a chair and started going through the stuff on the top shelf. When he stepped down from the chair, he was carrying a small nylon bag with a zipper closure. He walked over to the bed and unzipped the bag and turned out the contents. Six knives tumbled onto the bedspread.

"Well, well, well," said Hollaway. "Look what we have here."

Kara started to reach for one of the knives. Hollaway grabbed her hand before she touched it. "Don't touch. We're going to want to print these."

"Frank, this is all just a little too neat, don't you think?"

"What do you mean?"

"I mean, Taylor is arrested for the murder of Lannie Love, and we go to search his apartment, and this stuff is just lying around here like somebody put it here for us to find."

"This guy was one of our suspects in the Sheila Worthy murder, Kara. He was on the N.S. Meyer list. Now we've got him with a missing U.S. insignia, and we've got what looks like a goddamned collection of knives, and you're saying this stuff was planted? Come on."

"It's too convenient, Frank. You think if he killed

either one of those women, he'd keep a bunch of knives in his house? That's pretty dumb, isn't it? He's a smart guy, Frank. Randy Taylor is General Beckwith's aide. He had to beat out thirty other candidates for the job. You don't get to be a general's aide because you're a fuck-up."

"I've seen smarter people do dumber stuff, believe me."

"Maybe. But this is beginning to smell to me, big-time."

Hollaway unfolded a handkerchief and carefully picked up the knives, putting them in the zippered bag. He grabbed the Class A uniform jacket and walked back into the living room.

"I'm taking this stuff over to the lab. I'm going to send the fingerprint guys over here, see if we can't get Sheila's prints off some of this stuff. They dated, remember?"

"Yeah."

"You don't sound too enthused, Kara."

"I'm not real sure about this, Frank. I didn't tell you what I found when I had a look around Lannie's room. You know what was in there, Frank? Not one but two ice buckets."

"So?"

"Randy said he was carrying the ice bucket from his room when he went down to Lannie's room."

"What are you saying, Kara?"

"I'm saying he wasn't lying, Frank. He had an ice bucket with him, and he was carrying it when he went into her room, and it's still in her room. I'm going to call up there and get the D.C. forensics guys to print both of those buckets."

"Maybe he used the ice bucket as a ruse to get in."

"He didn't *need* a ruse, remember, Frank? She left a message for him to come down to her room."

"What's the matter with you, Kara? Here we've got a guy practically caught in the act of killing your best friend, and now we have a look through his belongings, and we find evidence tying him to the murder of Sheila

Worthy, and suddenly you're *believing* this fucking killer?"

"I'm just saying some of this stuff isn't adding up for me, Frank."

"Well, it's adding up for me, and I'm going in to see Lambert this afternoon, and I'm going to recommend that we charge Taylor with Sheila's murder. Are you with me on this or what?"

"Why don't you get that lab work done first, Frank? What if somebody else's prints are on those knives? We ought to have all our ducks lined up before we charge him with Sheila's murder."

"All right. But in the meantime I'm going to question Taylor about this stuff, and I'm going to notify Lambert that we've found additional evidence in Taylor's apartment that implicates him in Sheila's murder. I've got to keep her informed, Kara. Even you know that."

"Okay, Frank."

They turned off the lights and walked outside. In the Cherokee, she let the engine warm up for a moment before she pulled out of Randy's parking space.

Beckwith.

The D.C. forensics lab called just before she left the office for the day. They dusted both of the ice buckets in Lannie's room. The one on the desk had a full set of Randy's prints and one partial print, unidentified. They had searched the room registered to Randy the morning after his arrest. Just as she thought, the ice bucket was missing from his room. It was dark when she left the office and drove straight out Jackson Boulevard.

The Fort Benning stockade was in the middle of a field surrounded by razor-wire fence. At night, huge kleig lights lit up the grounds like a stadium. Inside, even after nine at night, when most of the inmates were locked down, Kara couldn't get over the noise. Clanging, crashing, banging, slamming, screaming . . . it was a wonder so many criminals were repeat offenders. You'd think they'd go straight just so they wouldn't have to put up with the noise of being put back behind bars.

They had Randy in isolation. His thick steel door had a viewing slot at eye level and a meal slot below. An MP guard unlocked the door, and Kara walked into a ten-by-ten cell with a narrow cot and a stainless steel sink and toilet. Randy stood up.

"What are you doing here?"

"I want to help you, Randy."

"Yeah. Sure. I heard all about the help you're giving me today. Hollaway was in here questioning me. You're going to charge me with Sheila's murder too, aren't you?"

"Not me. I'm not going to charge you."

"What?"

"I think you're innocent, Randy. I think Beckwith set you up. I think he killed Sheila, and I think he killed Lannie, and he framed you for both murders. I want to defend you, if you'll have me as your lawyer."

Randy collapsed on the cot. "Kara! You believe me!"

"To tell you the truth, I didn't know what to think at first. But this stuff is falling into place a little too neatly for me. I think Beckwith's behind this whole thing, and I'm going to get him, Randy. The best way for me to do that under these circumstances is for me to defend you."

"What do I have to do?"

"I don't want you to say anything to me or anybody else right now. Tomorrow morning, you put in a request to have me as your defense attorney, and I'll put in my papers to defend you, but there's always the chance they'll deny it. In that case I don't need to hear anything from you that would give them an opportunity to call me as a witness against you."

"Do you think this will work?"

"I don't know. I've been the prosecutor on Sheila's murder. It would be highly unusual to allow the prose-

cutor to switch over to the defense on a case, let's put it
that way. But I'll do my best."

"I don't know what to say. This has been so
incredible—"

Kara stopped him before he went on. "Listen to me.
You sit tight. If Hollaway or anyone else comes in here
to question you, don't breathe a word. Don't even talk
to the other inmates. One of them might be a plant."

"I'll be careful."

They shook hands. "I haven't told anyone I've been
here to see you, and I got a guard I know to let me in
without signing in. So don't tell anyone you've talked
to me."

"I won't."

"Keep your chin up."

There was a message on the machine when she got
home.

It was Mace. "Hi . . . uh, I wanted to tell you I've
moved out of the barracks, and I'm living with another
Sergeant downtown in an apartment. I, uh, would like
to, uh, talk to you." He left the number. Quickly she
picked up the phone and dialed.

Mace answered, "Sergeant Nukanen, sir."

Awkwardly: "Mace, it's me."

"Hi. How are you doing?"

"Fine . . . uh, Mace, I wanted to apologize for—"

He interrupted, "No, wait, I'm the one who's sorry. I
never should have walked out on you in New Orleans
like that. I've been thinking about it ever since. I'm
really sorry."

There was a long pause as she savored his words. "I
shouldn't have let you go. I was so stupid. I've been
thinking about it too, every minute of every day. I miss
you so much, Mace. You don't know how much."

"Yes, I do. I miss you too."

"I want to see you."

"I don't think that's such a good idea, Kara. There's

too much going on. I saw in the paper you're on that murder case. If anybody finds out . . ."

Disappointed: "You're right. Of course you're right."

"I just wanted to talk to you, is all, to tell you how much—"

"I know. I feel the same way. Can I call you again?" She hoped her voice didn't sound as pleading to him as it did to her.

He hesitated. "My roommate's out in the field, but he gets back in the morning. I don't want him to know what's going on. I don't think it's such a good idea. Why don't you let me call you?"

"I understand."

"Maybe tomorrow night. Will you be around?"

"Of course. Mace, I'm so sorry. You were right—"

He interrupted: "I've got to go. I've got stuff to get ready for the morning."

"Me too. Thanks for calling, Mace."

"Bye."

She cradled the receiver against her shoulder for a moment before she hung up. There were so many things she wanted to say to him. Why couldn't she just get them *out*? She felt frustrated, not being able to pick up the phone and listen to his voice. And angry. The Army's obsession with fraternization rules were compounded by the situation with Beckwith. She wished that it would somehow go away, but she knew it wouldn't.

She fixed a cup of weak instant coffee and sat down at the laptop and started typing out her request to represent Randy. Just like her relationship with Mace, it was a long shot, but she had to try.

Subject: Change of Representation
    To: Lieutenant Colonel Lambert
        Staff Judge Advocate

The next morning she called Lieutenant Colonel Lambert from the car. When she got to the office, Lambert was sitting primly behind her desk as usual. Kara walked in and reported. She handed the request to Lambert, who scanned it quickly.

"This is an outrage, Major. I'm not going to allow it."

"Colonel, I can't prosecute a man I believe to be innocent."

"Well, you're going to have to do it. You were assigned to the Sheila Worthy case right from the start, and we're charging Captain Taylor with her homicide as well as the murder of Captain Love, and when this case goes to trial, you're going to be right there at the prosecution table."

"Ma'am, I don't believe Captain Taylor killed those women. Not for a minute."

"That's really beside the point, isn't it, Major? You're a JAG officer. Sometimes you defend them, and sometimes you prosecute them. That's the nature of the job when you're a lawyer in the Army."

"Yes, ma'am. I understand that. But I have developed evidence that someone else committed the murder of Sheila Worthy, and most likely committed the Lannie Love murder as well."

"Why haven't you revealed this evidence to me? Or to Major Hollaway?"

"I have told you about my doubts regarding this case, ma'am. Only a week or so ago, you were urging me to present evidence to a posthumous hearing on Lieutenant Parks, and I told you I was insufficiently convinced of his guilt. Now I have new evidence which I withheld because I came to believe Captain Taylor is innocent, and if I revealed it to you or Major Hollaway, I would be giving away the defense case."

"Only if you are the defense attorney, Major."

"Yes, ma'am."

"If you're the prosecutor, and you have exculpatory evidence, you would have to give it to the defense anyway."

"Yes, ma'am. I understand that. But the defense is under no obligation whatsoever to reveal its case to the prosecution, and for the last two or three days I have felt that Captain Taylor is innocent, and started looking toward becoming his attorney."

"But on the other hand, Major, you have knowledge of the prosecution's evidence in the Sheila Worthy matter. You have a conflict there as well, don't you? Maybe the best solution is, we'll take you off both cases and assign a defense attorney to Captain Taylor and a new counsel for the prosecution as well."

"Ma'am, I don't believe there's a conflict. Under the UCMJ, the prosecution is obligated to reveal to the defense all of the evidence it has gathered and will present in court. The defense is entitled to know the entire prosecution case before trial. So right now I don't know anything that I wouldn't by law find out anyway when we go into discovery."

Colonel Lambert pressed her hands together as if in prayer. "You're right about the prosecution revealing its case. I should have remembered that."

"Ma'am, there isn't a conflict here, and I want to defend Captain Taylor. Under the UCMJ, he is entitled to the military attorney of his choice, if that JAG officer is reasonably available. I'm here, and I want the job, and I'm ready to defend him."

Lambert gazed out her window for a long moment, then turned to face Kara. "This is an extraordinary request you are making. I do not believe I have the authority at this level to approve or disapprove it."

"But you do, ma'am. You're the staff judge advocate. It's part of your job."

"Major, with what's going on here at Fort Benning, I'm not going to touch this thing with a ten-foot pole. I'm going to forward your request up the chain of command. It will take a higher authority than me to make a decision on this matter."

Kara saluted and left. Yeah, it'll take a higher authority, all right.

Beckwith.

The message came much sooner than she expected. It was around 1600 when Specialist Lester knocked on the door and handed her a slip of paper. It was an order to report to General Beckwith's office immediately.

Third Army Headquarters wasn't far, so she walked. By the time she got there, a very nervous major was waiting at the door for her.

"Where have you been, Major Guidry?"

"I got the order five minutes ago."

"The General is ready."

"Good. So am I."

She was escorted to the door of the General's office and the door was open, so she walked in and reported.

"Close the door, Major," said Beckwith.

She closed the door and walked back to his desk. He held up her written request in one hand and shook it violently.

"What the fuck do you think you're doing?"

Kara's jaw was tense, and her words, when they came, practically vibrated with anger. "Don't you *dare* talk to me in that manner, General."

He smiled. "Now I've got you on insubordination too. I'm finished playing games with you, Guidry. I'm going to charge you with fraternization, insubordination, and dereliction of duty."

"You're not going to charge me with anything, General Beckwith. You've got my request. Either you approve my request to defend Captain Taylor and sign it right now, or I'm going to walk out of this office and pick up the phone and call the *New York Times* and CBS and CNN and the rest of the network news programs, and I'm going to hold a press conference right out there on your helicopter pad, and I'm going to tell them everything I know about you and Sheila Worthy and

Lannie Fulton Love. When I'm finished with you, there won't be a senator left who will vote to confirm your appointment to be chief of staff."

Beckwith stared at her for a long moment. "You're bluffing."

Kara practically spat the words at him. "Take your best shot, General. We'll see who wins this little war in the court of public opinion."

Beckwith's voice sounded a note of quiet anger. "You think you've got this all wrapped up, don't you? You think you're going to waltz in here and threaten me, and I'm going to sit here and take it. I guess you've forgotten who you're dealing with, Major."

"I haven't forgotten, sir. You told me in a motel near West Point fifteen years ago that you wanted chief of staff. I know *exactly* who I'm dealing with."

Beckwith studied her. "I'm going to deny your request, Guidry." He reached for his pen.

Kara struggled to keep her voice steady, to keep the depth of her anger far below the surface. "Lannie was deeply, incredibly in love with you. I found that hard to accept, but she loved you, and after she died, I swore that I would respect her memory. But you know what, General Beckwith? If you deny my request, her name and reputation will go right into the mud along with yours."

"You'd do that to your friend?"

"My friend, sir, is dead."

Beckwith blinked once, twice. His face reddened as he scrawled his signature and threw her request on the floor. She picked it up.

Approved.

Chapter Thirty-three

The commo shack was tucked away behind an old warehouse on a rail spur that ran along the western edge of the post. Kara knew the technology scrambling the secure lines on the post was classified as a national security secret. Still, Sheila Worthy had made two cell phone calls the night she was killed, and they had been patched through the secure switchboard at the commo shack. Now that they had charged Randy with Sheila's murder as well as Lannie's, the calls she had made took on an added significance. She had to give it a shot.

The evidence against Randy in Lannie's murder was nearly overwhelming. Even under the best of circumstances it would be nearly impossible to overcome. But the Army had made a potentially fatal error in linking the murders, ordering a court-martial of both charges at once. If she could show that Randy didn't murder Sheila Worthy, then the case she would put on challenging the evidence in Lannie's murder would be that much more compelling and believable.

It was obvious that the last call Sheila made on her cell phone the night of her murder had been to someone other than Randy, because he didn't have access to a secure telephone. So who had she called?

Kara was convinced she had called Beckwith, but proving it was going to be difficult. She pulled up outside the commo shack and found the door locked. She knocked hard, twice. The door opened halfway. A grizzled old sergeant with the name Crowell on his chest peered from the door. He was holding a cup of coffee.

"Mornin', ma'am. Something I can help you with?"

"Sergeant Crowell?"

"Yes, ma'am."

"I am Major Guidry. I'm a JAG officer. May I come in?"

The sergeant looked momentarily confused, but he stepped aside and opened the door wider. "Yes, ma'am. I don't know what commo's got to do with the JAG corps, but you're welcome."

"Thank you." She walked inside. It was a large room crammed with communications gear. There was row after row of metal shelving holding what looked like switching equipment. Along one wall was a very sophisticated radio console, and next to it, a telephone console. A spec-4 wearing a headset was sitting at the console.

"I've got a problem, Sergeant Crowell. There was a murder awhile back here at Benning. Maybe you read about it."

"Yes, ma'am. Lieutenant. Female."

"Right. I'm defending the man they accused of killing her."

"I don't envy you that job, ma'am. Not many court-martials I heard of end up in the guy gettin' off."

"You are right about that, Sergeant." She reached in her purse. "Let me see . . . on the night she died, she made two cellular telephone calls . . ."

"We don't have nothin' to do with cellular here, ma'am. That's downtown."

"I understand that, Sergeant. Let me finish."

"Sorry, ma'am."

She unfolded Sheila's phone bill. "The calls she made were to the secure switch. I've been told the secure switchboard is here in the commo shack. Is that correct?"

"Yes, ma'am. Comes in right over there." He pointed at the console where the spec-4 sat. "But that's classified, ma'am. I can't get into that without orders."

"I'm not asking you to, Sergeant. What I want to know is, when a call comes into the secure switch, where does it go?"

"It goes out on regular lines, but it's scrambled, ma'am. You got to have a secure phone to receive one of those calls."

"Right. And that technology is classified."

"Yes, ma'am. Top secret."

"When you get a call into the secure switchboard, is a log kept?"

"No, ma'am."

"So there's no record kept at all of where those calls might have gone."

"No, ma'am."

She handed the phone bill to the sergeant. "Look at these calls, Sergeant. It looks to me like she called once, and there was no answer. So she called again."

"Might be. No way of telling."

"Let's say I'm right. She called once and there was no answer. She calls again. Let's say she was calling the same person. Where might that second call go, Sergeant? If you were just guessing, I mean?"

The sergeant thought for a moment. "We get calls in here from the Pentagon. They call on the secure lines all the time. Sometimes we patch them through, and the party is out of the office. They might be in their vehicle, or in the field. So we pick up the call and put it through on their radio."

Of course! Beckwith had been in his staff car!

"Let me ask you this, Sergeant. A call made through this switchboard that's patched through to a radio, that would be in the clear, right?"

"Not necessarily, ma'am. They've got scrambled radios in their command vehicles."

"That would be in their combat command vehicles?"

"Yes, ma'am. Command helicopters got 'em. Some of the Humvees got 'em. There's quite a few of 'em around."

"I'll bet they've got scramblers in staff cars too," she said, fishing.

"Yes, ma'am."

Kara folded the cell phone bill and stuck it in her purse. "Thank you, Sergeant, you've been very helpful."

"Anything else I can do, ma'am?"

She stopped at the door. "One other thing, Sergeant. Staff cars here on post, like commanders' staff cars, they've all got radios, right?"

"That's right, ma'am."

"Do they have cellular phones too?"

The sergeant thought for a moment. "I know some of them do. The Generals' staff cars, they're completely outfitted—radios, cellular, the whole bit."

"Thank you again, Sergeant."

"No problem, ma'am."

She found Randy pacing when they opened his cell door.

Eagerly: "What happened?"

"I got it. I'm defending you."

"That's great! How'd you do it?"

"Let's just say your boss and I came to a meeting of the minds."

"He tried to stop you."

"And then he thought better of it."

Randy sat down on one end of the bunk. Kara sat on the other.

"I tried to get you released into house arrest, Randy. Beckwith's not going to allow it."

"Even Lieutenant Calley wasn't locked up during his trial."

"All they charged him with was killing a couple hundred Vietnamese. With you it's different. You killed not one but two of the General's mistresses."

"But I didn't do it!"

"Just joking, Randy."

"Sorry. I guess I'm a little tense."

"You've got a right to be." She opened her briefcase on the bunk between them. "We've got some stuff to go over. Let's talk about the night of Lannie's murder. You said when you got to the room, you found her on the bed, and there was a knife sticking out of her neck and you pulled it out."

"Yes."

"That means they're going to have your prints on the knife. There was a lot of blood. Did any of it get on you?"

"Lots. They took about thirty pictures of me, from every angle."

"Christ."

"It's bad, isn't it?"

"It could be worse. They could have caught you in the act of sticking the knife in her."

"But—"

She held up her hand. "Stop. I know you didn't do it. Beckwith killed her. I just know it."

"Kara, I'm frightened."

"Look, Randy, I've got to know if there was anyone who could have seen you in the hall or on the stairs that night. Did anyone see you, like, in the elevator, or in the hall at that time?"

Randy looked away for a long moment.

"Randy, talk to me."

"My lover saw me."

"Great! What's her name?"

"His name. I'm gay, Kara."

As Kara looked up, she was thinking, *of course.*

"Okay, what's his name?"

"Ed Teese."

"He's the general you were sitting with in New Orleans!"

"Yes."

"You were staying with him at the hotel?"

"No. Each of us had a room, but he was with me in my room that night."

She made a note. "Randy, why didn't you tell me this before? You have an alibi."

"I was scared. Kara, I'm *gay*. You know what that means in the Army."

"Look, Randy, Lannie was dead when you got to her. That means she was killed sometime before you arrived. What time did you say it was when you picked up her message?"

"Three-fifteen. I remember looking at the clock radio next to the bed."

"So you got to her room at, say, 3:16, 3:17."

"It couldn't have been any later. I had to go down only one floor."

"That confirms your alibi. You were in your room with General Teese, and you called the message desk. So we've got the hotel operator who gave you the message, and we've got General Teese, who can testify as to your whereabouts at the time of death—"

"He can't do that. I won't ask him to."

Kara looked at him, incredulous. "Randy, this is serious. You're being charged with capital murder. You could get life in Leavenworth without parole. You've got an alibi, and you have *got* to use it. We can probably get the charge that you killed Lannie dismissed with General Teese's testimony. In the United States Army there is no more credible witness than a general. That court-martial will believe him in a heartbeat."

"Not when they find out he's gay, and we are lovers, they won't. They'll put me away for life, and they'll court-martial him to boot. It will mean two of us end up in Leavenworth instead of one."

"That seems like a chance he would be glad to take, to ensure his lover doesn't go to jail for the rest of his life."

"Kara, you don't understand. You don't know what it is to be a gay man in this Army. You think 'Don't ask, Don't tell' is going to save anybody? They're purging gay men and women right and left! The prejudice against gay people in the Army is incredible, and it's not going away. If you think they're going to empanel a court-martial of senior officers who will put aside their prejudices and listen to a gay general stand up and give an alibi for a gay captain, you are out of your mind."

"I guess I didn't think of it that way."

"How could you have? It's not your experience talking here. It's mine."

"Randy, I still think it's worth trying. Why don't I talk to General Teese and see what he thinks?"

"I won't allow it."

"Why not?"

"It doesn't make any sense. If you try to get him to testify and give me an alibi, it will backfire. The members of that court-martial will go in that jury room, and they'll figure I'm a faggot and I hate women, and that's why I killed them. It would be the worst thing you could do, putting Ed on the stand. Believe me. I know. So does Ed. He'd tell you the same thing."

"Randy, I still think I should talk to him."

"Okay, talk to him. But it's my life that's on the line, and if I say he doesn't testify, he doesn't testify. Deal?"

"Deal."

"All we've got to prove is, I didn't do it."

"We don't have to prove a thing, Randy. They have to prove you did it. But the way things look right now, they're not going to have a very hard time."

"I know. It looks bad, doesn't it?"

"I'm going to be honest with you. It doesn't look good." She flipped through her notes. "Oh. One thing. I found out Sheila made two cell phone calls just before she was murdered. She called the secure switch."

"She was calling Beckwith. That was the way they got in touch."

"*I knew it!*"

"But you can't prove it. That's why they used the secure line."

"Yeah. I was going to ask you. Is the radio in his staff car scrambled?"

"Yes. They talked that way all the time."

"So they might have patched her call through to his staff car radio."

"That might have happened."

"But he's got a cell phone in his car too, doesn't he?"

"Yes, of course."

"So her call could have been patched through to his cell phone as well?"

"It could have."

"That means the last call Sheila made before she died was to the man who killed her. We can't prove it yet, but that's what happened."

"What good does that do us?"

"I don't know right now. I've got to think about it."

He looked away, lost in thought.

Kara touched his hand. "You really love him, don't you? General Teese?"

"Yes, I do."

"I wish there was some way—"

"There isn't. Don't you think I've racked my brain about this? Don't you think if I knew we could use my alibi and it would work, I'd have gotten Ed to talk to you and Hollaway back in Washington?"

"Yeah."

"I don't want to beat a drum or anything, but I've got to tell you, Kara, if it's hard being a gay man in America, it's impossible being a gay man in the Army. You are damned if you do and damned if you don't. If you admit you're gay, they throw you out for being gay.

If you conceal the fact and they catch you, they throw you out for lying. It's hell on earth, is what it is, Kara."

"So why did you go to West Point in the first place? Why be an officer if it's so terrible?"

"I could ask the same question of you."

Kara chuckled softly. "Yes, indeed you could."

Chapter Thirty-four

Dahlia King was dicing onions, and the General was sitting at the counter with a cup of tea. Outside, the wind had kicked up, flapping the awnings on the kitchen windows.

"Everybody's talking about Bill Beckwith's speech at the AUSA convention, Bernie."

"I never heard such a load of crap in my life."

"He was a big hit. I heard Senator Maldray telling one of his aides to get him a copy of the speech."

"Maldray's already made it clear he's backing Beckwith. I wrote him off weeks ago."

"Is there anything you can do to counter it?"

"I've got an op-ed piece coming out in the *Washington Post* next week. I compared corporate downsizing to what's going on in the armed services. Everyone is giving short shrift to the human element in this thing. Large corporations like AT&T and institutions like the Army really aren't that different. In both cases we ask these people to dedicate their lives to the organization, and then we come along ten, fifteen, sometimes twenty years later, and tell them thanks a lot but no thanks and they're on the street."

"And what did you come up with?"

"The problem we've got is, we're asking soldiers right from the start to look forward to retirement at twenty years with half pay, when in fact we know many of them will never get that far. We're cheating them out of their dreams. I'm suggesting voluntary retirement at an earlier time would yield one sliding scale of retirement benefits, and mandatory retirement in a downsizing would yield still another scale of benefits. I think if we give some of these younger people a chance to opt out at, say, fifteen years with benefits, we won't have to RIF so many of them."

"That sounds like a good idea to me."

"Yeah, but it's going to be a political hot potato. The problem is, we'd have to increase expenditures in the near term to pay for it, even though it would save us money over the long term. That would mean the money would have to come from somewhere, and the logical place is to cut the Reserves and the National Guard, and those congressmen and senators with all those Reservists and National Guards in their states aren't going to stand for it."

"Those bastards on Capitol Hill are so shortsighted."

"Like moles."

She laughed.

"That smells good. What are you cooking for lunch?"

"I found some blue crabs this afternoon. I'm making gumbo."

"Man, that's going to hit the spot on a cold winter day like this."

"That's what I know."

"I'll tell you what the deal is in the Army. We're in a people business. That's all we've got out there is people. We don't make a product. We don't yield a profit. All those tanks and helicopters and weapons systems exist solely to support our people. It's easy to lose sight of that, sitting up there in the Pentagon, surrounded by paperwork, looking across the Potomac at the ebb and flow of politics in Washington. That's the thing that gets me about Beckwith's speech. Hell, I'd call the President myself and recommend him for chief if I thought he believed even a word of it. But the only thing that cunning son of a bitch believes in is his own career."

* * *

Kara slammed down the phone. Detective Fogel from the Chicago PD had called back and told her they had located Patti O'Brien's place of work. It was a chain record store on Broadway called the CD Shak, but the place was closed for renovations. All the employees had been given vacation time, and Patti O'Brien was nowhere to be found.

Kara called the 800 information operator and got a listing for CD Shak, Incorporated, in Minneapolis. The people there didn't have a list of employees of CD Shak franchises, but they did have the name of the store manager in Chicago, a Jeff Klein, who they said would know the home addresses of all his employees, but he was on vacation too. Kara talked her way through the bureaucracy at CD Shak, Inc, and ended up on the phone with the corporate president. She said Jeff Klein had taken his motor home and was driving through the Mississippi Delta, going to blues clubs and juke joints. Most of the places he was going didn't even have phones, so there was no way to leave a message for him. Then she thought of a record store in Clarksdale, called Stackpole Records, where Klein was bound to stop. Kara left an urgent message with the CD Shak president for Jeff Klein to call her, then called Stackpole Records and left a message for him there too. It was vital that she locate Patti O'Brien. She was positive O'Brien would provide information about her roommate that would implicate Beckwith in her murder.

Major Frank Hollaway and Major Howard Sanders were waiting for her in the conference room. She walked in and put her briefcase down and shook hands. Sanders had a confident grin on his face.

"So we go to war again, Kara. I'm going to get you this time. I've learned your little tricks."

"Different case, Howard. New client. New little tricks."

"We'll see."

"So we will. Let's get down to business, gentlemen. What have you got?"

Hollaway pushed a single sheet of paper across the table. Kara scanned it and looked up.

"You must be kidding."

"We've got him, Kara. He's going away."

"Look, Frank, I was there in his apartment with you when we found the knives and the gold insignia. Where in the hell did these photos come from?"

"We went back and took another pass at his apartment. They were in the pocket in one of his jackets in the closet."

"I need to see them."

Hollaway pushed a manila envelope across the table. Kara removed a small packet of photos from the envelope and studied them.

"Frank, this thing is a frame that fits my guy to a T. I can't believe you don't see how he's being set up."

"Really? By whom? And when? And for what reason?"

"Jesus, Frank. This is pathetic."

"We've got motive. We've got means. We've got opportunity. We've got him."

"You're getting led down a path here, boys. I'm very surprised. I thought you were smarter than that."

"How about your witness list? Have you got it?"

She reached into her briefcase and pulled out a sheet of paper. "Here you go."

They read the list. Sanders looked up. "What's this? What is General Beckwith doing here?"

"Character witness, Howard. I'm sure you've heard of them."

Sanders gave a little chuckle. "No way the General's going to appear as a character witness for a murderer. No way in hell."

"Then I'll have you subpoena him, Howard, if that's what it takes."

Sanders leaned back in his chair, lacing his hands

behind his head. "You think you're going to get me to issue a subpoena to General Beckwith? Never happen."

"Then I'll go over your head, Howard. Rule 703 of the UCMJ provides that both sides in a court-martial will have equal opportunity to obtain witnesses. I'll go to Forces Command, if I have to, and get the commanding general to *order* Beckwith to appear."

"Why are you so insistent on calling Beckwith?"

"Beckwith wrote Randy's OER, Howard. Have you seen it? Reads like a recommendation for canonization from the Vatican. He gave him a hundred. Twice."

"So? That was before Taylor was charged with two murders."

"You haven't proven my client is a murderer, gentlemen. All you've got is an allegation and a skinny little packet of evidence. Until such a time as your case is proven beyond a reasonable doubt, and judgment is rendered by seven officers on a court-martial that Captain Taylor is guilty as charged, he is entitled to be considered innocent, and he will be if I have anything to say about it. As his defense counsel, I *do* have something to say about it. General Beckwith *will* appear as a defense character witness, if I have to go all the way to the Court of Military Appeals to see to it that he does." She stood up. "Good day, gentlemen."

Randy was eating his supper when they unlocked his isolation cell and let her in. The evening meal consisted of a fried hamburger patty, a slice of rye bread, and an orange, each sitting in a separate compartment on a plastic mess tray. They had given him a plastic spoon, but it broke when he tried to cut the tough hamburger patty, so he was eating with his fingers.

"I'll bring you something from home, next time I come," said Kara.

"Please do. The food's pretty terrible."

"I'm sorry you have to go through this, Randy. I know it's hard on you."

"Like you can't even believe."

"Randy, I went to the discovery meeting today. They gave me their witness list and their evidence summary." She handed it to him. He looked up, wide-eyed.

"I can't believe this! They're saying one of my gold U.S. insignia is missing? It's not! I've got both of them! I can prove it!"

"I know."

"And these photos! I never had any photos of Sheila or Lannie in my house! I don't even have a picture of Ed! And the knives? Where did they come from? The only knives I own are in my kitchen drawer!"

"Randy, I know that. Somebody planted the photos and knives. And somebody removed one of your gold U.S. insignia. We've got to figure out who could have done it."

"I don't believe this, Kara. Who set me up?"

"Beckwith. He killed Sheila, and he killed Lannie. He must have gotten someone to break into your apartment and plant the evidence. I want you to think hard about this. At any time over the past several weeks, do you recall coming home and finding anything out of place? Or noticing any signs of a break-in?"

"No."

"Maybe I should get somebody to go over there and dust the windows for prints. They could have jimmied open a window and climbed in."

"I'd know if anyone broke in my place, and no one has. I'm positive."

"Maybe it was someone else. Who's been in your apartment lately?"

"Well, for starters, you have. Ed came down a few weeks ago on Army business in Atlanta and stayed over. And Mrs. Beckwith. We were at my apartment doing invitations for the party together. I've got a maid who comes every Wednesday at seven. I let her in, but she lets herself out when she's through. I'd trust her with my life. I'm sure she didn't do it."

"Any delivery people or repairmen?"

"No." He thought for a moment. "Wait. My fax. A guy had to come from the phone company to put in a new line for my fax. That was, like, a week ago or so."

She made a note. "Anybody else? Think, Randy. This is important."

"No. Nobody else."

"One other thing. When I questioned you before, you said you were at home the night Sheila was killed."

"After the O-Club thing, yes."

"I'm going to see if I can't establish an alibi, see if someone in your complex didn't see you coming home. We've got time-of-death span to play with, and if we can put you in your apartment during that period, we can beat the charge on Sheila right there."

"Do you know what the charge is yet? I mean, the formal charge?"

"Yes."

"So tell me. What is it?"

She took a deep breath. "On Lannie, they're going for the big one. Violation of Article 118, sub-1. Premeditated murder. In civilian law they'd call it murder in the first degree. It carries the death penalty, Randy. I feel like I've got to tell you what you're facing."

"Where are they holding the court-martial?"

"In that little building over by the football stadium."

"That's where they tried Lieutenant Calley."

"Yeah. It's all set up for media. They're expecting big coverage. It was all over the Atlanta papers, on the national network news, the whole nine yards. Beckwith wants all the coverage he can get. He's going to play this like he's defending the lives of women in the Army by taking you off the streets. He's going to turn you into the Rusty Calley of the nineties."

"I saw Calley downtown one day, coming out of a diner. He looks like Audie Murphy gone to seed."

She chuckled. "That baby face of his is half of what saved him. The other half was Nixon, of course. He wasn't going to let any red-blooded American boy who just went out there and followed orders and killed those gooks do any hard time. They gave him house arrest, remember? I don't think that guy ever spent an hour behind bars. Nixon saved him."

"Who's going to save me, Kara?"

She clicked her briefcase shut.

"Me. I'm going to save you."

Chapter Thirty-five

Major Sanders had just raised his right hand in salute when General Beckwith boiled out of his chair and thrust his face into Sanders' ear, screaming: "What in hell do you think you're trying to do to me, Sanders? Stop my fucking career in its tracks right here, right now, with this shit?"

Sanders' eyes were straight to the front. He could feel the General's breath on his neck, but he couldn't see him. "No, sir."

Beckwith waved a piece of paper. "Then what in the fuck is this?"

"Sir, it is a request that you appear as a witness for the defense in the trial of Captain Randolph Taylor."

"I can read the fucking thing, goddammit! I want to know what the fuck it's doing on my desk!"

"Sir, when a defense counsel makes a witness request through the prosecutor, under the UCMJ, I am bound by the law to forward the request to the witness."

"You know what this is, Sanders? This is a fucking outrage, is what it is!"

"Yes, sir."

"Take this fucking piece of paper and shove it up Guidry's ass! Do you hear me?"

Sanders hesitated. "Sir, we can't do that."

"What in the hell do you mean? You'll do any god-damned thing I tell you to do."

"Sir, Rule 703 stipulates that the defense and the prosecution will have equal access to witnesses."

"I don't give a fuck about any Rule 703, goddammit!"

Sanders half turned to face the General. "Sir, if you ignore or refuse this request for your appearance, defense counsel can apply through me for a subpoena, compelling your testimony. Major Guidry has already made clear to me that she will demand such a subpoena if you refuse to testify."

"You mean to tell me that bitch can force me to appear before this court-martial?"

Sanders cleared his throat. "Yes, sir. It's the law, sir."

Beckwith walked slowly around his desk and sat down. "Do you have any idea how incredible this is?"

"Yes, sir."

"The President is making his selection for chief of staff in two weeks. I expect to be selected. But if I'm dragged into that court-martial and made a fool of by Guidry, my stock's going to go down precipitously in Washington. Understood?"

"Yes, sir."

"What is this crap about character witness, anyway?"

"She made reference to the OER's you wrote on Captain Taylor, sir. I'm sure she's going to present them as evidence and make you go over every praiseworthy thing you had to say about Captain Taylor."

"I wrote the last one of those OER's months ago. How was I supposed to know my aide was a murderer?"

"I pointed that out to her, sir."

"What do you think she's up to, Sanders?"

"I believe she thinks if she can force your testimony as to Taylor's good character on the OER's, she can draw attention away from the case we're presenting, sir."

"You've got Taylor cold on these murders, don't you?"

"Yes, sir. We have more than enough evidence to convict."

"Then her motive is to embarrass me. It's plain as the goddamn nose on your face."

"If she thinks calling you as a witness will embarrass you, sir, she has made a big mistake. The jury will take that strategy as an insult to this command and to the United States Army, and they will act accordingly."

"All the more reason I shouldn't testify. If you've got enough evidence to hang the sorry son of a bitch, why should I be put through this wringer?"

"I agree completely, sir. I wish there was something we could do."

"Well, goddammit, Sanders, I want you to figure a way out of this."

"That's going to be pretty difficult, sir. She's got the law on her side."

"Well, come up with some roadblocks you can throw in her way. Do something!"

"Sir, I, uh . . . there's something we might do right now. You could delay your response to this request, and we'll wait and see how Guidry reacts. There's a possibility she'll get busy and lose track of the fact that you haven't responded. That will put her in the position of getting a subpoena issued during the trial."

"What does that do for me?"

"The military judge will have heard our case against Taylor by then, and he would very likely listen to a motion to quash the subpoena if he thinks your testimony won't add much to the trial."

"Who's the military judge on this thing, anyway?"

"Colonel Freeman, sir."

"Christ. Freeman. You think we can count on him to go along?"

"I don't know, sir. All we can do is try."

"I want you to do more than *try*, Sanders. I want you to keep me off that witness stand, I don't care what the fuck you have to do. Do you understand where I'm coming from on this?"

"Yes, sir. Completely."

"You're dismissed, Sanders. On your way out, send my chief of staff, Colonel Roberts, in here."

Sanders saluted. "Yes, sir."

Beckwith swiveled his chair, looking out over the parade field. Colonel Roberts walked up to the desk and cleared his throat.

"You wanted to see me, sir?"

The General turned around. "Guidry is up to something, Harry, I can smell it. I want you to put a tail on her. I want to know the identity of every person she talks to. I want to know where she goes, and who she sees, and what she does. I want you to wake her up in the morning and put her to bed at night."

"You want me to use that military intelligence team we used before, sir?"

"Yes. We can't have Sanders or Hollaway mixed up in this. They'd be under an obligation to report it to the military judge. And you know who drew the court-martial? Freeman. He'd throw the whole damn case out if he found out about it."

"Yes, sir, he would."

"Get on it, Harry. I want this done, and I want it done right, and I want a report from the field on my desk by close of business every day."

"Yes, sir."

"Dismissed."

There was a message on her machine from the president of CD Shak when Kara got home. Jeffrey Klein had called the home office. He was in Mississippi and would be at Stackpole Records in Clarksdale that night at eight. She checked her watch and dug through her notes in her briefcase and came up with the number and dialed. The man who answered sounded like he was speaking to her from another planet.

"Record shop. How can I help y'all?"

"Is this Walter?"

"Yes, ma'am, it is?"

"My name is Kara Guidry—"

"Y'all's the lawyer down in Georgia, huh?"

"Yes, that's me—"

"How's the weather down there in Georgia?"

"It's pretty cold."

"They got a wind blowin' across this delta like to curl your eyebrows it's so damn cold, I'll tell ya that much. Now, what is it you wanted?"

"I'd like to speak with Jeff Klein, if he's there."

"Gimme a minute. He's right here."

When Klein came on the phone, he sounded nervous.

"Jeff, I'm Major Kara Guidry, and I've been looking for you for days."

"I told the people at the home office I didn't want to talk to you."

"I'm looking for one of your employees, Patti O'Brien, Jeff, that's all. I need to talk to her."

"How do I know you're not just some bill collector, or lawyer trying to serve her with papers?"

"Look, Jeff, Patti isn't in any trouble. I just need to ask her a few questions. If I don't talk to her, the man I represent might be sentenced to death for something he didn't do."

"The death penalty?"

"Yes. My client has been charged with murder. He's innocent, and Patti O'Brien may know something that will help our case. But we'll never know unless we can talk to her. You have *got* to help me, Jeff. A young man's life is at stake."

"Patti has done her best to put the Army and everything it represents behind her. All she has from those years are bad memories."

"I am sure that's true. Listen, Jeff, Patti may be a key link in my case. Something happened when she was stationed at Fort Polk, and I need to ask her about it."

"If I give you her address, you won't tell her where you got it, will you? I know she's going to be really pissed when you show up."

"I'll tell her I used a private detective."

"I don't have a phone number. She doesn't give it out to anybody. But I've got her address."

"That would be a great help, Jeff."

"Okay. She lives in Evanston."

Chapter Thirty-six

She rented a car from Avis at the Chicago airport. The counter man told her if she took Oakton Street, it would take her straight east into Evanston, and she would avoid the rush-hour mess on the freeways. She drove around for a while before she found Oakton, but a half hour later she was on Birch Tree Avenue in Evanston.

The address Klein had given her was an attractive 1920s three-story apartment building, one large apartment per floor, typical of the Chicago area. Up and down the tree-lined street were kids' bikes and wagons in the yards in front of the neat houses and apartments and well-maintained apartment buildings. She pressed the buzzer for O'Brien, and an older woman's voice came over the speaker.

"Who's there, please?"

"Patti O'Brien? I'm looking for Patti O'Brien."

Curtly: "She's not home yet."

"Okay. Thank you. I'll come back later." After the encounter with the voice on the intercom, Kara figured it would be easier if she approached her outside the apartment. There was always the chance if she got behind a locked door in her apartment, she wouldn't agree to be questioned at all.

A bitterly cold wind blew down the east-west street right off the lake, so she waited in the rental car at the curb. About an hour had passed when a young woman came down the street, holding hands with a little girl.

Kara had seen a photo of Lieutenant O'Brien in the file at Fort Knox. It was her, all right. She opened the door and stepped out of the car just as Patti reached the sidewalk leading to the apartment.

"Patti O'Brien?"

She turned, alarmed. "Yes?"

"I'm Major Kara Guidry. I'm a JAG officer down at Fort Benning. I'd like to ask you some questions."

"I don't want to talk to you."

"I'm the attorney for a man on trial for murder—"

Patti glanced over her shoulder at a face in an upstairs window. Her voice was a whisper: "Why don't you go back to Fort Benning and leave me alone? I don't want anything to do with the Army."

"My client didn't commit the crime. He's innocent, Patti. I *really* need to talk to you. It could mean life or death for this young man."

Patti stood there holding her daughter's hand for a long moment before she spoke. "Will you come upstairs? My mother will watch Tisha, and we can have a cup of coffee."

"Thank you. I'd like that."

"What did you say your name was?"

"Kara Guidry."

Patti knelt next to her daughter. "Tisha, this is Kara. She's going to come up and have cookies with us. Do you want a cookie?"

"Yes, Mommy," said the little girl.

Upstairs, Patti introduced Kara to an obviously disapproving mother, who spirited the little girl away to a room in the back of the apartment. They sat down across the kitchen table from each other.

"Good coffee," said Kara.

"It's a habit I picked up in the Army, I guess. I drink coffee all day long."

"Me too."

"What's this about, Major Guidry?"

"Call me Kara. It's about Sheryl Jansen's murder."

Patti took a deep breath. "I thought so. Why does Sherry's murder have anything to do with your client at Fort Benning?"

"Two female lieutenants from Fort Benning have been murdered, Patti. Both of them were stabbed in the neck, just like Lieutenant Jansen."

"Oh, my God."

"I am convinced of my client's innocence. That means somebody else killed those women. I know Jansen's murder is still unsolved. I was wondering if you had any ideas about who might have killed her."

There was a long pause as Patti swirled the coffee in her cup. Finally she looked up. "I don't know who killed Sherry."

"I think you do, Patti."

"What makes you say that?"

"We both know who killed Sheryl Jansen, don't we?"

"I'm telling you the truth. I don't know."

"Jansen was having an affair with Colonel William Beckwith. She had a date to meet him the night she died."

Patti took a deep breath. "No, she didn't."

Kara's voice was steely: "You're lying."

"I'm not." She stood from the table. "Major Guidry, I didn't invite you into my house to be insulted. I'm not in the Army anymore. I don't have to take this from you or anyone else."

Kara hesitated before she spoke. She knew she was close to losing her cooperation. She had to calm down.

"I'm sorry, Patti. I didn't mean that. But how do you know she didn't have a date to see Beckwith that night?"

"Because I did. Sherry and I were supposed to go to the movies, but he called up at the last minute and said his wife had driven down to New Orleans to go shopping. I met him at a motel over across the border in Texas."

Kara sat there staring at the young woman's face in disbelief. "You're covering up for him."

"Major Guidry, I'm telling you the truth."

Kara's frustration boiled over. "Beckwith was having affairs with both of the women killed at Fort Benning! He was doing the same thing at Fort Polk! I just know he was!"

Patti walked over to the pot and calmly refilled her cup. She was still standing when she said: "You met my little girl, Tisha, Major Guidry. She is Bill Beckwith's daughter. He refused to acknowledge paternity and demanded that I get an abortion. When I refused, he flew into a rage and beat me up."

Stunned, Kara said nothing.

"He arranged my discharge to get me out of the way. I came home to Chicago, and Tisha was born. He's never laid eyes on his own daughter. He has never sent me one dime of child support. Do you think I would lie to protect a man like that?"

She knew Patti was telling the truth. "No, I don't."

"I have such guilt about Sherry's murder. I can't tell you the nights I've lain awake thinking, if only I hadn't gone away with him that night. If only I'd gone to the movies with Sherry, the way we planned, she'd be alive today."

"You really have no idea who killed her?"

"None. All I know is, it wasn't Beckwith, because I was with him the whole night."

She heard a door open, and the little girl came running through the kitchen into her mother's arms. "Can I have another cookie, Mommy? Please?"

"Sure, hon." She reached for the cookie jar and held it out so her daughter could take one out herself. "Take one for Grandma, hon." The little girl went running back down the hall with two cookies in her hands. Patti was smiling widely.

"She's a doll," said Kara.

"The joy of my life. She's the only reason I've kept

my sanity. When I got pregnant, I was so mad at myself,
I almost went along with what he wanted and got an
abortion. But at the last minute I thought, Why shouldn't
she live? It's not her fault. Why should I be ashamed of
my own baby? I finally realized I was ashamed of myself, not her."

"She makes you very happy."

"Like you can't even believe."

Kara stood up. "Well, thank you very much, Patti."

"You're not going to mix me up in this thing, are
you?"

"No. I can't see any benefit to my client in that."

"I wasn't much help, was I? You thought Beckwith
did it. I mean, you thought he killed Sherry? And now
you don't know who did it."

"Right."

"I'm sorry, Major Guidry. Really, I am."

"That's okay, Patti. You have been very kind. I know
it's been difficult for you."

They walked to the door. "I hope your case goes
okay, ma'am."

"So do I, Patti. So do I."

There was a late evening flight out of Chicago for
Washington, and on an impulse, she changed her ticket
and got on board. It was more important than ever that
she talk to General Teese and see if there was any way
at all that he could testify for Randy. Her theory of the
case had been shredded by Patti O'Brien's story, but the
idea that Beckwith was somehow behind both killings
was stuck in her mind. As soon as she got back to Fort
Benning, she would have to go over her list of officers
with access to secure phones and see if one of them had
been stationed at Fort Polk at the time of Sheryl
Jansen's murder. Whoever had killed Jansen had killed
Lannie and Sheila too. Maybe there was someone else
who fit the evidenciary profile. There had to be some-

one at Fort Benning who had the means, the motive, and the opportunity to have committed all three murders.

She must have dozed off for a few minutes, exhausted. When she awoke, she was staring straight at the Airfone mounted in the seat back ahead. She unsnapped it from its cradle and swiped her phone card and dialed. Mace answered on the first ring.

"Hi, it's me."

"Where are you?" he asked. "You sound like you're in the next room."

"On a plane."

"Really? Where are you going?"

"Washington. Mace, I know I wasn't supposed to call you, but I've just got to talk to you."

"It's okay. My roommate's out."

"I'm so mad at myself. You were right about Beckwith. I found evidence that Beckwith didn't kill either of those girls. I let my own prejudice blind me. I put my entire case in jeopardy."

"What are you going to do?"

"I don't know. I had predicated my entire approach to defending Randy on the belief that there was another killer, and his name was General Beckwith. Now I know I was wrong, and I'm going to have to start over from the beginning, and I haven't got much time. The court-martial is next week."

"Is there anything I can do to help?"

"I don't want to mix you up in this, Mace. If Beckwith gets wind of it, he'll destroy you."

"Well, if you need me, I'm here."

"Mace, that is so sweet . . ." She paused, collecting herself. "I just wanted you to know . . ." Her voice failed her, and she held the phone tightly to her ear, as if his words would save her. "I feel so stupid."

"You're going to be okay."

"I will, but Randy—"

"He's innocent. You'll find a way."

"It looks bad, Mace. Really bad."

"Kara, you said you'd have to start over. You know, I learned something, it's just a little thing, but maybe it'll help. When you're dealing with troops, sometimes you get a guy, and you're having trouble with him, and nothing works. You try it one way, and you try it another, and you can't get through to him. I've had guys I thought were lost, they'd end up in the stockade, or they'd end up on the street with a bad discharge. Then I learned, if you start all over again, and you let yourself really look at things brand-new, sometimes you find the solution was there all along, and you just couldn't see it. It's like, you get the freedom, you know? To really see."

The captain was on the plane's intercom, announcing the approach into National Airport. She was thinking, How can you not love this man? How could you have let someone like him nearly slip away?

"Sounds like you're about to land," he said.

"Yeah."

"Well, good luck."

"Mace, I—I love you. Thank you."

There was a long pause, and then he said, "I love you too, Kara. Everything's going to be okay. You'll see."

She called General Teese from the airport, and he gave her directions to his apartment. By the time she got off the elevator at his floor, it was almost midnight. He opened the door dressed casually in jeans and an Army sweatshirt.

"I thought I'd be hearing from you, Major. Come in. How is Randy?" He poured her a glass of wine, and they sat on a sofa overlooking the city through a wide picture window.

"He's holding up, General. It's tough. They've got him in isolation."

"It's that son of a bitch Beckwith. He's playing Randy's case all over the Washington press. He thinks a conviction will wrap up chief of staff for him, and he's probably right."

"He's been a problem, all right." She waited a moment, studying him. "General, Randy told me about you."

"So I figured."

"He was with you when Lannie was murdered. You're his alibi."

General Teese got up and refilled his glass. His back was to her when he said: "You want me to testify."

"Randy is against it. The prosecution will cross-examine you, and you'll be under oath, and if they ask, you'll have to admit that you and Randy are lovers. Randy feels the jury will discount your testimony as one gay man covering up for another."

"He's right. They'll write us off as two lying fags."

"Randy says prejudice against gay men and women in the Army hasn't changed since 'Don't ask, don't tell.' "

"Not one iota. The men on Randy's jury will be loyal to Beckwith. You know the way it goes in the Army. It's a big case. They'll know what's expected of them."

"Do you think Beckwith has fixed it?" asked Kara.

"He won't have to. The system will take care of that. A jury of your peers is a joke in the United States Army. What Randy's going to get is a jury of frightened men. I've seen commanders destroy the careers of officers who served on juries that didn't reach the verdict the commander wanted. A man like Beckwith doesn't have to do much. It's very subtle: You can be left off the invitation list to an important party. They can change your duty assignment, take away your responsibility and authority. The next time you come up before a promotion board, someone on the board will have gotten the hint. You're finished."

"I'm sure what you're saying is true, General. But if ever there was a time to test the system, it's now. You've got the truth on your side. What if I found the hotel operator who took Randy's call when he picked up the message? That would prove he was in his room. We can corroborate your testimony. We could make it very difficult for the jury to disbelieve you."

"I'm surprised at you, Major. As a woman in the Army I would have thought you'd be more aware of how deep the prejudice and distrust and hatred is."

Kara gazed out the window. In the distance she could see the Lincoln Memorial, bathed in white light. She thought back to her experiences as a chopper pilot, when they wouldn't let her command a squadron.

Why? she asked. There's never been a female squadron commander, he said. So I'll be the first! Not on my watch, you won't, he growled. But that's unfair! It's not legal! So go over my head. See where that gets you.

So she filed an appeal, and within a week they took her off flight status.

Teese was right.

"I'm only too aware of the illegality and idiocy involved in gender discrimination in the Army, General. It's just that trials are a funny business. You get a sense about a jury. You get a feel about the way things are going. I'd like to ask you to keep an open mind about testifying, General. I want to see what kind of mistakes the prosecution makes. Even the best lawyers always make a few. They could open a door that a witness like you could waltz right through. Your testimony could save him."

General Teese didn't hesitate: "I love him. Do you know that?"

"Yes, I know."

He took her hand. His eyes blazed with emotion. "I've given most of my life to the Army. I'll gladly give what's left of it to Randy. I'll be there if you need me."

Chapter Thirty-seven

They said in law school that the worst hours in your life would be those before you went to trial. This would remain true from one trial to the next, no matter what the stakes were. They were right.

She had reported what she had found out from Patti O'Brien to Randy. It was crushing news. Their case wasn't in jeopardy, it was in tatters. Then she told him what General Teese had said, but even that didn't lift him up. He looked as if he hadn't slept in days, and the night ahead was going to be an even longer one.

Sleeplessness went with the territory. Kara found herself waking sometimes six and seven times a night, groggily switching on the light, fumbling to make notes on the yellow legal pad next to the bed.

One night she woke up around three a.m., and it was different. This time she was truly awake, and so she put on her robe and went into the kitchen and made coffee. Her files from the night before were strewn across the kitchen table.

She was going through her notes about the evidence that had been found in Randy's apartment. In Hollaway's office, she had been afforded the opportunity to examine the evidence in detail. The photos they had found in his jacket pocket had been developed in a one-hour shop. Anybody could have taken them. All they needed was a motive: framing Randy.

The knives were a different matter. They had been in a nondescript nylon bag. Nothing to be concluded from that. But the knives themselves were interesting. There was a German knife with a deer's antler handle. One of them had markings on the blade in Thai figures. Another was a folding knife, an antique, with a name she had traced to a defunct firm in upstate New York. Then there were several new knives, hand-made custom jobs. She'd read in the Atlanta papers about so-called "knife shows" in the area, where collectors sold and traded these hand-crafted beauties.

The thing about the knives was that they seemed to come from everywhere and nowhere. The prosecution was going to get up and say Randy was an obsessive collector. She knew they would tie the knife found at the scene of Lannie's murder to the ones in the bag. It was identical to one of the newer custom-made jobs.

It was the haphazard nature of the rest of the so-called collection that got her. Where could they have come from? Did they belong to a single person, the man who committed the murders? Or were they assembled specifically with planting them in Randy's apartment in mind? If so, where could such a strangely diverse collection could have come from in Columbus, Georgia?

The obvious answer, with an Army post next door, was a military man. He might have traveled the world on duty assignments and have assembled such a collection. But would the killer take his own knives and plant them in Randy's apartment when there was a chance someone might recognize a knife as his and implicate him? She thought not.

She made a note to ask Randy: Did he know anyone who collected knives? What kind of camera did he have? Could his camera have taken the photos?

She went back to bed and was about to drift off to sleep when one of the cats jumped on her stomach, purring loudly.

"Yeah, I know. You can't sleep either." She closed her eyes as she gently scratched his neck, and sleep finally enveloped her in the soft cloak of fog and dreams.

* * *

The MP guard unlocked the cell door. Randy was lying on his bunk, staring at the ceiling. Kara pulled the door shut behind her with a loud *clank*.

"Randy. Get up."

"What's the use? They're going to kill me, or send me away to Leavenworth for the rest of my life. I don't even know what's worse at this point."

Kara yanked him upright on the bunk by the arm. "We've got to talk about your apartment."

"What about it?"

"Let's go over the list of people who had access to the apartment."

"We've been over that before."

"Yeah, and we're going to go over it again. What about the maid? You're positive about her?"

"Absolutely."

"What about Mrs. Beckwith?"

"Oh, come on, Kara. You don't believe she—"

She interrupted, "I need to go over every single person who was in your apartment, Randy."

"Okay, it was a Saturday. She called me in the morning, said they had painters all over the house. Could we use my place to do the invitations? I said yes, of course. We'd done invitations together before, always at the General's quarters. I showed up, and sure enough, the place was crawling with painters, so we went to my apartment."

"Did you take your car?"

He thought for a moment. "No. She couldn't stand getting in and out of my little car. We took her Lexus. She wanted to run some errands. We picked up laundry, stopped and got a quick lunch, and dropped off her spare tire to get fixed."

"So then at your apartment, did you ever leave her alone?"

"No. I was there the whole time."

"I see."

"She couldn't have done it, Kara. I'm closer to her than I am to the General. We're friends."

"What about the phone guy? The one who installed your fax line."

"He was only there maybe fifteen minutes."

"And you were there the whole time?"

"Yes."

Kara thought for a moment. "I'm going at this case from one angle and one angle only, Randy. Someone planted evidence in your apartment. That person had a motive for doing it. They wanted to frame you, and the evidence in your apartment would be enough to hang you."

"You still think General Beckwith did it, don't you?"

"He's the only one who fits the profile. He was involved with both women. He had a date to meet Sheila the night she was killed. He was in the hotel the night Lannie was killed."

"But you thought he killed the girl in Fort Polk, and he didn't do that."

"No, he didn't. But maybe Sheila and Lannie were getting in his way. Maybe he wants to be chief of staff so bad he would do anything. *Anything.*"

"But he has an alibi for the night Sheila died."

"Yes. Mrs. Beckwith is his alibi. And if I asked him where he was the night Lannie was killed, he would say he was in his hotel with his wife."

"Have you asked him?"

"No. I've got no probable cause to question him about the murder. Not with you under indictment." She paused, consulting her notes. "You told me Mrs. Beckwith knew about Sheila, but you said you were certain she didn't know about Lannie. Why?"

"Because Beckwith had been so careful. You remember the reception for the Sec Def?"

"Yeah."

"She went off with that civilian from the base closure commission. I know Beckwith didn't see her that night because I went home with him in the staff car. They played it like that since she got down here."

"I forgot to ask you something. The cell phone in Beckwith's staff car, it's an Army phone?"

"What do you mean?"

"I mean, the bill doesn't go to General Beckwith."

"No, Third Army pays."

She made a note. "Randy, I've got some work to do. I'll come and see you before the court-martial starts."

"We've only got a few days."

"I know."

"Kara, how does it look?"

"I'm going to be honest with you. On a scale of one to ten, we're about a five."

"That's not good."

"It's not great. But we've still got some time. It's going to be okay, Randy."

"Do you think he did it? General Beckwith?"

"He's the only suspect I've got, besides you. And I know you didn't do it."

"That's something, anyway."

"Yeah. It's something."

She spent the rest of the afternoon canvassing surplus and sporting-goods stores around Columbus, the kind of places where they sell custom knives to collectors. The clerks were uniformly short-haired, clean-shaven, stupid, and paranoid. They all seemed to think that Kara represented a new anti-knife lobby that was going to take away the God-given right of every good upstanding Georgian to buy and own a custom knife. She got nowhere.

On her way home she passed the AirTone cell phone building and, on a whim, stopped in. They were less than cooperative. They couldn't release a cell phone bill without the permission of the billed party. She told them she could get a subpoena for the record she was looking for, but that didn't faze them. Go ahead. Get your subpoena.

She was leaving the office, considering that phone companies were all the same, when it hit her.

The so-called "billed party" for Beckwith's staff car was the United States of America. If the taxpayers didn't have a right to know how the commanding general was spending their dollars, who did?

Chapter Thirty-eight

Seven officers were empaneled, all of them senior to Randy, serving on the Army's version of a jury: Two colonels, three lieutenant colonels, and two majors. In the military, they were not referred to as jurors but as "members of the panel," and the jury itself was referred to as a "panel," or more commonly but less accurately as the "venire," which many military attorneys mispronounced as "veneer," as if the seven grave officers sitting on seven mahogany chairs behind a mahogany banister were nothing more than paneling, and perhaps in some cases—perhaps even in this one—that is all they would be, a facade obscuring the rot of a corrupt system.

They had started with twelve officers, and Kara had challenged two of them off the panel for cause. Sheila had served under one of them, if only tangentially, and Lannie had served under the other. Their prejudice in favor of the dead women was probable, so Kara turfed them, put them on the street. Then there were ten. The prosecutor, Major Sanders, successfully challenged one officer because he had served over Randy and had been a "reviewer" of Randy's Officer Efficiency Report, even though he hadn't written it. That made nine.

Kara challenged one preemptorily, because she didn't like his looks. He was a pug-ugly little colonel who had been pissed off since nursery school, and he had a runt complex to boot, and probably hated Randy for being taller and better-looking than him. The rules enabled her to make the challenge without giving a reason. As the Colonel left the panel, he gave her a nasty look, confirming her suspicions about him. Sanders preempted a female major, Kara figured, because she was black and a woman. Sanders was able to make his challenge unchallenged, as it were.

There was a short recess after the seating of the final panel. They put Randy in a locked interview room, where Kara tried to reassure him that everything was going to work out okay, but not even she believed it by then. Back in the court, she looked at the gallery. It was packed with media types and soldiers from the post. What's-her-name from CBS had stuck a microphone in Kara's face that morning as she was trying to enter the courthouse, and asked something completely obvious like, "How do you feel?" Kara stopped and looked at her and shook her head and moved on. Probably not a good media move. She would have to work on that. Maybe Randy had some suggestions. He did.

"Smile," he said. "They can't argue with a smile."

He was right, but it sickened her. The media was feeding on Randy like vultures. He was road kill to their carrion lenses and microphones and satellite trucks and uplinks and downlinks and cables and cell phones and makeup persons and hair persons and sign-offs to the anchors back home. The stupid reporter types would grin and spin and ever so subtly trash her client and then pass it off to the smiling anchor back home, wherever that was: "Barry?" "Gary?" "Terry?" "Jerry?" "Sherry?" "Larry?" "Carry?" "Mary?"

She concluded there was nary a brain among them, and wondered if to become a news anchor in the nineties meant first and foremost that your name had to end in a chirpy little y. Probably not, but it sure as hell sounded that way.

An MP stepped to the front of the court and snapped to attention.

"All rise!"

Colonel Freeman appeared in court wearing the black robes that obscured his rank. "Be seated, please. Major Guidry, Major Sanders. We meet again. Good morning."

In unison: "Good morning, Your Honor."

He turned to Sanders. "Major, read the charges."

Sanders stood at the podium and read from his notes. "In the case of *United States* versus *Captain Randolph Taylor, Regular Army,* the charges are as follows:

"Charge One. Violation of Article 118 of the United States Code of Military Justice, sub-paragraph D, felony murder. Specification one: that the defendant did kill or cause to be killed Lieutenant Sheila Worthy.

"Charge Two. Violation of Article 118 of the United States Code of Military Justice, sub-paragraph one, premeditated murder. Specification one: that the defendant did with premeditation and malice aforethought kill or cause to be killed Captain Lannie Fulton Love."

Sanders returned to the prosecution table and sat down.

"Very well. How do you plead?" asked Colonel Freeman.

Kara stood, with Randy at attention next to her. "Not guilty, Your Honor."

Colonel Freeman put on his half glasses and read from a page in front of him. "Major Sanders, having read the charges and accepted the plea, are you prepared to proceed?"

"We are, Your Honor."

"Major Guidry?"

"We are, Your Honor."

"Very well. Proceed with opening statements."

Kara stood. "Your Honor, the defense would like to exercise its right to give an opening statement when we begin our case."

"That's an unusual request, Major."

"I understand, sir. But it's within the law."

"Indeed it is. Major Sanders? You may begin."

Sanders took the podium and faced the panel.

"Gentlemen, you have been empaneled to hear the evidence and render judgment in a case that is as straightforward as it is brutal and disgusting."

Kara stood. "Your Honor, really—"

Freeman held up his hand. "Sit down, Major Guidry. Both sides have great latitude in opening remarks. You will get the same chance the prosecution has when it's your turn. Proceed, Major Sanders."

Sanders looked over at Kara with a "gotcha" expression, and turned again to the panel. "As I was saying, this case is brutal and disgusting but simple. We will show that this man"—he pointed at Randy—"Captain Randolph Taylor, was obsessed with these two women, Lieutenant Sheila Worthy and Captain Lannie Fulton Love. He dated both of them, and when he learned that his affections for them were not reciprocated and that indeed both women shunned his advances, his obsession grew and he became enraged and he murdered them, one after the other. We will show that he had the opportunity to commit both murders, and in fact, in the case of Captain Love, he was caught in the act. In the case of Lieutenant Worthy, we will show that the defendant made a mistake in the commission of his crime. He left evidence at the scene. We will connect that evidence directly to the defendant and show that his method of murder, the usage of a knife to stab both women in the neck, is connected to an obsession with knives on the part of the defendant. Both murders were brutal and ugly, and prematurely ended the lives of beautiful, talented young women with a fine future as officers in the United States Army. We will ask you to find the accused"—he pointed at Randy and looked at him sternly—"guilty of premeditated murder in both cases, and it is my duty to inform you at this time that we will be asking for the death penalty. Thank you."

Colonel Freeman looked over at the panel, then turned to Sanders.

"The prosecution will call its first witness."

"Sir, the Government calls to the stand Captain Charles Evans."

Sanders led Evans through the autopsies he had done on both victims. Special attention was paid to the use of a knife in both killings. The size of the knife was estimated by the autopsy doctor to have been about the same in each case.

"A knife like *this*?" asked Sanders, dramatically holding aloft the knife they had recovered in Lannie's room at the hotel in Washington. Dried blood was visible through the plastic bag containing the knife. He handed it to Captain Evans.

Evans examined the knife and looked up. "Yes. Like this one."

Sanders entered the knife into evidence and turned the witness over to Kara. She went through the time-of-death window for Sheila, then turned to the autopsy Evans had done on Lannie.

"Let me get this straight, Doctor. What time was it when Captain Love was first approached by paramedics in the hotel?"

"Oh-three-thirty."

"Right. But that wasn't the time my client walked into the room and found her—"

"Objection! Reference to facts not in evidence."

"Sustained."

"Sorry, Your Honor. Let me go back. Oh-three-thirty was not the time that house detective Reilly came upon the scene, was it?"

"Same objection, Your Honor."

"Counsel?"

"Reilly's interview is in the autopsy record, Your Honor. Counsel has either not read it, or he's being very disingenuous."

"That will be enough sarcasm, Major Guidry. Objection overruled. Proceed."

She turned back to Captain Evans. "Well?"

"Reilly came on the scene about 3:17, 3:18. There is a

record of his radio call to the hotel security room at 3:19. He must have been there just before that."

"Captain Love was dead before Reilly arrived, correct?"

"Yes."

"How do you know this?"

"When the EMT's arrived at 0330, there were no vital signs and she was not bleeding. She was removed to D.C. General Hospital Emergency, they weighed her, and she had lost, I'm estimating here, enough blood that she had to have been bleeding for at least a half hour before she died, given the size and placement of the wound. That would put her time of death some time between 0230 and 0315, give or take fifteen minutes either way."

"That's a pretty specific time of death, Doctor. Why so narrow a time frame, as compared, say, with Lieutenant Worthy's?"

"Lieutenant Worthy's blood loss was compromised by the cold water of the river. There was no such compromise here. I can give a much tighter estimate. She died between 0230 and 0315. That's my testimony. Forty-five minutes' leeway."

"Thank you, Captain. Interesting." Kara turned toward the defense desk, as if she was finished and was going to sit down. Then she returned to the podium and cocked her head, as if confused.

"I'm curious about this finding in your autopsy of Captain Love, Doctor. On page three." Evans flipped the pages of his autopsy. "Bottom of the page. You report that you found semen in Captain Love's stomach and esophagus. That would indicate that she had performed fellatio almost immediately before she was killed, correct?"

"Objection! Counsel is casting aspersions on the character of the deceased!"

Freeman turned to Kara. "Counsel?"

"The semen is in the autopsy report, sir. Just because

the prosecution is not charging the defendant with rape or sodomy, in addition to murder, does not prevent me from questioning the doctor on each and every aspect of his report."

"Objection overruled. Proceed."

"Captain Evans?"

"The presence of semen in both the stomach and the esophagus would indicate recent fellatio, yes."

"Doctor, in your years as a pathologist, have you ever seen a case in which a victim was *forced* by an attacker in a *forced* act of sodomy to swallow the attacker's sperm?"

"Objection! Captain Evans has no expertise in this area! This is pure speculation on the part of the defense!"

Kara looked over at the judge. "Your Honor, I don't know why the prosecution is so squeamish on this issue."

Freeman signaled both attorneys to approach the bench. He whispered: "Where are you going with this line of questions, Counselor?"

"I am seeking to show that the deceased engaged in a sex act with a male individual other than the accused almost immediately before she died, Your Honor. It will be my contention in presenting my case that circumstantial evidence will prove that it was this sexual partner of Captain Love's who killed her, not my client."

Freeman dismissed them from the sidebar. "Objection overruled. Proceed."

Kara turned to Captain Evans.

"I have to say I've examined rape victims, including victims who had been forced to perform fellatio, and I never found evidence of semen in their stomachs or esophagus, no."

"Did you type the semen for DNA, Doctor? Did you run a PSA on it?"

"Yes."

"Did it match my client's DNA?"

"No. I can say categorically that the semen found in Captain Love's digestive tract is not your client's."

"So it *is* a fact that Captain Love performed consensual sodomy, on *another male person* almost immediately preceding her death. Is it not?"

"I think you could say that is a fact, Major. Yes."

"Thank you. That's all I needed to know."

When she sat down, Randy whispered: "Why did you go after the time of death if we're not using my alibi?"

"Just laying the groundwork, Randy. You'll see."

"Next witness."

"Your Honor, the Government calls Major Frank Holloway."

Holloway was sworn and took the stand. As Sanders took him through the evidence in the murder of Sheila Worthy, Kara noticed that he managed to work around the issue of who had found the body. But when he got to the gold U.S. insignia, he zeroed right in.

"So you checked with the N.S. Meyer Company to see how many Fort Benning officers had ordered the gold U.S. insignia, and Captain Taylor's name turned up on the list, correct?"

"Correct."

"He was at that point a suspect?"

"Yes."

"And under questioning he admitted that he had a relationship with the deceased?"

Kara jumped up. "Objection. I was present for that interrogation. He didn't admit it. He volunteered the information."

"The witness should be allowed to answer the question, Your Honor."

Colonel Freeman rolled his eyes. "Objection overruled. Let's allow the witness to characterize the defendant's answers under questioning. Major Holloway? You may answer."

"He said he had dated her, yes."

"Why didn't you check to see if Captain Taylor's insignia was missing at that point?"

"We didn't have any corroborating evidence. He was a suspect, but we didn't have probable cause to go in and search his apartment."

"But you got your probable cause when the defendant was found astride a dead woman in a hotel in Washington, D.C., right?"

"Yes. We searched his apartment, and we found one of his gold N.S. Meyer insignias in his drawer. It matched the one we found in Sheila Worthy's car. Captain Taylor had plated insignia on the Class A uniform hanging in his closet. They were similar in appearance to the N.S. Meyer U.S.'s, but they weren't solid gold."

Sanders entered the gold U.S. insignias found in Sheila's car and in Randy's apartment into evidence as exhibits B and C.

"And it was during another search of the apartment that you found these photographs, correct?" He held up a packet of color photos of Sheila and Lannie.

"Correct."

"Ask that these photos be introduced as prosecution exhibit D, Your Honor."

"So ordered."

He handed the photos to Hollaway. "Have a look at the photos, Major. Describe them for the panel."

"These photos appear to have been taken with a telephoto lens. They show both of the deceased women in various places around Fort Benning. Getting out of a car at the PX. Going into an office. Entering their apartments. That sort of thing."

"So the defendant was following these women and taking their pictures with a long lens, so that they would be unaware of this intrusion into their lives?"

"Objection," called Kara from the defense table. "The question asserts facts not in evidence. It has not been proven that my client took these pictures, Your Honor. Only that they were found in his apartment."

"Sustained."

"Would you say that photographs such as these reflect an obsession with the subjects of the photos on the part of the person who took them?"

"Objection. Major Hollaway is a talented and experienced military policeman, but he is not an expert on the psychology of photography."

"Overruled. The witness can characterize the photos."

"Yes," said Hollaway. "I would agree that the photos reflect an obsession with the subjects."

Sanders pulled out the nylon bag and handed it to Hollaway. "You found this in the defendant's apartment, correct?"

"Yes. Under a pile of clothes in the closet."

"What does the bag contain?"

"A collection of knives."

Sanders took the bag and dumped it onto the prosecution table. He asked for and was granted permission to enter the knives as prosecution exhibits.

"There is one additional knife, correct?"

"Yes."

Sanders held up the bloody knife in a plastic bag. "This one. It was found next to the dead body of Captain Love, less than one inch from the defendant, with his prints on it, correct?"

"Yes."

"Objection. Major Hollaway isn't the person who found the knife. He has no knowledge of where the knife was, or under what conditions it was found."

The judge turned to Hollaway. "Is this correct?"

"Yes, Your Honor."

"Then why did you answer the question in the affirmative?"

"I was remembering what I read in the report from the District of Columbia PD and the house detective, sir."

Freeman turned to Sanders. "Presumably you will present this testimony?"

"Yes, Your Honor."

"Then you may proceed to question Major Hollaway on *his* knowledge of the evidence, not the knowledge of others. Understood?"

"Yes, Your Honor." He handed the bag containing the bloody knife to Hollaway. "When you examined this knife, did it resemble the knives you found in the defendant's apartment?"

"Yes. It's a hand-made, custom knife, identical to one of the knives we found in the bag."

"Did you run a check of the prints on this knife?"

"Yes. The Washington, D.C., police ran a check, and we ran a backup check. They came out the same."

"Whose prints were on the knife?"

"Captain's Taylor's. Four fingers and palm."

"No further questions." Sanders sat down.

Kara stood, leaning on the podium. "Let's start right there, Major. He could have gotten his prints on that knife in any number of ways, couldn't he?"

"I'm not sure I understand the question."

"Oh, I think you do. Let's run down a list of possibilities. Captain Taylor could have gotten his prints on the knife when he pulled it out of her neck, couldn't he?"

"I guess that's possible."

"His prints would be on the knife if the knife was lying next to her, and he picked it up and handled it, correct?"

"I guess so."

"And his prints would be on the knife if he moved it out of the way, so he could perform CPR on her, right?"

"That's improbable."

"But possible."

"Yes. On the outer edge of possible."

She walked over to the pile of knives on the prosecution table. "You didn't happen to run fingerprint checks on the rest of the knives, did you?"

Hollaway shifted nervously in his chair. "Yes."

"Did you find any of Captain Taylor's prints on these knives?"

"No."

Kara feigned surprise. "Really? Isn't that a bit strange, Major? You're in this court testifying that these knives belonged to the defendant, and presumably the purpose of your testimony is to bolster the prosecutor's claim in his opening remarks that the defendant was some kind of knife nut, and he was obsessed with knives the way he was obsessed with strange photography, and you *didn't find his prints on them*?"

"No."

"Did you find any prints at all on the knives?"

"A few. They were all partials, one half thumb print, the rest of them just scraps, really."

"As if, perhaps, the knives had been wiped down and a couple of prints on a tang, say, had been missed?"

"Possibly."

"Were you able to identify these prints?"

"We ran them through the FBI's fingerprint system, but nothing came up."

"How could that be?"

"I don't know."

Kara paused for effect, a quizzical look on her face. She looked up at Hollaway. "You've been an MP for how long?"

"Fifteen years."

"You've investigated murders before, haven't you?"

"Quite a few."

"Knife murders?"

"Yes."

"You collect knives yourself, don't you, Major Hollaway?"

He shifted again in his chair. His voice dropped a half octave. "Yes."

"It's rather common in the state of Georgia, isn't it? Knife collecting? They have knife shows and knife shops and knife conventions, isn't that right?"

"Yes."

"How many knives do you have in your collection?"

"Six." ·

"Custom knives. Nice knives. Collectible knives, like these?"

"Yes."

"Are your fingerprints on your knives, Major Hollaway? Do you pick them up and hold them and look at them and show them off to other collectors and maybe even whittle with them occasionally?"

"Yes."

"So indeed it is rather unusual that *these* knives"—she put her hand on the table next to the knives—"the ones you say belong to Captain Taylor, do not appear to have been touched by Captain Taylor at all. Not once. Maybe never."

"Objection! Asks for speculation!"

"I'll withdraw the last part of the question, Your Honor. But I want an answer to the first part."

"Answer the first part of the question."

"It is unusual, yes."

"How unusual, Major? Have you ever heard of a knife collector who never touched his knives?"

"No."

Kara snuck a satisfied glance at the panel. "One more question, Major. How many officers were on that list of people who owned solid gold U.S. insignia from N.S. Meyer?"

"Twenty-two."

"Sixteen men and six women, correct?"

"Correct."

"Did you check to see if any of the twenty-one officers other than Captain Taylor were missing a solid gold U.S.?"

"No."

"So as far as you know, there could be an additional twenty-one U.S. insignias missing from uniforms all over this post, isn't that right?"

"I don't know that to be a fact."

"So you don't know whether or not twenty-one U.S. insignias are missing?"

"That's right."

"Major, you didn't mention finding the negatives for the photographs you discovered in Captain Taylor's apartment. Did you look for them?"

"Yes."

"Did you find the negatives?"

"No."

"Isn't *that* a little strange, Major? You're saying this man was so obsessed with these women that he went around taking their pictures, and you find the prints, but there were *no negatives*?"

"Maybe he threw them out."

"Maybe they didn't belong to him. Maybe someone else took the photos and they have the negatives."

"Objection!"

"Withdraw the question. Thank you. That's all I have."

Colonel Freeman checked his watch. "We'll take a break for lunch and reconvene at 1400 hours. This court stands in recess."

Chapter Thirty-nine

She grabbed a sandwich from the PX and sat in the Cherokee behind the football stadium, reading through her notes. A training company of young second lieutenants ran past in formation, carrying their M-16's at port arms. In a moment she heard them inside the stadium, going through bayonet drills. An instructor was standing on a PT stand, screaming at them over the P.A.: "WHAT IS THE SPIRIT OF THE BAYONET?" And the company of lieutenants was screaming back: "TO KILL, SIR!"

Here she was in a murder trial only a hundred yards away from the stadium, and inside the court that morning they could hear the echo from the football stadium across the street: "KILL! KILL! KILL!" There were jarring incongruities in the military to which, even after all these years, she still had difficulty adapting.

Just before the court-martial reconvened, she ran the gauntlet of reporters and cameras, and this time she stopped directly in front of what's-her-name from CBS, who shoved the requisite microphone in her face.

"What did you think of the prosecution's case?" she asked perkily.

Kara smiled warmly. "I thought they did a good job of pumping a lot of hot air into a very flat tire."

What's-her-name faced her camera and said: "There you have it! A legal flat tire, says the defense! Barry? Back to you!"

Inside, Kara strode into the anteroom the prosecution

was using as an office. Sanders and Hollaway were bent over a conference table, going over notes. They turned when she slammed the door closed.

"I've got a request for a subpoena, Howard. I wonder if you could process this right away." She handed him a typed sheet of paper.

He scanned it quickly and looked up. "What in the hell is this?"

"Just what it looks like, Howard. A subpoena."

"You want the records on a military cell phone?"

"Yep."

"What could this possibly have to do with the court-martial of Captain Taylor, Kara?"

"Look at the date, Howard. I want the billing records covering the time of Sheila's murder."

"Whose cell phone is this?"

"I don't have to reveal that to you."

"Then I don't have to process the subpoena." He handed her the typed request. Angrily she snatched it from his hand.

"The law says you've got to honor my requests for a subpoena, Howard."

"The law says I have to honor *reasonable* requests. How can I tell if this is reasonable if I don't know what's involved? You tell me whose cell phone it is, and I'll make my decision."

"I can't do that. It will give away my case."

"Then I'm sorry."

She glared at him for a second and stalked out of the room. In the courtroom, Randy was already at the defense table. She sat down. "Did the guard bring you the hamburger and fries?"

"Yeah, thanks. It was great."

The judge walked in and gaveled the court to order. "Call your next witness, Major Sanders."

"Sir, the prosecution calls Nicholas Reilly."

The burly house detective from the hotel was sworn in, and Sanders took him through the morning he had arrested Randy. His description of discovering Randy on top of Lannie's bloody dead body was devastating. Sanders showed him the photos of Randy taken by the Washington police. Reilly confirmed they reflected Randy's appearance at the time of his arrest. It was obvious when Sanders sat down that he thought Reilly's testimony practically guaranteed a conviction, at least on the charge of killing Lannie.

Kara stood and approached the podium. "What did the defendant say when you first came into the room, Mr. Reilly?"

"He said something like, he was trying to revive her."

"Didn't he say he was giving her CPR?"

"Yeah. That was it."

"And what else did he say?"

"He said I was making a big mistake."

"And you said?"

"You're the one making the mistake, mister."

"Now, Mr. Reilly, I want you to be very careful as you answer my next questions. They are very important, and I want to get your precise recollections of what transpired. Understand?"

"Yeah."

"When you entered Captain Love's room, did you see the defendant with the knife in his hand?"

"No."

"Did you see him stab her with the knife?"

"No."

"When you described the scene for Major Sanders, you said there was blood all over the place. In fact, there was blood on Captain Love, and there was blood on the bed next to her neck, and there was blood on Captain Taylor, and that is all the blood you saw, correct?"

"Yeah, it was all over the place."

"How much blood was there on the bed?"

"Lots."

"We had testimony from Captain Evans, the doctor who did the autopsy on Captain Love, and he said that she had lost so much blood that quite a bit of time had gone by since the time of her death. Would that surprise you?"

"She was lying there and he was on top of her, is all I saw."

"Yes. So you told us." Kara glanced over at the members of the panel. At least one of them looked like he needed a nap. She turned back to questioning Reilly. "I was referring to the amount of blood and the probable time of death, Mr. Reilly. The doctor said that perhaps as much as thirty to forty-five minutes may have passed since she was killed. You understand that?"

"Yes."

"Let me ask you this, Mr. Reilly. How long have you been a house detective at that hotel?"

"Six years."

"And during this time you have made quite a few arrests, correct?"

"A lot."

"And at least one of those arrests was for murder, correct?"

"Yeah. Two years ago. Guy killed his wife."

"Mr. Reilly, how many times in six years at the hotel have you seen a crime committed with the door open so the whole world could walk by, as you did, and look right into the room?"

The witness sat very still for a moment, thinking. "Uh, I can't remember that that ever happened."

"So your answer would be, none. Zero. Correct?"

"Yeah."

"People who rent hotel rooms ordinarily keep their doors closed and locked, do they not?"

"Yeah."

"And you've had to use passkeys to get into rooms where you suspected a crime was being committed, right?"

"Yeah."

"Let's go back to the arrest you made for murder. The

man killed his wife, you said. Did he kill her with the door open?"

"No. He did it in the bathroom."

"So both the door to his room and the bathroom door were closed, isn't that correct?"

"Yeah."

"You could conclude that murder is normally a very private business, couldn't you?"

"Objection! The witness is not an expert in homicide investigations."

"Your Honor, he's an expert house detective, and he has testified to his extensive experience in that regard. The question merely asked him to draw a conclusion based on his own experience."

"Overruled. You may answer, Mr. Reilly."

"I forgot the question."

"I was asking you, Mr. Reilly, if you couldn't conclude from your experience that ordinarily murder is a very private business."

"Yeah, I guess so."

"So if murder is not a public, but rather a very private affair, sir, why do you think that Captain Taylor had the door to a public hallway open?"

"I don't know. That's his business, not mine."

"Didn't he tell you the door was open when he walked by, and he looked in and saw Captain Love lying on the bed covered in blood?"

"Yeah, he told me that, but I didn't believe him."

"You didn't believe him because you found him astride her."

"Yeah."

"Do you know the correct position for the administration of CPR, Mr. Reilly?"

"No. We got a house doctor for that."

"Would it surprise you if I told you that the correct position for CPR is the position Captain Taylor was in when you walked into the room?"

"I don't know that."

"I know you don't, Mr. Reilly. You have made at least that much abundantly clear. No further questions."

Sanders stood. "Redirect, Your Honor."

"Proceed."

"Mr. Reilly, Captain Taylor was covered with Captain Love's blood, isn't that right?"

"All over him. Yeah."

"The knife was right next to his hand, wasn't it?"

"I thought he was going to reach for it when I surprised him."

"Thank you. No further questions."

Kara was on her feet. "Recross, Your Honor."

"Proceed."

"Where were the defendant's hands when you entered the room?"

"On her chest. Like this." He put his own hands on his chest.

"He didn't reach for the knife, did he? His hands remained on her chest until you put the cuffs on him. Isn't that correct?"

"I had the Glock on him. He wasn't going anywhere."

"The question was, he didn't move his hands from her chest. He didn't move toward the knife, isn't that right?"

"Yeah."

"Mr. Reilly, I'd like you to step down from the stand and assume the position the defendant was in when you walked into Captain Love's room. On the floor, please."

Sanders was up. "Your Honor, please—"

Kara addressed the judge: "Your Honor, this is a reasonable request. He has testified as to how he found the defendant. All I'm asking him to do is reenact it for the members of the panel."

"That is a reasonable request. Step down. Do as she said."

Reilly got down on his hands and knees. His rear end was in the air, and he was leaning forward in the crawling position. "Like this."

"Thank you. No further questions."

After Reilly, Sanders put on his housekeeping witnesses. The fingerprint expert who took the prints off the knife testified that the prints were Randy's. A representative of the N.S. Meyer company verified that Captain Taylor had purchased gold U.S. insignia from his company. He examined the two U.S. insignias in evidence, and confirmed that they were both solid gold and quite likely a pair. The testimony of a gas station attendant who had filled up Randy's car on the night Sheila was killed showed that Randy had been out of his house at ten forty-five p.m. and had the opportunity to commit the murder.

Sanders introduced into evidence Randy's Nikon camera, with a 70-200mm zoom lens that an expert claimed could have taken the photographs. And with a final flourish he introduced huge color blow-ups of the autopsy photos of both women, showing the similarities in the placement of the neck wounds.

With a self-satisfied glance at Kara, he said, "Your Honor, the prosecution rests."

Freeman addressed Kara: "Will the defense be prepared to present its case tomorrow morning?"

"We will, Your Honor," she said reluctantly.

"Very well, this court-martial will stand in recess until 0900 tomorrow."

When Kara got home that night, she spent most of the evening going over her notes for her presentation in court. Around midnight she washed her face and put on her pajamas. She grabbed her court files and got into bed. She started going through her notes, but after a few moments she could stand it no longer, so she picked up the bedside phone and dialed Mace's number. An unfamiliar voice answered.

"Is Sergeant Nukanen there? I need to talk to him, please."

"No, ma'am, he's not here."

"Do you know where he is?"

"No, ma'am, I don't."

"I'd like to leave a message for him. Could you ask him to call Kara Guidry?"

"I'll tell him, ma'am. Gotta go. I've got a call on the other line."

She hung up the phone dejectedly. Around one, the phone rang, and she picked up excitedly. She could hear the hollow sound of someone on the line, then the phone went dead. Around two, she fell asleep, court-martial papers covering the bed.

The bedside light was still on when she awoke with a start, glancing at her watch. It was just past three. She thought she heard something . . . *there it was again!*

She switched off the light, plunging the room into darkness. She moved the papers from her lap and slipped out of bed.

There it was again! Someone was trying to open a window in the back of the house!

She dropped to her hands and knees and crept down the hall, pausing at the door to the living room. A fluorescent light was on, mounted under one of the kitchen cabinets. She was looking quickly from one window to another when she heard the sound again.

It was coming from behind her!

She crept to the bathroom door and flipped on the overhead light. A pebble hit the frosted window next to the sink. She opened the window and looked down. Mace was kneeling in the bushes next to the back stairs. He held a finger to his lips.

She ran around to the back door and unlocked it. Mace glanced around at the wooded edge of the backyard and hurried up the steps. Inside, he moved quickly to the light in the kitchen and switched it off. He crouched behind the counter next to the sink.

"Get down," he whispered.

"Mace, what are you—"

He interrupted her with a *sssshhh*. "There's a car with

two men sitting out there, parked in the bushes about fifty yards down from your drive."

"Who are they?"

"I don't know. They're in a Chevy Caprice. If I had to guess, I'd say they were military, judging by their haircuts."

"It's Beckwith. He's having me watched."

"If they've got physical surveillance on you, they could be tapping your phone—"

"They wouldn't dare! They would be listening in on privileged communications!"

"You think they care? He's the next chief of staff."

"I'm going to get Hollaway's people in here tomorrow and have this place swept. If I find out anyone is bugging or wiretapping me, I'll get the whole case thrown out for prosecutorial misconduct."

"That's kind of like asking the fox to check out the chicken coop, isn't it? He's on the other side, your friend is."

"I trust him. He would never condone anything like wiretapping the defense attorney."

"You'd know better about that than me, I guess, but I wouldn't go taking anything for granted. They've got you in their crosshairs, Kara."

"I know they do."

They were sitting on the kitchen floor in the dark. He reached for her hand. "I had to see you tonight. Things were so good between us . . ." He squeezed her hand tightly and pulled her toward him.

"Mace, I—"

He held his finger to her lips. "Ssshh." Then he kissed her and rocked her in his arms. "I've been so worried about you," he whispered. "I had to risk it."

"I'm glad you did," she whispered. "I need you." He was looking into her eyes. There was a sheen of perspiration on his forehead, and his eyes were hooded with a mixture of fear and excitement.

"I want to help you," he whispered. "Tell me what I can do."

She reached for the pad of paper next to the phone and scribbled quickly. "There is a bill for the cell phone in Beckwith's staff car." She wrote down the month. "Sheila Worthy made two calls from her car just before she was killed. Both of them were to him. I've got to get that bill."

"Why would her call show up on his bill? Wouldn't it be charged to her?"

"Ordinarily, yes, it would. But she called the secure switch, and they patched it through to him in his staff car. Once she got the secure switch on the line, she was charged for that call. But when they patched it off a land-line phone, through to his car, if the call came in on his cell phone, the cellular company would read it as a call from a regular phone to a cell phone, and the bill would go to him."

"The call could have been patched out to his radio."

"That's why I need the bill."

"You still think he killed her."

"Yes, I do."

"I'll see what I can do and call you tomorrow."

"Mace, I don't want you to do anything that's going to get you in trouble."

He grinned, his eyes glistening brightly in the dark. "Major, you've been trouble since the day I met you."

Chapter Forty

The members of the panel filed into the courtroom and took their seats. Colonel Freeman hit his gavel. "This court-martial is in session. Major Guidry, you may make your opening statement."

Kara walked to the podium without notes. "Gentlemen, this is going to be brief. The case against my client is such an outrageous frame, the person responsible for it must have had training in an earlier life under Goya." She was relieved to see that there were a few smiles on the panel. She had broken through to them, and so she drove on. "Captain Randy Taylor is a graduate of West Point and has had an outstanding career as an officer in the United States Army. Until a short while ago he had the coveted position of aide to General William Beckwith, here at Fort Benning. His father is a West Pointer, and so is his uncle, and so was his grandfather. The case we will present will ask and answer this question: Why would a young man from a family like the Taylors throw his heritage, and his family name, and his career, down the drain by committing two brutal murders of women we will show he knew and admired? The answer is, he wouldn't have, and he didn't. He did *not* kill either Sheila Worthy or Lannie Fulton Love. He is innocent of these charges. We will show that the prosecution's case is so full of holes, it looks like the cooling shroud on a fifty-caliber machine gun"—more smiles on the panel—"and we will raise the reasonable doubt you need to set this fine Army officer free and return him to his family and his distinguished heritage, where he belongs. Thank you."

Colonel Freeman cleared his throat. "Major, are you ready to call your first witness?"

"We are, Your Honor."

"Do so."

"Sir, the defense calls Major Frank Hollaway."

Sanders jumped to his feet. "Objection. The defense has had its chance with Major Hollaway during cross-examination."

Freeman peered at her over his half glasses. "Major Guidry, I believe the prosecutor is correct."

"It's true, sir, that I had the opportunity to cross-examine him—"

Sanders interrupted: "Perhaps the defense should have finished with its questions then, Your Honor."

Kara shot a look at Sanders. "Your Honor, if I may be permitted to finish . . ."

Freeman looked over at Sanders. "There will be no further outbursts from you, Major Sanders. Understood?"

"Yes, Your Honor."

"Proceed, Major Guidry."

"Sir, under the rules of evidence, I was permitted to question Major Hollaway only about those subjects which the prosecution brought up during its case. I have new questions for Major Hollaway concerning matters which the prosecution did not touch."

"I see. This is quite out of the ordinary, but I'll allow it. Proceed."

Hollaway was reminded he was still under oath and took the stand.

"Major, you recall Lieutenant Barry Parks, don't you?"

"Yes, I do."

"Lieutenant Parks is now deceased, is he not?"

"Yes, he is."

"Parks was on your list of officers who owned solid gold insignia from the N.S. Meyer company, wasn't he?"

"Yes."

"He was also something more than an acquaintance of Sheila Worthy's, correct?"

"Yes."

"In fact, they were lovers during college, isn't that right?"

"Yes, they were."

"You and I questioned Lieutenant Parks, and he told us these things, didn't he?"

"Yes, he did."

"You considered Lieutenant Parks your chief suspect in the murder of Sheila Worthy, did you not?"

"For a time, yes."

"Why was that?"

"He fit a profile I have seen in other cases. He had had a relationship with the deceased, and most murders are committed by persons who are acquainted with their victims. And his name appeared on the N.S. Meyer list."

"You winnowed your list of suspects down to two, did you not? Who were they?"

"Lieutenant Parks and Captain Taylor."

"And of the two, you liked Parks as the killer, right?"

"Yes."

"His relationship with Lieutenant Worthy had broken up after college, and he had tried to restart the relationship, and he had failed at this, correct?"

"Yes."

"And that enhanced his status as a suspect in your eyes."

"Yes, it did."

"Even after Lieutenant Parks was killed, he remained your chief suspect, isn't that right?"

"Yes."

"You were going to call for a hearing and present evidence that he killed Sheila Worthy, and close the case, weren't you?"

"Yes."

"When did you decide not to do that?"

"When the District of Columbia Police Department called and said they had arrested Captain Taylor for the murder of Lannie Love."

"Until that very moment you were convinced that Lieutenant Parks had killed Sheila Worthy, weren't you?"

"Yes."

Kara walked over to the defense table and picked up a document.

"I'd like to ask you a few questions about Lieutenant Parks' death. He was killed by an artillery round during a field exercise here at Fort Benning, correct?"

"He crossed over into a live-fire zone, right."

"You've read the incident report on his death."

"Yes, I have."

"This is a copy of that report." She held up the document.

"Objection! That report is not in evidence."

"I supplied the prosecution with a copy of the report, Your Honor."

Freeman looked over at Kara. "Are you asking that the report be introduced as evidence?"

"No, Your Honor. I merely want to refer to it when I question Major Hollaway."

"All right. You can use the report for the purpose of questioning the witness, but that is all."

"Understood, sir." She turned to Hollaway. "Major, the report says that Lieutenant Parks failed to heed a warning to stay clear of the live-fire zone, correct?"

"Yes, that's correct."

"You thought Parks committed suicide, didn't you?"

"Yes."

"You thought he committed suicide because he was guilty of killing Sheila Worthy, isn't that right?"

"Yes."

"Do you still believe that?"

"No."

"But you changed your mind only when Captain Taylor was dropped into your lap, when he was arrested for the killing of Captain Love, correct?"

"Correct."

"So these two murders are inextricably linked, aren't they? If Captain Love hadn't been killed, you would have closed out the Sheila Worthy case and pinned it on Parks, wouldn't you?"

"Objection! Calls for speculation!"

"Your Honor, I'm trying to show that there was in fact no case against the defendant regarding the murder of Sheila Worthy until his arrest for the murder of Captain Love."

"Approach the bench."

Sanders and Kara stood before the judge as he whispered: "I know what you're trying to show, Counselor. If you can explain to me why this line of questioning is germane, I'll allow it."

"Your Honor, it is the prosecution's theory that Captain Taylor obsessively pursued these two women, and that because he was unsuccessful in his pursuit of them, he became enraged and killed them. It is entirely germane to show the members of the panel that there was another suspect in the murder of Sheila Worthy, Lieutenant Parks, who fit the prosecution theory, and that Parks was dropped as a suspect only when my client was arrested for the murder of Captain Love."

Freeman turned to Sanders. "Well?"

"Sir, she's on a fishing expedition here, wildly casting about, trying to find something that will save her case."

"Your Honor, I'm trying to cast doubt on the prosecution theory, which is my job."

"I'll allow an answer to the question at issue, but that is all, Major Guidry. You will return to evidence in the case, is that clear?"

"Yes, Your Honor."

They took their places, and the stenographer reread the question.

Holloway glanced nervously at Sanders. "I'm not sure."

"Isn't it true that you were in the process of scheduling a postmortem hearing that would have closed the case on the Sheila Worthy murder?"

"Yes."

"No further questions."

Sanders got up to cross-examine his own witness. "Major Holloway, in the matter of the murder of Sheila Worthy, which suspect did you find more evidence on? Lieutenant Parks or Captain Taylor?"

"Captain Taylor."

"You found enough evidence that he had murdered Sheila Worthy that you brought the charge against him, correct?"

"Yes."

"No further questions."

Holloway stepped down, and Kara decided to get her housekeeping witnesses out of the way. She called two knife experts who testified that the collection of custom knives found in Randy's closet was not a true "collection" at all, but a random assemblage of rather ordinary, run-of-the-mill hand-made knives. Neither expert had heard of a knife collector who had never touched his knives. Both experts confirmed that if Randy was a true collector, he certainly wouldn't have stored the knives all jumbled up in a bag in a closet. Sanders chipped away at their testimony by getting each of them to concede that a person might store knives in a nylon bag if he wasn't a collector, but someone who intended to use the knives for a purpose such as murder.

Kara jumped up on redirect to point out the change in the prosecution theory. Now they were saying Randy wasn't a collector, but a *user* of knives, and if he was a user, then why weren't his prints all over the knives?

Watching the members of the panel as she made the point, she thought she had won that round.

Next, she called the owner of a photography shop in Atlanta who was an expert in photo analysis. He testified that it would have been impossible for Randy's Nikon with a 70-200mm zoom lens to have taken the photographs found in his apartment. Randy's lens was not a Nikon. It was a cheaper brand that had a very slow shutter speed that allowed only a small amount of light to reach the film when shooting objects at a distance. He showed some photographs he had taken with a Nikon just like Randy's, fitted with the same cheap lens as his, under conditions that were similar to those in the photos in evidence. His photos were much darker and quite grainy, and there was a pronounced distortion of the picture at the edges of each photo, as if it had been squeezed together from the sides. He testified that the camera used to take the photos in evidence was most likely a fast, top-of-the-line Canon or Nikon, with a Canon or Nikon lens in the range of 300mm, not 200mm. He showed a couple of photos he had taken with such a camera at the same time he took the photos with the camera like Randy's. They were bright and clear, just like the photos in evidence.

Under cross-examination by Sanders, the expert testified that though he was certain he was right about Randy's camera, he couldn't be a hundred percent certain, because photography was subject to many variables that couldn't readily be duplicated. His expert testimony had been effective, and he probably raised some doubts. But he had not slammed the door shut on the photos.

She called a forensics pathologist who testified in a similar, though more detailed vein as Captain Evans, that Lannie had been dead over a half hour when the house detective found Randy trying to revive her, remaking the point that it was unlikely Randy had killed

Lannie with the door open, and then remained astride her body for over a half hour.

She called a couple of officers who worked with Randy in the headquarters building, and they testified as to his good character.

It was late in the afternoon by the time she called her final witness for the day.

"Can you state your name and occupation, please?"

"Greg East. I work for Southeastern AirTone, the cellular phone company."

Kara picked up a single sheet of paper. "Your Honor, we would like to introduce this as defense exhibit D."

"So ordered."

She handed the paper to Mr. East. "Can you describe for the court what you're holding, sir?"

"It's a cell phone bill. An AirTone bill, to be precise."

"For whose account?"

"For Lieutenant Sheila Worthy."

"Did she make any calls on the day that she died?"

Mr. East studied the bill for a moment and looked up. "I'm confused. Which day are you referring to?"

"The last page of the bill. The final calls she made. There are two of them, I believe, are there not?"

"Yes. At ten-forty and ten forty-two."

"What's the duration of the calls?"

"The first one is for one minute. The second call was also for one minute."

"She called the same number twice."

"Correct."

"Do you recognize that number?"

"No."

"Thank you." She turned to Sanders. "Your witness."

"No questions."

Kara addressed the judge. "Your Honor, I have another witness to call, but I believe the testimony will run on for some time."

"Perhaps we'd better recess, then." He banged his gavel.

After court, she talked to Randy in a small interview room. Three MP's stood outside the door. She wasn't sure if they could hear them through the door, so they whispered.

"Did you get Beckwith's bill?"

"No. Sanders won't issue the subpoena."

"What are we going to do?"

"I don't know. But I've got some good news. You told me you and Mrs. Beckwith dropped off a flat tire to be fixed, remember?"

"Yeah . . ."

"I went to the gas station downtown, and the tire hadn't been picked up. I took a sample of mud from the tire and ran a check on it with the lab at the University of Georgia. They confirmed that the mud came from the same area where Sheila was killed."

"What does that do for us? General Beckwith was in his staff car that night."

"Maybe not the whole time. Beckwith could have gone home, and gotten in his own car and driven out there to the firing range."

"Does Sanders know?"

"Of course not."

"How are you going to get those results into the case?"

Kara paused. "I don't know yet. I'm still working on it."

"You've *got* to come up with something!"

She closed her briefcase and knocked on the door to be let out. "I know I do."

Chapter Forty-one

Specialist Lester was waiting for Kara on the porch when she got home. She fixed a couple of sandwiches and put on a pot of coffee, and they worked until nine, when Specialist Lester went back to the office to type up notes for court the next day. Kara was undressing, getting ready to take a shower, when the phone rang.

Mace said: "It's me. Get in your car and start driving around. Wear your Class A's. It's important."

She answered with a single word: "Okay." She got dressed and pulled on her overcoat. The temperature outside had dropped ten degrees since she got home. The Cherokee's engine roared to life, and she pulled out of the gravel drive.

She didn't see the headlights right away. They waited until she crested a hill to fall in behind her. They kept their distance from her on a long stretch of straight road. She drove for another mile or so and pulled into a convenience store parking lot. The car that had been following her stopped at the red light and turned right. She went inside and bought a cup of coffee and got back into the Cherokee. She pulled out of the lot and turned left at the light. The headlights appeared again. She made a turn and glanced in her rearview mirror. She knew it was the same car when they made the turn and she saw that the parking light on the right side was broken.

Her cell phone rang. It was Mace. "Are they tailing you?"

"Yes, they've been on me since I left home."

"I got the stuff you want. We're going to have to break the surveillance so I can get it to you. Where are you now?"

"I'm on Claiborne. I'm just driving around the west side of town."

"Okay, we're going to lose those guys. You've got to listen close and do exactly as I tell you."

"Okay."

"You remember that friend of mine, Barney Tennant?"

"The warrant officer. The guy you were friends with in the Gulf."

"That's him. Here's what you do. Drive onto the post and go to your office. Park in front, in the lot where you usually park, go upstairs, turn on your light, make it look like you're catching up on work before court tomorrow. Then go downstairs and out the back door. I'll be waiting for you."

They hung up, and Kara headed toward Victory Boulevard and drove onto Fort Benning through the front gate and did as she was told. She found Specialist Lester at the computer, working on notes for court. Lester followed Kara back to her office and stayed out of sight. From the office window Kara watched as the car that had been following her passed the parking lot and turned down a side street and cut the lights. When she was certain that they had seen her upstairs in the office, she unbuttoned her uniform jacket and handed it to Specialist Lester.

"Put this on and sit at my desk with your back to the window. Every once in a while, get up and walk over to the bookshelf and remove a book and return to the desk. Make sure you don't face the window. I want them to think I'm still up here, getting ready for court."

"Will do, ma'am," said Lester, donning Kara's Class A jacket.

Kara put on her overcoat and ran downstairs and opened the back door. An Army Huey helicopter was parked in the middle of a grassy field, its rotors beginning to turn. The door slid open, and she ran for the chopper. Mace pulled the door shut as the Huey lifted off and made a steep left turn, heading south.

"Curb service," he yelled over the sound of the engine.

Warrant Officer Tennant waved from the pilot's seat. Kara pulled on a headset and heard his voice through the intercom. Tennant handed her a clipboard. "Sign on the dotted line, Major. It's a requisition for a military hop. Initial the flight manifest on the second page."

She signed the requisition and grabbed a webbing strap as the Huey leaned into another turn.

"You like my taxicab, Major?" the pilot called over the intercom. "We've got everything but yellow paint."

She laughed. "I haven't flown in one of these in years."

"Taxicab's right on schedule, Major. Be there in a short-short." He leaned the Huey into another turn and gained altitude.

Mace pulled her headset from her ear and yelled: "Tennant's one of the good guys."

"He could get in big trouble for this."

"No, he can't. He did everything legal. You signed a requisition that'll get filed and forgotten, and he signed out at his squadron logging night flying time."

Tennant's voice came through the intercom: "You want me to put you down where you left your car, Mace?"

"Yeah, Barney, that'll be great."

"Good as done."

Mace opened the side door as the chopper lost altitude and slowed. Tennant circled and put the skids down in the middle of a rural road next to a phone booth. Mace gave him a pat on the top of his flight helmet, and they jumped out, scampering to the side of the road. The Huey lifted off, heading north.

They climbed in the car parked next to the phone booth, and Mace started the engine.

"Mace, you took a big chance tonight. I'm sorry I got you mixed up in this."

"I'm not. When I saw they were watching you, I got pissed. I figured, here it is, Mace. You've got to take sides." He looked over and took her hand. "I'm on your side."

She leaned across the seat and kissed him. He put the car in gear, and they headed back to the post.

"You still think Beckwith did it, don't you?" asked Mace.

"Yes, I do."

"Who do you think has been following you?"

"I don't know, but I'm going to find out first thing tomorrow morning."

Mace flipped on the overhead light and handed her a manila envelope. "Here's the phone bills for the General's cell phone."

Kara opened the envelope and looked inside. "Where did you get them?"

"I've got a pal over in Finance, known him since we were in NCO School together. I traded him four tickets to a Garth Brooks concert for them."

"These are the actual bills."

"Yeah, my pal said you should make copies and give them to me. I'll see to it he gets them back into the files before anyone's the wiser."

She closed the envelope. "I've got to figure out a way to get home. They're probably still watching my house."

"I'm sure they are. Why don't I drop you off downtown? You can catch a cab."

"Good idea." She paused, watching him, relaxed behind the wheel. "Mace, I don't know how to thank you."

He glanced over with a smile. "I just wish I could be there in court tomorrow morning."

"I do too."

Kara stopped Hollaway in the hall outside court. "Frank, there's something I've got to ask you."

"Shoot."

"Are you having me followed?"

Hollaway looked surprised. "What?"

"There's been an unmarked car watching my house and following me for two days, Frank. I want to know who ordered it."

"Kara, you've got to believe me. I don't know anything about this."

"Can you find out who's behind it? I want some ass kicked here, Frank. Whoever is having me followed is stepping into the middle of a capital murder case. I'll get this damn thing declared a mistrial and move for a dismissal."

"I'll make some calls right now. I'm very surprised. Normally, nothing like this happens at Fort Benning without crossing my desk first."

"Thanks."

"I'll tell you as soon as I find out anything."

"Okay."

Randy was waiting at the defense table in the courtroom. Kara opened her briefcase and walked over to the prosecution table. "I've got some business with Freeman before we start, Howard."

Sanders looked up, surprised. "Really? What's up?"

"You'll find out soon enough."

The judge walked into the court and gaveled them to order.

Kara stood. "Your Honor, I would like to address a matter concerning this case before the members of the panel are brought in."

"What's on your mind, Major?" asked Freeman.

"Your Honor, I've had surveillance of my home and

office and an unmarked car following me for two days. It's my belief that the other side in this case is trying to gain advantage by tracking my movements and observing who I'm meeting with."

Freeman turned to Sanders. "Is this true, Major Sanders? Because if it is, we've got a real problem here."

Sanders stood, open-mouthed. "Your Honor, the prosecution is not carrying out and has not ordered surveillance of opposing counsel. We are well aware that to do so would compromise this court-martial and damage our case."

"Your Honor, the surveillance started when this court-martial began. It is obvious the surveillance is linked to this trial, and to my representation of the defendant."

Freeman held up his hand, stopping her. "Give me a moment, Counselor." He turned to Sanders. "You're not pulling any kind of deniability crap with this court, are you, Major? Maybe they're following Major Guidry, and you don't know about it, but you are enjoying the fruits of the surveillance?"

"No, sir. I don't know anything about counsel for the defense being under surveillance, and my office has not received any information concerning her movements or any witnesses she is interviewing or anything of that sort."

"Major Guidry, that's a solid denial of involvement by the prosecution. I don't know how much further we can go with this."

"I do, Your Honor. I would suggest that the court-martial–convening authority be brought into this matter, and an order issued to call off the surveillance. I will move for a mistrial if the surveillance of my home and office and movements is not called off immediately."

Freeman turned to Sanders. "I'm going to order the prosecution to do exactly as Major Guidry has suggested. Furthermore, I want you to use your best efforts to find out who has ordered this outrage, and I want a report on my desk by tomorrow morning outlining everything you have found out. Understood?"

"Yes, Your Honor," said Sanders.

"Is that satisfactory, Major Guidry?"

"Yes, it is, Your Honor."

Freeman turned to the MP guard. "Bring in the members of the panel." They filed into the courtroom and took their seats. "Call your next witness, Major Guidry."

"Sir, I'd like to recall Mr. East from Southeast AirTone."

Sanders objected. "We've already heard his testimony, Your Honor. She's stalling."

"No, I'm not, Your Honor. New information has come into my possession. I need to question Mr. East about this information."

"Call your witness."

Mr. East was reminded he was under oath.

"You have testified that according to her cell phone records, Lieutenant Worthy made two calls the night she died, one at ten-forty, and one at ten forty-two."

"That's right."

She handed him a sheet of paper. "Do you know what this is?"

"It's a cell phone bill, for another phone."

"There's a call on the bill, at ten forty-two, the night Lieutenant Worthy was killed, correct?"

"Yes, there is."

"When a call is made to a cell phone, the call is billed to the receiving cell phone, correct?"

"Yes, unless the call was made from a cell phone. In that case the bill would go to the calling party."

"But if the call made by the cell phone was patched through a land-line, then the bill would go to the receiving cell phone, correct?"

"Yes. The computer would recognize that the receiving cell phone had been called from a wired phone, and the bill would go to the receiving phone."

"Do you recognize the number on the bill, sir?"

"The call came from Lieutenant Worthy's cell phone."

"So with these two bills, Mr. East, we have closed the loop, have we not? We know she made a call, and we know who she called. In your professional opinion, would my statement be accurate?"

"Yes."

"Thank you." She turned to the judge. "I would like to have this phone bill entered as defense exhibit E, Your Honor."

Sanders stood up. "I'd like to see that."

Kara handed it to him. He studied it for a moment uncomprehendingly. Finally he turned to Colonel Freeman, a look of panic in his eyes.

"Your Honor, permission to approach."

"Approach."

Sanders and Kara walked to the side of the bench. Sanders whispered. "This bill is for General Beckwith's staff car, Your Honor. I object to its admission as evidence. General Beckwith has nothing to do with this case, and its admission will only serve to damage his good reputation as an officer in the United States Army."

"My chambers."

They followed Freeman into his anteroom off the main courtroom.

"Give me that." Freeman looked at the bill. "What are you up to, Major Guidry?"

"Sir, we have evidence that Lieutenant Worthy made two calls just before she was killed on the night of her murder. She made one call. Then she made another to the same number. The number she dialed both times was the secure switch here at Benning. The second time they patched her through to General Beckwith's cell phone in his staff car. The linkage between her phone bill and his proves it. She made no further calls that night. He is the last person to have spoken with her before she died."

"So you intend to call General Beckwith and question him about the call?"

"Yes, sir, I do."

"Do you have General Beckwith on your witness list?"

"Yes, sir. I put in a request with the prosecutor to call General Beckwith several weeks ago."

Freeman turned to Sanders. "Is that true?"

"Yes, sir."

"Did you inform the General?"

"Yes, sir. He said he would refuse to testify."

"Did you inform Major Guidry of General Beckwith's response?"

Sanders hesitated. "No, sir."

"Why not?"

"Because the General told me he wouldn't testify under any circumstances, sir."

Freeman looked at Kara. "Maybe I'm missing something here. You questioned this man from the cellular telephone company a second time because you said that you had come upon new information. I'm assuming that the new information you were referring to is the cell phone bill for General Beckwith's staff car, correct?"

"Yes, sir."

"What was General Beckwith doing on your witness list several days before that?"

"I had General Beckwith down as a character witness, Your Honor. He is Captain Taylor's boss. He wrote two OER's on him. As well as practically anyone on this earth, General Beckwith knows the defendant and is uniquely qualified to comment as to his character."

Freeman addressed Sanders. "Well, what's the matter with that?"

"Sir, calling him as a character witness was a trick. She's up to something, sir. She wants to muddy the waters of this case, and embarrass Fort Benning and the Third Army by calling the commanding general and putting him on the record in this case."

"Is that what you're trying to do, Guidry?"

"No, sir," said Kara.

"Major Sanders, do you have any evidence she has an ulterior motive in calling General Beckwith?"

Sanders stammered: "It's obvious, sir."

"Sanders, call the General's office. Tell them I want to speak to him."

"Yes, sir." Sanders picked up the phone.

"Have a seat, Major Guidry."

They sat down. Sanders was on the phone for a moment and handed it to the judge. Freeman turned his back and spoke in a low voice for several minutes and hung up.

"Major Guidry, we're in a difficult spot here. The General said you should introduce the OER's he wrote on Captain Taylor as evidence, and that would be sufficient."

"Your Honor, Rule 703 states that I can call any reasonable witness for the defense, and General Beckwith is certainly a reasonable witness in this case. He was the last person to speak with Lieutenant Worthy before she died. I want to question him about that phone call, Your Honor, and if he is not called as a witness for the defense, I will ask for a mistrial."

"Major Guidry, you are talking about the commanding general of the Third Army. I am certain that the commanding general has valid reasons for not wanting to testify in this case. The court is compelled to respect the wishes of the commanding general in this matter."

Kara stepped forward and locked eyes with Freeman. "Sir, I don't know why you're trying to protect General Beckwith, but if you force me to continue my case without hearing his testimony, I'm going to walk out there before those television cameras, and I'm going to tell them that Beckwith was the last person to talk to Sheila Worthy before she died, and that he has refused to testify about the conversation. I'm going to tell them that you, Colonel Freeman, and the prosecutor in this case, are conspiring in a cover-up of the truth. By the time I finish, you're going to have media set up out on the lawn outside this building for weeks. Some of them will decamp to the Third Army headquarters building and stake out the General himself. I'll give this post a migraine headache all the Advil in the world won't cure."

"Major, you are acting in an insolent and disrespectful manner toward the institution of the United States Army, toward this command, and toward this court."

"Sir, I am a defense attorney who is trying to put on the best defense she can for a client who is innocent of the charges against him."

"Military attorneys are officers, and as such they are subject to the traditions and protocols of military service. You are over the line, Major. Way over."

"Are you countenancing General Beckwith's exercise of command influence in this case, sir? If you're telling me that because I'm a major, and you're a colonel and Beckwith is a general, that I've got to toe the line and take orders and shut up and do what I'm told, and ignore my duties as a JAG attorney defending a man in a capital case—if that's what you're telling me, sir, then I'm going back into that courtroom and moving for a dismissal of all charges against my client because command influence has fatally infected his ability to get a fair trial. And if you deny my motion, I'll take it to the Court of Military Appeals."

Freeman stood up, glaring at her. "Out. I will take this matter under advisement and will inform you of my decision later."

In the hall, Sanders started to say something to her, but she snapped: "Shut up, Howard. I don't want to hear it."

Outside, Kara walked through the crowd of reporters, ignoring their shouted questions. She started the Cherokee and pulled into traffic. There was one more place that had knives for sale she needed to check.

* * *

Children filled the playground next to the child-care center as she drove up. Inside, with all the kids at play on the swings and slides and teeter-totters outside, it was quiet. She found Mrs. Bennett in her office.

"Mrs. Bennett?"

She looked up. "Oh, Kara, you scared me."

"Sorry. Ma'am, I need to ask you a question."

"What about?"

"You know I'm defending Captain Randy Taylor in the murder case."

"I read it in the papers."

"They found a bunch of knives in his apartment that don't belong to him. I think someone planted them there."

She took photographs of the individual knives from her purse and handed them to Mrs. Bennett. "I noticed the night I was here, when you took me through the thrift shop, that you had some knives in your case line."

"Quite a few, actually. We get them in every once in a while."

"Have you ever seen any of these knives for sale here at the thrift shop?"

Mrs. Bennett began studying the photos. She handed one back to Kara. "This one. I remember it very well. The woman who brought it in was the German wife of an enlisted man. It was some kind of family heirloom that they wanted to keep, but they needed money. They put it on consignment."

She turned to the next photo. "This one too. I remember it because it was so . . . how should I put it? So delicate, and light."

Kara looked at the photo. It was the picture of the knife that matched the one recovered at the scene of Lannie's murder.

Mrs. Bennett looked through the other photos. "I can't be sure . . . I think I took this one on consignment from a young soldier about three months ago." She handed Kara another photo. It was one of the custom knives.

"Can you remember who bought these knives?"

"You know, it's a funny thing. That German girl was in just the other day, wanting to know if we had sold their knife, and so I went through the records and looked it up. There was no sales slip for it, and one of our volunteers had reported it missing."

"Do you mind looking through your consignment records to see if the other knives you recognized have been sold?"

"Not a bit." She went to a file cabinet and started flipping through the files. In a minute, she returned with several handwritten receipts. "None of them have been sold, Kara. And two more were reported missing or replaced."

"Mrs. Bennett, can I see the duty roster for your volunteers for the last couple of months?"

She stood up and walked across the room and flipped the calendar back one month. "This seems pretty important to you, Kara. Is it?"

Kara's eyes were focused on the calendar. "Yes. Very important. Can I have this calendar, ma'am?"

"Certainly." She took it off the wall and handed it to Kara.

"The last time I was here, you said you remembered that General Beckwith had arrived here the night of the storm about nine forty-five. Do you remember how long he stayed?"

"Oh, he was here for quite a while."

"How long would that be, Mrs. Bennett? This is important."

"I'd say he was here a half hour, at least."

"So he would have left around ten-fifteen."

"He left just after the fire department turned the power off, and I know what time that was because the clock stopped and I had to get up on a ladder to reset it when they turned the power back on. I remember exactly what time it was. That clock read ten-twenty for two days."

"I might have to call you as a witness, Mrs. Bennett. I'll let you know later today."

"Oh, I don't want to testify at a court-martial!"

"You would if it meant that an innocent man would go free, wouldn't you?"

"I guess so."

"I'll let you know if I need you later, Mrs. Bennett. Thank you very much."

Hollaway was waiting for her in the hall when she returned to court. He pulled her aside. "I made a couple of calls, Kara. I don't know who ordered the surveillance, but it's a military intelligence team that's been following you."

"That's what I figured."

Just then Major Sanders walked up. "Freeman wants to see us. Now."

She followed him into the judge's chambers. Freeman was standing behind his desk.

"I've given this matter very careful consideration, and I've looked up relevant Court of Military Appeals decisions regarding Rule 703. You may call General Beckwith as a witness, Major Guidry."

"My objection stands, Your Honor," said Sanders.

"It's a legitimate inquiry, Major Sanders. If General Beckwith has information regarding the whereabouts of the deceased, or her state of mind, or anything else so close to the time of her death, this court is entitled to hear that testimony."

"Sir, it could have been his driver who received that call."

"No, it couldn't have," said Kara. "He drove himself. I can prove it."

"How?" asked Sanders.

"I'll call Mrs. Bennett, the woman who runs the child-care center. She'll testify that when the General drove up to the center, he was alone. There was no driver in the car."

"That answers your question," said Freeman.

"Sir, she's up to something!"

"Major Sanders, my hands are tied." He turned to Kara. "I'm going to warn you, Major. You are going to be questioning the commanding general of the Third Army. You will exhibit proper deference to his rank and stature at all times, do you understand?"

"Yes, sir."

"If you go out of bounds with this witness, it will be the last witness you question in this court-martial."

"Yes, sir."

The court was packed with military spectators and press by the time the court-martial resumed. The word had gotten out all over the post that Beckwith was going to take the stand. Kara stepped to the podium. "The defense calls General William Telford Beckwith."

Beckwith came through the door of the courtroom and walked straight past Kara without looking at her and held up his right hand and was sworn as a witness.

"Good afternoon, General. Welcome."

Beckwith stared at her stonily.

"You are familiar with the defendant, are you not, sir?"

"You know I am."

"General Beckwith, sir, a simple yes or no will suffice."

Beckwith scowled. "Get on it with it, Major."

"All right, sir, we will. How long have you known the defendant, sir?"

"One year."

"And during that time you wrote his Officer Efficiency Reports. Can you tell the court how many reports you wrote, sir?"

"Two."

"And what scores did you give Captain Taylor?"

"One hundred."

"Both times, sir?"

"Both times."

"Sir, I'd like to read from the first OER you wrote on the defendant. Quote: 'This officer is one of the finest, if not *the*—' " She broke in. "And here, sir, you underlined the word *the,* and you said, quote: '. . . if not *the* finest young officer who I have ever had the pleasure to have working for me. His dedication to duty is unstinting. His sense of honor is without peer. His patriotism is unquestioned. His performance of his duties as my aide should put him in the very top one percent of the officers in his grade, and I will work to see to it that he gets promoted on the accelerated list to major.' Signed, General Beckwith. These are your words, are they not, General?"

"Yes."

"I have a second OER here. Would you like me to read your comments from it, or will you agree with me that they are equally as glowing, if not more glowing than those you wrote on the first OER?"

"What's this about, anyway? So I wrote a couple of OER's. Have them put in evidence if you want my testimony as to his character."

"Sir, I want the members of the panel to hear your words, from your mouth, regarding Captain Taylor. That's why you were called as a witness."

"So ask your question."

"You stand by these reports, sir? That Captain Taylor was an outstanding officer."

"I wrote them, didn't I?"

"Yes, sir, you did. What I want to know is, do you stand by them today?"

"What do you think?"

Kara turned to Colonel Freeman. "Your Honor, I'd like a yes or no answer from the witness."

Sanders leapt to his feet. "Permission to approach the bench, Your Honor."

"Granted."

Kara and Sanders walked up to the bench and whispered, out of earshot of the panel of officers and those seated as spectators.

"Sir, she's baiting him, trying to get him to say something nasty about the defendant so she can get him declared hostile."

Freeman turned to Kara. "Well?"

"Sir, General Beckwith had Captain Taylor working for him for over a year, and he wrote two of the best OER's I've ever seen. According to everything I've heard, both he and his wife thought the sun rose and set on my client. I'm just trying to get him to go on the record endorsing what he said in the OER's."

"She is within her rights to question the General as to Captain Taylor's character," Freeman whispered. "Major Guidry, you may proceed."

Kara retook the podium. "General Beckwith, I'm going to ask you again. Do you stand by your OER's on Captain Taylor as written?"

"As much as I stand by anything else with my name on it."

Kara walked back to the defense desk and picked up a sheet of paper. She walked back to the podium.

"General Beckwith, you and the defendant were together on the night Captain Worthy was murdered, isn't that correct?"

"Yes. He accompanied me to my speech at the officers club."

"And then you left the club in your staff car, and you received a call on your radio that there had been storm damage at the child-care center, and you drove over to the center, didn't you, General?"

"Yes."

"And after you left the child-care center, you received another call on your cell phone, is that correct?"

Beckwith looked over at Freeman. "Do I have to answer that? I thought I was called here as a character witness."

"You were, General Beckwith. Major Guidry has informed me of her intended questions, and I have approved them. Proceed, Major."

"General?"

"I don't know what you're talking about."

She handed him the cell phone bill. "It's right there on the bill for the cellular phone in your staff car, sir. I outlined it in yellow to make it plain for you to see."

Beckwith studied the page. He looked up at Kara with cold hatred in his eyes. "You insolent, insubordinate little—"

Kara interrupted: "Unresponsive, Your Honor. Request that the court instruct the witness to answer the question."

"General Beckwith, you have been asked a question relevant to the issues before this court-martial, and you are instructed to answer the question."

Beckwith snapped: "You're going to permit this?"

Freeman spoke calmly. "You are under oath, sir, and you are a witness in a court-martial of a man accused with a capital offense, and you must answer the legitimate questions of counsel for the defense."

"Well, I think this whole thing is a load of crap, and I'm not going to be a part of it any longer." He stood and started to walk away.

The judge raised his voice. "General Beckwith, I can order you to answer, and if you refuse, you can be held in contempt of this court and you can be held in the post stockade until you agree to come back to this court and answer questions as required by law. Sit down, please, General."

Beckwith turned and looked at the judge. It was evident to everyone in the courtroom that he meant business. He sat down.

Freeman said to Kara: "You may proceed, Major Guidry."

"General Beckwith, the bill for your cellular phone reflects the fact that you received a cell phone call in your staff car on the night Sheila Worthy was killed. The call came from Lieutenant Worthy. We know that because her number is listed as the originating caller. Can you tell us what you were doing talking to Lieutenant Worthy on the night that she was murdered, General?"

"I never received such a call. I never talked to Lieutenant Worthy that night."

"Perhaps you have forgotten, General. Sheila called the secure switchboard, and they patched the call through to your phone. She knew exactly who she was calling, and I can show from her phone bills during previous months that she called your staff car using that method many times."

"Lieutenant Worthy called my staff car on numerous occasions. She worked in my headquarters, and I received calls from my headquarters through the secure switchboard as a matter of security policy. I am certain that Lieutenant Worthy called my staff car on official business on other occasions, but I received no such call from her the night she died."

"Look at your bill, sir. That was the only cell phone call you received the whole night. It's right there on paper. Now, sir, can you tell us what you and Lieutenant Worthy talked about?"

Beckwith looked over at Freeman. "Can she do this?"

"It is a legitimate question, sir. The evidence shows the deceased called your staff car on the night she died. The defense has a right to an answer."

Beckwith glared at her. "I am telling you under oath that I never talked to Lieutenant Worthy. I left the child-care center, and I drove straight home. I didn't get back in my staff car until I received a call at home that there had been a fatal accident on the post."

"At that point you got up and put on your uniform and drove to the hospital. Isn't that right? I remember seeing you at the hospital late that night."

"That's correct."

"So you went straight to bed after you drove home from the child-care center?"

"Yes."

"And that is the sum and substance of your testimony regarding your whereabouts on the night of Sheila Worthy's murder, and you swear this under oath, sir?"

"You're damn right I do."

Kara turned to Colonel Freeman. "Sir, the defense is finished with this witness."

Freeman glanced over at Sanders. "No questions, Your Honor."

"The witness is dismissed."

"Your Honor, the defense requests a brief recess."

"Granted. The court-martial will resume in thirty minutes." Freeman banged his gavel, and reporters ran for the exits, frantically dialing cell phones and scribbling in their notebooks.

In the interview room, Kara was hastily scrambling through her notes when the MP's walked in with Randy. She looked up. "Randy, this is important. The night of Sheila's murder, what time was it when you left the officers club?"

"At nine-thirty. I remember that the General said I should arrange it—"

"Not Beckwith, Randy. *You.* After he was gone, you went back into the club, didn't you?"

"Yes. General Beckwith told me he wanted me to make certain that his wife got home okay."

"And did you?"

"She was gone. She had already left."

"Wait a minute. I thought you told me that you had met her at the General's quarters that night and driven her to the club yourself."

"I met her at the General's quarters, but she drove to the club herself."

"So she drove herself home."

"I would imagine so."

Kara snapped shut her briefcase and stood up to leave. "I've got to arrange for a witness, Randy. I'll meet you back in court."

Chapter Forty-two

"The defense calls Mrs. Virginia Bennett."

Sanders jumped up. "Your Honor, we're going to object to the swearing of this witness. She does not appear on the defense witness list."

Freeman signaled both lawyers to approach the bench. Whispering, he asked Kara: "Major Sanders has a point, Counselor. The name Virginia Bennett does not appear on your list of witnesses."

"Sir, I interviewed the witness only this morning. The interview became necessary because of new information developed in the course of the trial. I was unaware until then that she would be necessary to my case."

"What is the relevancy of her testimony?"

"Sir, I am pursuing the matter of Sheila Worthy's final phone call to General Beckwith's staff car. I believe General Beckwith when he says that he didn't receive that phone call, and Mrs. Bennett can help establish that fact."

"That doesn't seem helpful to your case at all, Major," said Freeman.

"Your Honor, I believe that the person with whom Sheila spoke that night is the person who killed her."

Sanders whispered: "She spoke to the defendant, Your Honor."

"That will be for you to establish, if you think you can, Howard," Kara whispered.

"I still fail to see the relevancy of her testimony, Major Guidry," said Freeman.

"Your Honor, the defense has wide latitude in calling witnesses. Mrs. Bennett will be helpful to my case in establishing who Sheila Worthy spoke to at ten forty-two, and she has relevant information concerning the knives found in the defendant's apartment."

"All right. I'll allow her testimony, but this is the last time I'll allow you to call a witness the prosecution has not had an opportunity to question. Understood?"

"Yes, Your Honor."

Mrs. Bennett took the stand and was sworn in as a witness. Kara approached the podium and neatly laid a sheet of notes before her.

"Mrs. Bennett, what is the job you hold at Fort Benning?"

"I am the director of the post child-care center and thrift shop."

"Recently, there was a storm that caused a great deal of damage to the center. Do you remember that night?"

"Yes, I do. Vividly. It blew the roof from the back of the center."

"It was also the night that Sheila Worthy was murdered. Did you know that?"

"Yes, I did."

"General Beckwith visited the center that night, didn't he?"

"Yes, he did."

"What time did General Beckwith arrive at the child-care center?"

"Well, let me see. The storm hit us at nine-thirty, and he came not long thereafter. I'd say about nine forty-five."

"And he stayed about a half hour, correct?"

"He left at ten-twenty."

"Ten-twenty exactly, Mrs. Bennett? This is important."

"Yes, it was ten-twenty exactly. I remember because he left just as the fire department cut the power to the center, and that stopped the electric clock on the wall.

That clock read ten-twenty for the next two days, until they turned the power back on."

Kara walked over to the evidence table and picked up the antler-handled knife. She handed it to Mrs. Bennett. "Mrs. Bennett, I want you to take your time and look at this knife very carefully. Have you ever seen it before?"

She studied the knife for a moment. "Yes. I took this knife on consignment at our thrift shop."

"You took it on consignment? Can you explain that for the court?"

"The wife of a young sergeant brought the knife in. It had belonged to her family, in Germany. They needed money, so they decided to sell the knife. By taking it on consignment, we agreed to sell the knife through our thrift shop, and we would keep ten percent of the proceeds."

"Did you sell the knife, Mrs. Bennett?"

"No, we didn't."

"Can you tell the court why not?"

"It was reported missing, along with several other knives we had for sale."

Kara pointed at the evidence table. "Do you see any of the other knives that were missing from your thrift shop, Mrs. Bennett? You may stand and walk over and examine them closely."

Mrs. Bennett walked to the evidence table and examined the knives. She pointed at three of them. "These knives disappeared from our stock too."

"So out of these six knives, four of them came from your thrift shop?"

"Yes, that is correct."

Kara turned to Major Sanders. "Your witness."

"Do you have any idea who took the knives, Mrs. Bennett?" Sanders asked.

"No, sir, I do not."

"Have you ever seen the defendant in this case?"

Mrs. Bennett looked over at Randy. "No, I have not."

"No further questions."

Freeman turned to Mrs. Bennett. "You may step down."

Kara stood. "Your Honor, the defense calls Mrs. William Beckwith."

Sanders stood. "Permission to approach, Your Honor."

Freeman signaled both lawyers to the bench. "What's on your mind, Counselor?"

"Sir, I'm going to object to this witness too. She's on the list, but counsel for the defense informed us that she would be called as a character witness, and it's obvious that counsel is going to question the witness on more than the defendant's character."

Freeman looked at Kara over his half glasses. "Well?"

"Your Honor, I am under no obligation under law to inform the prosecution about my intentions regarding the witness. I answered counsel's question about my purpose in calling Mrs. Beckwith only as a courtesy. My answer that she was a character witness does not bind me as to the depth or breadth of the questions I have for the witness."

"My objection stands, Your Honor," said Sanders. "This is another defense trick. She wants to cloud the issues in this case. She is seeking to besmirch the commanding general and his wife in an attempt to discredit the command that brought charges against the defendant."

"Is that what you're doing, Counselor?" Freeman asked Kara.

"No, Your Honor. The prosecution is objecting to this witness because its case is predicated on the linkage between the two murders. They have made a case that the defendant was obsessed with both of these young women, and his obsession drove him to kill not one but both of them. They're afraid if I cast doubt on the defendant's guilt in the murder of Sheila Worthy, the same doubt will carry over and destroy their case in the murder of Captain Love. That is exactly what I am seeking to do, which is entirely consistent with my duties as counsel for the defense."

"I'm going to allow the witness, Major Sanders. Take your seats."

Mrs. Beckwith was summoned from the hall and walked into the court and took the stand and was sworn in. As Kara walked to the podium, she saw General Beckwith come into the court through the side door and sit in the back.

"Mrs. Beckwith, will you please state your full name and occupation for the record?"

Her voice was steady and quite loud. "I am Mrs. William T. Beckwith, and I am the wife of the commanding general of the Third Army."

"Mrs. Beckwith, we have spoken previously, have we not?"

"Yes."

"When was that, ma'am?"

"I'm not certain, exactly. Perhaps two months ago."

"I came to your home at your invitation, did I not?"

"Yes."

"Will you recount for the court the substance of our conversation that day, Mrs. Beckwith?"

"I'm not sure I remember exactly what we talked about, Major Guidry. It was some time ago."

"Allow me to refresh your memory, then. You told me that on the night of Sheila Worthy's murder, General Beckwith had been at the child-care center, examining the damage they suffered in the storm, and that he drove straight home from there. Do you remember telling me that?"

"Yes, I do."

"All right, then, let me ask you this. Do you recall what time you told me General Beckwith returned home that night from the child-care center?"

"Yes, I do. It was ten p.m."

"We have just heard testimony from Mrs. Virginia Bennett, who runs the child-care center, that your hus-

band left her center at ten-twenty that night. She remembered the time exactly, because his departure coin-
cided with the power being cut at the child-care center,
stopping an electric clock at the exact moment General
Beckwith left. I just drove from the child-care center to
your quarters. It took me exactly six minutes in midday
traffic. At night, with very little traffic, I would estimate
that you could easily drive that distance in six minutes.
That means your husband was at home at ten twenty-
six. Can you account for this discrepancy, Mrs. Beckwith?"

"I didn't look at the time. I was estimating what time
he came home."

"After hearing about Mrs. Bennett's testimony, would
you agree that your husband came home later than the
time you told me before?"

"He told me himself that he drove straight home from
the child-care center. If Mrs. Bennett is positive about
when he left the center, he would have been there by ten
twenty-six. I'll accept that."

Kara continued calmly: "All right, Mrs. Beckwith,
let's go over the things we know for certain about that
night. Let's start with Sheila's time of death. The Fort
Benning medical examiner, Captain Evans, has testified
that she could have died anytime between nine o'clock
and eleven-fifty, when she was dragged from the water
and found to be dead. But we have information that
gives us new insight as to her time of death. We know
that Sheila Worthy was alive at ten forty-two that night,
because we have her cellular telephone record, and that
record reflects that she made a call from her car at that
time. And we know that the last person Sheila Worthy
called before she died was your husband. We know this
because the cellular telephone bill for his staff car reflects that the call Sheila Worthy placed was answered.
We know that General Beckwith didn't answer the cell
phone in his staff car, because both you and General
Beckwith have testified that he was at home at ten

twenty-six, and General Beckwith has testified that he didn't get back into his staff car until after midnight. That means we have a problem, Mrs. Beckwith. Do you know what the problem is?"

"I have no idea what you're talking about."

"The problem we have is, who answered Sheila Worthy's call in General Beckwith's staff car at ten forty-two? Do you have any idea who that might have been?"

Mrs. Beckwith pointed her right forefinger at Randy. "It was him. He had the keys to the staff car. He stole the car and drove out there and killed her."

Kara took her time. She looked down at her notes for a moment, then walked around and leaned on the podium with one elbow. "That's just it, Mrs. Beckwith. Another thing we know for certain is that the defendant could not have been the person who answered the cell phone in General Beckwith's staff car, because the prosecution called a disinterested witness, a gas station attendant, who testified that he filled up Captain Taylor's car with gas at ten forty-five that night at a station downtown. And he produced for the court a credit card receipt with a date and time stamp on it that proves this fact." She handed the credit receipt to Mrs. Beckwith, who stared at it blankly.

"It takes more than three minutes to fill up a car and take a charge card from a customer and run it through the system and get a signature from the driver, Mrs. Beckwith. I know, because I drove down to the Union 76 and tried it myself. It took me seven minutes, and I put in only a half tank of gas, eight gallons. Captain Taylor's car was nearly on empty. He put nineteen gallons in his car. That means Captain Taylor was sitting in his car at the Union 76 at ten forty-two, Mrs. Beckwith. There is no way he could have been answering the phone in your husband's staff car and been more than ten miles away downtown at a gas station in his own car at the same time. It just isn't possible."

Mrs. Beckwith looked up from the credit receipt. Her

eyes were hooded with hate as they followed Kara's path back to the podium.

"So you see what I mean about the problem we have, Mrs. Beckwith? We can account for Sheila Worthy at ten forty-two. She was in her car, dialing the number for your husband's staff car on her cell phone. We can account for the defendant. He was getting his car filled with gas at a Union 76 station downtown. We can account for General Beckwith. He has testified that he was at home, in the commanding general's quarters at Fort Benning. The only person we can't account for at ten forty-two is you, Mrs. Beckwith." Kara paused, and looked directly at her. "Where were you at ten forty-two, Mrs. Beckwith?"

"I was at home in bed."

"Are you certain about that, Mrs. Beckwith? We have already established that you didn't really know what time it was when your husband got home. Let me ask you this: when you drove up to the house, did you see his staff car parked in the driveway?"

"Yes. I remember now. His staff car was there."

"So if General Beckwith was home by ten twenty-six, that means you must have arrived sometime after that, correct?"

"Yes."

"And what you're telling us is that you probably arrived sometime soon after he did, and your testimony is that you were at home in bed by ten forty-two."

"Yes, that is correct."

"So if I called your husband back to the stand, and I asked him if he could verify that you were at home in bed at ten forty-two, he could do that?"

"Of course he could."

"Well, Mrs. Beckwith, that presents us with a new problem. Do you remember what you told me that morning a couple of months ago? You told me that you and General Beckwith sleep in separate bedrooms, and have done so for years." She paused, looking the witness straight in the eye. She let her words sink in, and then she continued. "Mrs. Beckwith, you have testified that your husband could verify that you were at home in bed at ten forty-two on the night Sheila Worthy was murdered, when plainly he could not. That leaves us with the problem of where you were at ten forty-two, ma'am. Do you know what I think? I think you were driving your husband's staff car, and I think *you* are the one who answered Sheila Worthy's cellular telephone call."

Mrs. Beckwith's face reddened, and she half stood from the witness chair. "That's a lie! I was driving my own car that night!"

Kara stood for a moment at the podium, Mrs. Beckwith's words ringing in the room. She waited until the witness sat down, and then she walked over to the defense table and picked up a notebook. "Yes, of course you were. I have it in my notes here somewhere . . ." She made a show of paging through a spiral notebook, looking for the correct page. "Here it is. I spoke to one of the gardeners who works at your quarters. He told me that on the morning after Sheila Worthy's murder, you asked him to change a flat tire on your Lexus sedan." She looked up at Mrs. Beckwith. "It would have been the Lexus you were driving on the night in question, isn't that right, Mrs. Beckwith?"

"Yes."

"Do you remember getting a flat tire, ma'am?"

Mrs. Beckwith's face went blank, registering momentary confusion. Her eyes followed Kara as she walked to the defense table, picked up a plastic bag, and put it in full view of the members of the panel on top of the podium. "Do you know what this is, Mrs. Beckwith? This is a sample of mud that I removed from the flat tire of your Lexus sedan when it was downtown at a gas station getting repaired. I ran this mud through a geological testing lab at the University of Georgia, and the report I received from the lab"—she picked up a folder with a light blue cover—"established with a probability of less than one tenth of one percent that the mud taken from your tire came from the river bottoms of Fort Benning where Sheila Worthy's car and body were found."

Major Sanders rose slowly from his chair. "Your Honor, I'm going to object. Counsel for the defense—"

Kara loudly interrupted him: "Mrs. Beckwith, can you explain to this court how mud from the riverbank where I found Sheila Worthy's car got on the tire of the Lexus sedan you were driving the night she was murdered?"

The courtroom was totally silent as Colonel Freeman removed his reading glasses and used the arm of his robe to carefully wipe them clean. "Counsel for the defense and counsel for the prosecution will proceed to chambers."

Freeman sat down behind the desk in his office and perched the reading glasses on the tip of his nose and peered over them at Kara. "Are you going to move to introduce the mud and the report from the University of Georgia into evidence, Counselor? Because if you are, I'm going to deny your motion. You've got evidence that was seized without a search warrant, making your geological report useless."

"If you deny me the evidence from Mrs. Beckwith's tire, I'll move to introduce into evidence the volunteer duty roster from the thrift shop, which Mrs. Bennett gave to me. The thrift shop duty roster will establish that Mrs. Beckwith was the thrift shop volunteer on each of the days preceding a report that a knife was missing from their stock. Then I'll make a motion to compare the witness's fingerprints with the partial prints found on the knives. Then I'll ask for a warrant to search Mrs. Beckwith's personal belongings, among which I am certain we will find the kind of camera and lens that experts have testified took the photographs of the deceased women that the prosecution put in evidence. Then I'll call a witness who will establish that

Mrs. Beckwith had both the means and opportunity to plant the knives and the photographs in the defendant's apartment. Then I'll call General Beckwith and remind him that he is under oath, and I will question him about the affairs he was having with both Sheila Worthy and Lannie Fulton Love. And after we establish Mrs. Beckwith's motive to kill the women who were having adulterous affairs with her husband, I will ask for a dismissal of the charges against Captain Taylor, and I will personally go to the provost marshal and file double murder charges against Mrs. Beckwith myself."

The standing room in the back of the court was filled with soldiers in uniform. Colonel Freeman looked down from the bench. "Do you have a motion, Major Guidry?"

"Yes, Your Honor, I do. I move to dismiss the charges of premeditated murder against Captain Taylor. We are prepared to present testimony implicating Mrs. William Beckwith in the murders of both Lieutenant Worthy and Captain Love."

"Do you have a response, Major Sanders?"

Sanders stood. "Sir, the prosecution understands that the defense has evidence that Mrs. Beckwith was on duty at the child-care center at the time the knives from the thrift shop were found to be missing, and that there is fingerprint evidence establishing that the partial prints found on the knives belong to Mrs. Beckwith. We intend to reopen the investigation into both murders, and notify Mrs. Beckwith that she is the target of this investigation. The prosecution has no objection to the defense motion."

"So ordered. The charges in this matter are dismissed with prejudice. They can never be filed again against this innocent and honorable man." He looked straight at Randy, who was standing next to Kara. "The United States Army and the people of these United States of America owe you an apology, Captain. I hope you will find it in your heart to accept it." He struck his gavel hard on the mahogany desk. "The charges against the defendant having been dismissed, this court-martial is adjourned."

As they were leaving, Sanders walked up and extended his hand. "Excellent job, Counselor."

"Thank you, Howard. I did my best."

"You never got around to telling us who received the call from Sheila Worthy to General Beckwith's staff car."

"He did. He was lying."

"You can prove that, I presume."

She clapped Sanders on the back. "Howard, I'm finished with this case. You prove it."

There was a mob of reporters waiting outside, and it took Kara and Randy almost an hour to make their way through them. Afterward, Kara was walking alongside Randy toward the Cherokee, parked across the street next to the football field. A platoon ran past, screaming, *"If I die in a combat zone, box me up and ship me home."* It occurred to her that Fort Benning felt like Fort Benning again for the first time in months.

Mace was standing next to the car with General Teese.

"You did a hell of a job in there, Major Guidry," said Mace.

"Not bad, huh?"

General Teese shook Randy's hand. "A new day."

"Yes. It is a new day." He hesitated for a moment. "You came."

"Yes. I asked Kara not to tell you I was here."

"You were going to testify."

"If you needed me."

Mace cleared his throat. "Did you hear the news, sir?"

"What news?" asked Randy.

"The President announced his pick for chief of staff."

"I guess General King beat Beckwith after all," said Kara.

"The President picked General Ranstead."

Randy raised a fist in the air. "Yes!"

Kara laughed. "Sometimes justice has a very, very good day."

Randy shook Kara's hand. "I've got to tell you, I had my doubts about whether or not we could get a fair trial."

"The law is as fair as you make it, Randy. This time the system yielded to all the pushing and shoving we did. Next time, who knows?"

After Randy and General Teese left, Kara unlocked the Cherokee and put her briefcase in the backseat. Mace was standing next to the car at parade rest, his hands clasped behind his back. His voice was a hoarse whisper:

"So, you want to give it another shot?"

"It's going to take all of our talents at cover and concealment. The Army's rules haven't changed in the last few days, that I'm aware of."

"That's okay by me. They'll never catch us."

"They'll come after me. The ones loyal to Beckwith are going to want revenge."

"Let 'em come."

"They're probably looking at us right now," said Kara, glancing around.

"So let's give 'em a show." He snapped to attention and saluted. "Permission to carry on, ma'am."

She smiled at him, returning the salute. "Carry on, Sergeant."